YOU & ME, Honeybee

Book Two in the Fayette Bay Series

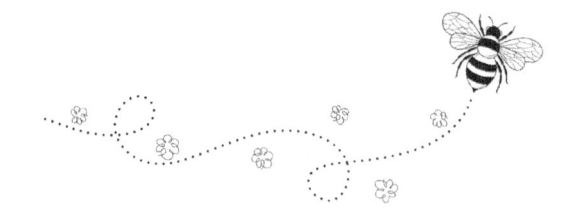

Gemma Nicholls

Copyright © 2024 by Gemma Nicholls

All rights reserved.

No part of this publication may be reproduced, distributed, or transmitted in any form or by any means, including photocopying, recording, or other electronic or mechanical methods, without the prior written permission of the publisher, except as permitted by U.S. copyright law. For permission requests, contact author.

The story, all names, characters, and incidents portrayed in this production are fictitious. No identification with actual persons (living or deceased), places, buildings, and products is intended or should be inferred.

Book Cover by Bia Shuja

Illustrations by Gemma Nicholls

First edition 2024

For the readers who just want someone in their corner, backing them through the thick and thin of every accomplishment.

Believe that you'll find that person, but for now, Artie Avila's cheering you on all the way.

Author's Note

Thank you so much for picking up You and Me, Honeybee! It truly means the world to me that my words are in your hands right now. Before you dive in, this book contains darker themes such as anxiety, mental health, violence, and death. There is on-page violence during the later chapters, and anxiety/ panic attacks are mentioned throughout the book. There is also mention of absent parents and parental death.

Please consider if these themes might be upsetting for you before reading. Make sure you put yourself first, always.

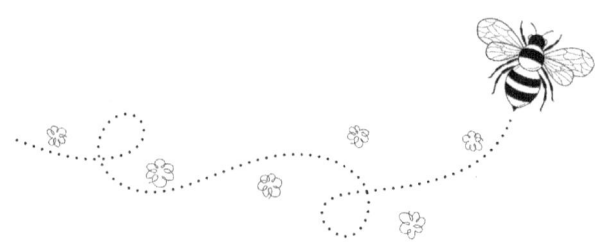

Also by Gemma Nicholls

The Fayette Bay Series

The Long Con
You and Me, Honeybee

Chapter One
Bea

"Bullshit!" I shout as the stranger across from me sets three cards down on the middle pile. I look up triumphantly, but an entire table of staring eyes quickly humbles me back to my usual quietness.

Too loud, Bea.

The only people here who aren't looking at me like I've just pulled my plain T-shirt up over my head are Silas and Jessica. Silas is trying—and failing miserably—to stifle a laugh behind his fist, while Jess is looking at me sympathetically, squeezing her fiancée's leg under the table in a bid to distract him. I scowl at them both.

My outburst is forgotten quickly, it seems, as the rest of the guests return to the game, but my blush is still burning its way up my neck and across my fair cheeks in full vengeance.

"I'm getting a drink," I mumble, keeping my head low. I knock into the corner of the table as I stand, almost sending my half-full glass flying before I catch it at the last second.

Get me out of here.

"But the game's not finished," Jessica starts, waving towards the pile of cards I'd discarded in my haste. "You're winning."

"Go on without me, it's fine." I move towards the kitchen space in Silas and Jessica's apartment, silently cursing their open-plan home. What I wouldn't give for a second of privacy…

I could leave—honestly, I'd probably love nothing more—but how could I skip out on my best friends' farewell party so early? They're finally about to get their happy ending, and that's definitely worth celebrating. Even if I am completely out of my element in a room full of strangers.

Silas and Jessica are moving away from Fayette Bay and I'm happy for them, even if I do secretly wish they'd pack me into one of these boxes and take me with them. They've been my rock since everything happened last year, with Desmond Rose keeping us trapped in his dungeons and almost killing Silas…multiple times. It's reached the point that if I'm not here, they're at my house. We're almost inseparable, and I've had a full year of them being my safety nets should the memories all get too much.

But now they're moving away, and I'm being left behind.

I have Maria, of course, but she's always so busy running her café. Silas and Jessica just understood the whole *locked up in a dungeon with a scary, unhinged conman* kind of thing. Not that I'd ever wish that on anyone, but there's some kind of unspoken bond between us now.

"Hi," a deep voice rumbles behind me, interrupting my thoughts and drawing me back to my mortifying reality. "I've been appointed as the spokesperson to make sure you're okay."

I meet his eyes and have to stop myself from recoiling from the watery green, crystal-clear pools shining with playfulness and childlike excitement. I don't think I've ever seen eyes quite so bright before.

A brown curl hangs loosely over the frame of his glasses, and I have the weirdest urge to reach up and push it away.

Wait—what?

"I'm fine," I say with a small, probably unconvincing smile. "Just thirsty."

"What was wrong with the other drink you hadn't finished?"

His toothy grin knocks all coherent thoughts from my brain, eyes glittering as he watches me scramble for an answer, leaning his hip on the kitchen counter with his big arms folded. Despite his boyish look, the stranger still towers over me easily, making me far too self-conscious about the messy plait I hadn't had time to tame after a long day of visiting patients.

He looks down at his wrist and pouts, checking the time on his non-existent watch.

"I don't know, it was warm?" I huff, turning back to the bottles. "Why do you care?"

"Woah, it was just a joke. Sorry." He holds up his palms in surrender. "I'm Arthur, by the way."

My shoulders slump slightly, because I hate confrontation and that was rude of me. I much prefer blending into the background and being quiet—which is exactly what I wish I were doing right now. Damn my competitive streak and weird luck in all card games.

"Wait, Arthur...Avila?" The name dawns on me.

Arthur Avila—the hacker who'd helped save Silas last year.

He was hailed a hero by everyone we knew...except for me.

Arthur smirks. "The one and only."

The blood drains from my face as I take a step back, abandoning my drink on the side as my vision pulses. I turn back to the table, which is lively once more in the middle of a crude game. I touch Jessica on the shoulder lightly, who has her head nestled into the crook of Silas's neck as he draws idle circles on her thigh. She looks up at me with a content smile.

"I have to go now—early morning," I stutter. Her inky curls shimmer in the warm light as she nods. "But will you text me when you get there safely? Call me when you're settled, and I'll miss you—"

"Bea," Silas interrupts. "We'll video call you tomorrow evening, and we're not that far. The guest room will be ready and waiting for you anytime."

I smile, relaxing slightly. For a complete grump, Silas Knight had turned into one of the kindest men I'd ever known. Miles apart from the man I'd first met all those years ago when I was put on his mother's medical service.

"Thank you," I whisper as I give them both a quick hug. "Love you both. You two deserve the biggest 'happy ever after'."

They give each other a knowing look at that, and I leave them gazing longingly at one another as I grab my oversized scarf and head towards the door.

"It was nice to meet you!" I hear Arthur shout as the door clicks shut behind me. I hurry down the stairs, wanting to get away from that voice as quickly as possible.

Why him?

Why was *he* there?

In the year following Silas's final discharge from hospital, I hadn't had to hear Arthur's name once. I'd just assumed that Silas and Jessica didn't want the constant reminder of Desmond and his lair either. Hail him a hero all you like, but he worked for Desmond Rose. He had the means to get into Desmond's camera system and see exactly what was happening to us in those dungeons, and yet he never turned anything over to the police to help us.

It's difficult, even now, thinking about everything that happened in the past twelve months. Silas and Jessica got the worst of it, but they've also received complimentary therapy sessions every week since. I, on the other hand, am still on a waiting list and probably won't be seen for another year or two.

It affects every single part of my life, the trauma of it all. I drive the long way through town to avoid the storage containers where the lair used to be hidden. *To avoid where he kept us.* I go shopping a few towns over. I even changed hospitals so I wouldn't have to walk past the floor Silas had spent so long recovering on after countless beatings and near-death experiences, begging them to put me on house visits instead of working on the floor.

And I just met Arthur Avila. The *hero* of everyone's story but mine.

Because a hero would've found a way to help his dying friend when he needed them most. A hero would've helped the other people trapped in the dungeons. Not just swooped in at the very end to take all the credit for himself.

My heart is racing as I reach the main doors to the apartment block. I push out into the bitterly crisp air, face instantly prickling at the sudden temperature change.

"Shit, Bea! Watch it," Maria gasps, dropping her canvas bag into the layer of fresh snow. Bottles clatter together dangerously as she composes herself. "Where's the fire?"

"I—I," I try, before bursting into tears.

"Oh, lovely. Come here, what's wrong?" Maria grabs me and tugs me into her, crushing me against her full chest. She smells like roses and sea salt, and I didn't know I needed a warm, enveloping hug until now.

Since the moment I met Maria, she'd become like a big sister to me. She seemed to understand me more than anyone I'd ever met before, never making me feel foolish for how I felt or acted. She's completely kind; she always listens to me without judgement.

I shake my head, unable to put my feelings into words.

Probably because I don't quite understand them myself. *The* Arthur Avila is upstairs and was just talking to me so casually, even though he *must* know who I am and that I was in those dungeons too. And I wasn't hating our conversation, and I hadn't envisioned him to be quite so attractive...

Not that it matters now.

I've been using the blame game as a coping mechanism for the past twelve months, and Arthur just so happened to pick the short straw. Desmond's dead and buried, so the blame had to go *somewhere*. And who better than onto the man who did nothing to help?

Shuddering through my sobs, I try again. "He's—"

But the door swinging open behind me stops me in my tracks.

"Can we help you?" Maria asks over my shoulder, eyeing the intruder up and down.

"I came to see if she was alright. She kind of ran out of the party," Arthur's deep voice rumbles and I swallow a scoff.

Seriously? He doesn't even know me, and now he's checking on me?

I steel my spine as Maria dabs my cheeks with her fingers, presumably trying to save my makeup that's now having a party of its own as it slides around my face. I call behind me, in my strongest voice, "I'm fine. I don't need a babysitter."

Maria's eyes go wide, but she looks wholly impressed.

"Right. Sorry," he chuckles as I hear the door open again.

I'm about to relax when Maria begins jumping around me like an overactive puppy. "Wait, wait! Don't let me interrupt...whatever this is. I'll leave you to it. Lovely, will I see you tomorrow?" she asks me, eyes gleaming.

"Yes, but you don't have to—" I begin through gritted teeth.

"Nonsense, the bottles are getting warm!" She swings the clanking bag over her shoulder, now dripping wet from where it had been lying in the fresh snow. "See you tomorrow, hon."

I exhale through my nose as she skips around us, leaving me alone with a complete stranger in the darkness.

"Well, I'd better be going. Early morning shift and all," I sigh, the words turning to thick haze in the chilly night. I turn on my heel, taking a second before spotting my new car. A midnight blue sedan.

I go to step around him, but Arthur grabs my hand. "Wait, I didn't get your name," he hums, lightly tugging me back to him.

I slip my hand from his. "Bea."

He stares at me for a moment too long, like he is waiting for the punchline. But when it doesn't come, he repeats, "Bea?"

"That's right."

"As in...honey?"

I glare at him impatiently, wrapping my arms around myself to preserve the smidge of warmth I have left. "What?"

"Like the Honeybee. That's your name?"

"I suppose?" I ask with a hint of uncertainty. No one has compared my name to an insect before. It's three letters—not exactly difficult to understand.

Arthur dips his head in agreement. "I like it."

"I'm glad you approve," I utter dryly, but the remnants of my tears make it sound sadder than I'd hoped. I glance behind me at the deserted street, ice crystals floating in the air around us. I can feel my toes curling in on themselves the longer we stand out here. "I should really get going."

"Can I walk you home? You seemed upset upstairs." Arthur's glasses fog every time he speaks, his warm breath creating a white sheen across his face every few seconds.

"I drove here," I say with a tight smile, sticking a thumb over my shoulder toward my car. "My ride's the blue one."

"Then I'll walk you to your *ride*." He shifts past me, signalling for me to join him. I follow, but stop as soon as he continues, "Come on, Honeybee."

"Oh, don't do that."

To anyone else, his smile is probably infectious. But it's just pissing me off. "Do what?"

"Call me a stupid name, make fun of me. I don't know, whatever you're doing."

"I'm not making fun of you!" he exclaims, clutching his chest like I've wounded him.

"Then just call me Bea."

He seems to mull this over for a second, looking deep in thought. But then he shakes his head. "No."

"No?" I bark a laugh, and he sucks his lips between his teeth.

"No," he agrees. "Bea doesn't work for me."

"But it's my name."

"What else can I call you?"

"You won't have to call me anything after tonight, but Bea is my name."

His eyes flare. "Wow, and here I was thinking you were the kind one of the friend group," he remarks with a soft chuckle.

"You thought wrong," I shrug, but the need to elaborate overcomes me. "I'm kind to people who don't make fun of me."

Arthur takes my arm in his and spins me to face him. We're standing next to my car now, and I consider getting in and driving away. I probably would have if his palm weren't radiating a delicious, toasty warmth through my skin.

"I'm not making fun of you." His voice is low and earnest, and for some stupid reason it makes me want to believe him.

"Thank you for walking me to my car," I sniff, turning away from him to unlock the door and slide in. Arthur might be trying to catch a chill tonight, but I'm certainly not wasting another second out in the freezing cold just because some stranger has a hero complex.

I shut the door on him, but he simply grins through the window. I scowl, give him an exaggerated grin and a wave, and start the ignition—but he still doesn't step back. He's staring at me with an infuriating smirk on his face.

Is he waiting for something?

"I'm going home now," I shout through the glass.

He simply points down with his finger. I grumble but crack the window anyway. "Can I help you with something?"

"I just wanted to say it was lovely meeting you tonight," he croons in a sickly-sweet voice, tainted with arrogant challenge. "I'll be seeing you, Honeybee."

Without another word, I close the car window and drive away. I watch him through the mirror until there's so much distance between us that he's nothing more than a tiny speck.

Good—as far as I'm concerned, there will never be *enough* space between me and Arthur Avila.

Chapter Two

Artie

I STRIDE BACK INTO Silas's apartment to find Maria cranking the music and dragging people up from the table, calling them dull if they dare resist her powers of persuasion. The only people still sitting are Silas and Jessica, who finally allow Maria to get them up, only to crash back down onto their hideous green sofa. I sit down in the ratty armchair next to them, firmly shaking my head at Maria's waggling eyebrows. She rolls her eyes, mouths *boring* to me, and turns back to the dance floor.

I think I'll live.

"And that looks like my cue to leave." I gesture to the swaying crowd. Silas barely looks up from Jessica's neck but throws me a thumbs up. Jessica gives me the same lazy smile she's been giving everyone all night. "Alrighty then. Safe trip."

"Thanks for coming, Artie," Jessica hums before turning her attention back to her fiancée. But he meets her with a peck and stands up quickly to follow me.

"Don't call me that," I tell her in a mock warning. No one ever listens, anyway.

"Actually Arth, I need to speak with you about something." Silas gestures toward the door. "I'll walk you out."

"Fine," I say, saluting to Maria and the few other guests I know before following him.

"There's no easy way to say this," Silas starts as we push out into the bitter night. I might've considered bringing a coat if I knew all my conversations were destined to be outside tonight.

Silas tucks a lock of sandy blonde hair behind his ears as he thinks of the right way to word whatever he wants to say, obviously meaning business.

"Look, Sy. I'm flattered and all, but I–"

"Shut up, idiot."

I zip my lip. Forcing Silas into a fury-induced tizz is one of my favourite pastimes. There's just something about seeing his eyes flash red that is so damn...*hilarious*.

"I need you to do something for me while I'm gone," he continues, ignoring my smirk. I gesture for him to continue because I can no longer feel my fingers. "Bea hasn't been doing so good recently. She's been dealing with the events of last year in her own way, and I think she's struggling to let go of the past."

"Right," I drawl.

Nope, don't like where this is headed.

"Jessica's been going back and forth on whether she actually wants to leave Fayette Bay because she's so worried about Bea. The only way I could fully persuade her to go through with it was by telling her that I'd enlist the help of the infamous Arthur Avila."

"Flattery will get you nowhere, Knight." I lean against the bitter door frame, folding my arms tightly. "And the answer's no. I won't babysit your friend while you run off into the sunset."

Silas smooths a hand down his face. "Come on, Arth—for Jess? She needs this escape. You won't have to babysit Bea at all. Just keep an eye on her. I know you have the means in that grotty little den of yours."

I choke on a laugh. "That grotty little den saved your life."

"I know, and I'm eternally grateful." Silas bows his head a fraction. "Just do this one last thing for me. She'll get used to us not being around, but I need to know she's in safe hands in the meantime."

"What do you suppose I do? I met her tonight—she hates me."

"She doesn't *hate* you." The look in his eye confirms to me that she definitely does. "She just needs someone to blame."

There's a heavy pause that hangs between us then, because deep down I *know* I'm not to blame.

I just need a quick reminder sometimes.

"I don't know if I can handle that, Sy." The words get caught in my throat. It's taken me longer than I'd care to admit, to come to terms with the fact I couldn't have done anything to save Silas, Jessica...and Bea.

Yes, I'm no stranger to hacking camera feeds, but I don't keep tabs on my enemies twenty-four-seven. Desmond Rose was my employer. No one knew he was targeting Silas until it was too late, and I helped in any way I could once I knew what was going on between them.

Still…so much happened that I could've prevented, if only I'd checked in on Desmond…

No, Arthur.

See? The last thing I need is for Bea's misplaced anger to set me back any more than my own brain keeps trying to.

"It's nothing to be ashamed of, you know." Silas sniffs, as if sensing my rising guilt. "Feeling like this, I mean. We're all dealing with it the best we can."

"I know."

"She has one of those video doorbell thingies," Silas changes the subject, clapping a hand on my shoulder. "Keep an eye on her, make sure she looks okay when she's coming and going from work. No real contact between the two of you needed."

I think it over for a second and grumble, "Fine." If only to shut him up so I can get into the comforting warmth of my car. He grins before ducking back into the lobby of his apartment building, waving me off.

I throw him the middle finger and jog to my car, cranking the heating up to full blast as soon as I slide into the driver's seat.

A text chimes in while I'm still warming my hands in front of the air vent. It's from my nemesis.

Silas

> Oh, and don't even think of touching her. She's far too good for you, even if she doesn't know it.

I scoff at that, because it's probably true, and also, I don't think Bea would ever let me touch her with a ten-foot bargepole.

When I get home, I toss my keys onto my desk. The metal makes a small thump on the piles of papers I've yet to read through. Honestly, being a renowned hacker hasn't turned out as sweet as I thought. Even after giving up my private business and working solely for my contact in the police force, the paperwork is endless.

The apartment is icy cold and pitch black. I turn the thermostat dial up to max and click on my little desk lamp. It casts a warm glow over my living room, and that's about as homey as this place gets.

I sit at my desk, using the pile of unsigned paperwork as a mouse mat to log onto my computer. My three screens ignite with life, and within thirty seconds I've found Bea's home address. Another minute has me watching her video doorbell feed.

I can't find any sign of a home camera system inside, which is something at least. One less thing for creeps on the dark web to crack.

After what feels like hours of watching grainy footage of an empty doorstep, I open my hacker's database on another screen and type in the name of Bea's hospital, Spring Grove Medical Centre. It's an establishment certainly in need of some cybersecurity training.

Within a few minutes, I'm into the rota schedule and breaking a million ethical codes simultaneously.

That's when I find her—Nurse Beatrice Di Menna. *Great name.*

She's scheduled for a home visit at 10 am tomorrow, so she'll need to leave her house around nine. I'll make sure she leaves then, and I'll watch her getting back after her final visit around 6 pm.

Great, that's a good plan. I'll get through tomorrow, and then I can go on with my life knowing she isn't *actually* spiralling about Jessica leaving and Silas is just overthinking with that big head of his.

And I can stop thinking about Nurse Di Menna for good.

Look, it's not that I hate her, or dislike her, or have any feelings towards her at all, really. But she *clearly* blames me for my involvement last year—*or lack thereof*, my brain adds helpfully—and I've put myself through enough of that for a lifetime. I need to protect my peace, and something tells me Bea is an imminent threat to the quiet life I'm trying to rebuild.

So I'll keep an eye on her from a distance for a few days, but that's it. I won't look after her forever. We'll both be better off staying far away from each other, anyway.

I lock the screens and lean back in my desk chair, the backrest groaning quietly at the shift. I drag a hand down my face and check my phone for the time—a few minutes past midnight. A text from Jessica pops up.

Jessica

> Thank you so much, Artie. I really, really, really appreciate you doing this!

I send her a quick thumbs up but groan outwardly. My first meeting with Bea flashes through my mind again—her loosely plaited golden hair, intense ocean-blue stare, feminine curves...oh, and the burning distaste she has for me. *What have I gotten myself into?*

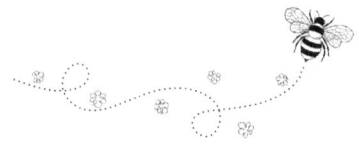

No, I'm not freaking out.

Just because it's 2 am and Bea's doorbell footage hasn't shown any activity all day, that does *not* mean there's anything to freak out over.

Yes, I'd been watching the grainy footage since 9 am to make sure she'd left for work, and no, there was no sign of her then, either—but there's probably a perfectly reasonable explanation that doesn't involve her freaking out or spiralling into a pit of despair.

I hate it when Silas is right.

But he's not right; not necessarily. I might've just missed her.

In my eighteen-hour watchathon of this livestream, I probably missed her.

Yeah—I'm not freaking out at all.

So why does something feel so off about this?

The ominous letter I found slid underneath my door earlier certainly isn't helping, glaring at me from underneath my mouse. I pick it up, examining the envelope again. No address, just my name written in cursive. The contents aren't as soft and pretty as the handwriting, though.

I reread it for what must be the hundredth time.

We don't take kindly to hackers feeding our information to the police. You will pay for what you did.
- D.W.

I feed the paper to the shredder. Believe it or not, that's *not* the first threatening letter to be hand-delivered to my apartment. I used to sell people's private information to others all the time. Now I get the police involved. Not everyone takes that well, and I've grown somewhat desensitized to the threats.

But this one's different.

It might be because I'm having the hardest time placing a *D.W.*

I've only been working with the police regularly for a year, which means it must be a recent tip. So how can I have absolutely no idea who *D.W.* is, or what information I'm supposed to have fed to my contact, Officer Monty Robinson?

By the time I'm finished scouring my files again for any hints, the clock reads 2:30 am and there's still no sign of Bea. But no, I'm *still* not freaking out, because I know nothing about her life and what she likes to do in her free time. Maybe she's a fan of staying out and partying all night on a Sunday. Perhaps she's got a partner and is perfectly safe at their house.

I scrub my face with my palms and grab my phone because a part of me knows if any of that was true, Silas wouldn't have asked me to check in on her.

"Artie, I swear to god you better be waking me up for good reason this time," Silas's gruff voice starts when he answers my call.

"Don't call me that. Does Bea have a boyfriend?" I ask, matching his pissed-off tone. Because yes, I'd quite like to be asleep right now too.

"What?"

"A *boyfriend*; does Bea have a partner whose house she might be staying at?"

"No boyfriend," he groans around a yawn. "But Arth—"

"You're a real pain in my arse, Knight." I hang up.

I slip on a dark green hoodie, shove my keys and phone into the pocket, and head out the door. Before my brain can conjure up any more worst-case scenarios, I'm driving towards her address.

For twelve full months, I have loathed myself for not knowing my friend was strung up in some shipping container without anyone to help him. Since I realised I could've—*maybe*—saved Silas, Jessica, and Bea from a whole lot of trauma and danger, I haven't been able to sleep. I keep tabs on Silas around town. I watch Jessica walk to and from the market. My phone is always on loud in case either of them needs me.

It's a fraction of what they deserve after my colossal oversight.

But now I'm speeding towards the house of a woman I barely know because she's missing from the camera feed I've been spying on all day. And I'm feeling guilty, because it never even occurred to me that I should be keeping an eye on Bea too.

I park in the deserted cul-de-sac just before 3 am. There are no streetlamps, so the stars shine extra brightly as I stride towards Bea's door. The houses all look the same: white siding, pruned gardens leading to the doorways, baby blue window shutters. It looks like something out of a Lifetime movie.

It's not until the brass knocker singes my fingertips mockingly that I contemplate the ridiculousness of the situation.

Then it clicks. Shit. *Shit.*

What the fuck am I doing here? This might just be the most stalker-y thing I've ever done. There is literally no good explanation for what I'm doing here...

"Hi, I know I'm a complete stranger, but I just thought I'd show up in the middle of the night because I hadn't seen you through your camera system I've hacked. Everything okay?"

Before I can sprint back to my car and drive far, *far* away, a warm light flicks on from inside and the door cracks open. Peering back at me through one barely open eye is Bea. Perfectly alive and well.

I am a complete fool.

"Arthur?" she croaks, opening the door wider so I can see her fuzzy pink pyjamas with cartoon pigs dotted over them. She's wearing a thin white T-shirt with her hair in a high bun, wispy blonde pieces flying out in all directions. My attention's drawn to a tiny dark freckle she has underneath her right eye. "What are you doing here? How'd you know my address?"

I stare at her for an agonisingly long time, begging my brain to say literally anything. The best it comes up with is the truth. "I noticed you weren't at the hospital today and I wanted to make sure you were okay."

She blinks at me. Once. Twice. Three times. The silence is excruciating.

And embarrassing.

"I shouldn't have come. You look fine; I'm stupid. Can we just forget this ever happened please?" I turn to hurry down the steps toward my car.

"Um, no?" She grabs the arm of my hoodie, and I almost slip on the icy bricks. I grab onto her wrist for balance. "How'd you know I was supposed to be working today?" she asks, her hard face accusing.

"Lucky guess?" I laugh awkwardly and oh god, I need to escape.

She rolls her eyes before they grow large, and she audibly gasps. "Did you hack into the hospital database and get my schedule?"

"You're smart," I hum as if I'm impressed. No use but owning it now. "Yes, that's exactly what I did."

She looks at me like I've just lost my head. "Are you insane?"

"Perhaps," I say with a wide grin. She snatches her wrist away from mine and I almost lose my balance again, so I drop my gaze and continue, "I apologise for checking your schedule. It was a mistake—I know that now. I just wanted to keep an eye on you with Silas and Jessica leaving today."

Her expression doesn't soften, but she also doesn't look any angrier. I'd better quit while I'm ahead. I throw her a small wave and back awkwardly down the stairs.

"Wait," she calls. I cringe inwardly—*so close* to the car. "How did you know I didn't go to work?"

I point. "Video doorbell. Notoriously easy to hack into."

She gasps, jaw dropping. "What is wrong with you? This is a serious invasion of my privacy! I could—I *should*—call the police!"

"You probably should," I agree. "But I beg you not to. It was an incredible error in judgment, and I really am very sorry. I can assure you it won't happen again."

She watches me, perplexed, as I unlock my car and shut myself in, giving her a two-finger salute through the closed window before leaving her standing there in her pyjamas.

By the time I get home, I'm furious with myself. I rip the new letter from my door, addressed in the same scrawled handwriting as earlier, and throw it straight in the shredder. *Stupid empty threats.* Can't D.W. see I'm too busy hating myself for the both of us?

Chapter Three

Bea

I LEAVE HOME EARLY today, making my way to the Twinkling Bliss café for my weekly round-up with Maria. I didn't sleep much last night. My conversation with Arthur wouldn't stop reeling through my thoughts, again and again.

And again.

He'd turned up to my house after breaking into my private camera system. Not to mention hacking into my personal work files and reading my sensitive information—like how am I not supposed to overthink every single minor detail of this situation?

Despite my swarming thoughts, the sight before me as I enter the café has me wanting to burst into laughter. Maria, blazing red bun pointed up in the air, with her head firmly rested on her forearms, draped along the counter helplessly. She moans something at me without looking up, but it's too muffled to decipher.

"Aren't you lucky I'm not a real customer?" I ask, throwing my bag on the counter next to her head and jumping on the barstool behind it. "Because I have to confess, this isn't the best customer service I've ever experienced."

"Get what you want and be quiet," Maria moans, turning her head to the side so I can see the true magnificence of the situation. Black mascara smudges spread halfway down her cheeks, glittery makeup turning her entire face into a mirrorball as the artificial lighting catches it. There are over twenty jokes cycling through my head, but something nags at me to be quiet.

That'll be my pestering people-pleasing trait making me think everyone secretly hates me.

"Fun night?" I chide, flicking her frizzy bun.

"The worst." She leans back comically slowly, peeking at me through squinted eyes. "I remember...dancing. There was *a lot* of dancing." I laugh as she drops her head to the counter again with a resounding whimper. "Tell me what's going on with you to make me forget about this ghastly hangover?" she begs.

And that's *my* cue to groan. "You're never going to guess who showed up at my door in the middle of the night."

"Arthur Avila?" she guesses, arm stifling the words.

I recoil. "How on earth did you know that?"

I hear her smirk. "I knew there was something going on between you two after the party the other night. So, how was it?"

"Oh, gross." I shudder. "As if I'd ever go anywhere near *Arthur Avila*."

"Ouch. Why was he at yours if not for a booty call, then?"

"He hacked into my video doorbell to watch me."

Maria's head flies up then, amber eyes wide. She slaps her forehead at what I'm assuming is a movement-induced migraine but doesn't take her eyes off me. "He did *what*?"

I nod enthusiastically because I knew it was creepy as hell. My feelings validated, I continue, "He said he was checking in, with Silas and Jessica leaving, but still."

Maria thinks over my words. "Well, I guess that's kind of sweet reasoning. Weird execution, but nice to know he's looking out for you?"

"No way. He's the last person I need looking out for me."

"Right," she drawls, turning away to make us a pot of rhubarb tea. "Remind me why we hate him again?"

I sigh outwardly—no one ever understands. "He was in Desmond's cameras, Mar. He must've seen *something*. Silas was literally on his deathbed, Jess and I were trapped..." I swallow hard at the memories flooding back in. "Arthur had the means to help, and he didn't. And no one seems to acknowledge that. They all hail him as some kind of hero."

Maria places a mug in front of me and fills it with steaming liquid. "You can't put all this on him, Bea."

"Why not?"

"Because you have no idea what it's like in that world. He didn't trap you or injure Silas. You're blaming him for something he had no real part in."

Isn't that my point?

"People died," I remind her. "Our friend *almost* died."

"I know that, but Silas is still alive. He's about to move away with his fiancée to a much better life! Everything worked out some way or another, so why are you still focused on hating Arthur so much? Let the past lie, Bea. You'll be happier for it."

I fake a cough to hide my sigh. She doesn't understand the feeling of drowning in grief, and that's fine. But if blaming Arthur takes even the slightest edge off this unbearable feeling, then what's the harm?

I excuse myself a minute later. It's no use debating it with her because she probably has a million other reasonable explanations for why she's right.

I just don't want to hear them.

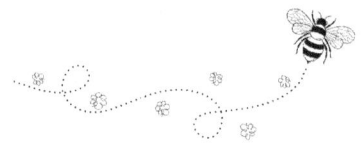

I'm not sure what I'm doing here, either. Pacing outside Arthur's apartment after coaxing the address from Jessica right outside the Twinkling Bliss. I didn't tell her what happened, but that only aggravated me more.

Who invades someone's privacy like that, then runs away like a coward?

I need answers if I'm ever going to sleep again, and he found my address without my knowing first. He crossed the line; I'm just jumping over it after him to even the playing field.

Squaring my shoulders, I garner all my mental strength and knock loudly.

Arthur opens his door and actually has the decency to look ashamed when his eyes catch mine. "Oh...hi."

"I want to talk about last night," I say, folding my arms. They're stiff from the chilly air and tension I've been carrying around all day.

My heart's pounding in my ears, and my hands are clammy as he takes a step towards me and closes his front door behind him.

"I'm just heading out on a walk," he says casually, like my being here isn't strange at all. I'm about to protest when he jerks his head towards the stairs and continues, "Let's go."

He guides me down the stairs, and we walk back into the heart of Bluetine Park. It makes my breath hitch. Each of the shops are decorated with twinkling lights, but there's still such a gaunt haze over the square. My vision pulses.

"Everything okay?" Arthur asks, walking around to face me. He squeezes my shoulders lightly and dips down to meet my eye level. I snap my attention to him.

"Yeah—*yes*. It's just...difficult being here. Too many ghosts." I try to laugh it off, but it comes out as a mere sigh. He looks at me like he has questions, but he doesn't ask them. He simply gives me a small smile and starts walking again. I do the same.

"I was planning on heading to the river. Fewer ghosts down there?" he asks.

I have no idea whether he's being genuine or just throwing me a bone, but I concede anyway. "The river sounds nice," I say through the scarf barrier I've made around the lower half of my face. He smirks and turns down a side street, leading away from Bluetine Park.

"So," he starts as the sparkling river comes into view. Moonlight breaks across the moving water, skittering in all directions.

Warm streetlamps line the bank on either side, creating spotlights for flying insects to prance in. A lone boat floats lazily down the waterway. "You had questions."

"Yes, I did—I do."

"Ask away, Honeybee."

I look at him through my lashes, chronically unimpressed. He's not going to get out of this with a stupid nickname. *I need to remain firm.* "Don't call me that. I want to know why you did it. What could've possessed you to find my address and schedule, and then come barging over at three in the morning?"

He looks down at his shoes. "That's a fair question, Beatrice."

Beatrice? The audacity of this man!

Arthur grins at me like the Cheshire Cat. I must look horrified, or furious, or downright pissed. "You're seriously smiling right now. Is this all a joke to you?"

"No," he drawls, looking back to the water. "I'm sorry. I'm not very good at the deep conversations. I'm much more suited to sarcasm."

"I'm not looking for sarcastic answers. And, since it's my personal data you stole from my place of work, I think you could be a little more willing to take my feelings into consideration."

My chest tightens as I take shallow breaths between my words. I *hate* confrontation, and my lungs feel like they're collapsing with every angry syllable.

Arthur stops and turns to me, hand on my arm. "Are you okay?"

"Yes," I snap. Although I'm definitely hyperventilating, and I don't *sound* okay. "It's my anxiety. It got a lot worse since…everything."

"Shit," he murmurs, and a part of me feels the tiniest bit guilty for the inconvenience I'm probably causing him. He tugs my arm gently towards him as he leans against the railing, watching the water. I might've resisted if I wasn't so focused on my breathing, but I am so my body follows him willingly. Plus, his shoulder is a welcomed warmth next to mine. "What makes you feel calmer?"

I gasp out a quiet laugh. "Not having to confront the stranger who turned up at my house in the middle of the night might be a good start."

He hums a concerned sound, and I notice his hand has moved down to my wrist. He's stroking his thumb gently over my skin, and I think he might be looking for my pulse. "Don't then. Just watch the water, and I'll explain everything in a minute. No confrontation needed, I promise."

I bite the inside of my lip as I do what he tells me, feeling my heartbeat slowly soften. I count how many ripples the docked boat makes as it bangs into the bank over and over. Arthur's thumb never moves from that one spot on my wrist, and I watch that too.

Seemingly satisfied with my slowing pulse, he sighs and drops his head. "I meant what I said last night, Bea. I was genuinely concerned that you might not be dealing with Silas and Jessica leaving, and I thought if I could keep tabs on you—just for one day—that I'd let it go. You seemed really upset at the party, and I just wanted to know you were okay. That's why I did it."

I want to sucker punch my heart for that silly little flip it does, and I hope my wrist pulse doesn't betray me. "But you don't even know me," is all I say.

He smirks. "True, but Silas never stops going on about you. I feel like I kind of know you through him. And I know he likes to look after you, so with him moving away, I think that responsibility may have transferred to me. Maybe I'm overcompensating for something."

I swear I see a quick flicker of something in his eyes at that, and maybe he really does think he has something to overcompensate for.

Does he agree with me? That he's at least partly to blame for all this hurt?

Before I can explore that further, he pushes off the railing and begins walking again. My hand slips free of his and it's instantly colder. I'm not about to admit to missing his touch so I shove it in my pocket and follow after him.

"Any other questions you want to ask?" Arthur asks with a wry smile, one dimple on his right cheek making it look slightly lopsided. That careless grin brings everything crashing back down on me—of course he doesn't think he's in the wrong.

No one ever agrees with me on that.

"How'd you get into the hospital database?" I ask, shaking my disappointment away.

"I used my special skills."

"You hacked into it illegally." I don't need to train my voice to sound wholly unimpressed.

"There's a bit more to it than that," he drawls.

"I'm listening," I challenge, but he only puts a finger to his lips. I grumble and he laughs at me. "Do you not sell sensitive information to criminals for money?"

I think he must physically recoil, because now he's a step behind me. "Not anymore."

"What does that mean?"

"It means, don't assume you know everything about a stranger, Honeybee."

"Stop calling me that stupid nickname!"

He stiffens, but only for a moment before that smug mask is back. "Would you prefer I call you Beatrice?"

"No."

"Well, I can offer you Beatrice or Honeybee. Which is it?"

"I'm going home." I ignore the question, turning away from him and stalking back the way we came. The stars wink at me as he catches up quickly, knocking my shoulder with his.

"Okay, I'm sorry Bea. I get uncomfortable when people think they know everything about my job. I can't defend myself because of all the secrecy," he holds up his hands and looks me directly in the eye, "but I'm not the bad guy...not anymore."

I take a moment to allow those words to sink in. *Not anymore.*

What does that mean?

His expression tells me I probably shouldn't pry, so we walk in silence back to Bluetine Park. It's not until we reach his front door on the side of the betting shop that he breaks our peace. "Can I walk you to your car? It's getting dark."

"I'm fine," I reply defiantly, although I could think of a million things I'd rather be doing than walking through Bluetine Park alone this late in the evening.

Arthur must read that on my face because he faces me and asks again, "Come on, let me walk you to your car—please? Where are you parked?"

I point silently and he leads me down a side street. He places a tentative hand on the small of my back and I don't resist. We walk for what feels like forever, and I don't miss Arthur looking down at his empty wrist as we walk. *Putting on a show, as usual.*

"Are you sure we're going the right way?"

"We're almost there," I say wearily.

"Right. Do you mind if I ask why you've parked two miles away from the square? There are spaces right outside my house."

"I tend to avoid Bluetine Park as much as I can," I admit. If he can be honest with me tonight, I'll return the sentiment. I give him a small, tight-lipped smile. "Ghosts."

He doesn't reply, but I feel his fingertips dig into my back a fraction deeper. The touch sends a flicker of something like comfort through me. A zing of electricity that I purposefully ignore. In that moment, I think I might even be grateful for his company. I let myself enjoy that feeling for a quick moment in our comfortable silence.

"Ah, there you are." He points at my sedan parked on the other side of the road. I smile to myself—*he remembered.*

"Thank you for walking me." I step away from his touch. "Can I drop you back off at your apartment? I bet you hadn't bargained for such a long walk in the opposite direction."

He shuts my door after I slide in and I roll down the window between us. "No thank you, I'll enjoy the walk. It's how I clear my head."

I nod thoughtfully. "Okay. Thank you for the answers. Guess I'll see you around." I ignite the engine and roll the car away from the kerb. He gives me a lasting smile and steps back, letting me leave this time. A glimmer of wickedness overcomes me and I drawl, "Bye, Artie."

"Don't call me that," is the last thing I hear him shout as I drive away. I smile despite myself. I got my answers, and they weren't as disturbing as expected.

Arthur walks to clear his head. After a long day of *not* participating in illegal activities, because he doesn't do that anymore.

Tonight's given me a lot of information to digest, and I realise that a lot of my preconceived notions towards Arthur Avila might've been wrong. *Oof, that's a tough pill to swallow.*

Still, I must remember his smug smile and irritating inability to remain serious for longer than a second. Frustrating doesn't begin to cover *that*, and he likes to joke about things I'll never find funny.

As I finally park outside my house, I settle on one thing before pushing Arthur to the back of my mind—to a place where I'll never have to think about him ever again.

Maybe he does have a conscience, after all.

Chapter Four
Artie

I arrive home later than I expected after my surprise two-mile detour. I don't mind the walk—sometimes I'm glad for an excuse to get out of my small apartment. The place was convenient when I started my business, but now it just feels cramped.

It's not that I don't have the money or time to move. It's just that there's always something better to do, like walking a pretty woman to her car in the dwindling twilight.

As I climb the final stair to my front door, I cringe. Suddenly, I'm completely grateful for the extra miles added to my walk. My eyes dart left and right, checking for bandits ready to pounce on me in the small entryway, before snapping back to the note taped to the door.

Despite my better instinct, I roll my eyes. "Another note," I muse loudly enough for anyone still lurking in the shadows to hear. "How original. I really do prefer my fan mail through email, though. Much better for the environment."

Nothing.

No shuffling or tiny coughs or big, scary crime lords leaping out at me.

Guess they didn't want to stick around. I'll take it as a win.

I unlock my door, rip the note down from the wood, and slip into the apartment. I turn on my lamp straight away and inspect the letter. A quick glance at the shredder, but then a longer one at that damned cursive handwriting.

Something tells me to open it, so I slide a finger between the envelope's edge and split it apart.

Arthur Avila. 30 years old, Caucasian male, lives alone. Friends with Police Chief Monty Robinson.

We know who you are, where you live, and how to hit you where it hurts most. Call the police off and tell them you made a huge mistake, or we'll have no choice but to teach you a lesson of our own.

- D.W.

How is it possible I still have no idea who this person is?! They are literally threatening my life, and yet my useless brain is drawing a blank.

I shake my head and run a hand down my face, too tired to think. My body aches and my eyes beg for the sweet release of sleep, my brain slowly turning itself off. I feed the letter to the shredder, ready to push that concern to tomorrow's to-do list.

But I'm not even a step away from my desk when the phone rings, and a shot of cortisol blasts through my body. *No one friendly ever rings at midnight on a Monday.*

My heavy limbs try to carry me towards the bedroom, but I make myself pick up the phone and hold it to my ear. I slink back against the counter, and I'm pretty sure it's holding me up at this point. "Hello," I say, a grin laced around my words.

"I'd suggest you stop throwing our letters away and begin taking them as a real threat."

My eyes dart around, but I don't allow my callous body language to falter. "Ah, so you're the infamous D.W., then. So nice to finally have you on the phone," I croon. "Lovely handwriting, by the way. Tell me, have you bugged my apartment?"

"Mr Avila, your friends in the police force will not be able to help you once we come after you. Call them off before you see what we are capable of." The line is crackly, but I can still hear that the voice is being distorted to stop me from figuring out who I'm talking to.

"Where's the harm in a little challenge? Call it friendly competition between you and the police force. You can never get too comfortable these days, you know." The breaths down the phone become louder, almost turning into snarls. I push on, "What do you say, *D.W.*? Shall we forget all about this and move on with our lives?"

The voice ignores my baiting. "Call your pigs off or we might just pay your *female* a quick visit."

It takes me a second to realise who my female is. I don't have a female—nor do I have a girlfriend, a woman, or anything slightly less derogatory.

But then it crashes down on me like a tonne of bricks. *They're talking about Bea.*

And now my brain is entering panic mode because I can't drag her into another one of these messes. It's simply not an option.

"You must be mistaking me with someone else. I don't have a *female*," I say, voice a lethal quiet.

A sinister chuckle down the phone—the first indication that I'm talking to a real person and not some AI-generated robot. "Beatrice Di Menna. 29 years old, currently residing at sixty-three Bempton Drive. She drives a blue Fiesta with the plate K-D-nineteen S-M-V. Does that sound familiar, Mr Avila?"

The blood drains from my face and my lips tighten. But I train my voice to remain cocky, taunting. "Nope, not my female, girl, or lady friend—nothing. Unfortunately for you, I barely know her. So you'll have to find someone else to threaten me with, I'm afraid."

Although I regret those words as soon as I speak them, because I'd prefer he not threaten me with *anyone*.

"We'll see about that, Mr Avila. Goodnight."

"Have a blessed week," I say before the line goes dead.

Shit. *Shit*.

Every muscle in my body is alert and tense. My heavy eyelids kiss the distant thought of sleep goodbye, shedding a silent tear as they mourn.

After our conversation tonight, hell will have to freeze over before I allow any harm to come to Bea again. I'm cursing Silas, because yes, this is his fault for getting me invested in Bea's safety in the first place. And now I'm calling him.

"Artie?" Silas's voice groans through the phone.

"You're an arse."

"Oh good, I was wondering when you'd be back to pick up on this conversation," he deadpans. "Do enlighten me."

"I was perfectly happy knowing nothing about Bea or her well-being. We were all fine with you leaving, and now I've dragged her into the path of a very angry criminal who wants to teach me a lesson for feeding their information to the police."

"Wait, what? Are you in trouble?"

"No, not at all. Just thought it would be a funny joke to call you in the middle of the night and lie about someone threatening my life. Bye!"

"Shut up, idiot. Who's threatening you."

"Someone going by the name D.W.," I groan.

"Do you need help?"

"No." *Yes.*

He misses a beat. "There's no shame in asking for help, Arth."

I miss two. "I know, Sy. It's probably all empty threats, anyway."

I won't be the person to drag Silas back into this mess. I can't—he's been through too much already. I'm just going to have to deal with this one on my own.

"Probably," he agrees, although he doesn't sound convinced. "Call me if you change your mind, okay? And remember—it wasn't your fault."

"Thanks," is all I get out before hanging up.

It wasn't my fault. The sentiment Silas has become so used to telling me during these late-night calls. The ones I use to calm me down after the nightmares claim me, or when I'm too amped with guilt to sleep.

I'm not to blame, and I'm learning that.

But this, with D.W.? That *is* my fault. And I know I won't be able to live with myself if Bea gets caught in the crossfire.

Next on my call list is the man I'm supposed to be standing down.

"Avila? What the heck are you calling me at one in the morning for?" Officer Monty Robinson barks through the phone, voice gruff from interrupted sleep.

I've known Monty for nine years. Once upon a time, believe it or not, I hadn't been the excellent covert hacker I am today. One slip landed me in the interrogation room, where we struck an unlikely friendship. He slipped me his number and told me to use it if I ever felt like jumping over to his team. It wasn't until last winter that I finally used it.

"I've got a situation, boss. Do you know anyone by the initials D.W. that I've given you information about recently?"

"Are you serious—send me an email!"

"It's important, Monts. I'm being threatened, and so is my friend."

The big man yawns, and it all but bursts my eardrum. "What do they say, Avila? Stupid games, stupid prizes." The line goes dead.

Wowza. I follow up with a strongly worded email that I have no doubt he'll skip over tomorrow, but I send it anyway.

Monty—

A serious criminal under the initials D.W. is threatening me and my friend. While I may deserve a fraction of this torment, she certainly does not. Please check the tips I've sent you recently and let me know if you find a match for the initials.

Thanks, Avila

I send a few similar messages to my Inner Circle group chat. We're a small group of hackers located all over the world, founded by Kyra on one of the more secretive hacking forums.

Despite sending the message in the coldest hours of the morning, the replies come through instantly.

Johnny

> In all honesty Arth, I'd call the cops off. It's the safest way if you don't want this innocent person dragged into your mess.

Aaryan

> Monts wouldn't allow it, John. Sorry Arthur, you're going to have to find another way to deal with whoever this is. I don't know anyone under D.W., but I'll keep an ear out for you.

Kyra

> This is exactly why I tell you idiots not to get involved with the police. It never ends well for anyone.

Johnny

> Time and a place, eh Kyra?

I grumble towards the ceiling. They're no help, but it's nice to know they'll look out for us in their own corners of the internet.

D.W.

D.W.

The letters get stuck on my tongue, coating it like the bitterest poison.

I find the tiny microphone taped to the underside of a picture frame eventually. Spy mics are often impossible to find, but it's not the first time my apartment has been bugged, either. I soak it in water before throwing it away and spend the rest of the night working out potential names to go with the bitter initials. By the time I finally throw my pen down and rub my eyes with the heels of my hands, the sun is casting a mocking glow over my desk.

I might be no closer to figuring out who my freaky stalker is, but one thing is for sure—I'll need to keep far away from Bea from now on. I've become a magnet for what she fears most in the world, and the only way to keep her safe is to stay away.

Chapter Five
Bea

I'M FINISHING MY LAST house call of the day when Maria's name flashes across the car's centre console. I answer through hands-free, excited to get home and crash into a pile of sheer exhaustion on the bed. The lounge floor will also suffice if the bedroom turns out to be too far away.

"Hello, lovely lady," Maria's voice booms through the speaker. "How was work? Hang on, let me guess—fourteen?"

Maria thinks it's the pinnacle of humour to call me as soon as I finish work and guess how many cups of tea I'd consumed that day. Without fail, no matter how busy the café is at 5 pm, she rings me to check in. I love that about her.

"It was somewhere around sixteen," I relent sheepishly. "I can't help it, Mar. I am a tea woman, through and through."

Her cackle bounces around the car, surrounding me with her infectious cheer. "And I wouldn't have you any other way. I did actually have an ulterior motive for this call today—*someone* has a big birthday coming up!"

I groan. Birthdays are not my idea of fun. A party in my name, with a guest list of more people than I've ever met in my entire life. Alcohol. Loud music. Maria forcing everyone to dance with her lest she call them boring. It literally sounds like my anxiety's worst nightmare.

"I already told you, Mar..."

"I know, I know. But listen—what about a small get-together with less than ten people, at the café so you're in a safe location, with a pinkie promise from yours truly that I'll remain your sober sister all night so I can whisk you away whenever you get too uncomfortable. Do I get the green light to start planning?"

I give the centre console a disbelieving look. Maria declaring herself the sober sister is as believable as Father Christmas flying around the world in a single night. I'd be better off booking myself a taxi right now.

But that's what people usually do for birthdays, isn't it? They have fun, they drink with their friends. I should be putting myself out there a bit more. Can't stay cooped up in my lonely bubble forever, right? And less than ten people sounds...manageable.

I sigh, already regretting my decision. "Fine, but only ten people. And I have to know them all."

"Yes, you have my word, superstar! You're going to have the best thirtieth ever, I'll make sure of it!" Then she squeals so high I'm surprised the windows don't shatter. I smirk as she finishes with, "Okay, I need to go now—lots of planning to do! But mark my words, Saturday is now officially declared The Thirtieth Birth-Bea of the Centur-Bea!"

I have to chuckle at that. "That doesn't even make—" I start, but she hangs up before I can finish. I drive the rest of my long way home in silence, trying to make the most of the excitement I'm feeling, while also ignoring the trepidation about what this weekend will bring.

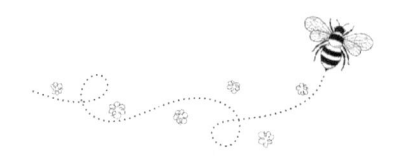

The rest of the week flies by in a bland blur of work, cleaning, and trying out new recipes from a cookbook I picked up last week. My current hobby is gourmet cooking. And through what I assume to be no fault of my own, everything is turning out too soupy or too spicy. I'm giving myself until next week before I give up entirely.

So by the time Saturday rolls around, I'm weirdly excited to get to the café. Maria texted me to expect a taxi at 7 pm, so I'm applying a light layer of makeup and tousling my curled hair for the zillionth time in the hallway mirror. Waiting. Very impatiently.

My dress is a river of sparkly sequins—further out of my comfort zone than I'd usually ever dare, but if I can't take a leap on my thirtieth birthday, when can I?

"That's probably the smallest leap anyone's ever taken," Maria chided when I told her yesterday.

But still, it's a leap and I think I look quite good.

The driver honks outside bang on seven and I skip out instantly. A light bubble floats up from my stomach and pops in my chest, letting loose a flutter of teeny tiny butterflies. Good butterflies, I think. But as the taxi drives towards the Twinkling Bliss, I still have to sit on my hands to stop them from shaking.

When we get to the darkened café, I notice all the lights are off but the door is still unlocked. "Hello?" I call out as I let myself in. A few long seconds of silence pass, and a deflating feeling cowers over me, wondering if Maria has truly forgotten...

"SURPRISE!"

The bellowing crowd springs up from behind the counter. I jump back into the glass door with my hand covering my smile, banging it dangerously against its frame.

Maria stands front and centre with a glittery party hat and a streamer hanging out of her mouth. I spot a few of the nurses from my old hospital along with Jessica, who's jumping up and down and whooping, Silas, a soft smirk tugging at his lips as he squints at the noise, and...Arthur. Looking wholly miserable, like he'd rather be anywhere else, leaning against the back wall. My own face falls.

Why is he here?

Who invited *him*?

I shake the tension from my face as I turn towards the others, who are slowly coming towards me in a huddle. I am *not* going to let him ruin my party.

I refuse.

I hug the guests one by one, Maria furiously blowing her streamer in everyone's faces as I do. As Silas advances in on me and envelopes me in a hug, he grabs the streamer and scrunches it in his palm, flicking it back at her. Jessica hits him playfully on the arm, but Maria simply plucks out another from the plunge of her neckline and we all cackle loudly. Silas rolls his eyes and stalks off to sit in a faraway booth, but a ghost of a smile betrays him.

"Let's get the birthday girl a drink!" Maria squeals, hauling me towards the counter littered with half-empty bottles and red plastic cups. Jessica hooks her fingers through my other hand and skips along with us.

"I don't think I'm drinking tonight," I start as Maria mixes up a lethal mix of white whiskey and lemonade for us all.

"Don't be silly, it's your birthday!" Jess sings, taking a sip from the cup Maria handed her. One eye slams shut, and the other rolls to the back of her head. She chokes back a coughing fit and pours the remaining drink into my cup.

"Yeah, Bea! You're supposed to get blindingly drunk tonight—we're all here to look after you," Maria hands me my drink, and I peer into the cauldron of fizzing poison. A little alcohol tends to make my anxiety worse, but if I push through to reach the happy buzz, I might just have the time of my life.

And the girls are right, it *is* my birthday. And damn it if I don't deserve some fun.

"Okay, but you—" I jab a finger at Jessica, "—have to promise me you'll get me in a taxi at the end of the night because this one can't be trusted." I throw a thumb back at Maria, who has already drained her cup and is pouring herself another. Her cherry-red lips stretch into a devilish grin.

"Normally I would totally agree with you there, but tonight I *can* be trusted, because I've already sorted out another sober sister for you. Arthur actually volunteered to do it, so talk to him when you want to go home."

"That was nice of him," Jessica says.

Was it?

"Wait, why is he here anyway?" I ask.

Maria shrugs. "You told me I couldn't invite any strangers—he's not a stranger, he's Silas and Jessica's friend. You're basically their adopted child, so he should be your friend too." Her eyes turn shifty and a fraction mischievous. "And...I don't know, but I feel like there was a *vibe* I squashed at the leaving party. I might've dragged him here just in case you wanted to explore that unfinished business."

"Wait, what?" Jessica asks as Maria jumps back to avoid my backhand. "You and Artie—what *vibe*?"

Ignoring her, I hiss, "Maria, what the heck were you thinking?"

"Funny," is all the explanation I get before she's cackling like an evil queen.

I dare a glance over at him, slumped in a booth laughing with Silas. My cheeks redden. It doesn't help that he looks incredible tonight, with a dark green silky shirt unbuttoned to his chest. His curls bouncing across his forehead with every movement, full lips and shining eyes. "This is mortifying!" I groan.

"So there's no vibe between you and Artie?" Jessica interjects.

"No!"

"Well," Maria raises her eyebrows and wiggles her hand like there's a fifty-fifty chance.

"No!" I repeat. "Absolutely not, no way. Dear *god*—"

"What are we praying for over here?" a deep voice asks, and we all jump back very suspiciously.

Great, now Arthur probably thinks we're hiding something and won't stop until he gets it out of one of us. It'll be Jessica who cracks. She's terrible at keeping secrets.

Arthur glances between us all as we aimlessly stare back at him. *Quick, Bea...something to say...*

"We were just discussing the possibility of Bea's feel—" Maria starts.

"NOTHING. We were talking about nothing," I shout, smoothing out my hair with clammy palms.

Jessica and Maria exchange a wide-eyed look, and Maria says, "Oh yeah, silly me. We weren't talking about *anything*." Then they're drifting backwards onto the dance floor, snickering with each other like schoolchildren.

I make a mental note to kill them both later.

But for now...I turn back to Arthur, who's staring back at me with an obviously confused and perhaps even slightly scared expression. "Thank you for coming," I smile politely, dropping my shoulders slightly.

"Are you kidding? I wouldn't have missed it for the world," he says with a coy smile as he pours himself a lemonade.

"Oh," I say, because he's obviously making some sort of weird joke. Maria probably dragged him from whatever he'd rather be doing, and he felt too awkward to leave. *Why do I feel guilty about that?* "I'm sorry, you can leave if you have other plans."

He gives me a confused quirk of an eyebrow. "No way. I've accepted the job as your sober chauffeur now, so you've got me until the end of the night."

"Sober sister," I correct.

He laughs, the corner of his eyes crinkling and his dimple coming out in full force. "My apologies, birthday girl. I've accepted the job as your sober *sister*, so I'll be around until you're ready to go home."

I smile and accept the drink he poured me. Maybe Maria didn't drag him here against his will, after all. "Thank you, but I'm more than capable of getting myself in a taxi."

"I won't hear any more of that slander. I'm here, I don't drink anyway, and I have nothing else I'd rather be doing. So go enjoy yourself, birthday girl. I'll be waiting." He finishes with a wink, and something in my chest convulses. I don't dare say anything else, so I tip my drink to him and back away.

Am I supposed to break eye contact first? He's still watching me...

And that's when I bump into Antonia from my old hospital. I hear Arthur let out a loud laugh, and I glare at him before apologising and hugging her, along with Deena and Carrie—who I also used to work with. I hardly notice finishing another two drinks while talking, with Jessica floating by every time my cup is empty to replace it with another. By the time they announce they need to get back to the hospital, I'm swaying. Luckily, I'm too happy to care.

Chuckling merrily to myself, my body moves on autopilot as I stumble towards the back of the café and plonk down next to Silas.

"Hey," he says, nudging my shoulder with his own. "You doing okay?"

"Yessir," I slur, squinting to keep his face from splitting into five different floating heads. I think he's laughing so I giggle along.

"Do you need some water?"

I think for a second before shaking my head. "Mm-no thanks. Jess has been keeping me *well quenched*."

"I'm going to get you some water," he laughs anyway, pushing up from the booth. I go to ask him for something stronger instead, but he's already swirling towards the counter. Right where Arthur's sitting.

I put an elbow on the table to prop my head up, and I can feel myself grinning like an idiot as I stare at them, but I can't look away. Everything is a blur and that's simply hilarious to me.

"You feeling good, honey?" Jessica asks, sliding into the booth. I snap out of my spiralling stare, and a horrifying image materialises before me: Arthur looking right back at me, a small smile tugging his lips.

Shit, he didn't see me looking at him, did he?

"Bea?"

"Yep," I say, snapping my head to look at Jessica. "I'm fine; I'm good. How are you?"

She laughs nervously. "Okay, I just wanted to make sure. You and Artie have been staring at each other for like five minutes now," she grins, and my stomach plummets. "If you wanted to keep something to the imagination, maybe stop gazing at him."

I run a hand down my face but stop quickly when I remember that I am wearing makeup. I put my palms together to create a shield in front of my face and whisper, "Did he look mad?"

She does the same and makes her own shield, creating a wall of digits between us and the rest of the room. "No, he looked *dangerous*." She wiggles her eyebrows.

"I don't even know what that means," I hiss at her. But before I can demand she elaborate, someone pinches my fingers and gently lowers them down to the table. Silas slides into the booth next to Jessica and robs me of her attention as Arthur's face appears in front of me.

"Hey," he says in a tauntingly quiet voice. "Are you having fun?"

I nod.

"Glad to hear it. I thought you might be asking me with your eyes for an excuse to get out of here." One side of his mouth quirks up in a soft smile.

"Why would I want to leave?" I ask. It's my party, after all. I can't leave early—can I?

"I guess I took it the wrong way," he says with a shrug. "My mistake."

"You've been making a lot of those around me, haven't you?"

Arthur's eyes sparkle behind his glasses and I think I might want to take them off him to get a better look.

"What's that?" Silas interrupts, dragging our attention from each other.

"Nothing," Arthur shrugs, far too demurely to be believable.

"What mistakes has he been making around you?" Silas is asking me now, ignoring the look on Arthur's face. But I'm watching the way his tongue darts around the inside of his cheek like he's trying to swallow the truth. Like he's trying to get a rise out of Silas by acting so casually.

So I answer for him. "Your friend stalked me through my video doorbell and turned up on my doorstep at three in the morning before running away with his tail between his legs." I give Silas an expression like it's no big deal, but my cheeks heat as I feel Arthur's eyes on me.

"I can't believe you'd betray your *sister* like that," he whispers, but his grin is impressed. "Look, Sy—"

"Just get her home in one piece," Silas interrupts him.

"You're still going to let me near her?" Arthur asks, and I wonder for a moment what that means.

"You're the only one sober enough to drive."

"High praise, my Lordship."

"Arthur..." Silas growls in warning.

"Fine. Honeybee, let me know when I'm needed." He begins to retreat from the death glare he's currently receiving from Silas, but I down the dregs of my water and rise from the booth's bench.

"I'm ready now. Let me just say goodbye to Mar." My bare legs catch on the sticky pleather seat, throwing me off balance, but large muscles cocoon me before I hit the floor. Arthur hoists me up and steadies me, tucking a stray curl behind my ear as he smirks down at me. I look up at him wide-eyed, cheeks burning. "Sorry," I utter as I push away from his grip.

"Don't apologise," he murmurs as I turn to find Maria. She's holding two thumbs up at me as she perches on the side of the counter, changing the song on her phone.

"We're going to take off now, Mar. You have a ride?" I ask as I dab the beads of sweat around her temple with a napkin. She's been dancing enough for all of us, it seems.

"My sister's on her way. Nice going snagging the hot hacker," she whispers with a crude gesture. "Make sure you invite him in for a nightcap."

I poke my tongue out at her. "Yeah. That's not happening."

"Tsk. You don't know what's good for you, lovely," Maria mutters but kisses me on the cheek and pats my head. She's as gone as I am. "Have you had a good time?"

"Oh, the *best*. Thank you so much," I say with a big smile. "Text me when you get home."

"You too—but not while he's still on top of you. I can wait," she cackles, and that's my sign to leave. "Goodbye, lovers!" she calls as Arthur meets me at the café's front door and guides me into the night with a hand on my lower back.

Cooling kisses from the frosty air litter my skin and make me breathless. The world tilts, spins, and shifts as I walk with Arthur to his car, not caring when he opens the door for me and helps me sit. My skin melts into the soft leather as I lean back in a bid to slow the splintering world around me.

I *really* don't want to throw up in this nice car.

Arthur appears in the driver's seat next to me and I can feel his eyes on me again. I drop my head to the side despite myself because a tiny part of my brain thinks that I might want to look at him, too.

Even through my hazy reality, I can see him trying to keep his face neutral. Biting the inside of his lip, green eyes glittering. I grin widely. He lets his own smile loose. We stay here for a while, staring at each other for absolutely no reason. It feels...nice. Comforting, somehow.

I could just lean forward and...

"Did you have a good night?" he asks, breaking me out of my questionable thoughts. He turns the heating on full blast, clearing the fogged windows before setting off.

"I did," I nestle deeper into the seat, enjoying the feeling it's offering as if I'm being hugged from behind. *I love being hugged from behind.* "Did you?"

He hums. "Of course I did."

But my smile twists into confusion. "Then how come you looked so annoyed when I arrived?"

"Did I?" he asks, a hint of amusement in his voice. He pulls away from the café. "I didn't realise you were watching me."

"It's pretty hard to ignore someone looking like they'd rather be anywhere else in the world than at your party."

"I had fun," he repeats.

"You could've told your face. You looked miserable."

He tucks his lips together to stop from laughing, and his cheeks puff. "You must not have been looking at the right times, Beatrice."

I scoff. I'd been looking at him for most of the night. I know I'm not imagining that scowl and those shadowed eyes. But the warm air is making me sleepy, and I decide it doesn't matter. I had a good time, and that's the most important thing anyway.

"Why can't I call you Artie?" I ask to change the subject.

"It's not my name," he says simply, as if he doesn't get the irony of that. He's focused on the road, and I wonder what he'd do if I leaned across and flicked that stray curl hanging in front of his eye away.

Stop, Bea.

I shake that thought right out of my head, blaming it on too much alcohol. "But when I ask you not to call me names, you ignore me."

"You really don't like Honeybee?" His voice almost sounds...hurt. No, wait. That's arrogant challenge. He's challenging me.

"I don't care."

"Sounds like you do," he chides.

I fold my arms in defiance. "I just think that if you're going to call me names, I should get to call you one, too."

"Call me whatever you want to." Artie wiggles his eyebrows at me. "Might I suggest Pretty Boy?"

I snort. "No."

Artie *tsks* but tries again. "Prince Charming, Your Hero? How about Dreamboat?"

"You really do think highly of yourself, don't you." My happy buzz makes me giggle.

"I do."

"Dream Boy," I drawl, each letter rolling off my tongue slowly.

"What? No. Dream*boat*. Dreamboat."

"I like Dream Boy, though."

"Are you admitting you like me, Honeybee?" Artie gasps dramatically and I give him a flat look.

"No. Just want to show you how it feels to be called a stupid nickname."

"I don't have a problem with it."

"Oh yeah, right." I hike my eyebrows up and implore, "You'd seriously be okay with me calling you Dream Boy in front of people?"

"It's a free world, Bea. I can't stop you from doing anything."

I bob my head resolutely and instantly regret it. My vision goes black before projecting stars throughout the car and beyond into the night. *Damn right he can't stop me.*

Although…"It's a stupid name."

"Better than Artie," he reasons. I consider asking how that'd ever be true, but this seat is heated and so comfortable, and suddenly I don't care that much.

Artie taps my knee lightly as he parks up outside my door, and I shoot up out of my relaxed position.

"Thank you, Archie." *It's the best I could come up with, okay?*

His eyebrows arch and his lips curl into a taunting smirk. "Are you confusing me with someone, Honeybee?"

"No—"

"Because if you're calling me by another man's name, my feelings are going to get hurt." His voice has lowered into almost a growl.

"I wasn't..." I feel myself flailing slightly, my palms turning clammy and the tightness returning to my chest after a blissful night without it.

Maybe he sees it, too, because he reaches over to put a hand on my knee, gives it a reassuring squeeze, and smiles up at me. "Can I walk you home?"

I look towards my door, then back at him. "It's like ten steps."

That smile might just have the power to melt me completely. "I'm aware, but you're in very high heels and so *incredibly* drunk. I'd really feel better if I could give you a hand and avoid a hospital trip tonight."

He looks at me expectantly, and I concede begrudgingly. "Fine," I sulk and open my door. He's already there to meet me as I swing my legs out. "But my heels aren't *that* high."

Never mind my ankles are throbbing and my calves had gone numb somewhere around my second drink. I could still walk.

But the universe wants to embarrass me even more apparently, so I trip over an uneven stone on the path to my door. Arthur steadies me with a powerful hand wrapped around my forearm, not letting go as we ascend the stairs.

"I need you to know that I always trip over that stone," I drawl flatly.

"You should get it fixed," he says with a matching tone, not daring to meet my eye. I suspect it's because if he looked at me, he might just burst into a never-ending fit of laughter.

We arrive at my door, and I fumble with the lock before it swings open. A wave of whiskey bravery washes over me as I ask, "Would you like to come in?"

He takes a sharp inhale and waits just enough time for me to completely regret asking, and I consider slamming the door in his face to avoid hearing him decline the invitation.

But before I combust on the spot from my utter embarrassment, Arthur shakes his head and says, "Sure."

CHAPTER SIX

Artie

I DON'T KNOW WHY I accept Bea's offer either. Not when I vowed to stay away from her less than a week ago.

Maria asked me to come to the party, and I swear I said no. But apparently, that was the wrong answer, because she proceeded to lead me out of my apartment by the collar of my shirt. I was then told to sit quietly in the café until it was time to set up, which was really just me hanging up decorations while Maria bossed me around.

She then pulled out an outfit for me from thin air. A green silk shirt, which I'm definitely keeping, and black dress trousers. No idea where she got them from or even where she hid them all day, but what I don't know can't hurt me.

Anyway, by the time Bea had arrived, I'd been so paranoid that someone was watching me through the tall windows that I must've forgotten to tell my face to fake happy.

So now I'm standing in Bea's kitchen, failing miserably at staying away from her, and not caring in the slightest because she's kind of cute when she's stumbling around like a tipsy newborn fawn.

And that dress—*jesus*.

I shove my hands into my pockets to stop them from doing what they want, which is to reach out and touch the sequins. To touch *her*.

She's brewing us each a cup of tea from her extensive collection. She must've talked me through a dozen options before proceeding to give me a slurred lecture about why the one I'd picked was the incorrect choice.

So now I'm getting a surprise. Whatever it is, it smells nice. God knows I could use a pick-me-up.

I'd barely slept this week since the threat from D.W. had arrived at my door, and we're still no closer to finding out who it is or what they want. I'd thrown myself into researching tips and old clientele, which had been a good distraction from the new guilt I'd acquired over failing Bea for the past twelve months.

But now I'm failing her again, accepting her invitation to come in after swearing I'd stay away.

I'm blaming the dress. The sparkles reflect light onto her face like mini mirror balls, lifting her cheekbones even higher, making her lips look even fuller. Light glitters up and down the dress in thin lines, accentuating every curve and defining every feature.

Breath-taking—that'd been my thought when she'd first stepped into the café earlier.

"I'd ask if you want milk, but it'd ruin the taste. So no, you don't want it," Bea says, interrupting my inner turmoil as she turns with two steaming cups in her hands. "And don't ask for sugar, either."

I take the mug and smile back at her. "You're bossy when you're drunk."

"I'm not drunk," she slurs.

She is, and she's also *different* tonight. Like she isn't overthinking every word before she speaks it. It's nice—she's funny without trying. But I'm not trying to get told off, so I don't respond.

Instead, I take a sip of steaming tea. It tastes like warm gingerbread cookies and Christmas. She looks at me expectantly over her own cup, and I nod.

She raises her eyebrows in satisfaction.

I roll my eyes, and she scrunches her nose.

Oh, *god*. I'm in trouble.

Bea must not get the damning reaction our silent conversation just had on me, because she drains her cup casually and takes it to the sink. But she doesn't just walk; she twirls. Like a natural-born dancer.

The movement surprises me—even at the party, as exhilarated as she was, she hadn't danced all night. As if she realises what she's doing, she stops instantly, dropping to her heels and returning to her normal movements. I frown.

"You like to dance?" I ask as casually as I can. *I want to see more of her moving like that.*

"Only when I'm alone," she hums. "It makes me feel free, like I can breathe deeply without the crushing weight of fear sitting on my chest."

The raw honesty of that statement takes me by surprise. I think she must shock herself, too, because she quickly continues, "I must've forgotten you were here for a second."

"Ouch," I laugh.

"Sorry," she shrugs, although she doesn't sound very sorry at all.

"Why don't you dance around people? You look good."

Bea's eyes catch mine at that before darting away again. "I don't know," is all the answer she gives me.

Fine—she doesn't want to talk about it.

So instead I stand, reaching out my hand. "May I?"

She scoffs, curling her arms around her ribs as if trying to make herself smaller. "What?"

"May I have this dance?" I ask her again, smile tugging at my lips as I watch her rack her brain for an excuse to say no.

"There's no music."

I grab my phone and play the first slow song I see on my playlist. "There is now."

"I haven't danced with someone in so long," she mumbles, shaking her head.

"Then try with me." She still looks unconvinced, so I step forward and run my fingers down her forearm, linking them with hers. "Come on, Honeybee. Feel free with me."

Maybe I could do with feeling a little lighter, too.

Bea looks at our interlaced fingers, then up into my eyes. Magnificent blue opals stare back at me, and she steps closer. Her other hand finds my shoulder and mine curls around her waist. We sway back and forth, inconsequential movements that feel like they could mean a lot more. She rests her head on my chest as we dance in our little circle, round and round and round as the music fades from one song to another.

I resist leaning down to place a quick kiss on top of her head, settling for resting my chin there instead. One of her blonde curls tickles my nose, but I don't dare move it. I don't want to risk losing that smell of brown sugar spice. I'd actually like to bottle it and carry it with me.

The music surrounds us, swirling in a whirlpool of harmonies and notes to guide us. In all honestly, it feels quite...magical. In the moment.

My original plan, when I first agreed to enter her home, was to get kicked out. With how our few interactions had gone in the past, I didn't think it'd be too difficult. I'd get left out on the street, throwing D.W. off Bea's scent should any scary stalkers be lurking outside. They'd see her true feelings for me, and maybe that would make me their only target from now on.

But now we're slow dancing in her kitchen and I think—I *think*—Bea might just let me stay tonight.

How selfish does that make you?

The little voice inside my head is a real wisecrack sometimes. I wish I could turn them off. Why so insistent on ruining a good thing?

But I know the voice is right, and I hate myself for it.

I savour her warm body pressed against mine once more before taking a step back and dropping my hand from her waist. "I should really get going," I say, rushing the regretful words.

She raises her eyebrows slightly but nods. "I figured anyway," she says with a hiccuping giggle, gesturing towards the hallway and walking me to the door.

"Figured what?" I ask, shrugging on my thick coat and willing my sleepy eyes to focus on her face just one more time. I want to see those ocean-blue eyes, that pinched nose, and those full lips. I want to remember the exact location of that tiny freckle under her right eye, the slight blush to her cheeks that never seems to go away. I want to take it all in before I have to leave and resume my distance.

"I figured you didn't want to kiss me." She leans against the open door, eyes closed, waiting for me to leave. But my feet won't move. I want to beg her to repeat herself—say it again. *Challenge* me.

But she doesn't.

She sways against the door and hums a quiet tune to herself, perfectly content with waiting in the doorway all night. I smirk—she's adorable tonight.

But the door is open and anyone could see her, so I steel my spine and slide past her.

Before I can commit to fully crossing the threshold, I allow myself the pleasure of leaning back and brushing the briefest of kisses along her warm cheek. I linger close for a long second, and she hums a fraction louder.

"For the record, you are *so* wrong," I whisper. And then I walk straight to my car and drive home before I have the chance to change my mind.

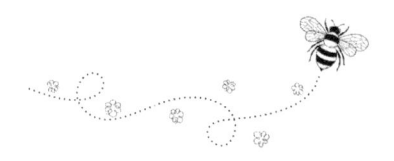

"So, where've you been these past few months?" Eden asks, looking at me through thick lashes over the chai tea she insisted I buy her from a local bistro. A small smile tugs at my lips at the memory of Bea's passionate tour through her tea collection. "We've missed you. The *kids* have missed you."

I sigh, leaning back in the uncomfortable metal chair. It groans with the small movement, and I sit up straight again. "I miss them too; I've just been busy."

"Are you going to come by and see them soon?"

"Yeah, next week. Definitely, count me in." I affirm, but she looks at me disapprovingly, like she doesn't believe me for a second. "I'll bring them some presents," I add, hoping to sweeten her up a little. I love my niece and nephew, but I haven't had time to see them much recently. Between D.W. and Bea, I haven't had the capacity to think of much else.

"No computer stuff," Eden drawls. "I can never stop Hector from going on about all the weird code-y things you teach him." She takes a sip before continuing, "What's going on with you? I feel like we haven't had a catch-up in years."

I smile sadly at the look in her eyes because the truth in that is so apparent.

Eden and I have always had a strong twin bond. No matter how far apart we are, wherever we are in the world, it always feels like she's right next to me. Since birth, we've been inseparable, but after last year everything changed.

I pretty much cut myself off from everyone I knew. The guilt—looking into Eden's eyes, knowing she had no idea what was really going on with me and that I couldn't tell her the truth—was all too much. So I locked myself away and told her I was too busy with work to see her or her two children.

It killed me and probably made me spiral even further, but I told myself it was best for them. The last thing I needed back then was for her to know of her brother's involvement with a psychotic conman and multiple murders.

We'd text back and forth occasionally, but our weekly visits became almost non-existent. This coffee date is my first attempt to regain some of her trust. Luckily for me, Eden's exactly like me; she doesn't hold a grudge and she understands that life can get tough sometimes. I don't deserve her, but she's stuck with me.

"Not much, Edie. How's the business?"

"It's good—Jackson's really getting into the financial side of it, so I don't have to worry about the books. I get to be the boss without any of the boring bits."

That sums her and her husband up perfectly. They're like two sides of a coin. "And how's Hector getting on with that reading challenge?"

"Oh, Arth—I'm being dragged to the library every other day to fill up his little cart of books. Janie sits on top of the stacks, and he drags her home afterwards. You should come with us one day! It's adorable."

I smirk. "Sounds it."

"But don't change the subject. I want to know about your life—tell me about the girl." She waggles her eyebrows at me suggestively and I throw my balled-up napkin at her.

"What girl?"

"My sweet, sweet Arthur. You forget we share a brain." Eden taps a long finger on the side of her forehead. "I know everything you're thinking."

I can't help but smile as I lean forward to rest my elbows on the metal table between us. "Go on then, genius. Who is she?"

"Ah ha!" Eden jumps up, almost sending our cups flying. "You said she! Who is *she*!"

Shit. "That was clearly a hypothetical statement."

"Nu-uh, Arthur Avila. Tell me all about this woman right this instant."

I keep my head down as I wipe up our spilt drinks, so anyone who sees my sister dancing on the spot might not associate her with me. "Sit down and stop acting like a fool, and I might let you in on a secret."

She obeys, tucking her short brown hair behind her ears so that she doesn't miss a single word, and waits expectantly with her fingers steepled underneath her chin.

"Right, it's incredibly important that you accept that she is *not* my girlfriend, nor will she ever be. She's a friend of a friend who moved away, and I was tasked with keeping an eye on her. But I have no reason to see her again, so that's it—okay?"

Eden nods, but her eyes are twinkling. She doesn't believe a word. "What's her name?"

I blow a breath through my nose. "Bea."

Eden gasps, clasping her hands together dreamily. "Beautiful name. What's she like?"

I think about my answer for a moment—what am I supposed to say?

That she's lovely, beautiful, way out of my league in every way imaginable.

No, that would put my sister in matchmaking mode. And I'm trying not to be selfish.

So, I say simply, "She's nice."

Eden's shoulders slump, and her face falls dramatically. "That's it? She's *nice*? Really, Arthur, no wonder you can't get the girl if that's the best compliment you've got." She drains her cup and folds her arms in front of her chest.

"I could get the girl," I muse, and her ears prick. "I just don't *want* the girl."

"You're a terrible liar." She laughs, and I feel heat stinging my cheeks.

Fine, maybe I do want the girl—just a tiny bit—after last night. But I don't *want* to want her, because that'd put her in insurmountable danger and I don't think I'd be able to live with myself.

And, most importantly, the girl will never want me. So what's the point of even entertaining the idea?

After a few more relentless prying attempts, Eden announces she has to get back to the office, so I loop her arm through mine and walk her to her black minivan. Before she gets in, she turns and kisses me on the cheek. "You'll come by and see the kids soon?"

"I said I would," I confirm with a large grin that I know she hates.

"I mean it, Arthur," she whispers. "Please don't disappear on me again."

"I won't, Edie. I promise."

She blows me another kiss through the window before driving away, and I make a silent vow to visit her next week.

With the familiar bitter inner thoughts already getting louder now I'm alone again, something tells me I'll need the distraction.

Chapter Seven

Bea

I needed a full week of recovery before I could stomach being around anyone after my party. Seriously—the last seven days have consisted of nothing more than trying not to act like a zombie during my patient visits, coming home to cook a microwavable dinner, and collapsing into bed. I've been afraid to look in the mirror.

I haven't spoken to Maria or Jess, although not for a lack of them trying. It's not that I'm ignoring them, but I have serious concerns that my head might explode if I have to talk to anyone for longer than a few short words.

Especially if they're going to remind me of what a fool I made of myself at the party.

But today's the day. I've braved the bathroom mirror, and the purple bruises underneath my eyes are *finally* fading. My hair is just starting to relax from its frizzy defiance, and I can eat a vegetable again without immediately thinking about throwing up. I think I *might* be able to stomach a conversation.

"And just where exactly have you been, *Beatrice*?" Maria's voice rings through the car speakers. I wince and turn the volume dial down as far as it'll go.

"In the midst of the worst hangover of my life," I moan. "Why'd you let me drink that much?"

"Funny."

Right. "Has anyone ever told you you're a terrible friend?"

"No, because I'm an excellent friend," she says with an amused hum in her voice. Can't argue with that one. "Although I was kind of hoping you'd be ringing to tell me you'd finally managed to make your way out of a week-long expedition between the hacker's sheets."

"Maria!"

"What? You couldn't take your eyes off each other at the party." I can almost hear her shrug through the phone.

I groan. "That's not what happened. I haven't even thought of him since then."

Liar.

"This is quite literally the most disappointing piece of information I've ever heard," Maria drawls, sounding completely sincere. "I play matchmaker and neither of you can seal the deal. What am I going to do with you?"

"I think you might have to accept that nothing's ever going to happen between me and Arthur."

"You're in denial," Maria sings.

"No." *Maybe?*

"What's the plan for the rest of the night then, if not sneaking over to see your secret boyfriend?"

I look at the clock on my dashboard—just past 6 pm. "Probably a quiet night in with a film. Want to join?"

"Wish I could lovely, but I'm meeting my new accountant after closing. He's got some more boring spreadsheets to show me or something. I'll text you when I'm finished if it's not too late, but don't wait for me."

As we hang up and I park in my usual space, the moon is already alight and high in the dreary sky. I throw my satchel bag on the floor and slip off my pumps, heading straight into the kitchen to get dinner started. I connect my phone to my speaker and sway to a slow song while heating up way too much leftover pasta.

I'm not usually a ballad kind of woman, but I haven't been able to get this one out of my head all week.

I pick a cheesy romantic comedy, which I'm regretting by the halfway mark. Who chooses to watch a fuzzy romance when their own love life is so...non-existent?

Me, apparently.

When I'm trying so desperately to forget one smile in particular, the way it creases the corner of his eyes...

Ugh. And the deafening lack of messages.

He has my number, doesn't he? Surely, I'd have given it to him after he'd driven me home...although I don't remember what happened past the drive. Flashes of dancing flit through my mind at the most inopportune times, but I hope that's just some weird dream. Because if he'd seen me dancing—well, no wonder he hasn't texted me.

Not that it matters, anyway. I don't want to hear or speak to Arthur ever again. He'd been nice enough at my party, but he never should've been there in the first place. I don't need an Arthur Avila in my life, and I'll be better for keeping well away.

If only someone would tell my stupid mind that.

As if the universe is toying with me, my phone buzzes as soon as the film's credits begin rolling. I grab it quicker than I'd like to admit, but it's Jessica's name flashing across the screen. I wipe my moist eyes, sniff harshly, and answer the video call. "Hello?"

"Bea! Where have you been?" Jessica's voice booms through the speaker. "Silas has been going out of his mind."

A gruff, muffled voice sounds from behind her, getting closer with every word. "Bea? Is that Bea? Let me talk to her."

"Here." Jessica hands him the phone, but whispers, "Sorry!" to me before Silas appears.

"Bea, are you okay?" he asks, voice laced with something other than anger. His face fills the entire screen, and his eyes are heavy.

"Yes Sy, I'm fine. I just—"

"What were you thinking?" His voice turns rougher. "You couldn't send a quick text in the group chat to let us know you were okay?" He's pacing now, and it's making my stomach churn.

"I'm sorry, Sy. I had a raging hangover; I didn't think." Truthfully, I hadn't even considered anyone would be worried about me.

A silence follows as he takes some deep breaths in and out. That's *his* coping mechanism, I'd recently learned. "I'm glad you're okay," is all he says before handing the phone back to Jessica.

"Hey," she sings nervously, propping the camera up in front of her. "Sorry about that. You know how he gets. He's been going out of his mind this week. He's been on the phone to Artie every day to make sure you were safe—"

"How would he know?"

A pause. "Oh, I don't know. I tend to drown out their conversations; they're so boring." A half laugh. "But don't be mad at them, they're just looking out for you. I guess Artie probably didn't know anything either, as their calls never calmed Sy down. Seriously Bea, he was going to drive back to look for you if you hadn't answered today."

"I'm sorry," I say again.

"No! Don't apologise for taking some time for yourself," Jess reassures in her warm, sunny tone. "Just...next time, could you let us know if you're planning to go radio silent?"

"I promise," I laugh. "I love you both."

"And we love you! I'll let you get back to whatever you're doing. I think I have an amped-up Knight to calm down."

We hang up, but suddenly I feel...lost.

Maria still hasn't called, Jessica and Silas are busy, and the man that I am definitely *not* thinking about has probably already forgotten my name. I shake my head and drop my shoulders with a resounding huff. I don't care.

I *don't*.

The grandfather clock in the hallway chimes 10 pm, so I resign to my bedroom and place my phone on charge next to my bed before heading into the ensuite to get unready from the day. And to give myself a quick pep talk in the mirror before work in the morning.

Tomorrow is Monday, and I need a fresh head before my weekly visit to the hospital. I love spending as much time away from there as possible, but the senior nurse, Helena Dayes, insists I come and see her once a week to check in and get my weekly timesheet.

I love Helena. I love the nurses I work with. But I can't…I can't spend longer than an hour at any hospital. It's a nightmare fuelled with memories and terror and utter panic. So I stay on the home visit rotation and suck up my fears for one hour of the week.

But that doesn't mean I won't freak out about it every Sunday night.

I walk back into my bedroom and fall into my fluffy green comforter, letting the feathers swallow me whole. Throw pillows billow up around me, adding to my sweet suffocation. I snuggle deeper into the covers, turn the seashell lamp that Maria had bought me off, and check my phone one last time.

For no one in particular.

Which is why, when the notification screen still shows no new messages, I'm completely fine and not bothered at all.

Chapter Eight
Artie

It's been an agonisingly long week. Without any word from my inner circle or Monty about who D.W. could be, there hasn't been much to occupy my thoughts other than the woman who is certainly *not* supposed to be there. I lose count of how many times I stare at her number saved in my phone, considering pressing the call button and giving in to every fibre of my being telling me to *just do it*.

But she'd been drunk.

She obviously didn't mean what she said, and it's no secret that she doesn't like me. My suspected reason for that might be ridiculous and a little—*a lot*—hurtful, but it doesn't change the outcome. Bea has no interest in me, and I need to leave her alone.

Forgetting about her would've been a whole lot easier if Silas hadn't been calling me every single day to ask about her whereabouts. Apparently, she'd dropped off the face of the earth after the party and no one had heard from her. Silas had some pretty colourful words for me when I told him I wouldn't be checking on her—but I'd given her my word it wouldn't happen again, and I'm honouring that.

I owe her that much, at least.

Bea's fine, I tell myself for the millionth time this week.

Silas had texted me as much last night, and it felt like the breath I'd been holding in for the past eight days finally loosened from my lungs. Good. Now all I need is my brain to get the memo so that it can stop thinking about her and refocus on my stalker situation.

I finish my research into possible D.W. threads around midday, but an email from Monty erases any hope I had of enjoying an early finish. I read the words once, twice, three times.

Avila.
No one in your recent tips under the initials D.W. If you send me images of the notes and any other material you have on them, I can have someone on the team take a look into it.
Best, Chief M. Robinson

Right, so the police aren't any help either. Sending them the notes is certainly *not* on my agenda after the friendly phone call I'd received, so I delete the email. Leaning back, I scrub a hand over my face. How is it possible that my life's being threatened because of a supposed tip I sent to the police, and yet the officer who would've received it is saying it doesn't exist?

I need a coffee and a break.

The Twinkling Bliss is just a short walk down the road from Bluetine Park, so I head straight there. The neon sign shines like a guide, casting a red glow across the entire street as if a mirage for coffee addicts everywhere.

The doorbell rings twice as I enter the empty café, but I stop dead in my tracks as soon as I glance behind the counter.

"Welcome to the Twinkling Bliss," Bea says without looking up from the notepad she's writing on. "Feel free to seat yourself."

"Thanks." I walk up to the counter and take the stool right in front of her. I look her up and down in all her glory, eyes catching on the waitress apron tied around her waist. "Sudden career change?"

Bea's eyes flutter up to meet mine, but only for a second before she rolls them and looks down again. "Maria needed the night off." She gestures to the empty tables around us. "Easiest gig ever."

I smirk at her joke, trying to ignore the tiny butterflies dancing within my chest. *Does she remember what we last said to each other after the party?*

Bea lies the notepad on the counter between us and starts writing again. No, she's doodling. Mini ladybugs with top hats. I smile, noticing the little details on each. One has a moustache and a monocle. Another has curly hair and glasses.

"So, can I get you anything? Or did Silas ask you to start stalking me again?"

"Ha!" I bark, and the sharp sound even surprises me. "No, I swear I only came for coffee. Completely innocent, I didn't know you were going to be here." I raise my hands to show I'm not lying.

She smirks, and I have to train my lips to stop from grinning. Tearing my eyes away from her proves to be more difficult than it should've been, too. Her hair is wrapped up in a small blonde bun, and she's wearing a short black skirt beneath the apron with a cream knit jumper tucked in. Effortlessly incredible.

"Wait, how'd you know it was Silas who asked me to keep an eye on you?" I ask her as she pours obsidian liquid from a glass pitcher into the mug in front of me.

"Please," she scoffs with another eye roll. "It's Silas."

I nod because I guess that is all the explanation needed. "He does see you as a little sister these days," I muse.

"It's not so bad, him looking out for me," she admits, avoiding my eye. "It's nice to know someone is that protective over you."

"But when you thought it was just me looking out for you...?" I taunt, although I'd actually quite like to know why she was so upset at the idea of me wanting to keep an eye on her.

"You're...different."

"Good different?"

"No."

I almost spit out my coffee at that, because she didn't even miss a beat. *Talk about brutal honesty...*

"Different how, then?"

I know the answer already—she didn't want me checking in on her because I'm the bad guy in her version of events. It's fine, really. Everyone deals with trauma in their own way. *But I want to hear her say it.*

"You...you're...we don't know each other that well," is all she manages.

"Cop out," I mutter with a smile into my coffee cup.

"Excuse me?"

"You're giving me a lame excuse because you don't want to tell me straight to my face the real reason you don't like me." I raise my eyebrows in a silent challenge.

"I never said I didn't like you, *Dream Boy*." Her eyes finally meet mine, twinkling with something like smug defiance. It's an effort to keep my jaw from hitting the floor.

"So, you *do* like me?"

She shrugs. "I wouldn't go that far."

I give her a small smile. She might be confused about whether she likes me or not, but my feelings are crystal clear. I like this Bea—a lot.

But something tells me I'll get kicked out of this café if I keep prying, so I tip my half-empty coffee cup to her and ask, "You're not going to join me?"

"And drink that poison? I'll pass." Bea pretends to retch before tugging a bag from underneath the counter. It looks like a balled-up vintage quilt, roughly stitched together with thick lime green thread. She catches me inspecting it as she pulls out a small silver tin. "The result of my patchworking phase. It didn't last very long." She shrugs as she opens the lid, unveiling a row of multicoloured, individually wrapped teabags.

I smirk at the memory of last weekend, and she catches me looking. Her eyebrows knit together in a silent question that I'm not going to answer. I quirk up my own to tell her as much.

She continues to stare at me suspiciously while ripping open a burgundy packet, filling a mug with freshly boiled water, and steeping the bag dramatically. I widen my eyes to provoke her. I'm not going to be the one to break.

She grumbles after a few long minutes of silence, "What are you smiling at? Is it so wrong for a girl to carry her own mini collection of tea in her bag?"

I shake my head. "Not at all."

"That's what I thought. Besides," she says as she clicks the lid shut and hides the box back in her handmade bag, "this isn't even the half of it. You should see my real collection at home."

"It was quite impressive," I drawl, taking another sip of my coffee coyly.

She doesn't remember what happened after the party...interesting. *Oh, I could have some fun with this.*

I flick an eyebrow up when I notice her staring at me, hiding her expression behind the steaming mug. She doesn't take the bait, but it is oh-so-sweet to watch the blush creep up her neck as she pieces together how and when I'd have been in her kitchen.

"Did I invite you in after you dropped me home after my party?" she whispers, like it's a big secret. As if it's something to be ashamed of.

"Mhm. Sure did." I bite back a laugh.

She gasps. "How do I not remember that?" Her eyes flick left and right at the speed of light as she racks her memories. But then those piercing blues are on me, and I can almost see the thoughts racing past them. I squint in response. "What did we...do?"

I choke out a laugh then—I can't help it. But as soon as I do, Bea folds into herself, stepping back toward the back counter and averting her eyes from mine. She looks for something to busy herself with, but I reach over the counter and grab her wrist to keep her close.

I'm not willing to consider why it's so important that she doesn't walk away from me right now.

"Sorry—I'm sorry. You invited me in, lectured me about my teabag choice. We talked for a while, and then I left. It was a nice conversation, but you were tired and needed to sleep off the alcohol, so I went home." One side of my lip curls in a half-smile.

"That's it?" she asks, glancing down at my hand wrapped around hers but not moving to free herself. If there wasn't a large counter between us, I might've been tempted to pull her closer.

God, I wish she was closer.

"That's it," I agree.

Something tells me she wouldn't want to know about the dancing or the almost-kiss. Maybe I'll tell her one day, but for now, I like the idea of that being my little secret—a tiny slice of truth I share with no one but my intoxicated version of Bea.

And by her visibly relieved—if not still slightly sceptical—expression, it's the right thing to do.

I let go of her wrist and she lingers within reaching distance for a moment, before turning away to focus on refilling salt and pepper shakers. A lock of her golden hair falls from her bun, swaying across her face as she looks down. The urge to lean over and tuck it behind her ear overcomes me, but I push it back down.

No more touching.

She fixes it herself, glancing up at me as if she could feel my eyes on her. "What?" she asks, irritated. I think she might be biting her lip to look angrier than she is.

"I want to know all about your patchwork phase." I grin.

Bea snorts at the bag left on the counter in a sad, deflated heap. "It's just one of the many crafts I've tried and failed at."

"Many? Oh, now you've piqued my interest." I lean my elbows on the counter, tucking my hands underneath my chin to give her my undivided attention. "Tell me more, Honeybee."

She looks unimpressed at the name but doesn't mention it. Again, *interesting*. "There's not much to tell, really. I like trying new crafts. Sadly, they don't always like me."

"How could anyone ever dislike you?"

"*Anything*. And I know," she sighs. "All I do is give, give, give. You'd think the materials would be grateful. But alas," a swooping gesture to the bag, "they are not."

I laugh at her sullen expression, the pathetic shrug she offers after such a declaration. "Maybe you should try your hand at acting, Queenie. That was impressive."

"*Queenie*? Really?" Bea groans, her tone slightly harsher than before.

I could burst with glee. "Like Queen Bee—get it?"

She glares at me flatly. "Your relentless positive mood is exhausting. Do you ever have a day off?"

"Sure, I have my bad days. But then I remember what a cute smile I have, and I'm back to my happy self."

That earns me a small chuckle. "Did you just quote *Friends*?"

"I did, and I won't apologise for it," I reply, matching her grin.

She holds her hands up in surrender. "I'm impressed."

I gasp. "Me, impressed the Ice Queenie? I'm taking that as a win." She glares at me for that, but I can see her trying to hide her smirk. "I'd better quit while I'm ahead."

"Let me get the door for you," she says and I wince, cupping my chest like she's physically hurt me. She rolls her eyes before seeing me out. "Always a pleasure, Artie. I *do* hope you find somewhere else to get your coffee soon."

I walk out into the dark evening and turn on my heel, taking in every inch of that smug face. "No, you don't," I say with a wink, walking away before she can say anything else.

I don't hear the door close until I'm around the corner, and I love the thought of her standing in the doorway, desperately trying to think of a comeback before I disappear.

I'm still smiling like an idiot as I get to Bluetine Park. It's deserted, all the shops long since closed.

I'm still thinking of Bea as I push my key into the door. The name *Dream Boy* on her curled lips is the last thing gracing my mind as blinding pain ricochets through my calves.

My legs are swept from underneath me, sending me crashing towards the cobblestones. There's a distinct snapping in my arm, and my head cracks on a particularly sharp stone to break my fall.

I have barely enough time to glance up at the masked assailant before everything around me fades into complete and utter darkness.

Chapter Nine
Bea

An easy smile hasn't stopped tugging at my lips since last night, no matter how much I try to curse and school it into neutrality. After Artie left the café, I only needed ten more minutes to clean and lock up. In those ten short minutes, I toyed with the idea of surprising him at his apartment. I didn't have a reason—at least not one I was ready to admit to anyone—but I think I just wanted to spend a little longer with him. I wanted to tell him my retort to his wink and wipe that insufferably coy look off his face.

I also kind of wanted to clarify that I didn't mean he was *bad* different.

But as I shoved the keys back into my homemade bag outside the café and let the fresh air roll over me, I shook the idea away. It was a stupid thought, and I'd already taken up too much of his time this evening.

So, I drove home and psyched myself up for today instead.

GEMMA NICHOLLS

Currently standing outside Spring Grove Medical Centre for the second day in a row, I lean against my car and look up at the old building. I force my lungs to inhale and dispel air to a gentle, casual rhythm.

You walked in yesterday, you can do it again today.

But yesterday's visit was planned. I know I'm needed at the hospital every Monday for my meeting with Helena. I don't need to come in on Tuesdays. I'm supposed to be at Mrs Kahn's house now, helping her find the edge pieces to her current puzzle.

Helena asked me to meet with her again today to discuss some changes, so my anxiety has been having a field day for the past twenty-four hours—well, except for my shift at the café. If nothing else, Artie provided a nice distraction from my overthinking.

Even now, the secret smile he left me with gives me something else to focus on other than my building nervousness.

With one last deep exhale through my nose, I push off the car and head inside.

Taking the stairs two at a time, I climb the endless flights to my floor. Elevators and I don't mix, and this is the closest to cardio I'll ever get, so I embrace the burning in my thighs as I reach the heavy door leading to the Palliative Care Unit.

"Morning, Myla." I smile at the receptionist sitting at the nurse's station, who doesn't look up from filing her nails as she grunts back a response.

Myla's barely twenty years old, in her first year of training. From the little I've seen of her, she doesn't care too much about the job. Helena's adamant that she shows promise, but to me, she looks like she'd rather be anywhere else.

Me too, probably. A familiar tightness begins to swirl deep within my gut.

"Do you know if Helena is ready to see me?"

Myla still doesn't look up. I'm not even sure she knows who she's talking to. "No."

"No, she's not ready, or no, you don't know?"

This seems to pique her interest. A riddle, if you will. "I don't know," is the answer.

I take a deep breath and bite my tongue. "Always a pleasure, Myla," I call over my shoulder before walking in the direction of Helena's office. The only reply I get is another grunt.

"Come in!" I hear through the door after knocking, so I obey. Helena's sitting behind her desk, thin half-moon glasses balanced on the tip of her nose as she reads the contents of a beige file. Her dark grey hair is scraped back into a low bun and her scrubs look like she woke up an hour early just to steam them. She glances up at me and throws me a winning smile. "Morning, Bea. How are you?"

"I'm doing okay," I say with a half-nod because it's half-true. That stupid smile of mine is still fighting its way free, acting as a sort of panic repellent.

"Glad to hear it," she beams, closing the file and gesturing to the chair in front of her desk. I take it, looking around the cramped office. There's not a single free space between Helena's ornaments, patient files, and mounds of paperwork. Her gentle voice brings my attention back to her. "Now, to business. I'm cutting your hours."

"What?" I ask, eyes bulging.

She looks at me like *we could've seen this coming*.

Still, it hurts to hear.

"There simply aren't enough patients who need house visits, and we can't keep paying you for doing half the work of everyone else, I'm afraid. It's either cut your hours or return to working on the floor. The choice is yours."

I bow my head stiffly, thinking over my options. The chance to choose between paying my bills and avoiding one of my biggest fears. *Lucky me.*

Helena must read this all on my face because she leans forward to squeeze my hand, her eyes full of unwanted pity. "I know being here is difficult for you—I truly sympathise, and I really did try and fight your cause, Bea, but the board isn't having it any longer. I'm sorry."

I attempt a forced smile and say, "Thank you for trying."

"You're an asset here at Spring Grove. I'd like to see you back working on the floor with us." She looks at me over the top of her glasses, and I have the desperate urge to curl up into a ball and disappear. "What's it going to be?"

I take a beat to think about it, although there's no point really. I can't afford a cut to my hours. "I'll come back to working on the floor, if you'll have me."

Helena's lips curl upward at that. "Of course. I've managed to convince the board that you're still the best of us to handle the house visits, so you'll only have to spend half your hours here. I'd be delighted to see you around more often."

Then she dismisses me with a shake of the hand as she goes back to reading the file in front of her. I rise and hurry towards the door, the small office suddenly seeming far too warm and suffocating.

"Oh, Bea," Helena says, halting me right before my escape. "You'll need to head down to admin and ask them to sort your schedule out. I've already sent them a memo of what's expected of you."

"Okay." I grimace inwardly at how weak I sound as I push through the door.

The cooler temperature in the hallway clouds my head and threatens to burst my chest. I fill my lungs with as much sterile air as they'll let me, blowing it out through my mouth loudly as I try and collect my thoughts. *Coming back to work here...I'm not strong enough.*

It's not until my fifth exhale that I notice Myla staring at me from over the nurse's station. Of course, *now* she looks at me. I shake out my arms and school my face into neutrality. "Have a great day, Myla."

"Uh-huh," she replies.

I can't wait to spend more time with her. I feel like we're building up to an unbreakable friendship.

I look around me, unsure of what to do next. I'm still relatively new to this hospital, and I've barely spent any time exploring the different floors. I chew my lip as I walk over to the nurse's station, suddenly feeling super annoying and clingy. Myla looks up at me as I shadow her, clear disdain in her eyes.

Yep, she definitely hates me.

"Do you know the best way for me to get to admin?" I ask with a gracious smile that hopefully says *I'll stop talking to you soon, promise.*

"It's on the same floor as the ICU, so head down there and you won't miss it." Her tone is flat as she very helpfully adds, "It's the big brown door that says 'Admin'."

I thank her through gritted teeth before heading down the stairs I came up earlier, tensing the closer I get to the Intensive Care Unit. I'd love nothing more than to never step foot in an ICU again.

Breathe, Bea. It's like ripping off a plaster—get in, talk with admin, get out. Five minutes max.

I push through the heavy fire door, walking into the absolute chaos that is the ICU. It's like walking into a twilight zone—the air feels cooler, colours are less vibrant, every sound seems quieter.

And yet, there's always a frenzied vibe cast over everyone. My vision pulses to the rhythm of beeping machines around me as I try to block it all out, walking straight to the big brown door that does indeed read *Admin*.

While I'm waiting for someone to answer my knock, my eyes land on movement in the corner cubicle closest to me. At least ten doctors hover around one gurney. I will myself to look away.

You don't know them.

"Hello?" the administrator asks, waving a hand in front of my face as she peeks around the door. "How can I help you?"

"Oh—I need a change of schedule? Nurse Dayes should've sent you down my requirements, I think."

"Name?" she asks.

"Beatrice Di Menna."

"Helena asked for the new schedule to begin next week," the administrator says simply, reading an email from her old computer. "You can pick your new timesheet up here on Monday morning."

"Thank you," I start, but she's already closed the door on me.

Okay, now to get out of this hellscape and enjoy the last of my freedom before Monday rolls around.

But something hooks my attention back to that corner cubicle, and I find myself gravitating towards the nurse's station. "Is everything okay in there?" I ask the first person I see—a nurse with burnt orange scrubs and cropped blonde hair. He follows my pointing finger and we both watch the doctors from afar, moving in perfect unison to treat the patient with incredible efficiency. It's like a choreographed dance; I can't look away.

"He was brought in about an hour ago," the nurse muses, still watching with me. "A guy in his thirties, I think. I heard it was a possible hitjob."

And that's my cue to leave.

I squeeze my lips into a tight line in a way of goodbye, but *something* stops me again from taking that next step towards the stairwell. It's like I'm magnetised to that one cubicle.

Some horrible, awful, *nauseating* feeling settles in my stomach at that, forcing me to turn on my heel towards the ominous corner of the ICU. Every fibre of my being is screaming at me to turn back around and get out of here, but somehow, I find myself at the entranceway.

No one notices me peering in.

No one hears the gasp that hitches in my throat.

They're all too busy rushing around the patient with the horrifically bruised and swollen face.

So no one hears me when I breathe, "*Artie.*"

Chapter Ten

Bea

The air conditioning unit rattles and splutters in the corner of the room, making everything far too bitter and unkind. I feel like I'm sitting in a morgue, not an ICU cubicle. If it weren't for the incessant beeping from the machines Artie lay wired up to, I might've believed I was in the former. But that taunting *beep, beep, beep* just keeps ringing in my ears, encompassing me as I rock myself gently, back and forth, in the cheap pleather chair.

With my head in my hands, I repeat a simple mantra to myself— "Not again, *please* not again." I don't think I could stop if I tried.

I've been sitting alongside an unconscious Artie for half an hour now, not too sure of what to do with myself. I've already called Helena from the nurse's station and asked for the rest of the day off. She'd granted it willingly, telling me to focus on my friend today and call her with an update tomorrow.

I'm grateful, of course, but after we hung up, I questioned whether I'd even need the time off. We *aren't* friends, after all. He probably has plenty of friends and family who will be here any minute to relieve me of my duties. Maybe even a partner...

As if on cue, a woman knocks on the doorframe. She glances between me and Artie before rushing to his bedside. Her face looks positively gaunt as she looks him over, but something tells me that if we'd met under better circumstances, she'd look effortlessly radiant.

"Hello," I try, but the woman doesn't turn from Artie, tubes and wires snaking from him at every angle. Her head's shaking slightly, her chocolate brown bob swaying with the movement.

I stand up and take a tentative step towards her, then another, until I'm right by her side. I brush a soft hand over her shoulder and say as gently as I can, "I'm Bea, a friend of Artie's and a nurse at this hospital. Would you like to sit down?" I even surprise myself with how level my voice is. It feels impossible to keep everything together at a time like this.

The woman still doesn't look at me, but she closes her gaping mouth and swallows hard. "You're Bea?" she asks in a small voice. Her eyes meet mine then, taking a quick scan of my face before looking back at Arthur.

"I am." Now is not the time to consider how this woman already seems to know me.

I lead her over to the chair I'd spent the last half an hour warming, sitting her down before dragging another from the corner of the room for me.

"I'm Eden," the woman announces quietly. "Arthur's sister."

My eyebrows raise. *I didn't know he had a sister.* "It's lovely to meet you, Eden."

Although now she mentions it, she's the spitting image of him. They have the same nose, the same line of their lips. The same piercing green eyes.

"You too. Although I was hoping it would be in better circumstances." A humourless laugh escapes her. The tears come then, and she scrunches her face between ragged breaths. "Do they know who did this?" Her voice is no more than a squeak.

I place my hand atop hers and she sandwiches it with her other one. "I haven't heard anything yet. The police haven't been by, though. I think they're probably waiting to see what the doctors say about when he'll wake up."

"Will he wake up?" she whispers like she's afraid to hear the truth. I squeeze her hand. *I've been there.*

"Yes, he will wake up. They've taken him for a couple of scans already and it looks like there's no bleeding in the brain from the head wound. From what I've gathered, the person who did this didn't want Artie dead, they just wanted to teach him a lesson."

Which, in my opinion, is so much worse.

Eden scoffs through wet sobs. "Teach him a lesson? For what?"

Oh. *Oh.* Does she not know about his work?

"I don't know," is all I say, because it's not a complete lie. I *don't* know why Artie's in trouble—at least not enough to land him in hospital with a sprained arm and a bashed-up face. "The doctors might be able to give you more details, but their main focus is healing him for now."

Eden nods, sniffles a few times, and then excuses herself with the intent to find a doctor. Before I know it, I'm left in this cold, blue hospital room again, with nothing but the sterile smell of cleaning disinfectant to keep me company.

I chew on the inside of my lip for a while, wondering what to do. Overthinking is my mortal enemy, and one I've let best me far too many times before. But sitting in silence, watching Artie's chest rise and fall, rise and fall, I allow it to consume me just one more time.

It's too quiet in here; too cold.

I'm alone, with no one to distract me from the unconscious man lying in front of me. Meeting his family, being in the same hospital room as someone who loves him so dearly—it's too much, too *real*. Like it's not just some weird dreamworld I'm stuck in anymore.

No, Artie really has been attacked and I'm the only one here and *oh god*, what if he does die and I'm the only person with him to keep him company...

Rising panic has me standing, shaking my limbs out, humming quietly to myself. Humming, because I need *some* kind of release for the tension building in my chest.

It's happening again.

An unending tightness that feels like it will never ease again grips my lungs. My jaw clenches so hard my teeth might break. My brain starts filling with taunts about forgetting how to breathe and how I'll die soon without oxygen.

They're coming back to get you.

A panic attack.

I'm on the cusp of an attack with no one here to ground me or remind me of my name.

It's just me, pacing around the occupied bed, the room spinning at the speed of light and I can't catch up to it...

I can hear someone's muffled sobs far, *far* away, although the wetness on my cheeks indicates they might be coming from me.

You're hopeless, Bea.

Taunting, teasing, *mocking* voices fill my head.

And just when I think I might die from dizziness and my incapability to breathe, I black out.

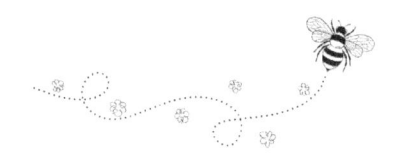

"Bea?" The voice and I are miles apart. Too far away to reach—*do I even try*? "Bea, can you hear me?"

I dare to open one heavy eyelid a fraction to see who the owner of that soothing voice is. *Eden.* She's tucked her hair behind both ears; cheeks flushing in her own mounting stress. I murmur something unintelligible, but she exhales a relieved breath, nonetheless.

"Wow, okay. You're alive," she looses a flustered laugh, heaving me up. "That's good."

"Is it?" I groan, every inch of my body stiff and singing. I must've got my back against a wall before the panic took my vision, because I'm slumped in the corner of Artie's hospital room. "I'm so sorry."

"Sorry? For what?" Eden asks as she helps me to the visitor's chair. I fall into it.

"I collapsed in your brother's hospital room," I breathe. "That's quite an obvious overstep, don't you think? Artie's laying right here after being *attacked*, and you're having to pull me off the floor like some pathetic mess."

"Stop that right now," Eden reprimands, her voice terse. "You are no *pathetic mess*. I don't know what's going on between you and my brother, but it's clear to see you care for him enough to warrant that sort of reaction. So I won't hear any self-deprecation coming from you, okay? If anything," she pauses before continuing, "I'm happy he has someone to care for him that much."

"Oh no, Eden. You've got that wrong, Artie and I...we hardly even know each other. We have a mutual friend who was hospitalised for similar reasons, that's all."

"Mhm. That's why the nurse out there told me you've been sitting in this room for the best part of an hour? That you took the day off work to be here?" Eden lifts her eyebrows at me expectantly.

"I wanted to make sure his family got here before I left, yes."

"And you're calling him Artie."

"So?"

Eden's eyes grow wide in disbelief. "He doesn't let *anyone* call him that. The last time I called him Artie, I was pushed from a playground swing and left with two bloody knees."

"He doesn't like me calling him that either. It's just something we do...He calls me silly names, too."

When had I stopped thinking of him as Arthur?

"Look, I know my twin. He wouldn't even entertain the idea of you calling him that if you weren't at least good friends."

"I'd say we're more acquaintances."

"Then why am I picking you up from the floor?" she chides, a wicked glint in her eye because she thinks she's caught me there.

I scoff quietly. My reaction was little more than the result of me spending half the day at this hospital when I've been avoiding it like the plague for so long.

That's why I had a panic attack. Not because I care for Artie—that's ridiculous.

But the last thing I want to be is insensitive, so I simply level Eden with a firm look and say, "There's nothing going on between Artie—*Arthur*—and me. I only met him two weeks ago."

Although I feel like I've known him much longer.

She stares at me for a long moment, her expressive eyes telling me she doesn't believe me for a second. God, she really is just like her brother.

I stare back, despite the raging migraine I can feel settling at the back of my head. A side effect I always get from my anxiety attacks.

"Okay," she finally relents, looking back to the hospital bed. "He told me about you, that's all. He hasn't told me about anyone in a *very* long time. I just assumed you were more important to him than he let on."

"If he said there was anything going on between us, then he's completely misled you."

A soft smile. "It's not *what* he said—it's what he didn't say. But don't be angry at Arthur. He was as adamant as you are that there will never be anything between you."

A weird pit opens at the bottom of my stomach then, and I will it to swallow itself and leave me alone. Confusing feelings for Arthur Avila, of all people, are the last thing I need today. *Or ever.*

I start to deny it again, but Eden waves a hand at me. A symbolic white flag. I dip my head once in agreement and nestle into the hard backrest of my chair, grateful for our truce.

The machines' beeping noise is still amplified, and my vision is still pulsing around its edges, but the quiet company of knowing Eden is sitting next to me helps. I close my eyes and try to savour the darkness instead of fluorescent lighting. I focus on the cool wood beneath my forearms and the solid ground beneath my feet. I listen to my own breathing, matched with Eden's.

"If you're waiting for more family to show up, I'm it. Our dad—well, he's not coming. So, don't feel like you have to stick around," she whispers, respecting the quiet.

I open an eye to look at her. *Oh, right.* I'm probably the last person she wants waiting with her, as a stranger with absolutely no feelings towards her brother whatsoever. So I push up from my slouched position, but as I glance back towards Arthur, something turns my movements leaden.

"Or you can stay if you want?" Eden throws me a lifeline. "Don't think I'm forcing you out."

I consider both options for a moment, but I can't look away from Artie.

The thick tube reaching down his throat.

The bright white sling wrapping around his arm.

His limp curls half-matted from dried blood.

"I think I'll stay for a while, if that's okay." I don't know why, but something tells me I'd never even make it out the door if I'd tried to leave.

Relief flashes across her eyes as Eden squeezes my hand, both of us settling back into our chairs. I choose to ignore the small curl of her lips that she tries to hide behind her magazine and go back to focusing on my breathing.

Chapter Eleven
Artie

I wince as my eyes shutter open involuntarily.

Bright lights swirl above me. I sigh, knowing I'm exactly where I don't want to be.

In a hospital bed, because someone jumped me outside my apartment.

The weight of that realisation has me instantly wishing I would slip back into the forgiving darkness, away from whatever fresh hell I'm about to be forced into.

I groan around the tube chaffing the inside of my throat.

Eden's face appears from nowhere then, her tired eyes glassy as she takes me in. "You are in so much trouble," is all she manages before a sob escapes and she disappears from my line of sight. I hear the click of a door open and close.

I blink. Once, twice.

Waiting. Waiting for someone to get this damned—

"Hey," a small voice says, and I almost jump right into another dreamless sleep. My eyes find her as she approaches my bed, something like relief instantly washing over me. I try to smile around the tube, eyes crinkling. She returns a tighter version, eyes sparkling slightly as she inspects every inch of my face. "I can take this tube out for you."

I nod as much as my stiff neck will let me and she makes quick work of it, the swiftness of her movements making the removal almost painless. Like she's done it a thousand times.

"They only used this as a precaution; they didn't know how much internal damage they were going to find when they got you here," Bea continues, almost to herself. "But you should be able to breathe fine on your own."

"Are you my doctor?" I rasp, which earns me a flat look. I grin weakly because I just love when she's mad at me.

"*No*, but I have read your chart and talked to all the doctors who have come to check on you. Working here has its perks for a woman whose friends like to get themselves beaten up time and time again."

She bundles the tube in a paper towel and throws it in the bin before returning to my bedside.

"Are you calling me your friend now?" My voice box is running on fumes, but I don't care. It's worth it to see annoyance creep up her face again.

"No," she assures me, but she doesn't move away.

Nor does she meet my eye when her hand lifts slightly, her fingertips grazing up and down the sheets next to mine. I can feel the slight movement along the thin mattress beneath my fingers, but I can't look away from her face.

That beautiful face, now laced with fear and grief.

Bea's fingers continue to edge closer to mine, never quite touching me. *Defiant Honeybee.* Damn if I don't want her to close that tiny distance and take my hand.

I stick my pinkie out carelessly, creating a speed bump in her way. Her expression jumps slightly as her fingertips settle on mine, so warm and soothing. That featherlight touch on my finger feels like something unique. *Hopeful.* Something I'd been missing for quite a while.

"Honeybee," I croak through a crooked smile.

She's biting the inside of her lip nervously, so I inch my hand closer to the edge of the bed, sliding my fingers further under hers. The pad of her thumb caresses my knuckles, delicately making her way over each one.

When she finally meets my eyes, I'm not sure if it's anger or fear or concern swimming behind them. I hate that I've had any kind of negative impact on her.

"Hey—" I try again, but we're interrupted by the door swinging open and Eden striding in with two doctors in tow.

Bea jumps back, her soft hand going with her. I swear I see Eden raising her eyebrows in Bea's direction, earning her an eye roll in return.

"Mr Avila," the first doctor, wearing dark blue scrubs and thick glasses, says. "My name is Doctor Barrett; I'm the primary physician on your case. I'm glad to see you awake. Your injuries were quite an eyesore when you first arrived."

"And when was that?" I ask, throat burning with every syllable.

"Two days ago," the doctor confirms, and I blow out a long sigh. "We've been giving you some pretty strong painkillers since you joined us. I don't think any of us would like to suffer through your injuries without them." The doctor exchanges an amused look with his colleague.

Sheer exhaustion threatens to claim me once more, but I beg myself to stay alert until I get my answers. "What injuries?"

"You came in with a large gash to the back of your head, as well as a nasty sprain in your left elbow. The good news is that we sent you for a number of scans which came back clear for any internal damage or bleeding. Considering the state you arrived in, you've been quite lucky."

I don't feel very lucky, to be honest.

My eyes flicker between the faces around me, and I catch Bea trying to contain a cringe. I wait for her to meet my gaze before signalling towards the door; *You can go if this is too much for you.*

Her face relaxes slightly but she gives me the smallest shake of the head before looking down at the floor. *Curious.*

"When can I get out of here?" I ask, not caring to learn more. Eden will have already asked them a million questions, and she'll fill me in with everything I'll need to know later—in terms I can understand, explaining it to me like I'm five years old.

"I believe Ortho is happy to sign off on your arm since it's not broken, right, Doctor Ines?" Dr Barrett says to the second doctor, who peers up over the chart only long enough to agree silently. "Although my team wants to monitor you for a few more days, once we're happy with your progress, we'll see about discharging you as soon as possible."

"A few more days? You said there's no internal damage, what's the hold-up?"

"An attack like this is no joke, Mr Avila. We'd like to keep an eye on your head wound to make sure there's no lasting damage. It's rare, but delayed symptoms could arise. Keeping you here for a few extra days is the best way to treat you should any nasty surprises come along."

Both doctors excuse themselves, with Dr Barrett calling over his shoulder something about the police coming to talk to me later. Excellent—that's all I need.

Once the door firmly shuts behind them, Eden perches on the side of my bed. "Arthur," she starts, combing gentle fingers through my hair. The movement tugs at the roots like there's something stuck in my curls. "What happened?"

I sigh dramatically, shaking my head as I pretend to rack my brain. "I have no idea, Edie. One moment I'm walking back from the café, the next my head's smacking on the pavement and it's lights out." My voice crackles and pops, each word getting quieter and harder to decipher.

Eden looks at me with nothing but worry in her eyes, but Bea's tell a completely different story.

Standing behind my sister, she looks almost...disappointed. I catch her eye, but she looks away immediately. "I'd better be off," she announces instead, gathering her things from one of the wooden chairs at the edge of the room. The closest to my bed.

I wish I could wipe the hurt from her expression. "You don't have to leave, Bea."

"Yeah, why don't you stay and chat a while?" Eden agrees. "You can help me catch Arthur up on current events."

I get out a small, raspy chuckle. "What could've possibly happened in two days?"

She winks, but Bea continues backing towards the door. "No, it looks like you're in good hands with your sister. Eden, it was lovely meeting you. Artie—*Arthur*—I'm glad you're okay."

I don't have time to thank her before she disappears, no more than a whisper on the wind. Peace is a fool's wish with Eden around, though. As soon as the door snicks shut, she whips her head back to me with a positively devilish expression. I scrunch my eyes and warn, "Don't start."

"What?" she croons, visibly giddy. "I wasn't going to *tease*. I think she's a very nice woman—you could do a lot worse."

"I told you, there's nothing going on between Bea and I."

"My god, you two are as bad as each other," Eden muses, chuckling to herself.

"Please tell me you didn't say anything to her," I grumble.

"Give me some credit, Arth. But come on, are you really both too blind to see it? She's been sitting at your bedside for two full days. She was here before I arrived, and stayed with you overnight when I had to get back home to the kids. She didn't eat anything except the snacks I brought her from the vending machine." Something warm settles in my chest at that. "I mean, seriously? She calls you *Artie*. If anyone else did that as much as she does, like it's so natural and genuine, you'd be seething. But Bea comes in, with her golden hair and subtle quips, and you act like it's the name on your birth certificate."

"Cut it out, Edie," I warn again as she cackles, getting far too much enjoyment from her detective skills. She senses my tone and throws her hands up in surrender.

"Fine. I'll let you two fools figure it out for yourselves. But I'm just saying, give me some credit in the wedding vows." She throws me a wink that has me wanting to kick her out, but I grin despite myself. We're far too alike. "I'm going to head to the cafeteria for some lunch, want anything?" she asks while rummaging in her bag for her purse.

"No, thanks."

"Alrighty-roo, I'll see you in a few." She gives me another wink as she retreats out of the room, pointing finger guns at me.

"That was terrible!" I try to shout after her, but my voice splinters and pain flares up and down my raw throat.

My two-day sedation has me absolutely spent, and I can feel the tempting tendrils of sleep trying to pull me back under. The stellar drugs still being pumped into the back of my hand are helping with any pain, though. My legs feel heavy, and my arm is twice the size it usually is.

But I'm alive; I'm safe.

While Eden's gone, two police officers arrive to take my statement. Considering I didn't see the assailant's face or any distinguishable features, it's a complete waste of time. I tell them everything I can, without mentioning D.W. or the fact I'm pretty sure they're the person who did this to me. Something tells me *that* would be a surefire way to end up in another hospital bed.

And if there's a next time, I might not wake up at all.

More importantly, D.W. knows about Bea. They've mistaken our relationship to be something more, and I don't want to think about what they might do next if they found out I sent these two officers after them.

What they might do to *her* to punish me.

I push our handholding to the back of my mind. That was stupid of me, letting my feelings get in the way without thinking of what it might mean for Bea's safety. Cooperating with the police without mentioning the infamous D.W. feels like the only way to keep her away from any more danger.

Eden returns, mentions something about having to pick up the kids, and leaves me with a quick kiss on the cheek. Alone again in my quiet cubicle, I drift off into a hazy, morphine-tinted slumber. And, despite my better judgement, the last thought I have before entering my bottomless dreamworld is one of caressing fingers, secret smiles, and how cold the bed now feels beneath my hand.

Chapter Twelve

Bea

It's been over twenty-four hours since I dragged myself away from the ICU and throwing myself into work seemed to be the only way to keep my mind off Artie and his attack.

He'd lied to his sister—probably lied to the police about it too.

Hearing him tell her he didn't know anything about the attacker, when it was so clearly a message from one of his *clients*, transported me back into a world I had no interest in diving into. Really, this had all been a blessing to warn me of the reality of getting too close to Artie, and why I should stay away.

A completely sick and twisted blessing.

If only someone would tell my overactive brain that I *didn't* want to call him and check in.

I mean, I *am* a nurse. It's in my nature to care for people. Nothing out of the ordinary about that.

This is what I keep reminding myself as I drive to my final house call of the day.

I'm certainly *not* thinking about his hand touching mine, or the jolts of electricity that skittered up my arm for the rest of the day after I'd left.

As I sit outside my patients' residential complex, I stifle a yawn into my palm and allow myself a second to close my itchy eyes. I'm exhausted after tossing and turning all night, and I'd really love nothing more than to go home and curl up into a ball underneath my thick comforter. But Oscar Ryan and Sonny Graham are some of my favourite patients, and they always end up roping me into a game of spades where we bet peanuts and they fill me in on the latest gossip going around the neighbourhood. So I blow a long breath through my mouth, push myself out of the car, and will myself to keep going.

"So Jill, from number sixty-one, has been going behind the other ladies in her club's backs to the managers, telling them about their curfew breaking!" Sonny chortles, delighting in the downfall of his long-time rival, Jill Walkers. Their feud began years ago when Jill moved into the better apartment that had been promised to Sonny.

"And Marcie has been calling secret meetings with the rest of them," Oscar adds as he shuffles the deck. "Some have been betting on what the revenge plan will be."

Sonny chuckles wickedly, and Oscar smiles at him. Something tells me Oscar only cares about the drama because Sonny's so invested in it. Before I can ask about the *revenge plan* theories circulating, a text buzzes through my pocket.

Artie

> Hey Honeybee, it's Arthur. I'm going out of my mind in this tiny cubicle, but I just wanted to make sure you're okay after the whole…situation. I know a hospital room probably isn't where you'd choose to spend your time ever again, especially for someone you barely know. So thank you, and are you okay?

I stare at the message for a second too long, eyes bouncing over each word again and again.

"Hey, Bea?" Oscar waves a hand in front of my face. "We're ready to play."

I blink at him, then at Sonny, before putting my phone face down on the table and picking up my cards. "Yep, sorry. Let's play."

Oscar begins the first turn, but Sonny interrupts, "Hang on, who's got you smiling like that?"

I laugh awkwardly as I shake my head, "What? No one."

Sonny throws his cards down dramatically, pointing a finger at me. "False. You're never on your phone when you come here." He looks to Oscar for backup, who relents with a lazy shrug. "So who's got you looking at your phone, grinning from ear to ear like the Cheshire Cat?"

I school my face into neutrality, but it's too late. Sonny is still jabbing his finger at me accusingly, a sparkle dancing wildly in his mocha eyes.

Oscar puts his own cards down and stands to get himself a glass of water. "Can we just play, please?" I ask, tapping my cards on the table. Oscar throws a *forget-it* signal over his shoulder, Sonny still staring at me expectantly. He looks like a piranha hunting for gossip, and I'm getting a little nervous. "It's no one, just a friend of a friend."

"A *friend of a friend*." Sonny cackles. "Sweet Bea, no one rereads a text from a *friend of a friend* that many times. Well, unless they're sending you filthy pictures." A gasp. "Are they?"

"No!" I laugh, feeling the heat prickle at my cheeks, my hands clamming up as I desperately wipe them on my scrubs. "He's in hospital and he's asking if I'm okay, and it was the first time he's texted me, so I was checking the number was really his."

"What's he in hospital for?" Oscar asks sincerely. Sonny leans further on his elbows to make sure he doesn't miss a word.

"An attack," I admit simply.

"Do they know who did it?" Sonny asks.

"No." It's not my story to tell—certainly not to Sonny, who would spread the news like wildfire as soon as the sun came up tomorrow morning.

"That's terrible." Oscar slumps in his chair, thoughtfully repositioning his flat cap. Sonny, suddenly looking sombre, nods in agreement.

We talk for a short while longer, but bringing up Artie's attack kind of killed the whole mood. I excuse myself ten minutes later and leave them to finish the game without me. As I walk to my car, I slide my phone from my pocket and draft my reply to Artie.

> Bea
>
> Hey, there's no need to thank me. I'm just glad you're safe. And yeah, I'm okay.

Is that too blunt?

Too forthcoming?

Too annoying?

The minutes tick up, up, up on the dashboard clock as I retype, adjust, rephrase, add words, delete words, Google how to reply to people's texts normally, and work myself into a flustered mess as I think of what to respond with.

After a ridiculous number of minutes have passed, I press send and put my phone on silent. Then I throw it in the passenger's side footwell and drive away, trying desperately to keep my eyes on the road.

It's not until I'm home and showered, changed into comfier clothes, and sat cross-legged on the sofa that I dig around in my bag to retrieve my phone. Holding it at arm's length with the screen angled towards the wall, I press the unlock button.

One unread message banner pops up. I hold the screen slightly closer, still angled away from me like a jump-scare's about to appear, until I'm just able to read his contact name.

My heart skips as I suck my bottom lip in between my teeth. Why am I trying to stop myself from smiling...in my empty house?

And why am I smiling at his name on my phone?

> Artie
>
> Good, that's good. Well, don't let me stop you from enjoying your Friday night. I just

> wanted to make sure you weren't struggling. I'm here if you need to talk, ever.

Oh. That's nice, I guess. There's no need to reply, which stops me from having to worry about drafting another sentence to send back. I throw my phone to the other side of the sofa with a content sigh.

But as I look around my empty living room, everything seems…too quiet.

Maria's busy with her accountant tonight, and my friends from the hospital are all on call. Jessica had promised to call after her date with Silas, but they won't be home for hours.

Nothing to do; no one to keep me company.

I tap the corner of my phone against my chin, wondering if I should follow my instinct. It's silly, and probably won't come to anything anyway. I might not even get an answer.

Even so…I don't know, I think I'm feeling a little silly tonight. I grab a glass of wine from the kitchen, get comfy on the sofa with a few fluffy blankets, and find my phone.

Bea
> How are you?

I press send on those three inconsequential words before I have time to overthink them. I sip my wine impatiently as I wait, phone resting face down on my chest so I won't miss the vibration. The vibration that comes after thirty *long* seconds.

Artie
> Can't complain. The nurses have got me on some lovely meds, so I can't feel a

> thing. Mostly just bored. What are you doing tonight?

I settle into the cushions as I type my reply, not bothering to sound interesting or exciting.

> Bea
>
> Literally nothing. I just got back from work. Jessica might call in a few hours, but I'll probably just throw on a film or read a book in the meantime.

No reply. Should I have made up some plans to make me sound more exciting? I bet he'd be out having fun tonight if he wasn't stuck in hospital, and I've just willingly told him my Friday night plans were to stay in by myself. Oh god, he's going to think I'm pathetic.

I may as well have sent, *Hi Arthur, I'm Bea—as in Boring. Delete my number, I'll only drag you down.*

Halfway through my spiral, another text chimes in.

> Artie
>
> Can I Facetime you?

Shit.

Shit, shit, shit.

I take a second to imagine how I look—no makeup, hair scraped up into a messy bun, in a stretched-out Care Bears pyjama T-shirt. I cannot video call him like *this*...can I?

Yes—yes, of course I can.

I don't care what Arthur Avila thinks of me. He's lying in a hospital bed, probably looking even worse than I do. He probably won't even notice my appearance.

I bet he only asked because he feels sorry for me, the girl with no plans on a Friday night. Nothing more than a pity invitation.

Hyped up on my newfound irritation at the nerve of this man, I text back a simple:

Bea

> Yes.

Instant regret.

When my phone starts vibrating in long strides, I jump up and throw it on the rug like it's caught fire. Draining my wine glass, I jog to the kitchen to pour myself another—and drain that one too. By the time I've filled the glass for a third time and returned to the living room, the phone's stopped ringing.

I pick it up tentatively at the same time it starts vibrating again.

And I throw it back down. A text buzzes through a second after the screen fades to black once more.

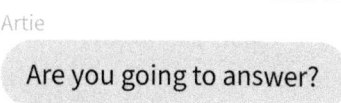

Artie

> Are you going to answer?

I sigh at myself and fall onto the sofa, opening my camera app to check how I look. I smooth the wispy baby hairs around my face and wipe a fleck of old wayward mascara from beneath my eye. I can do this. *I can do this, I can do this, I can do this.* I practice smiling a few times before I text him back.

Bea

> Yep, sorry. I'm ready now.

The call comes through straight away, and my heart hammers against my ribs as I answer.

"Hey," I say as breezily as I can.

"Hi," Artie replies with a lopsided smile, voice gruff. The swelling is still prominent around his eyes and jaw, but that doesn't stop his dimple from shining through my screen. "I was worried you'd changed your mind."

I bark a laugh. "No, nope. Just…getting ready. Changing out of my work clothes, blah."

"How was work?" he asks with a smile. "I didn't see you around here."

"Um, no. I try and stay away from the hospital. I'm mainly on the house call rotation." I try to keep my voice light, but there's something dark lacing the words.

Artie catches on, agreeing, "I think house calls sound much more fun, anyway."

"Yeah, they are." I smile. "I like taking care of people. I never got to do that with my own parents, so I might be overcompensating for something there, but I enjoy it."

Oh my god, why did I just bring my parents up?!

Artie stares at me through the screen for a few seconds, eyes soft. "Do you mind me asking what happened to them?"

Strangely, no.

"They died. When I was very young. I never knew them, and unfortunately, I never found my forever family. I've kind of been alone my whole life. I think that's why I like to keep my friends so close; why I became a nurse in the first place."

I have no idea why I'm telling him all of this, but it feels...freeing. As if I'm weightless, almost. For a second, my confession leaves me floating.

"Thank you for telling me that, Honeybee." Artie's voice is gentle, as if he is really thankful for that piece of information.

Just like that, the difficult conversation is over and my secret's out. But unlike most other people I've told, Artie didn't make me feel weak or less than.

Not at all, because then he sniffs and changes the conversation completely. "Dressing up for me, I see." He flicks his eyebrows up as his eyes dip to take in my pyjama top. I feel a shimmer of embarrassment tingle through me, but my white wine confidence stamps it down and kicks it away.

"Like you've done for me?" I ask, exaggerating my own eye movements as I look over every inch of his face, from his messy curls to that mesmerising dimple.

"I mean, I guess I do have the excuse of being in a hospital bed," he drawls. "With a sprained arm and a head wound..."

That shatters my confident mask. "Oh, you're right. I'm sorry."

But he simply bursts out in laughter. "You're too easy, Bumblebee. I give you my word—next time I will *definitely* dress up for you."

I roll my eyes, but I'm grinning from ear to ear. "I hate you, Artie Avila."

"I know you do, Beatrice. But let's not get into that now. Save that one for another day, shall we? Today I want you to tell me something *fun*."

"Fun?" I ask, suddenly put on the spot. "Like what?"

"I don't know. Show me your failed crafts."

"No."

"Why not?"

"They're failed for a reason. I've hidden them so no one will ever find them."

"You have a failed craft morgue? Oh, I *have* to see this."

I groan, but that twinkle in his eye tells me he's not going to give up. So I roll off the sofa and take him to my spare room where my craft supplies get hidden away shamefully. "This is my craft room, and this—" I point the camera to a beaten-up set of drawers in the darkest corner "—is where all failed crafts go to die."

"Love it," he croons through the screen. "Put on a fashion show for me, Honeybee."

I do what I'm told. I balance the phone on top of the drawers, sitting on the edge of the bed so I can pick out the random junk I've kept hidden within for so long.

First, a felted cow I gave up on after the third leg.

"That poor duck," Artie exclaims.

"A duck?" I gasp, hand clutching my chest. "This is clearly meant to be a cow."

"A cow? It has no spots."

"I gave up before I could add them," I sigh, throwing the cow back into the drawer.

"I'm going to call him Duck."

"Whatever helps you sleep at night, I suppose." I select my next item and show it to the camera. "This is a granny square

I crocheted when I wanted to make a cosy blanket. I gave up before I could make the other thirty-five needed to actually make it blanket size."

"That's a cosy blanket for Duck."

I laugh and toss it back into the craft coffin, grabbing something else to show him.

My fashion show lasts the full hour, with every new craft being related back to Duck in some way.

"Can I ask why you've tried so many crafts?" Artie laughs as I shove the second drawer closed.

"I'm looking for my yellow." My voice comes out strained as the contents fight back and I struggle to hide my shameful failures.

"Your yellow?"

Oh, right. That probably sounds stupid to anyone normal. *Probably why I haven't told anyone—why've I just told a stranger?*

Nothing else to do but own it now. "Yep. Like sunshine, homemade lemonade, and marigolds. I've been looking for some peace; something to calm my mind. Something yellow." Artie's staring at me intently through the screen, so I laugh it off. "I'm probably not making any sense."

"No," he interjects firmly. "That makes perfect sense to me."

I break into a grin then, feeling…seen. He mirrors the expression right back at me, but before either of us can say anything else, a nurse interrupts us to take Artie's vitals.

"Hey, I'll leave you to it now," he announces quickly as the nurse fusses around him. "But thank you for this—for picking up. I've had a great time."

"Me too," I say. And I truly mean it. "Bye, Artie."

"Goodbye."

During our call, Jessica had messaged to say she wouldn't be able to speak tonight, apologising over and over. I send her a quick reply to tell her not to worry before retreating into my bedroom to get ready for bed.

It's not until I slide under the covers that I check my phone one last time. A message from Artie stares back at me, waiting impatiently.

Artie

> I just wanted to say thanks again for keeping me company. Best Friday night ever! I definitely want to see the rest of your craft morgue next time. Goodnight, Honeybee.

Bea

> Night, Dream Boy.

As I send back a quick text of my own, I notice a tightness in my cheeks. *When was the last time I'd smiled so much my cheeks hurt?*

That thought makes me smile even wider.

I fall asleep quickly, those two silly little words replaying over and over again in my head—*next time*.

Chapter Thirteen

Artie

It's hard to believe I've only been rotting in this bland hospital room for almost a week now. The monochrome surroundings have been doing an excellent job of making it feel much, *much* longer. Grey monitors hooked up to the machines, beige pleather chair coverings, off-white thin blinds no one ever seems to fully shut. I'm going out of my mind.

Eden visits as much as she can, and I'm incredibly grateful for every minute she spends here. But between her family and a business to run, her returns are often fleeting and over far too soon. Not that I'd hope for anything different; Janie and Hector come first always.

It's just that without any visitors and only so much scrolling one can do on his phone without going crazy, my mind has decided to overthink every single thing.

If my attacker had managed to get into my apartment and steal my confidential files.

Whether a sprained arm and two days lost would be enough to appease D.W., or if I'd need another lesson.

If they were looking for Bea while I'm stuck in this bed.

The saving grace of this week had been my Friday night Facetime with Bea, who'd given in far too easily when I asked to see the inner workings of her creative mind. We haven't spoken since and I know it's my fault. Don't get me wrong, I've been desperate to text her. But one relentless thought steps in every time I type out a message.

You're putting her in danger.

The heavy thought always stops me, moving my thumb from the send button to the backspace. The message ceases to exist and I go back to arguing with myself. Which always ends in self-torment, but it's better than getting her mixed up in all of this.

Plus, she openly tells me she hates me. Daring to change that will only bring trouble to her doorstep.

I've been moved from the ICU to neurology, where they can monitor me quietly before discharging me. A small mercy, I suppose—I'll be out of here sooner rather than later. They've let up on the painkillers, too. A dull ache thrums across my arm and shoulder whenever I readjust, but I'm feeling good. I'd love to lose the headache, though.

"Mr Avila!" Dr Barrett booms as he glides through the door of my private room, and it's an effort not to wince. "How are we feeling today?"

"Like I'm ready to get out of here," I say, lifting the end of the last word in a hopeful question. If he weren't so interested in reading something off my chart, I might've fluttered my eyelashes at him to sweeten the deal.

"Of course," he hums, snapping the folder shut. Well, your most recent scans look good. I'm happy to have the nurses sort your discharge later today."

A tidal wave of relief washes over me. "Thanks, doc."

"I'll make sure your nurse gives you my pager number in case anything goes wrong at home, but I don't envision there being a problem. I think you've had a lucky escape, Mr Avila."

There's that word again. *Lucky.*

A tight smile is all I manage, and he leaves just as quickly as he came.

I don't think I can take another second of overthinking the past, so I pick up my phone to send that goddamned text. But as I do, my phone starts ringing. It's not the contact I've been craving, but it'll do.

"And to what do I owe this pleasure?" I croon in way of greeting.

"I knew I was going to regret calling you," Silas moans.

"You could never."

A sigh. "Bea told us what happened. Please explain to me why I'm hearing from her that you've been attacked, several days afterwards?"

"Did she also happen to mention I was under sedation for two days?" I deadpan.

"Arthur..."

"Were you worried about me?" I taunt. "Are you on your way to feed me grapes and brush my hair until my stitches dissolve?"

Silas growls away from the phone receiver, and I grin. It's just too easy to wind him up.

"Look, I didn't tell you because it's not a big deal. Stupid games, stupid prizes—right? You should know better than anyone."

"That's why I'm as far away from that game now as I can be," Silas says, tone turned into a warning. "This needs to stop, Artie. Don't make the same mistakes as I did. You don't know who'll get caught in the crossfire."

And suddenly, involuntarily, one person flashes through my mind. With her eyes as blue as the stillest sea. Her deep golden hair cascading down her back. The way she always looks at me like she has a secret. *That damned freckle beneath her eye.*

"I know," I finally relent. "It's not like I wanted this to happen, Sy. I'm not even sure how to stop it."

I don't know why I haven't admitted that to myself before. No, I *don't* know how to stop D.W.—I'm literally hoping a sprained arm and hospital stay will be enough to pay my debts. I can't simply get the secrets I'd handed over back from Monty, because there aren't any secrets to begin with.

I can't fulfil the only thing the anonymous bastard has asked of me.

"Tell me everything that's happened, starting from the beginning. Like you should've done in the first place."

Feeling like a disciplined child, I do. I tell him about the letters, the call, the notes. I tell him about Monty, how I often send him classified information that the police could use to take down their biggest targets, and how he can't find any evidence of my submitted tip concerning D.W.

Silas thinks everything over for a while, his small murmurs and pacing footsteps sounding softly through the phone. "Why are you waiting for your police friend to do the searching for you? I'd have thought the best hacker in the country could get into the system and check the files yourself. That way, you'd know for certain whether you sent the tip or not."

I have to take a second to think it over, because it's actually kind of genius. "How have I not thought of hacking into Monty's system?"

Another sigh from Silas. "Because you're not that smart," he says simply.

I ignore him because that's so obviously untrue. I'm blaming one woman for my apparent oversight of this potential solution.

"If I get into Monty's system, I can delete the tip myself," I muse. But it can't be *that* simple, can it?

Of course, the police will have the mother of all firewalls up to protect people like me from entering whenever we want. Not to mention if I got caught, I'd be facing a nice slice of jail time.

But Silas is half right—I *am* the best in the country. If anyone can do it, it'd be me. Well, me and my inner circle.

"Thanks, Sy. I actually think you've been a big help," I say before tacking on, "Which makes a change."

"You're an arse," is all I get back before he hangs up and I'm left with my swirling thoughts once more. But this time, they're full of code and tricks I'll need to break potential firewalls.

Something like a sense of revival overcomes me—like I've been given a new lease on life after that short call. Suddenly, I'm even more excited to get back behind my computers and keep this D.W. psycho out of my life for good.

And away from Bea.

Once D.W. has been taken care of, I'll need to rethink my alliance with Monty and the force. Whether the hacking game is worth it at all anymore.

But one thing at a time.

For the time being, my only mission is to get out of this hospital as quickly as possible. Then I can move on to planning the riskiest heist of my career.

Chapter Fourteen
Bea

ALL IN ALL, THE welcome back to working on the hospital floor had been warmer than I could've hoped for. With the exception of Myla, who still uses grunting as her main form of communication with me, everyone has been so lovely and understanding.

I guess Helena probably sent out a group IM before my big return—something along the lines of, *Nurse Di Menna has a tendency to freak out in hospitals, so don't give her anything too stressful to work on.*

I'm grateful, really. It's not so bad being here. After each shift, I have a quick cry in the car before setting off, but the tears are drying up quicker each day, and I choose to look at the positive on that one. I've started being able to listen to my happy playlists on my long drives home, too, which is another silver lining. I couldn't bear to listen to upbeat music for the longest time...

One thing I'm *not* looking for the silver lining in is the fact that Artie hasn't so much as texted in the week following our Facetime.

The urge to go storming down to neurology, where I know he's been transferred, is undeniable. I'd do it, too—if I wasn't still working through my fears of being on my current floor.

I have drafted a few messages this week, starting off nice with little titbits about my day. I deleted each one because I highly doubt he'd care about the lucky penny I picked up on the way to work, but I still typed them.

As the week progressed, the messages became slightly less *nice*. But today is the day. I pull out my phone and send a simple message as I clock out for my lunch break.

Bea

> ?

Yes, it's petty and silly. But he's the one who called me and said there would be a next time! And to not even send a quick text throughout the entire week when I know he's lying in a bed a few floors down, bored out of his mind?

I think I've earned the right to be a bit petty.

The reply I get is just as annoying as the sender, though.

Artie

> ? to you too, Honeybee.

I sigh through my nose as I type out a reply.

Bea

> **You are infuriating.**

Artie
> Did you just start this conversation to insult me?

That stops me dead, because now I have to wonder why I texted him in the first place. It's not like I want to talk to him. In fact, I think I miss when I *wasn't* talking to him.

Bea
> **Yes.**

Artie
> Fair enough. Are you frowning right now? You're so hot when you frown.

Bea
> **And you're so annoying always.**

Artie
> Yet you're the one who messaged me.

Bea
> **I regret it immensely.**

Artie
> You're breaking my heart, Honeybee.

Bea
> **As if you have one to break.**

I spend the rest of my lunch break silently stewing, considering possible reasons for why I'm so caught up on our week-long silence, and why my eyes keep landing on my phone screen, quietly hoping he'll text me back.

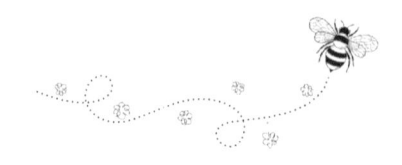

I turn up at Bluetine Park a few hours later, still in my scrubs from the hospital. Eden had called asking if I wouldn't mind dropping in on Artie if I ever had some free time to make sure he was doing okay. Apparently, he'd been discharged earlier today but she couldn't get out of prior work commitments.

I park a mile away from Artie's apartment and use the walk to clear my head, wondering why I'm really doing this.

To make sure he's okay, the voice in my head says.

Because you want to see him again, the juvenile other voice interjects.

The second voice is always wrong, so don't listen to it.

By the time I get to the first door, I've successfully psyched myself up to see Artie and I'm prepared for whatever I'll find. I make my way up the stairs and knock twice on the front door.

Within a few seconds, it opens onto Artie's confused face, which instantly transforms into a broad grin. The door opens wider so I can see the inside of his apartment.

"Hello," he says, slightly confused. "What are you doing here?"

"I came to make sure you were okay." My eyes travel down his body, noting the sling on his arm and the smaller bandages littered over the rest of his body. I definitely *do not* notice the light grey joggers he's wearing or his slightly mussed hair.

"That's awfully nice of you, Honeybee. Do you want to come in?"

I bite the inside of my cheek. I kind of do.

So I nod and step over the threshold, into the dim room with only a small lamp on to give the space a warm glow. I pass him with my head high, reminding myself that I'm still annoyed by his radio silence this past week.

A large desk sits in the middle of the room, scattered with stacks of papers surrounding the three screens standing proudly along it. Behind that is a sofa facing a large television against a tall window with the blinds drawn down.

"May I?" I ask, pointing to the dark grey sofa.

"Of course. Can I get you something to drink?"

"Tea, if you have any. Do you want me to make it?" I ask with a glance down at his sling that earns me a hearty laugh.

"I think I can just about pour a kettle. Tea coming right up. Please, make yourself comfortable."

I edge slowly past the desk that takes up most of the small space before sitting gently on the sofa. There's a small coffee table between me and the TV, a large armchair to the right and an ornate bookshelf to the left. I'm squinting, trying to read some of the names as Artie sits next to me, placing two steaming cups on the coffee table.

The sofa shifts beneath me as he repositions himself, and suddenly we're entirely too close. I practically springboard up and land in the armchair. Artie's eyebrows lift as I slide my mug closer to my new seat. "You okay over there?"

"Yep. The armchair just...looked comfier." I smile, but inside I'm wincing.

"Right," he says, drawing out the syllables and ending with an exaggerated wink. "So, what do I owe the pleasure of this delightful little visit? Dr Barratt hasn't sent you over here as some sort of spy, has he?"

"No—why would he do that? Did he say something? Is anything wrong?"

Artie chuckles and even has the gall to look *endeared* at my mild freak-out. "Just a joke. I'm all good and on the mend."

"Oh," I nod. "I just wanted to check on you, really. I know—I know how difficult it must be to come back to the scene of the crime."

"Ah, *that*." He gives me a tight-lipped smile. "Yeah, no one prepared me for feeling quite so terrified in my own home, but I'll get over it."

I'm a fraction taken aback by that. Looking at Artie now, I wouldn't think he was scared at all. He's his usual energetic self that I'm coming to learn a lot about. If it weren't for the sling on his arm and the fading black eye, I'd never think he was attacked only a couple of weeks ago.

"Terrified?" I ask, my voice smaller than intended.

He winks at me, and that damned dimple does the same. "Nothing a little time won't fix. You don't have to worry about me."

"I'm not *worried* about you," I say harshly, although it's completely untrue and we definitely both know it. I sigh, tucking my hair behind both ears before admitting, "But I know how it feels."

Artie stares at me intently, and I take a sip of scolding tea just for something to do. "Oh yeah?"

"Yeah," I agree solemnly. "I can't drive near Desmond's old shop or get anywhere close to the old hospital without freaking out. I take the back roads around town to avoid certain places, and it takes me triple the time it should to get anywhere. Just driving here from the hospital took forty minutes. I wanted to make sure you didn't feel that way too. I wouldn't wish it on my worst enemy."

Silence falls over us, and I chance a look up to see Artie staring at me like I'm a wounded puppy. Fabulous.

"Bea, I had no idea. I'm so sorry."

"I've never told that to anyone before," I muse quietly. I cringe slightly as I glance up at him. "Please stop looking at me like that."

He smirks softly. "How am I looking at you?"

I take a second to consider whether I want to tell him the truth or not. *I do.* "Like I'm weak."

"Honeybee, you're one of the strongest people I've ever set eyes on."

I scoff dismissively, but looking into his eyes, he looks sincere. *Too* sincere, and I'm suddenly super self-conscious because he can't mean that—not really. I'm not strong and I'm definitely not brave, and I don't think I'd ever be able to return to my house if someone attacked me right outside. "Not as brave as some," I whisper.

"But still braver than many," he counters. The smile that comes with his words has me flying, high on the hope that one day I might just believe him.

Not today, though.

I clear my throat, eager to get away from the conversation. "I guess I should leave you alone, you probably have big plans for your first night of freedom."

"I have literally no plans," he replies with a soft chuckle.

"Oh." Nothing else to say to that, really.

"Would you perhaps do me the honour of keeping me company, Honeybee?"

Oh god. "I'd love to, but I have to be at the hospital early tomorrow morning," I say with a helpless shrug.

"The hospital is closer to mine than it is yours, just stay the night."

"A sleepover?" I lift an eyebrow in a challenge.

It earns me an emphatic laugh. "If you want to call it a sleepover, you may. Otherwise, just call it crashing at mine."

"I don't have any pyjamas."

"Borrow some of mine."

"Or a toothbrush."

"I have a spare."

Am I really considering this? It *is* getting late...

The moon glimmers brightly just outside Artie's window as if in agreement. It's not like I have any plans...but I barely know him. *What was I mad at him about, again?*

"Look, I can see some kind of inner turmoil warring behind your eyes, so let me just put my cards on the table." Artie exhales some of the tension in his shoulders before continuing, "I'd really like it if you could stay for a while, Bea. It doesn't have to be overnight if you're not comfortable with that, but I'm finding it difficult to be here alone. I'd love it if you could stay."

I think I physically feel my heart crack, knowing the feeling well. So I tell him, "Okay." Everyone needs a friend to lean on when they're at their lowest, after all.

"Thank you." He leans forward and squeezes my hand with his, the warmth of his palm radiating up my arm. It leaves a spatter of goosebumps in its wake. "So, what do you feel like doing?"

CHAPTER FIFTEEN
Artie

I'M WELL AWARE OF the original plan to keep Bea away from me at all costs, but she turned up on my doorstep. What was a gentleman to do?! She asked if I was okay and I answered truthfully, because I'm shit scared in my own house and I don't think I could sleep here alone tonight. So I asked her to stay over, and I know that makes me a coward for putting her in harm's way. I wasn't thinking, and it's too late now, and *god* she's beautiful.

I'll protect her if D.W. comes knocking again. But on the off chance he's disappeared into thin air, let me have tonight with her. *I don't know what I'll do without her company.*

We decide to watch a film from my small collection, with Bea fishing a bag of popcorn from my cupboard that I have no recollection of ever buying. It's a romcom—the best genre, in my opinion, but I'm having the hardest time focusing on the movie.

No, apparently the woman sitting to the side of me is much more interesting. Her confessions from earlier continue to cycle throughout my head, over and over. She believes she's weak. She doesn't even realise how brave she is.

If only she could see herself through my eyes.

After Silas was taken to hospital last year, I hacked into Desmond's camera footage to catch a glimpse of just how much of a mess I'd missed. The image of Bea helping a dwindling Silas will forever be etched into my brain. The way she ran to him without a second's thought of her own safety. When she screamed at her captors despite their weapons being pointed directly at her. How her hands were shaking so violently that I could see them through the grainy footage, yet she managed to still them enough to patch her friend up so gently.

I was in awe of her then, and I think I have been every moment since.

To hear what she thinks of herself; how she's still dealing with all the trauma and grief…I can't bear it.

And now I can't take my eyes off her. She's kicked her legs over one side of the armchair with her back against the other. She seems to have monopolised the popcorn bowl and kept it all to herself, chuckling every now and then at the TV. Her side profile is literally glowing.

I blow a quiet sigh through my nose. I wonder if she knows she's driving me slightly wild without even trying.

"Is there a reason why you're staring at me?" she asks, turning towards me with a wicked look painted across her face.

"Please, you *wish* I were staring at you." I give her a lazy smile as she scoffs, because we both know I most certainly was staring. "I am going to grab another drink. Do you want another tea?"

"Yes please—wait," she says, eyeing me suspiciously. "You don't drink tea."

I roll my eyes preemptively, already knowing what's coming after I confess, "I bought some after you let me try a cup at yours."

"Oh *really*? Who knew I was so influential." She hums a smug laugh, looking up at me through thick lashes.

"Do you want a cup of tea or not, Beatrice?" I ask flatly.

"Yes, please. Do you want me to make it?" she asks, swinging her legs off the chair to stand.

"Absolutely not. Sit," I instruct, and she looks taken aback but obeys anyway. I notice the way she's biting her lip, and all hope of looking *anywhere* else tonight vanishes with that—

I curse under my breath as the corner of the desk rams into my thigh.

Bea swivels around, trying to swallow her laugh as she asks, "Are you okay?"

"Just dandy," I sing through gritted teeth, shaking the pain away. *Teach me for not looking where I'm going in this literal shoebox.*

"Why do you need a desk taking up the entirety of your living room, anyway?" Bea asks, reading my mind.

"Have you ever hacked into a top-secret government program? There happens to be a *lot* of code to get through, and lots of protection. The biggest hacker in the game can't have a small desk." I smirk.

"A top-secret government program?"

I hum a sigh. "Another lifetime." I can see the trepidation in her eyes from here. She's considering going home, I know it. Something tells me I won't be able to bear watching her leave tonight, so I add, "I've been thinking I need a downgrade, anyway."

I don't think I imagine how her ears prick as she repeats, "A downgrade?"

"That's right." I deliver her a steaming cup of tea before returning to retrieve my glass of water. "I've been wondering lately if the big desk is really worth it anymore."

"I think a smaller desk would be a good idea." She shrugs.

We lock eyes, and I think we both know we're not talking about just a desk.

"Or a bigger house," I counter.

She laughs then. "It is quite small, isn't it."

"I prefer to think of it as *quaint*," I smile.

"Maybe a bigger house and a smaller desk would suit you better?"

I hold her eyes for a long moment as I sit back down. "It's looking more and more appealing every day."

Bea grins knowingly, and I swear I physically feel a tendon of tension snap between us.

It's probably one of my favourite feelings ever.

We finish the rest of the film in silence, the only sound coming from Bea sorting popped corn from the kernels at the bottom of her bowl. By the time the credits roll just after 10 pm, she's already yawning.

"Tired?" I ask, and she looks over at me through squinted eyes.

"Why are you asking me that like it's not completely acceptable to be tired at ten o'clock? That's literally bedtime."

"I guess I'm just a night owl."

"Sorry, you young and spritely man," she mocks. "What would you be doing if I weren't here?"

"Working, probably."

I swear I see her bristle. It's becoming harder to ignore the elephant in the room.

I'm starting to think Bea might not hate me so much, but she *definitely* hates the idea of my job.

"I'm happy to leave if you have work to do," she suggests.

I do, actually. I was in the middle of devising a plan with the inner circle to get into Monty's interface when Bea turned up at my door. But while she might be happy to leave, I'm certainly not ready to see her go.

"I'd rather you didn't," I say, and I hate how casual it sounds.

Bea looks around. "I'm guessing you don't have a spare room?"

"Nope. Thought we could just top and tail in mine."

She scrunches her nose. "That's going to be a hard pass."

"Damn," I drawl. "I guess I'll take the sofa and you can have my bed all to yourself."

She gives it a long look back and forth, like she's inspecting it for traps. "I can take the sofa."

"No way, I insist."

"You're the one who's just been discharged from hospital. I'll be taking the sofa."

"So authoritative, *Nurse Di Menna*," I croon, clasping a palm to my cheek. "Do you often make overnight house calls?"

"Only for the lucky few." It's a simple sentence, but her cheeks redden at the suggestion she absolutely did not mean. I decide to let her off this one and ignore it.

"Do you want to borrow some pyjamas?"

"That is a requirement of our sleepover, I'm afraid."

I scoot past her and walk into my bedroom, grabbing a pair of fluffy red bottoms Eden bought me once as a joke and a burgundy T-shirt. At least they started off as a joke. Now they're my favourite pair. "Of course, sleeping naked at a patient's house would be completely unprofessional."

She appears in the doorway just as I turn, getting a good look at my cramped bedroom. "You're not actually my patient." Her tone is so innocent that it's an effort not to ask her to repeat herself. I want to ask her if she meant the unspoken implication, but before I can she steps towards me, eyebrows raised, and grabs the clothes from my hands. "Thanks," she throws over her shoulder as she walks into the bathroom.

Oh, she meant it. I'm a little wonderstruck.

And I'm glad she walked away. If she hadn't, I think I might've done something she'd come to regret.

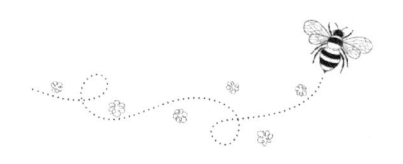

"Morning," I croak as I enter the living room, mouth twitching with amusement as I take in Bea's large eyes and O-shaped mouth. Like I just caught her doing the walk of shame, with one foot already out of my apartment. "Sneaking out on me, Honeybee?"

She scoffs, slowly closing the door again. "No," she says, dragging out the word. Awful liar. I pour myself some coffee from the pot she must've made before trying to make her quick escape. "I told you I have to be at work early."

I look at the microwave clock. It's just shy of 5 am. "How early?"

"My shift starts at six."

I chuckle, taking a sip. Somehow the woman who only ever drinks tea has managed to make a pot of coffee that tastes infinitely better than anything I've ever managed. "The hospital is a ten-minute drive from here."

"I like to get there early." A shrug.

"To do what?"

"I'll probably just read in the car until my shift starts."

I give her a levelling look, but she's completely serious. "You cannot sit in a freezing cold car for fifty minutes!"

"I do it every morning."

"Every morning?"

"Yes." Her arms are tightly folded now.

Then it dawns on me; the real reason she's leaving this early. "What are you avoiding?" I ask carefully, taking another sip to discreetly hide the implication behind my cup.

A heavy breath. "The shop."

"Ah." Desmond's Deals. Just on the outskirts of town, conveniently right in between Bluetine Park and the hospital. "I'm sorry for making you stay over. I didn't even consider that."

That earns me a smile and a shake of her head. It's a small smile, but I think it's genuine. "I had a good time."

"Me too." I'd slept better last night than I had done in a long time, and I have to wonder if having Bea in the apartment had something to do with it. "If only I hadn't caught you trying to sneak out on me, then it would've been perfect."

"I'm sorry! It won't happen again, but I really do need to go." That apology might seem more sincere if it hadn't been served with an eye roll.

"No, you don't." I take another sip of delicious coffee.

She's slowly backing towards the door, her lips curling in a quiet challenge. "Yes, I do."

I place my mug on the counter and match her slow steps, closing the gap between us as her back bumps into the door. I don't stop until I'm right in front of her, resting my uninjured arm on the door next to her head. "I think you have plenty of time to have breakfast with me."

She smells like morning coffee and cinnamon. The way she's looking up at me right now, the light in her eyes dancing, as she bites her lower lip...

My turn.

I dare to drag a soft finger down the side of her face to tuck a lock of hair behind her ear, before continuing my path to her chin. I lift it gently, earning myself a better angle of her full, supple lips. She's not smiling anymore, eyes darting around my face before landing on my own mouth. I don't think I imagine the sound of her breath hitching.

Moving painfully slowly, I lean down to close the small gap between us. But before I can, she breathes "Artie" onto my lips uncertainly. It's like a bucket of ice water over me, because I'm not doing anything she's not completely sure about. "I *really* have to go. I—I can't drive the quick route."

She can, but that's a conversation for another time.

"I'll drive you," I counter, stepping back from the pure temptation of her. I notice a blush creeping up her neck, and it's a serious effort not to explore that warmth with my lips. But the crease between her eyebrows tells me the moment's passed and I best keep my distance from the door she's still leaning against, so I continue as casually as I can, "Or at least come with you. I'll talk to you the entire time and tell jokes so hilarious you'll not even notice where you are."

"I couldn't ask you to do that..." she murmurs, dragging her thumb over her bottom lip in contemplation. *Temptress.*

I can't quite bring myself to look away from it. "It's a good thing you're not asking, then."

Chapter Sixteen

Bea

I ARRIVE HOME AFTER my visit with Sonny and Oscar absolutely exhausted. It's hard to believe Artie insisting he drive me to the hospital was today, but it was. Just over twelve hours ago.

Last night had been...something. Something special, something stupid. Just...*something*. This morning even more so. Something that probably shouldn't happen again.

I'd been thinking about our conversation against the door all day. Artie's lips so close to mine that I could smell the cinnamon I'd put in his coffee maker, his strong arm braced beside my head. Leaning into my space so intimately, his warm breath tickling my cheek. How if I'd been a tiny bit braver, he would've closed the gap completely and kissed me senseless. *Which is exactly what I wanted...in the moment.*

Like I say—it shouldn't happen again.

"So you just...slept on his sofa?" Maria asks, leaning across my kitchen island, looking at me through squinted eyes. "That's it?"

"What are you expecting me to say?" I snap, because this is the fifth time she's asked me to explain myself since she walked through my door as many minutes ago. She hasn't even taken her coat off yet.

Her blazing red hair pools against the countertop as she shakes her head. "What are we going to do with you? I'm going to need to have a serious talk with Jessica about how we move forward. I mean, come on! He literally asked you to *spend the night*, and you took the sofa."

"He meant it in a friendly way; he's closer to the hospital and I had an early morning." I add a shrug that really sets her off.

"Bea. You know I love you, but you're hopeless!"

"You have no idea what you're talking about—people *can* hang out without needing to sleep together."

A gasp. "You mean I'm not getting lucky tonight?" she asks with an eyebrow wiggle. I laugh and lead her into my living room without bothering to answer. I'm holding the giant bowl of popcorn; she's got the wine and glasses.

"What are we doing here, anyway?" Maria asks, sitting opposite me on one of the two floor cushions I'd set on either side of my coffee table. A table that is now neatly wrapped in old newspaper.

"Beeswax candle-making." I bought a kit online. It's apparently the new big thing in the craft world.

Maria clasps her hands together. "That sounds *so* fun."

You'd think I have shares in the small business I bought the kit from with how offended I get from that sarcastic comment. "It will be fun!"

Her eyes sparkle. "That's what I just said."

"For god's sake. Just pour the wine and tell me all about your new accountant." The new accountant Maria hadn't been able to stop talking about for the past two weeks.

Andrew, his name is. All I know about him is that he's super tall and *super* boring. Like, just goes on about expense reports and budgets all day long. Which, for someone like Maria, would be super boring.

I don't have the heart to tell her he's only trying to save her business.

We spend the next three hours trying to make our homemade candles—which are *not* beginner-friendly, by the way, like the ad suggested—and laughing at all the stupid jokes we come up with at poor Andrew's expense.

By the time I wave Maria off and clean up the dregs of our girl's night, I'm even more exhausted. Like, can't-believe-I'm-still-standing-right-now exhausted. And tipsy. And very giggly.

I get ready and jump into bed in record time, snuggling deep into the pillows. I check the time on my phone—just past midnight. But the idea of sleep is wicked away as soon as I illuminate my screen, because under the clock display is a new message.

Artie

> You up, Honeybee?

I actually gasp out loud. If I were wearing pearls, I'd have clutched them. The wine in my system hikes my confidence level up and I send back a reply without even rereading the first draft.

> Bea
>
> My mind better be playing tricks on me, Mr Avila. Because if I'm really receiving a booty call text message from a thirty-year-old, I might just have to bleach my eyeballs.

I giggle at my own joke, rereading my hilarious words until he replies.

> Artie
>
> I genuinely didn't expect you to answer.
>
> Can I call you?

That stops my laughing.

> Bea
>
> Of course.

Artie's name flashes across my screen as soon as I hit send, and I answer just as quickly. "Hey," I say, instantly conscious of whether I'm slurring my words or not. "Sup?"

I hear him hold the phone away from his ear to bark out a laugh. I smile at the sound; it's so genuine. So light and happy and real. It takes a moment for him to compose himself enough to reply, "Nothing much, Honeybee. *Sup* with you?"

"Just going to bed," I say with a muffled yawn, blissfully ignoring the bait.

"I was surprised when you texted back—I thought for sure you'd be asleep by now."

"Tomorrow's my day off, so Maria came round for a crafts night."

"Please tell me it ended with a new addition to your graveyard drawers."

I let out an irritated sigh. "Candles are surprisingly difficult to make."

Another laugh, this time directly into the speaker. The sound dances through my brain. "I have to see this."

"I'm not showing you any more failed crafts!" I sigh around my stubborn smile.

"Why not?" he asks in a sorrowful voice. I imagine him with a comically large frown, begging on his knees to see just one more of my secret stash.

It'd be a nice sight, I suppose.

"Because it's embarrassing, and I'm not getting anything out of it. Why would I show off my failures for free?"

"You get to see me and my reactions. I've been told I have a very expressive face."

I consider that for half a second. "Not good enough."

"What would be a suitable payment?" he asks, a deep chuckle rumbling down the line a moment later.

Another long pause while I think. "I want to know your deepest, darkest secret."

Artie hums a warm sound. "Only if you repay the favour."

"A secret for a secret?"

"That's right. Show me yours and I'll show you mine."

It takes me a moment to decide on just one secret to tell him. "I'm deathly scared of mascots."

He splutters a laugh as he repeats, "Mascots? Like people dressed up as big animals wearing T-shirts and baseball hats?"

"Yes," I say defiantly.

"Why?"

I sigh. "One time, my foster family took me to a theme park where there were lots of cartoon characters walking around. I never really had the big kids' channels growing up, so I had no idea who this massive yellow sponge was supposed to be. He literally came barrelling up to me with his hand outstretched." Artie's light chuckle cuts through my dramatic reconstruction. "In hindsight, I believe he wanted a high five. But at the time? Terrifying. I cried the rest of the way home and have been afraid of them ever since. It's definitely irrational, but I've never managed to get over it."

"That's amazing," Artie hums.

"Go on, then. What's your big secret?"

"I name inanimate objects around my home. For example, my computer is called Byte." His voice is so flat that I don't know if he's joking or not. As if he reads my mind through the phone, he adds, "No, I'm not joking. I say good morning to Byte every time I log on for the day. It's just standard practice; has been for years."

"I've never heard such a unique secret before." *Truly.*

"Well, I aim to please," he croons.

I hum in response. This call should be awkward, shouldn't it? I don't usually almost kiss people I dislike and then act like nothing happened. Not that it's ever happened before, but this feels like something I should be overthinking. Yet here I am laughing with Artie like it was nothing more than a fantasy. How is that possible?

"Why'd you want to know if I was up, anyway?" I ask, changing the subject before I can get hung up on whether I should be overthinking something or not.

The way he says, "Missed you" in such a relaxed, matter-of-fact way has me almost falling out of bed.

And I'm lying directly in the middle of the mattress.

"Sorry?"

"I wanted to talk to you," he says, and I can almost hear the shrug in his voice.

"Why?"

"Because I haven't spoken to you all day." The words are lengthened and spread apart to make them easy for me to understand. If I weren't so taken aback, I'd roll my eyes.

"You saw me this morning."

"That was almost twenty hours ago."

I do the math in my head before realising that *oh, this is another joke.* "Are you kidding?"

"Of course I'm not kidding," Artie laughs brightly, as if I'm being ridiculous. "I couldn't sleep, and you were the only person I wanted to talk to. I had fun last night, I had fun this morning, and I'd been thinking of you all day. So I called. It's not a big deal."

Oh yeah. Not a big deal. Not *at all.*

I'm completely fine with the fact that Artie, of all people, is the first person to tell me that they'd been thinking of me. The first person to admit that *I* was the only person they wanted to talk to when they couldn't sleep.

This, to me, is kind of a big deal.

"I'm going to ignore your silence and take the fact that you haven't hung up yet as a good sign," Artie interrupts my warring thoughts, and I curse myself silently for his self-deprecating tone I've caused. "Look, Honeybee, I'll let you get back to sleep. Thanks for keeping me company for a while. I'm sorry if I've overstepped tonight."

"Texting me for a booty call was a bit of a violation," I get out quickly before he can hang up. I don't want him to think he's made me feel uncomfortable.

Quite the opposite, really. He's made me feel rather special.

Artie guffaws again, and I realise I'm grinning from ear to ear. One of my favourite sounds in the world is laughter that I've had a hand in creating. "You are something else, Bea."

"And don't you forget it," I say, proud as punch.

"Something tells me I never will," he purrs. "Goodnight, Honeybee."

"Goodnight, Dream Boy."

He hangs up, but I don't go to sleep straight away. Instead, I tug the duvet right over my head so I'm in complete darkness and replay our conversation over and over again.

He'd been thinking of me.
I'm the only person he wanted to talk to.

He missed me.

By the time I do eventually fall asleep in my warm cocoon of pillows and the memory of his kind words, I'm beaming wider than I ever have before.

Chapter Seventeen
Artie

I'D BARELY MANAGED TWO hours of sleep by the time I hear my phone ringing on the nightstand next to me, the milky sunrise confirming that it's still far too early for a wake-up call. Rubbing my irritated eyes, I grab the phone and hold it to my ear without checking the caller ID.

"Please make the reason you're calling me so early a good one," I moan to whoever's on the other line, too exhausted to care.

"Good morning, sunshine. Thought you might like to come round for breakfast on this magical morning."

"*Eden*," I hiss as if I'd just figured out my twin sister was behind the evilest grand plan in the world.

She cackles then, playing the part beautifully. "Come on, Uncle Arth. It's the kids inviting you over, not me."

"Using them against me is blackmail," I yawn, rolling out of bed. For a moment, I forget my arm is double its usual size and knock it into the doorframe on the way out. I wince as dull aches snake up towards my shoulder. "What time?"

"Eleven." I can hear the grin in her voice as she adds, "You can invite Bea if you like."

"Thanks, Mum."

"You're welcome sweetie," she hums before hanging up.

I click the coffee pot into place and turn it on, in desperate need of a pick-me-up. Last night, like so many these days, had been spent tossing and turning with very little sleep in between.

Tossing, because the memories always come back with a vengeance when the lights turn off, and turning because I couldn't stop hearing Bea's laugh replaying throughout my mind. Without the fresh memories of her voice, I think I might've lost it. Or called Silas at 4 am again.

I know it's completely nonsensical, but I *had* missed her yesterday—right until the moment I finally gave in and texted her. I smirk again at her booty call comments.

If only.

No, it hadn't been a late-night booty call. It was probably more like a cry for help.

Help, I can't get you out of my mind and I think I might be going crazy from sleep deprivation, and I need to hear your voice one more time before I give up. Tell me I'm not to blame, Bea. Please.

The coffee maker chimes and snaps me out of my wallowing. I seriously consider drinking it straight from the pitcher for a second before opting for my favourite mug; one with a cat dressed as an avocado with AVO-CAT-O printed along the bottom.

Stupid, I smirk. Gets me every time.

I drink an entire mugful while staring at my phone, wondering if Bea would even want to come with me at all. She likes Eden, and Eden likes her—I guess there's no harm in asking. But I don't want her to feel *obligated* to come if she has better plans on her day off.

While I'm still deciding, a message buzzes through.

Bea

> Eden just texted me saying you have something you want to ask me?

I actually growl at that, because my sister is clearly out of control. She's like me times one thousand. Me, on three times my body weight of coffee. A complete pain, sticking her nose in where it doesn't belong. And now I *have* to invite Bea to stop me from looking incredibly rude.

Artie

> Eden has invited me for brunch with the kids and asked if you wanted to come too.

> You can definitely say no if you want.

> I'm going to kill my sister for texting you.

It takes all of two seconds for my anger to dissipate once a new text chimes in straight away.

Bea

> Pick me up?

Hm. My sister lives to see another day, it seems. I text Bea back a simple smiley face and get dressed in record time. I'm probably out the door and in the car within fifteen minutes, and that's with the extensive pep talk I had to give myself to leave the safe confines of my apartment.

When Bea slides into my car, she's all sunshine and smiles. She's wearing a forest green jumper and blue jeans, with her hair twisted into a long, glittery clip. "Hello," she says with a quirk of an eyebrow when she catches me staring.

"Hello. You look lovely."

"Thanks," she smiles, running a hand over the clip that my eyes keep circling back to. "You don't think it's too much? I only put it in so the kids might like me. I can take it out, though, if it's stupid."

"No, it's great. Janie's going to love it. If you're not careful, she might even manipulate you into handing it over." I give her a wink before driving away, and I see some tension melt away as she settles into her seat, arms wrapped casually around her stomach.

"Who's going to be at your sister's?"

"Eden, her husband Jackson, and the kids."

"No one else?" she asks through a small tight smile.

"Not that I'm aware of," I smirk. But when she doesn't laugh along with me, I ask, "Why?"

"Just not a huge fan of surprises is all. I like to be prepared for things."

"And agreeing to plans half an hour before they happen is not much time to prepare," I realise, and Bea gives me a quick thankful smile. "Don't worry. Eden's not one for big events or long guestlists."

"What about your parents; will they be there?"

A word—not sure which one—gets stuck in my throat, and I clear it loudly. "No," I murmur around it.

"Sorry," is all she says, because I did a terrible job of hiding my discomfort at that one.

"It's fine." I clear my throat again, trying to make my voice deeper to counteract whatever *that* was. "No parents."

"No parents. Got it." She stares out the window for a while before confessing, "Still scary enough with just your sister's family, though. Do you think Jackson will like me? What's he like?"

"I'm pretty sure you're impossible to dislike, Honeybee," I smirk as she scoffs. "Jackson's great. Normal enough for a guy who willingly chooses to live with my sister."

Bea laughs, and the sound brightens our entire atmosphere. "You're so mean to Eden."

"She's meaner." I give Bea a look to make sure she knows I'm kidding. "Don't worry about Jackson and the kids. If it gets too much, just give me a signal and we'll leave early."

There's something like gratitude shining in her eyes as she asks, "What's the signal?"

"Two winks."

She gives me a tired look. "You're just trying to get me to wink at you."

"Definitely," I agree. "Wink at me and I'm all yours."

"And I want you, do I?" she deadpans.

"That's up to you to know, I suppose."

A rosy blush creeps up Bea's neck as she switches the conversation to the complexities of beeswax candles, which I'm secretly thankful for. It gives me a second to appreciate her not dwelling on the topic of my parents. I've had enough unwanted conversations about them for a lifetime, and Bea sparing me from another is pure magic.

When we pull up outside Eden's house, she's still talking about the candles, although now she's gone off on a tangent about the different types of wax. It's a small suburb on the outskirts of Fayette Bay, perfectly quiet and serene. One day, I'd love to swap Bluetine Park for something more private like this.

Bea's voice trails off as we get to the door and I knock on the brass lion's head. "Sorry, was I completely talking your ear off then?" She laughs breathlessly. Her cheeks are flushed, like she's regretting accepting my invitation to come here. I slide my hand around hers, lightly caressing her fingertips until they open just enough for mine to slide between, enveloping her cold palm in mine.

"Not at all," I say earnestly. "I'd actually like to hear more about the dangers of paraffin when we get out of here."

That makes her smile, but I'm not joking. I fully intend to get her back on that conversation when we leave. There's nothing more special than getting to watch someone talk about something they're passionate about, and I want to watch her light up like that all day.

I, for one, have never been more excited to learn everything there is to know about candle-making.

She's about to say something else when the door swings open, Eden standing behind it with flustered eyes and red paint streaks across her forehead.

"Well, well, well. Look what the cat dragged in," she grins while kissing me on the cheek. My hand leads Bea into the warm house behind me, and it doesn't let go when my sister turns to give her a welcoming hug. "Lovely to see you again, Bea."

"You too," Bea smiles. "Your house is—"

"Loud?" I offer, gesturing to the music blaring over children's cartoons and shrieking coming from upstairs.

"Only way to live. Come through," Eden says, ushering us all the way into the kitchen, where it looks like she's getting ready to host a feast fit for a king. Every burner is on and covered with pans of eggs, baked beans, sausages, and pancakes. Bacon sizzles and spits, and Eden jumps towards it in a bid to prevent a grease fire.

"Where's Jackson?" I ask, my voice loud over the noise. The extraction fan whirs into gear, and I can see Bea's eyes dart around as she tries to keep up with everything. I give her hand a squeeze, and her eyes instantly land on me.

Is everything okay? I try to ask silently.

She seems to take in a long inhale, roll her shoulders back, and breathe some of the tension out through puckered lips. Then her smile is full of reassuring confidence and she gives my hand a stroke, as if in answer.

"He's entertaining the kids," Eden throws over her shoulder, pulling my attention back to the hectic room. "They'd only be under my feet otherwise."

"Do you need any help?" Bea asks, rounding the kitchen island and walking towards the chaos of Eden and her overflowing pans. Neither of us seems to be willing to let the other's hand go, so I follow.

I'd be happy to be pulled along by this woman for a while, anyway.

"No, you're absolutely fine!" Eden says, far too busy stirring and turning things down to look up from the stove. "Would you be able to shout up to Jackson and the kids that food's ready, though?"

"Of course," Bea beams, finally dropping my hand and rushing out of the room.

"Something smells good," I mutter, ignoring the look of glee Eden's throwing at me.

"That'll be the food."

"Why are you smiling like an idiot?" I deadpan, ignoring her lame attempt at a joke.

Her eyebrows fly up in response, and it only makes her smile wider. "No reason," she hums. "No reason at all."

Chapter Eighteen

Bea

Brunch is lovely, if not a tad chaotic. Eden barely sits down for longer than thirty seconds at a time, constantly jumping up to check something in the kitchen between bites. If she's not cooking or bringing new pans full of breakfast goodies to the table, she's exchanging exacerbated smiles with Jackson, who's trying his best to keep the kids in their seats.

The kids who, by the way, are the cutest little humans I've ever met.

Hector, a glasses-wearing sweetie who keeps asking to be excused to show me another of his prized rock collection, and Janie, who's very distressed to have been taken away from a tea party one of her dolls had been hosting.

I smile down at my plate as Janie grumbles loudly again, just in case her disinterest in her meal hadn't been caught the first hundred times she'd asked to get down from the table.

"Sigh all you want, Janie. Your dolls will still be sitting there when we're all finished," Eden says from the other side of the kitchen. I follow her voice, but Artie catches my eye instead. He's already glancing at me, trying to hide his smirk behind his coffee cup.

I stare straight ahead, biting my lower lip. I will *not* break first.

"But Mum! Who is going to pour the tea for them?" Janie asks, throwing her arms up in the air. "They can't move!"

"They also can't drink," Hector adds flatly. "On account of them not being real."

A rising bubble of glee escapes me, coming out as a small squeak. Artie clears his throat.

"They are too real," Janie pouts. "Mum, tell Hector that my dolls are real!"

We all glance at Eden, who has a look on her face that simply asks *why me?*. Jackson gives her a sympathetic look over his paper, but Artie straightens, leaning both elbows on the table and steepling his hands beneath his chin, looking at her expectantly.

"Janie, honey, you know your dolls aren't real. We've had this conversation before—when you asked why they didn't talk back to you." Eden's voice is soft like velvet, the way only a mother could talk with such sincerity.

But that doesn't stop Janie from bursting into tears and running out of the room.

Eden sighs as Jackson folds his paper in half and says, "I'll go."

"Can I go too?" Hector asks the room, already halfway off his seat.

"Sure, sweetie." Eden relents. The food's mostly gone now, anyway.

To his credit, Artie waits until Hector is safely out of the room before cackling. Eden throws him a glare as she begins tidying away plates from the table. If looks could kill, Artie would be ten feet under already.

"Oh, come on Edie—even you have to admit that was funny. I mean, where does your son come up with this stuff?" Artie croons, looking at me for backup. I shake my head and help gather the empty pans.

"Perhaps he's been getting pain in the ass lessons from his favourite uncle," Eden suggests dryly, and I do laugh at that. Artie's head whips around to look at me incredulously.

"Something to say, Bea?"

I shake my head again. "No, just sounds about right. You being the master instigator of Hector's sarcasm is definitely probable."

"You know what," he scoffs, looking from me to his sister, "I don't have to take this from you two. I'm going to find my niece and nephew, who actually like me, and spread some more of my amazing comedy genius onto them." Artie strides towards the doorway, taking a final glance back before passing the threshold. "Seriously? Neither of you are going to correct me and tell me you like me?"

Eden and I share a look before she shakes her head at him. "No, that sounds about right actually. Wouldn't you agree, Bea?"

I open my mouth to speak, but Artie jumps in. "Don't ask her! I'm trying to get her to *forget* about her active hatred towards me."

Eden chokes on a laugh and Artie winks at me before disappearing.

And now I'm alone in an unfamiliar kitchen with an almost stranger. I should feel panicked, frozen. But I don't—at all. This entire brunch should've been my definition of a nightmare, but I've found a strange comfort in the feeling of family.

Not that I'm a part of this family, of course. It's still nice to feel included.

"I'll help with that," I say, meeting Eden at the sink.

I've never seen a true *mountain* of washing up before today. But this...Eden's sink is something to marvel at. Not to mention how she'd managed to stack it all so neatly. The definition of organised chaos.

"Thank you, lovely. It's fine if you want to go find my wretched brother, though."

I hum a laugh. "He snuck some gifts in for Hector and Janie, so I should leave them to it." I take a towel from the oven door and begin drying dishes as Eden washes.

"At least there's one redeeming quality about him, I suppose," she muses, winking at me.

"He's not all bad," I agree, the sentiment striking something deep within me. I push it away. Now is not the time to be considering Artie's moral compass.

"He's actually pretty great, although never tell him I said that." She looks at me sidelong. "Why do you hate my brother, anyway?"

I smile down at the plate I'm drying, popping soap suds one by one. "I don't hate him," I say in a quiet voice, because I don't really know when *that* happened, or why. I used to loathe him; couldn't stand to be in the same room as him. But today I accepted an invitation to spend more time with him and meet more of his family. So...what's changed?

And why hadn't I noticed it happening?

"That's what I told him! Like, Arthur—she wouldn't stay by your hospital bedside for days on end if she hated you. But he's been so insistent, although he won't tell me why...I was kind of hoping you'd have some gossip for me."

"Hah. No gossip, I'm afraid. We're just friends."

Eden scoffs at me. "Yeah, and Jackson and I are *just* best buds."

I give her a hapless shrug. "No, really."

"Okay," she surrenders with a secretive smile.

My eyebrows draw together. "Oh, that's it? I thought you were going to put up a bit more of a fight."

Eden laughs heartily, and it's a harmonious sound. "You two will sort it out. I—"

She's cut off by Janie barrelling into the room. "Mum, Mum! Look what Uncle Arth got me!" she says, holding up a pink plastic princess computer. "He says he's going to teach me to be just like him."

"That's wonderful! Did you say thank you?"

"Oops!" Janie exclaims, sprinting out of the room again.

Eden chuckles, shaking her head. "Great, like we need any more Arthurs in the family." She looks at me like I should know what she means, and my heart skips a step. "As I was saying, I know you're not in a relationship, and I don't want to overstep my mark. But I *do* know my brother; I know how he thinks. How he feels most of the time. He really cares for you. I'm not saying that it's reciprocated, or that you should act on it if you don't want to, but I just wanted you to know that." She puts a soapy hand on mine before adding, "In case you didn't already."

Stunned silence is my only response as I look into her bright, clear green eyes. She squeezes my fingers before dropping them, along with the subject, as we continue cleaning the kitchen in silence.

But I can't enjoy the quiet because my head is loud. No, my head is *exploding* with questions.

Does Artie truly care for me?
Is Eden messing with me? What would be her motive for that?
Would it matter if he did like me?
Do I like him?

"Ladies," Artie's low voice drawls as he stops in the doorway and leans against the frame, arms crossed over his chest. "Can we all agree to be civil now, please?"

"That depends," Eden says with the exact same tone. Honestly, the more time I'm spending with both of them, the more it's getting slightly terrifying how similar they are. "How many more of your wise-crack jokes did you teach my children?"

"Only ten."

"An all-time low for you—not feeling very funny today?"

"Other things on my mind." I dare a peek up at him over the pan I'm drying, only to find those piercing eyes already on me. He throws me a cheeky grin—the one that makes something flip in my stomach.

Yep, there it is. That *feeling* again.

Damn him.

Damn him, and that funny feeling. Damn Eden for inviting me, and for making me question the entire dynamic of our relationship. And damn me...for being too afraid.

Too afraid to work at the hospital for an entire year and help the patients who really needed me.

Too afraid to ask Artie about what happened last year.

Too afraid to listen to myself, *just once*, about what I might want.

Damn you, Bea. This is no one's fault but your own.

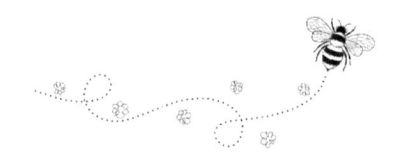

"Thanks for coming with me," Artie says as he parks in his usual spot outside his apartment.

"Thank you for inviting me. I love little get-togethers like that. I never had big family meals, obviously, so I used to host dinner parties all the time. I wish I hadn't stopped."

I watch him sidelong, and again, he doesn't look at me with pity in his eyes. Just simple curiosity. "Why don't you plan another?"

I shrug. "I don't know, really. I shut myself off for a long time, but I think I'd like to throw one again. Maybe."

"I think you should," Artie says with a resounding nod.

"I can't cook very well. Maria helps me," I confess.

"I'll be in charge of catering."

Giving him a suspicious smile, I ask, "You can cook?"

"Of course, I can. I love it, actually." *Right then. Decision made.*

"We'll see." I lean my head against the backrest and listen to the raindrops pattering along the car roof. "Hector and Janie are just like you."

Artie breaks into a sunshine smile. "I love seeing those little guys. Wish I could do it more often."

"Why can't you?" I ask, watching fine droplets of rain dust the windshield.

"Work," he says, clearing his throat. Followed by a cringe. "Speaking of which, I have *so much* to do today."

I gasp a laugh. *Back to reality.* "Yeah, I should get to the café." I'd agreed to cover Maria's shift last night, which I'm only wholly regretting now.

"I wish I could spend more of the day with you," he moans, and I almost jump at the feel of his thumb running down the outside of my thigh. I'm wearing jeans, but I swear I can feel his touch like we're skin to skin. "You're fun to be around."

"Really?" *Have I ever been called fun before?* "You're not so bad yourself, I guess."

He chuckles. "If that's as much praise I'll get from you, then I'll take it."

"You're more fun than a shift at the café," I hum in agreement. "The bar is literally on the floor."

"Well, do you want to come over later? I can drive you home after, then." He's looking at me hopefully, and I like the idea of him *wanting* to see me again.

Maybe even missing me when I'm not around.

Before I can overthink it, I answer, "Sure," and fling open the car door to escape into the icy rain, ripping myself away from his molten touch. I can hear him laughing at me as I take off down the road.

Maybe I should've taken a quick glance through the window before jumping out, because the rain's much more than a dusting now, heavy lashings whipping the parked cars I'm passing, the pavement, and my skin. By the time I get inside, the café bell ringing relentlessly as I enter, I'm absolutely drenched and howling with laugher.

"Um..." Maria glares at me wide-eyed from behind the counter, smiling like she can't believe her eyes. "You okay there, Bea?"

"Never been better," I sing breathlessly, meeting her behind the counter and reaching for her stashed bag where I know she always keeps a spare set of clothes.

"I need the details of *this*—" she zigzags her hand in front of me "—once you're dressed."

I duck into the kitchen where the staff bathroom is, peeling off my disgustingly wet jeans and replacing them with Maria's black skirt. My jumper is replaced with a grey knit cardigan. It's a cute outfit—if it weren't winter and zero degrees outside. I wrap my sodden hair in a bun atop my head—because Janie did in fact run away with my clip—and find Maria waiting behind the counter.

"So...?" she asks, resting her chin on her palms, eager for a good story.

"Why do you have a skirt in your bag like it's not *February*?"

She shrugs. "It's cute. Why have you just burst in here like you've come out of the shower fully clothed, laughing like a hyena?"

"It's raining."

"Where's your car?"

"I ran from Bluetine Park." I train my voice to be as casual as possible, but her squeal confirms that she does in fact remember who lives there.

"Well, well, well. What a fun revelation," she muses, sickly sweet and completely smug. "No wonder you came in with the biggest smile I've ever seen on you."

I fold my arms tightly and glare at her. "Don't be so dramatic. Don't you have somewhere to be?"

Maria looks at her watch and sighs. "Ugh, I guess. But this isn't over. I'm calling you tonight and you're telling me all about it."

"I'm..." I can barely meet her eye, for god's sake! "I'm actually going to see him after Trina takes over, so I might not answer."

Maria simply snickers, grabs her bag, and kisses me on the cheek on her way out. "Thank you for this. Call me tomorrow?"

"Definitely." I wave her goodbye from the door before turning on my heel and looking around the empty café. Looks like I'm in for a slow afternoon.

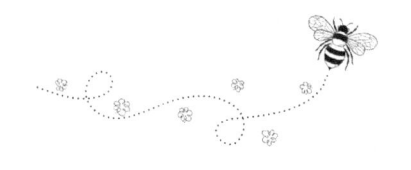

"Jeez, what are you wearing?" Artie asks as he opens his door to a shivering me. Maria didn't happen to pack a spare coat. "Are you aware it's forecast to snow this week?"

"I didn't realise you were such a sucker for women's fashion," I drawl and his eyes light up. "Are you going to let me in?"

He takes a step back to let me through, and I walk straight to the radiator to warm my hands. The biting sting of heat is a welcomed relief. "Only women I don't want to see catch their deaths due to tiny little skirts," Artie murmurs.

"Sorry, Grandpa. I'll be sure to wear only snow pants from now on." I turn around so the heat can reach the backs of my thighs—which are *incredibly* frozen—and frown. Artie's sitting behind his desk, a sheepish look on his face. "What are you doing?"

"I've got a tiny bit more work to do; it's taking a lot longer than anticipated."

"Oh," I shrug, pushing myself off the radiator and heading back towards the door. "I can just get a taxi home."

But Artie grabs my forearm as I pass the desk and squeezes it once, drawing my eyes to his. Those emerald cities behind them. "I'm sorry, I know you don't like my line of work. Give me twenty minutes—twenty measly minutes and I'm all yours."

I grumble dramatically. "Fine. But only because your house is warm and I'm *so* cold."

He smirks. "Feel free to borrow some more of my pyjama bottoms, if you like."

I don't know if it's subconscious or not, but I notice his hand has slid down my arm and is now balancing around my wrist.

His pinkie is tracing the hem of my skirt, back and forth, back and forth. Thoughts of our almost-kiss flood my mind then, and suddenly I want nothing more than for that hand to move higher.

Are my cheeks literally on fire? They feel like they've caught fire.

"Thanks," I mutter before stepping away from his touch and rushing past his office chair into his bedroom. I shut the door behind me and sink onto the edge of his mattress, cradling my burning face in my hands. *What is happening to me?*

I feel like I'm back at school with my first crush. It's not like I've never been around men before…I've *lived* with men before, for god's sake. So how—and why—is this one affecting me this much?

And oh god, *why* have I chosen to escape into his *bedroom*?! I'm sat on his bed. *Artie's* bed.

While I endure whatever this existential crisis is turning into, I've chosen to perch on his bed. *Excellent idea, Bea.* This is really helping with the not-so-clean and confusing thoughts parading around my head.

I should definitely not wear his clothes right now. That would be…too much.

Artie and I are not a good idea. So why is my thundering heart so insistent on considering it?

Pushing myself off the mattress, something colourful catches the corner of my eye on the bottom shelf of Artie's bedside table. I crouch down to get a better look, because I have no boundaries apparently when it comes to being in strange bedrooms, and let out a small smirk in the face of Artie's secret selection of romance books.

He's a romance reader. That loosens some of the tightness in my chest because it reminds me that he's just a guy. A guy who loves to read and watch romcoms and worships his niece and nephew. Maybe even a good guy—or trying his best, at least.

He's not who I thought he was, at all.

That silly realisation shines through me and I instantly feel lighter. I shake my head at what I must've looked like escaping into his bedroom like that.

I flick through the spines, all cracked and well-read, before landing on one about a cowboy and an actress falling in love. Fine—good. Artie isn't a cowboy and I'm certainly not an actress. He might be *just a guy*, but that doesn't mean I need any weird fantasising ahead of me. We'd be better as friends, anyway.

I rise from my knees, roll my shoulders back, and walk through the living room as confidently—but as *naturally*—as I can. *Please don't notice me, please don't—*

"Find something good?"

I wince before turning on my heel and flicking the cover up to show him, to which he raises his eyebrows and nods knowingly. "One of the best," he muses as his eyes return to the screens in front of him.

"I found your secret stash," I taunt, falling into the armchair and wrapping one of his fluffy oversized blankets around me.

"It's not a secret," he laughs.

"Then why don't you keep them out here with all your other books?" I ask, pointing at the bookshelf full of vintage-looking classics.

"That bookcase came with the apartment," he shrugs. "It would look somewhat strange if I mixed my pink-spined romance books with all those boring, dark-coloured ones."

"It might brighten this place up," I joke. "But I still think you're secretly hiding them in your bedroom. Maybe you're ashamed..."

"Why would any well-respecting man be ashamed of his reading preferences?"

That's a fair point. "Good answer," I say with an impressed smile, to which he chuckles.

"I'm glad I have your approval, Honeybee. I'm almost done here."

"Good."

I open the book to the first page, but some stupid part of my brain tells my eyes to glance up. I must be sitting at a funny angle, because now I can see Artie's concentrated face through the gap between two of his monitors. A small crease has formed in the centre of his eyebrows, and his eyes are flicking left and right a mile a minute, like he's reading something at a speed only superhumans could achieve.

Probably just some less-than-legal document.

I turn my nose up at that, lifting the book higher to hide my now-perfect view of him and his incriminating equipment. But that's not comfy on my arms, so I drop the book back to my knees and try to read some more.

Artie's still fixated on whatever he's reading.

Why are my eyes and thoughts betraying me so much? How hard is it to just read a damn book!

He must hear the frustrated sigh I let out as Artie's gaze meets mine between the screens. He gives me a suspicious smile. "Is everything okay?"

"Mhm," I reply, silently begging my brain to focus on the pages in front of me. But it doesn't. Nope, it does the exact opposite, actually—it gets my mouth involved, too. "What are you working on?"

I hear the words come out before I even register my lips are moving, and I must look as surprised as Artie, because he asks slowly, "Are you sure you want to know?"

No—I'm not sure. Anything I don't know can't come back to bite me in the arse. I'm not in the least bit interested in getting caught up in something illegal.

And I know it's illegal because if it wasn't he'd come out and tell me and stop being so evasive.

But *how* illegal?

For god's sake. It can't be worse than I'm imagining, and I'll spend the rest of the night wondering now, so I steel my spine before asking, "Why wouldn't I?"

CHAPTER NINETEEN

Artie

It's a trap. I know it's a trap, because—contrary to what many of my peers seem to believe—I'm not a complete idiot. The woman in front of me, subtly biting her lip as she waits for my response, does not like my line of work.

She doesn't like *me* because of my line of work.

I know that; she knows that. The whole world probably knows that.

Bea is asking what I'm working on because she wants to be reminded of *why* she hates me the way she does. We've been getting closer—although not close enough for my liking—and she wants me to give her a reason to back off.

Well, don't let me be the one to deprive her of all the havoc I can wreak from behind this desk. I love showing my equipment off, and with every passing day it's becoming clearer that I'm on borrowed time.

"Come here," I challenge with a flick of the head, gesturing her over. She drags a stool along with her and perches next to me.

"Woah," is all she says at the moving screens.

"Pretty chaotic, right?" I smirk, pointing at the middle screen I'd been working on. "See this? That's the entire security system of the Handley Hotel. And this—" I point at another screen with a switchboard on it, "—means I can control all the electronic features with just a push of a button. Turn the lights on and off, change the thermostat, yadda yadda."

She glances at me quizzically before returning her gaze back to the screen. "You can do all of that...from here?" Her words are slow. *Sceptical*.

"Why does no one believe me when I say these things?" I huff lightly, a hand to my chest. "It hurts my ego, you know." I catch her rolling her eyes as I hover the mouse over one of the switchboard's buttons and set it down in front of her. "Here, click."

She pushes the mouse away with the tip of her finger like I've just laid out rotten meat before her to eat. "No way, you're not roping me into your *illegal* dealings," she whispers as if a police officer might hear her on the street and burst through the door on a surprise raid.

I clamp down on my lip to stop from smiling. "One, I don't think you'll get in trouble for turning off some hotel lights. And two, it's not *illegal*..." I cringe. "Well, it's not *not* illegal to have hacked into this system, but I'm working on a police-driven mission, so it's fine." I shrug.

"You're working for the police?" she asks, still a hint of doubt in her voice.

"Yep," I confirm with a nod, clicking different levers on the switchboard over and over. I smirk at the streaming footage, which is barely keeping up its flicking from night vision mode to normal.

"But isn't that a bit...dangerous?"

"Danger's my middle name," I drawl, but she doesn't laugh so I stop messing around with the lights and turn to face her. "What do you mean *dangerous*, Honeybee?"

Bea looks at me flatly for the nickname and I wink. "I mean, you work for all these crime lords—what if the police start coming after you? Do you work for them just so you have their support if you ever get caught?"

She's staring at me with an odd coolness in her eyes. It's kind of terrifying if I'm honest.

"I told you; I don't work for criminals anymore. I have a contact in the police force who occasionally gives me odd jobs, but that's it." I squeeze her hand and look her directly in the eye to drive my last sentence home, "No danger here. Promise."

"Oh."

"So," I taunt, "want to see if you can blow some bulbs?" I push the mouse back to her with a waggle of my eyebrows and she *actually laughs.*

"Maybe just once..."

She clicks the mouse and the lights go off. I watch as her eyes widen and her mouth spreads into a big grin as she lets out a gasped laugh.

It's one of the cutest things I've ever seen, I think.

But then she's standing from the wooden stool and looking down at me, slipping her fingers out from underneath mine. "Thank you for showing me," she says before heading back to her armchair. Suddenly there's far too much distance between us, and I want to tell her I'll give everything up right this second if she'd stay by my side for a little while longer.

But I can't; I have to get back to what I was *really* working on when she'd asked—an email from my best friend, D.W.

See what I can do when people don't do what I tell them? This is your last chance, Mr Avila. Call off the police or I will be back personally to finish the job. And don't think I haven't noticed our friend Beatrice spending more time around you.

Don't keep me waiting.

- D.W.

Obviously, there's no way I could've shown Bea that message. She'd be out of my apartment quicker than I could explain, and I...I don't want her to leave. Yes, I'm a selfish idiot. Yes, the mention of Bea's name in the email made my blood turn to ice. But she's the one thing keeping me tethered to this absolutely miserable reality I'd been thrown into recently, and I can't let go.

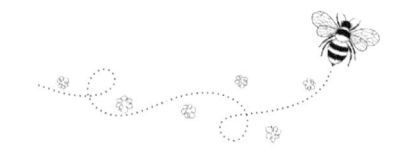

"Hello, Officer Robinson speaking. How can I help?"

"Monty—hey," I croon awkwardly.

"Avila?" Monty's voice turns to a lethal hiss, "What the fuck are you calling me at the station for? I told you to never do this—wait, how'd you get my extension?"

"Do you really need to ask that?" I drawl.

Monty grumbles something unintelligible. I think I hear the words *hate* and *hackers*—puzzler. "What do you want?"

"I need to know whether you've done any more digging on my D.W. guy. I don't know if you've heard, but he's managed to sprain my arm and taken quite a lot of my sanity."

"Jeez. You okay?" Monty asks and I rake a hand through my hair impatiently.

"Just dandy, Monty. Couldn't be better. You know, I've always wanted to have a bandage sling. It really makes life that bit easier. I'm thinking of getting some coloured markers so all my friends can sign their names on it in the playground. Would you sign it for me?"

"Shut up," Monty growls. "I took another look and couldn't find anything under your tips with that name."

I scratch at my creased brow, sighing out any hope I had of an easy solution. "Okay, can you search your entire database? I really need to find out who this guy is."

"Can't help, Avila. I have far too much on my plate without adding your petty concerns to it."

I chuckle quietly at the thought of any of this being a *petty concern*. "Monty, he's going to kill me and my friend. He's already landed me in hospital—what am I supposed to do?"

"Hope to high hell that we find him before he finds you?" Monty's gruff voice lifts with a smirk. "I'm sorry—really, I am. But I did you a favour by checking your own tips, and I don't have it in me to offer any more. Stupid games, right?"

He doesn't sound all that sorry to me.

"I've helped you catch countless criminals over the past year. You can't throw me a bone just this once?" I ask, voice low.

Monty sucks his teeth before delivering the final blow, "There'll be other hackers like you willing to help me. I'm sorry Avila, but there's nothing I can do." And with that, he's gone.

I don't have too long to stew on how much of a grade-A prick Monty Robinson is, though, as Bea pushes through the front door a moment later. She falls onto the sofa next to me, the smell of Chinese take-out filling the room instantly.

"It is absolutely freezing out there!" she says, leaning back into the sofa and rubbing her hands together. "Here, feel."

Then her fingers are on my cheeks and the impulse to jump as far away from her touch ignites somewhere within me, and yet I stay right where I am. Lean into her, almost. "Holy shit, you're cold."

She beams as she balls them up in her lap, but the absence of those insanely icy hands somehow makes me feel even colder. Would it be weird if I asked her to warm her hands up on my cheeks?

Obviously.

She's back up and in the kitchen gathering plates in an instant, so I begin removing cartons from the plastic bag, lining them up on the coffee table. "Did you order the entire menu?" I call behind me as the boxes just keep coming.

That comment earns me a light smack on my good arm before she passes me a plate and points the remote at the television. "What do you want to watch?" she asks.

"Anything," I reply, mouth already full of fried rice.

She hums for a few minutes while she flicks through the films before landing on one I'd never heard of.

"Another romantic comedy?" I ask, passing her a carton to dish up her own plate before I eat it all.

"Horror," she sings with a ghostly sound after it. Her eyes are wide and sparkling.

"I didn't have you pegged as a horror girl."

"I'll watch anything," she shrugs, nestling back into the sofa cushions next to me with a full plate, tucking her feet up underneath her.

I watch her sidelong for a long moment before a loud scream finally tears my eyes away from her and back to the screen. Regretfully.

God, she's gorgeous. *Does she know that?*

All pink, kissable lips and misty sea-blue eyes that reach for miles.

And that tight little black skirt she still has on...

There's a sudden pang of something in my chest then, like I *need* to know if she thinks about herself as highly as she should. I can't bear the thought of anything but.

Once we're both completely stuffed, Bea turns off the lights and grabs a blanket from the back of the armchair. Silently, she throws the single blanket over both of our laps. I don't dare look at her for fear she'll realise that we're now sharing a blanket and jump right back up to get me one for myself.

I like sharing. Sharing is good for me.

Although now all I can think about is that we're within touching distance, and yet *not* touching—for some unknown reason.

Come on, Arth. Be brave and see what happens.

I creep my fingers along the sofa cushion towards her, using the stifling heat as a guide. *Warmer...warmer...*

My pinkie finds her thigh and I draw a tentative circle across it. A tiny circle. A barely-there circle. But she doesn't flinch; doesn't move. Doesn't look at me, ask me what I'm doing, or flick me away.

Was that her leg?

It certainly felt like skin.

A draw another ring to be certain. It *must* be her leg, but I don't get a reaction. The next three lines don't earn one either, so I drop my hand silently to the cushion, allowing it to make its defeated way back to my lap.

My hand doesn't even reach the halfway point of the sofa before it's captured by Bea's own warm fingers, tugging me back towards her. She rests my hand just above her knee and scooches a fraction closer to me, the corner of her mouth curling so gently that no one else would be able to spot it.

And she never looks away from the screen.

My thoughts could not be further away from the film, though, as I follow a rosy flush spread across her cheeks and up to the tips of her ears. My hand turns to blazing fire under the blanket, sending embers up my arm and throughout my entire body. I'm not wholly sure I'm not vibrating.

I keep my hand on her thigh—*as if I'd ever be stupid enough to take it off*—for the rest of the film. Then for the credits, which we watch in their entirety. And I keep it there still, even when the screen fades to black, filling the entire room with darkness.

A long pause settles over us, my thumb and forefinger drawing idle shapes up and down her thigh, her breathing sounding far too rhythmic to be natural. "Artie?" she finally whispers, fracturing the dark silence I was quite happy to remain forevermore in.

"Honeybee," I say with an equal quiet, voice husky.

She turns to me, one leg bending to shift onto the sofa. My hand moves with it, turning my torso to face her. In the shadowed twilight, I can barely make out anything else but her most prominent features. It's just me and her; my hand on her thigh and her breath on my chin.

A staggered breath. From me or her, I don't know. She bites her lip; I lick mine. Her eyes are flitting across my face, and I know what she wants. I know what *I* want, and I'm sure as hell not going to let another chance pass me by.

So I take her jaw in my hand, drawing her lips to mine. I move painfully slowly, giving her every chance to back out, but she doesn't. Her eyelids grow heavy as our mouths graze.

We part for only a second before her lips are between mine again and her delicate hands are in my hair and I hate my damned sling so much for not allowing me to move like I want to, *feel* everything I want to.

The kiss is gentle but thorough, deepening with every flick of her tongue or nip of her skin. She tastes like chow mein and candlelight, and I think it might be my new life's mission to get that taste bottled up as a keepsake.

Kissing Bea feels like something worth celebrating, making me want to cherish the occasion.

I don't know how long we stay connected on the sofa, but it's long enough for her lips to be swollen when we finally part. They're reflecting the moonlight coming in through the window, and I have the sudden urge to lick that sparkle away.

Bea gently untangles her hands from my hair, smoothing it down before wiping the pad of her thumb over my bottom lip. I hum a chuckle. "That was...unexpected."

I see her smile in the darkness, a little bashful and completely beautiful. *Okay, that's it. I'm utterly gone.*

"It was nice," is all she says. But as if she's afraid of what I'm going to say next, she jumps up, turning a dim lamp on to bring us crashing back into reality without obliterating our corneas. Still, I have to squint to see her.

"I guess we should get to bed," she muses. "Oh—sorry. Is it okay if I crash on the sofa again tonight? It's gotten so late..."

"Bea," I rasp, grabbing her wrist and guiding her so she's standing in front of me. I drop her hand and run my palm gently up her thigh to her hip—*this freaking skirt*—never breaking eye contact. I want to make sure this is okay. "It was more than *nice*."

Her cheeks redden as my hand moves up and down, but she hums in agreement. For a second, I think she's going to sit right back down and start kissing me again, and it takes all my willpower not to beg. But then she's gone, slipping out of my touch, and putting too much distance between us.

"You don't have to stay out here, you know," I offer as casually as I can, gesturing in the direction of my bedroom. "There's plenty of room."

I can see the inner workings of her mind flash across her face, wondering if I'm joking. Wondering if she'd even want to. "That's a bit soon, don't you think?"

Nope, not at all. Not soon enough, in my opinion.

I stand and close the space between us, stroking my thumb down the side of her face, tucking a lock of gold behind her ear. "I don't think so. We don't have to do anything you're not comfortable with. We can just sleep if you like."

There they are again—the cogs of her mind whirring. I don't know why I'm so set on her spending the night with me, but it's like my brain won't accept any other alternative. Her lips must've put a spell on me. *Sorceress.*

Truthfully, I've been wanting to kiss her since her birthday party. But there had been no preparing me for just how *magical* it was going to feel, with her hands in my hair and her lips between mine. I don't think I could bear her being out in the living room after what just happened.

"Okay," she says, so quietly I almost miss it. My heart rate soars for a second. Her voice is so timid, so *delicious.*

"Okay," I repeat, worried that any other word might scare her into taking back her acceptance. She shines me a small smile before disappearing into the bathroom.

Holy shit.

Holy *shit!*

Chapter Twenty
Bea

I stare at myself in Artie's bathroom mirror, wondering what exactly I think I'm doing here.

Agreeing to spend the night in Artie's bed as if I don't have a very valid reason for hating him. So I might be rethinking my feelings towards him—that doesn't mean I had to instigate the whole thing by putting his hand on my thigh! If I'd let him take it back, I could've kept ignoring his sparking touch underneath that blanket...

But at that moment, one thing flashed through my mind. *Do more for you, Bea.*

Originally Maria's words that I'd turned into a mantra for myself recently, one I repeat over and over whenever I'm feeling too heavy with life. One I hope will eventually help me back to my old self.

What I wanted in that moment on the sofa was the simple contact Artie was offering, and to sleep in his bed is what I want now, too. *So stop worrying, Bea.*

But it *is* quite fast. A kiss is one thing—an amazing, best-kiss-of-my-life thing—but sleeping in the same bed? That's breaking like ten different codes of friendship and hatred, surely.

I'm doing it for me.

For the girl I lost last year. She deserves this, and so do I. To be honest, I think I'm a little giddy just thinking about it. I wipe toothpaste from the corner of my mouth before grinning at myself. Hello, hopeful Bea. I've missed you.

He saw you tortured and did nothing, that damned hidden voice in my head whispers.

My smile falters just a fraction. I know I have every reason to hate him, but this feeling I get every time I look at him or hear one of his stupid jokes...I don't think it's hatred.

I don't think I hate him at all.

The woman staring back at me looks optimistic, like she's silently willing me to take what's mine and listen to my heart. I give her a nod, and she nods back.

With one last sharp exhale and check between my teeth, I put my brave face on and get my ass out of the bathroom.

Artie's waiting for me, leaning against his desk and already smirking as I catch his eye. "Honeybee," he drawls, looking me up and down before settling on my eyes. "I thought I should give you an out in case you wanted one. I'm more than happy to stay on the sofa and for you to take my bed if that's how you'll be most comfortable."

Oh, that's sweet. But...I don't think I want sweet tonight.

So I walk up to him, pressing my palms to his chest as I rise on my tiptoes to brush the lightest kiss over his lips. He chases me as I lean back, looking into his eyes as I say earnestly, "I don't want to be apart tonight."

I'm treated to that lopsided smile and dimple wink I'm becoming so fond of. "If you insist," he murmurs into my neck, our hands lingering together as I step away. "I'll be in in a second."

I close the bedroom door behind me and change into another pair of Artie's fluffy pyjama bottoms—bottle green with white horse shapes dotted over them—and one of his old T-shirts. When I close the drawer and turn towards the bed, I startle seeing him leaning against the doorframe, arms folded.

"Knock much?" I ask, hand over my racing heartbeat.

"It's my bedroom," he reminds me very unhelpfully. "I didn't see anything, promise."

I admire him suspiciously. "You're already in your pyjamas."

He smirks. "I stashed them on the sofa while you were in the bathroom. I thought it might make you more comfortable if I got dressed elsewhere tonight."

"Thank you," I stammer, quite obviously taken aback. "That's very kind of you."

Artie raises my hand and presses a gentle kiss to my knuckles. "I'm a kind guy."

I think I'm starting to believe that.

He gestures behind him, towards his king-sized bed covered in dark bedding and plenty of throw pillows. "Shall we?"

I nod and he leads the way. As soon as I lie down next to him, I'm almost engulfed in bedding. Not complaining—it's just very different from any experience I've ever had before in a guy's bedroom. "You sure like your pillows, don't you?"

"I'm a firm believer that you can never be too comfortable," he agrees. "Are you a throw pillow hater?"

I laugh. "No, but most guys I know have told me I have too many pillows on my bed, and you must have double what I own." I snuggle deeper under the duvet. "I'm a big fan."

"Glad you like my bed setup, Honeybee. But I'm not loving the topic of other men while you're lying next to me." His voice is rough, and I can't really tell if he's joking or not.

But I'm in a playful mood. "Are you jealous, Artie?"

"Why would I be jealous?" he asks, turning towards me and stroking his fingers down the contour of my waist, all the way to my hip. "You're in my bed right now, not theirs. I just don't want to hear about the men who let you down before me—it'll make me angry, and I don't want to ruin tonight."

I run my thumb down the side of his cheek, and he takes hold of my wrist to drag it across so my thumb is hovering over his lips before pressing a kiss to it. A soft, deep peck that sends zings of electricity up my hand, arm, and straight into my chest.

Oh...

Before I know what I'm doing, we're kissing again, but this time in his bed and I am made of molten lava. Every morsel of my being is alight with desire and intrigue. I feel *alive*.

We make out like teenagers. It's like my lips are drawn to his—*tethered*—never willing to break apart for a second. It's a wonder we're both still breathing.

One second, my hand is tightly coiled in his curly hair, the next it's travelling down his neck, his chest, his toned torso...and his bandaged arm collides with mine. He winces and leans back, my face half following him—*that'll be the tether.*

"Bea," he breathes as I'm unashamedly still trying to chase our kiss. "We can't..."

"Why not?" I murmur.

"I want to—believe me, there's nothing I've ever wanted more in this world—but it has to be right. I want to make it perfect for you, and I can't do that with one weak arm." His breathing is ragged, making this moment only *completely* sensual.

"Don't be silly," I laugh a tad breathlessly. But he looks at me sincerely and I recognise the moment has passed. There's a slight hesitation behind his expression, as if there's more he wants to say.

"I need us to be on the same page," he admits, and now would be a good time to let him know that I want this—*him.*

But he's right. There's still so much left unsaid, and we're probably *not* on the same page about a lot of things—now isn't the time for *that* conversation. I want to keep this moment as is, with the warming thought of Artie caring so much about my experience that he wants to make it perfect. A rare, heavenly moment.

So I nestle into the crook of his arm as we both recover from our juvenile make-out session. In a last surge of confidence, I slide my hand down to the hem of his T-shirt, slipping it up underneath the cotton and resting it on his thumping chest.

"I'm sorry," he whispers into my hair.

"Don't be," I hum back. "I like kissing you."

"Best kiss of my life," he agrees, planting a peck on my forehead. "I love you in my pyjamas, by the way."

"I put these ones on especially for you."

"I wish you'd take them off for me," he muses, and I bat his chest with an exacerbated laugh. His grin lights up the warm darkness around us, and a strange sort of possessive feeling overcomes me. Like I want to keep that smile forever.

"Goodnight, Dream Boy."

A throaty chuckle. "Night, Honeybee."

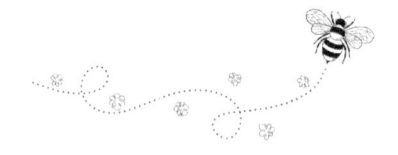

I wake up with Artie's strong forearm pinning my waist into the mattress, cuddled together on our sides with the window facing me. The sobering sunlight shimmers through the thin curtains, directly into my eye for some cruel, hateful reason. It takes me a few moments to realise where I am, and *whose* bed I'm in.

Oh, jeez.

What was I thinking? *Do more for you*—no! Doing more for me is finding time to craft or practice self-care, not sleep in a guy's bed who…ugh, no time to go down that route again. I need to get out of here—

But before I can craft some master escape artist sorcery and slide out from underneath his clutch, Artie stirs and rolls onto his back. *Okay, good. Freedom.*

Instead of rolling over to face him like a part of me wants to, I sit up and climb off the bed quickly. I only dare a glance at him once I'm safely three paces away from the mattress. He's staring at me with a confused quirk of the brow, but a toothy grin stretches his lips.

"What are you doing?" he asks, voice rough with sleep yet still amused.

"I'm—this—I—" I stammer, words failing me as I trip over my tongue in a blind panic. Artie sits up and swings his legs over the side of the bed, and I step back. His face falls then, and he looks...hurt, I think.

"Bea, what's the matter?" he asks in a gentle quiet, and I feel terrible.

Do I lie? Or rip off the plaster here and now...

"This was a mistake," I say, voice wobbling. *Rip it off, I guess.*

Artie starts to chuckle until he realises that I'm not joking. I escape into the living room, passing him quickly with my head low. I'm searching for my bag when I look down and remember that I'm still wearing his horse pyjamas and my clothes are in his bedroom.

Fantastic.

"Bea," Artie calls as he follows me, pulling a plain jumper down over his T-shirt. "Talk to me. What was a mistake?"

"Us! The kissing, the *sleeping in the same bed.*" I'm getting flustered, and I wish he'd disappear so I could get dressed and run away. But it's his apartment and my idiotic mistake that got me here, after all.

"Why do you say that?" he asks, not a hint of sarcasm clouding his concern.

I stumble over my words again, desperately trying to find the reason why I think this has been such an oversight on both of our parts, but my brain is severely failing me.

"Ah," Artie hums, dipping his head sharply. "You're still looking for a reason to push me away, aren't you?" A humourless laugh. "You know, Bea. This really is getting old now. You seem to have some preconceived notion regarding me that creates this active hatred towards me, and I'm not sure why. I'm not even completely sure that *you* know why anymore." He sighs, shoulders dropping. His voice isn't angry, but rather tired. The words are laced with something like grief.

I don't have anything to say to him because I think he's right. *I might be the worst person in the world.*

"Look, I'm not annoyed with how you choose to process your trauma. But I'm not the one to be mad at, and I think you're coming to terms with that. I'm asking you for a chance to prove myself, without all the made-up bullshit you've created in your head." Artie closes the space between us, and I don't back away. I turn my head to the side, though, and have the overwhelming urge to rest it against his chest. Just to feel his warmth again, the gentle beat of his heart. "Please, Honeybee. We're better together. I *know* we are. We can heal together—just give me a chance."

I bite the inside of my cheek and force myself to look away from his pleading gaze. "Alright," is all I mutter. I know I'm being rude, but that's all my warring thoughts can allow at this very moment.

"Alright," he murmurs back, breath tickling my temple. "Can I pick you up at seven?"

CHAPTER TWENTY-ONE
Artie

Kyra

H+kWC4o5Y,3l

Arthur

I'm in.

AND BY *IN*, I mean into Monty's system. I almost want to smirk at how easy that was—all it took was an hour with my inner circle helping get the passwords, break the firewalls, and set off a minor emergency that would have everyone at the station too focused on that rather than their emails. I have Aaryan to thank for that one.

We've decided to go ahead with the search despite Monty's insistence that he couldn't find anything because, well, there's only so far you can trust the opposition. While Monty and I may have a semi-friendly working relationship, our loyalties ultimately lie with two conflicting teams. Double-checking the system is the only way I'll truly know whether I've been right to rely on Monty.

I search the two worst letters in the English alphabet in the inbox and scan down the endless list of entries. Scrolling, scrolling, scrolling...*bingo*.

My eyes trip on an email flagged with the label D.W. sitting pretty in Monty's inbox—from his Mother. I open it to recognise my own discreet email design, with a tip I'd sent in two months ago concerning one Damian Wolfe and violent intimidation. It's nothing more than a few sentences and a file attached of video footage for proof. A tiny tip, by all accounts. Barely worth mentioning. *Why would Monty lie about receiving it?*

Which makes Monty's code name for me *Mother*. Amazing. Someone should send him an award for his stealth.

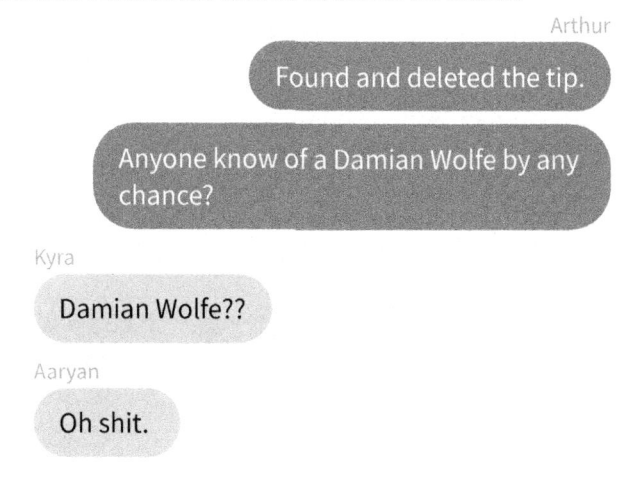

Arthur

> Found and deleted the tip.

> Anyone know of a Damian Wolfe by any chance?

Kyra

> Damian Wolfe??

Aaryan

> Oh shit.

Johnny

> Duuude.

Kyra

> THE Damian Wolfe???

I let out a silent groan. I'm the best hacker in the country, and yet I'm the only one of these suckers who apparently doesn't know who we're dealing with.

Arthur

> Care to enlighten me?

Kyra

> Damian Wolfe is the biggest crime lord of the past decade, Arth…

Johnny

> Not someone to be messed around with.

> No wonder Monty wouldn't tell you about the tip if it involved Damian Wolfe. They've been trying to catch him for years.

Arthur

> You think Monty double-crossed me?

Kyra

> Absolutely.

> Delete everything you can find associated with your involvement right now.

Fantastic news. I was worried the reveal of D.W.'s identity might've been underwhelming.

Monty's words flash through my mind then—*there'll be other hackers like you willing to help me.* He knew the possibility of Damian Wolfe killing me was astronomical without the deletion of this tip, and yet he still chose his own agenda. I'm not saying we were best buds or anything, but that's *cold*.

As I have absolutely zero desire to get on the bad side of the *biggest crime lord of the past decade*, I haul ass and delete any files I can find associated with my lead. If Monty were to glance at his computer at this very second, he'd see icons disappearing and reappearing all over the place. As much as we hate to give Aaryan any credit, creating a diversion was a stroke of genius.

Then I delete every single email I've ever sent Monty, just for good measure.

Or rather, every email his *mother* has ever sent him.

Before I jump out of Monty's desktop, I block my name, number, and email address from his contacts. I check my VPN software is still intact, although I'm pretty sure even someone as slow as Officer Robinson will be able to work out who snuck into his files by the time he sees what I've done. But without any proof to pin it on me, he'll have a hard time charging me. Plus, bringing me down to the station would be admitting to working with an underground hacker, and to do so would be putting his entire job at risk.

So I shut down the program I used to access Monty's desktop and lean back in my chair, smiling smugly.

Arthur
> Mission accomplished.

Aaryan
> Niiiice. What now?

Johnny
> Witness protection, just for the fun of it?

Aaryan
> Throw your computers out the window and hop on the next plane to a Greek island?

Johnny
> Spend your riches on a spaceship and shoot yourself to the moon?

Kyra
> Obviously, he's going to tell D.W. that he's deleted the lead and prevent another home visit.

Arthur
> Obviously.

That's why we love Kyra—she's the only one of us who actually considers the whole picture. Because honestly, contacting Damian Wolfe is the last thing on my mind, especially when Bea's name starts flashing across my phone.

"Honeybee," I say in way of greeting, phone sandwiched between my shoulder and ear as I ask the group chat how I should phrase my email to the apparently infamous Mr Wolfe.

"Hey, I just wanted to tell you I'm home," she says, her voice just the tiniest bit flat. She adds a rushed, "Like you told me to."

"I'm glad you called."

"Really?"

"Absolutely. I wanted to make sure the drive home hadn't changed your mind about later." I send the email and turn my attention to my third monitor, which is showing the website of a new restaurant recently opened not too far from the Bay.

A pause fills the line and a hint of worry flashes through me. *How is it possible last night didn't mean as much to her as it had to me?* But then she announces, "No, I'm still free," and I relax.

"Amazing. I'll see you later."

"Sounds good," she replies politely and I stifle a groan. One night together and she's retreated into her shell again. *I need her to see I'm not the villain.*

"Good, seven it is. Oh, and Honeybee?" I ask before she can slip away. "I think I might be missing you again."

Bea huffs a laugh. "I only left yours an hour ago," she chides warmly, but something icy passes through me. A little guilt, maybe. A *lot* of disappointment in myself.

"It took you an hour to get home?" I ask, although I already know the answer. "Why?"

Static fills the distance between us. "You know why," she confesses in a quiet voice. "I'm not brave enough to drive the short route by myself just yet."

Of course. I should've remembered that when she said goodbye earlier; given her a quick pep talk or offered to go with her. I let my irritation get in the way of her fears. "You are plenty brave enough," I argue firmly. I wish I was near her, so I could cover her soft skin in warm kisses until the words melt into her and she believes them.

"I think I need someone to hold my hand for a few more practice runs," she murmurs with a self-deprecating laugh that I hate.

"You don't need me to hold your hand, Bea."

A pause. "I think I might want you to."

Even after this morning? I want to ask, but to be honest I'm left speechless. That's probably the sincerest thing anyone's ever told me. Most vulnerable, for sure. Like she's just cracked open her chest and given me a tiny slither of how she feels about me. It gives me hope that I can salvage whatever happened earlier.

I take hold of it, grabbing onto it for dear life before she can snatch it away again. "Then I'll be there, right by your side, for as long as you'll have me." *I'm never going to let go.*

"Thank you. I'll see you tonight."

"Already looking forward to it."

She hums an agreeable sound. "Call me if you need me?"

"Always."

"Bye, Artie."

"Goodbye, Honeybee."

I throw my phone onto the sofa and scrub my face with my hands as I let the exhaustion of today wash over me. It's hard work, infiltrating a police force. I think I need coffee and to see a friendly face.

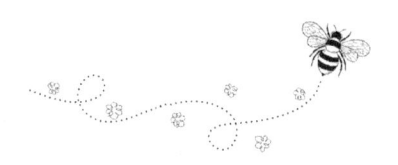

I drive home after effectively wasting an hour annoying my sister at her place of work, drinking her coffee and generally getting in the way. I have now been roped into attending Janie's first ballet recital this weekend, though, so I think we can call it even.

On my way back, I have to make a conscious effort not to turn right and drive to where I really want to go—who I really want to see.

She's probably busy trying a new craft or something. Maybe she's knitting me a jumper. I make a mental note to ask her to make me one, just to see her reaction. I smile to myself just thinking about making Bea squirm. Space is good, I guess.

It'll maybe even give her time to miss *me* before tonight.

Back home, the apartment is quiet. Too dark, too cold, too lacking. I fall into my office chair with a sigh, wiggling the mouse to see if any messages from Officer Robinson have found their way into my inbox yet. They shouldn't have, considering

I blocked any way of him contacting me. But that's the thing about police—they always have their *ways*.

So when I don't find anything from Monty, I'm both surprised and relieved. I log off and shut down the screens, because I feel like staying online might be testing my luck. I've severed ties with my one police contact anyway, so there's not much point continuing the work I was doing for him. I'll probably give it a few days, then send over any leads I have on the current cases with a sweet apology note and a smiley face.

That'll make up for tampering with police evidence—right?

Chapter Twenty-Two

Bea

It's nearing 6 pm when my laptop chimes with the sound of a video call, and I hurry to sit down on the sofa with my steaming cup of tea to answer it.

"Hey!" I say as the picture loads.

"Hello," Jessica sings as Silas waves from behind her.

"It's been too long since I've seen your faces," I say with a frown. Jessica mirrors my expression and Silas rolls his eyes.

"It's been a week," he argues flatly.

"Exactly," I reply in the exact same tone.

Silas clears his throat, ready to come back with another retort, but Jessica cuts him off. "How've you been? How's work?"

"Work's okay—busy with the new shifts at the hospital, but everyone's still being really supportive and lovely. Every day gets somewhat easier, I think."

"Oh, I'm so glad to hear that!" Jessica beams before adding, "I talked to Maria yesterday. She mentioned something about you *maybe* getting closer to Artie?"

Instantly my cheeks flare with an intense heat. Silas's eyes slide to mine across the screen, making me feel a little lightheaded. Artie's his best friend—I need to be smart about this. "Oh? Hardly worth mentioning really. I wanted to make sure he was okay after the attack," I shrug as casually as I can. "No big deal."

Although actually, now that I think about it, I slept in his bed last night and then completely freaked out on him this morning. If you want to call that getting closer, then fine.

"The attack was a while ago, though."

"I know, but he lives alone. His fear of the attack won't just go away overnight."

"I thought you hated him, is all," Jessica shrugs, a wicked smile quirking her lips. If she's trying to hide it, she's failing miserably.

"You forgave him, I guess I might be trying to, too." My voice is lower than normal, like I'm somehow betraying my friends. Silas's face remains unreadable, completely stoic. "I'm just trying to be there for him."

"Absolutely!" Jessica says airily, as if she's only just caught onto this weird tension building between Silas and me. Her own cheeks pinken a fraction, and I think she's wondering if this was really the best time to bring it up.

Which, I can say with absolute certainty, was not.

"How's he doing?" Silas asks, voice casual. "I haven't heard from him this week. Is he okay?"

I tilt my head in a so-so gesture. "He's definitely doing better. The attack knocked him, for sure. I think more than he was letting on. I'm seeing him tonight, so I'm sure I can ask him to call you—"

"What do you mean you're seeing him *tonight*?" Jessica interrupts, eyes dancing. I don't think I've ever seen her so giddy.

I look at her in a way that says *Can you just stop talking, please?* before explaining, "He's taking me for dinner," matter-of-factly, as if that's completely normal. "It's good for us to be spending time together, you know. We might be able to stop complaining about each other soon."

Jessica flashes me an understanding look and Silas nods ever so slightly. *Okay, I can work with a nod.*

But then his fiancée pipes up again, "Maria said you looked like you—"

"I think that's enough about me today," I interrupt before she can finish that thought. "I have to go, but it was so lovely seeing your faces. Let's do it again! Soon!"

I hang up without waiting for a reply, shut the laptop and kick it away from me. *That* is not how I wanted any of my relationship with Artie to come about. I make a mental note to pinch Maria the next time I see her. My chest is tight. I hate the way Silas looked at me like I'd betrayed him...I haven't, have I?

Of course I haven't—I was looking out for his friend. If anything, he should be thanking me. I sigh a heavy exhale and head into my bedroom to get ready for tonight, begging my brain to stop overthinking every minor nuance Silas just threw my way.

GEMMA NICHOLLS

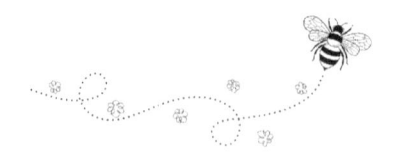

I finally get Artie to relent and tell me where we're going for dinner so I know what to wear. He sends me the link to L'Aura's website, the new restaurant only recently opened downtown. Incredibly lavish and sophisticated, and definitely not somewhere I'd usually go, but I'm excited. It's given me a chance to wear a champagne silk slip dress with little rosebuds dotted over it, a glittering shawl, and high heels. I had to call Maria to make sure I looked okay, twirling in front of the camera as she ooh-ed and aah-ed.

Artie rings the doorbell at 7 pm sharp, just as I'm primping my straightened hair for what feels like the millionth time. I answer the door and his jaw physically drops, and I wave him away dismissively but secretly it makes me feel wonderful.

"Hey," I greet as he stands before me, mouth still agape, looking me up and down.

"You look incredible," he marvels, finally meeting my eyes and taking a step in to give me a kiss on the cheek. I let him tentatively, because I want nothing more than to have him close to me even for a second longer. I'm keeping an open mind, after all. Artie asked for a chance and I think I owe him that much.

"You don't look too bad yourself," I smile, resisting the urge to lean into him. He doesn't—not with a black tailored suit and a white shirt underneath with the two top buttons undone. *Handsome.* "No sling tonight?"

"I've been set free as of two o'clock today," he smirks, tentatively shaking his arm out to show his progress. "I'm ordered to take it slow, but it's almost as good as new."

"That's amazing, Artie."

"It is," he agrees, still admiring me. His eyes trail over me slowly, inch by inch. I should probably feel self-conscious with all this attention, but I don't. I feel...special. It's intoxicating, to be admired so wholly. "Ready to go?"

Artie leads me to his car and opens the door for me, helping me in. Once he's sitting next to me in the driver's seat, he takes my hand and kisses my knuckles. He keeps my hand on his lips for a moment, looking up at me as he does. "You look incredible."

His breath on my skin sends a wave of goosebumps prickling up my arm, and I laugh brightly. "You said that already."

"It needed to be said twice," he concedes, placing my hand back in my lap and starting the car.

We get to the restaurant and are seated within minutes thanks to Artie's reservation.

"How did you get us a table here?" I ask once the waiter has left us alone with our menus. "I swear I read it takes months to get a reservation at the moment."

Artie agrees, "I booked it a few weeks ago."

That trips me. "Oh," is all I get out because what is someone meant to say to that? He'd booked a table before his attack. Three weeks would've been around my birthday—*who had he been planning to bring here?* "Original date fall through?" I ask a tiny bit frostily. I can't help it. Just ten minutes ago I'd been feeling like the only woman in the world, and now I've been relegated to second best.

Artie's eyebrows pinch together and an amused look spreads across his face, but I don't get my answer because the waiter's back and pouring our drinks. We order our food—the French pork rillettes for Artie and the honey roast duck for me—before being left alone again. Eating's the last thing on my mind with all these unanswered questions running through it, though.

"What do you mean *original date*?" Artie questions over his glass of water. His eyes are annoyingly bright with amusement.

"You said you booked the table weeks ago."

"I did."

I make a gesture that says *exactly* and he almost does a spit-take. "And you think I booked it for someone else?"

"It does kind of seem that way," I shrug. He fully chuckles now, so I sit quietly, waiting for him to finish finding my annoyance comical.

When the laughter finally dies down—long minutes later—he says simply, "I booked this table for you, and only you."

"Why would you ever do that when we didn't even know each other?"

"We did too know each other. I drove you home from your party, and you invited me in."

Okay, so we knew *of* each other. "Still a bit strange, don't you think? I mean, we weren't exactly each other's biggest fans back then."

"I've never not been a fan of you, Bea. In fact, since the very first time I introduced myself at Silas and Jessica's party, I'd say

I've been a big fan. And when I finally wore you down—because I knew I would eventually—I wanted to be able to treat you right. Which is why I booked the table. You're special and you deserve to be treated as such." Then he shrugs like he didn't just deliver the most devastating compliment I've ever received.

I will my face not to show my true feelings as I chide dismissively, "You haven't worn me down."

"Well, up until this morning I had. Even so, I'm getting there, aren't I?" His eyes glint with amusement and pride.

I shake my head with a small smile, but he moves the conversation onto something more surface-level. I tell him how I'd been researching cats, but how my plans to get one would probably never come to fruition because I always say I'm going to adopt a cat and chicken out at the last minute.

"I like cats," Artie says as our food is placed in front of us. "I like how they just do their own thing. It's like having a furry, antisocial roommate that screams at you for food and bites your ankles." He smirks. "You should definitely get one."

"Have you ever thought about getting a cat?" I ask over my duck.

"All the time," he admires. "But I just don't have the space for one. Not in that tiny apartment."

"You should find somewhere bigger," I agree.

Artie pretends to choke on his food and takes a gulp of water. "It's a bit too soon to be talking about moving in together, isn't it, Honeybee?"

I roll my eyes with a smirk. "Do you ever take anything seriously?" I ask.

"Nope," he says, beaming. "And I'm proud of it, too. Life's too serious—let's have some *fun*." His eyes flare on the last word.

I grin right back at him, biting the inside of my lip as a wave of something like realisation crashes over me.

He's right—I've been so busy holding onto the past and finding things to be mad at, that I've forgotten to get on with my life and *enjoy* the little things that used to make me, *me*. I've been avoiding large parts of my hometown, holding grudges that probably never should've been set in the first place...and to be honest, I'm sick of trying to convince myself that I don't like the goofy, kind-hearted idiot sitting in front of me.

I *do* deserve this. I deserve all of this.

Let's have some fun. Indeed.

CHAPTER TWENTY-THREE
Artie

THE RESTAURANT IS GORGEOUS, but not as gorgeous as my view across the table. Bea's devouring our shared sundae, although I've barely had two bites. Too full, anyway. Too busy staring at the most beautiful woman I've ever seen.

I pay the bill once she's finished and we head out into the cool night. The hours flew away from us in a haze of Bea's glorious laughter and my wonderfully witty jokes, and I can't help but wish time had moved a fraction slower. I don't want to go home yet.

"Fancy a walk?" I suggest and she nods straight away. I'm not trying to get my hopes up, but this evening has gone as well as I wanted it to and I think we're going in the right direction. But she's already shivering, and I shake my head slightly with a grin. "You're freezing."

"A-am n-not," she grits with a straight face. She's almost jumping on the spot trying to keep warm. I wrap my suit jacket around her shoulders, grab her hand and guide her towards my car. "Artie! I said I wanted to go for a walk; I'm fine."

"I am not going to be held responsible when you land in the hospital with pneumonia."

We must look ridiculous to anyone watching. Me, in only a shirt on the bitterest spring evening, towing around a stubborn woman in an unreal dress behind me.

"I can handle Silas," she pouts. "Come on, let's just go for the walk. Your jacket is heating me up already."

I turn to her as we reach my car, looking down into her doe eyes. "Your lips are turning blue, Honeybee."

"They are not!" she huffs, but quickly gives up and slides into the passenger seat. Not without folding her arms across her chest to show her displeasure, though. "Just so you know, this is a *complete* overreaction," she grumbles as I open the door behind her.

I grab my backpack from the back seat and shut the door again. I rap my knuckle on Bea's window until she glares at me. "What are you doing?" I ask, snickering like a giddy child. I can't help it.

Bea looks at me quizzically and I hold up my backpack, reaching inside to unveil the two jumpers I brought from home. "I thought these might come in handy if you said yes to the walk."

I think I can see her counting to ten in her head. I tend to have that effect on people. But then the corners of her mouth tip up ever so slightly and she opens the door to climb out again.

"You are too much work," she sighs as I hand over the jumper I picked out for her. It's a bright pink Christmas jumper with *Sleigh the Patriarchy* written across it that Eden bought me three years ago. Bea slips it on and barks out a laugh as she reads it upside down.

"Too much work, or just the perfect amount?" I grin, pulling my own goofy jumper over my head. Mine says *Talk Turkey to Me.*

"The jury's still out on that one."

But she takes my hand as I lead her down a pathway behind the restaurant towards Roseding Point, so I think—I *hope*—I'm forgiven.

Roseding Point is one of the biggest beaches around Fayette Bay, always bustling with people who've travelled far and wide to enjoy it. But tonight, on this gloriously frosty night, it's just me and Bea, the glistening moonlight, and the gently lapping waves.

She stops to take her shoes off as we get to the edge of the sand. "Are you going to ask me to skinny dip?" I ask, taking the strappy shoes from her in one hand and wrapping the other around her waist.

"Don't push it," she warns. "That suit's too nice to get all salty anyway."

"You like it?" I hum, gesturing down to the outfit I'd asked Maria to help pick out. She's the only person I know who'd have a clue about men's fashion.

Well—I *did* ask Silas first, but he hung up on me.

"I've definitely seen worse," she avers, running the collar of my shirt between her fingers. Our breath mingles together in the small gap between us, but she pushes away from me gently before I can close it. She leads me towards the water, the waves bubbling around her bare feet. "It's freezing," she laughs.

"It's March," I deadpan and she flicks me on the chest.

"Smart arse."

"You love it," I cluck and I swear her cheeks redden.

We walk along the shoreline for a while, falling into a comfortable silence beside each other. I wish she'd let me into those loud thoughts of hers. I don't know what I want from her; I'd just like her opinion on everything. What she thinks matters to me.

She sighs as if she senses my wish. "Okay, here goes. I've had fun tonight," she smiles at me, so I wink back, "and I've been considering what you told me earlier all day. I don't want to hold onto this grudge anymore, Artie. I know it's silly, but I still have unanswered questions that are preventing me from letting myself completely fall for you."

"Do you want to fall for me?" I challenge, and she looks at me sidelong like she has a secret.

"As much as you annoy me, and as much as my brain begs me to realise that this is a bad idea, I can't stop thinking about how good we might be together."

A grin spreads across my face like wildfire. Still, I urge, "Why is your brain so sure we're a bad idea, though?"

"Because of the questions I don't have answers to." Bea looks down to where she's digging a hole in the damp sand with her toes. I hook her chin and drag her eyes up to meet mine.

"Then please, ask away."

She takes a few seconds to steel her spine and compose herself, and I have an overwhelming desire to go back in time and stop whatever this conversation is about to be. But she can see a future with me, and I can't let this opportunity slip away. No matter what she asks, I have to be completely, *utterly* truthful—

"Why didn't you help us?" she pleads in a small voice, directing the words out towards the horizon.

And I'm obliterated from the inside out. "When?" I ask powerlessly.

"When Silas was in trouble—when *I* was in trouble—why didn't you help?" Somehow her voice becomes even smaller. Or perhaps it's the ringing in my ears getting louder, drowning her out.

"I helped Silas in any way I could."

Bea nods, squeezing my hand. Like she can hear the regret in my voice. I know I should've done more, but it's not like I did nothing.

"I know you helped Silas before and after," Bea continues, her voice trembling. "But what about when we were being kept in the dungeons? Why—why didn't you help me?" Her voice cracks on the last word and I'm pretty sure I hear my heart break right alongside it.

"I didn't know you were in there," I say, trying to catch her eye. "I didn't know about any of it until you'd got Silas to the hospital."

"Desmond had a camera system. Silas said you'd hacked it."

"I don't make a habit of breaking into camera feeds to watch people go about their business very often." I exhale a laugh, although nothing about this is funny. "I only broke into Desmond's feed once I knew Silas was out of hospital and on his way back there to end it."

She takes a second to digest this information. We've stopped walking now, Bea staring out to the blackened ocean, me unable to tear my eyes away from her flushed side profile. "Okay," is all she concedes, but it feels so far from the truth that I almost laugh.

I don't want this to be the end of our previously wonderful date, so I step inwards to face her, cupping her chilly cheeks in my hands.

Her eyes are searching and glassy in the moonlight. I want to kiss the doubts right out of her, but I need to know something first. "Bea, please don't tell me you've been thinking all this time that I knew you were being kept in that dungeon and did nothing to help you?"

It sounds so preposterous out loud, but she nods in my palms and I want to yell at the ocean. I blow a long sigh through my nose, close my eyes, and tug her into my chest, wrapping my arms so tightly around her I think she might protest. She doesn't.

"Believe me when I say it's been killing me for the past year to know that you, Silas and Jessica were being kept in that *place* right under my nose—I would've torn the place down to find you all, had I known."

"Torn the place down?" she repeats quietly.

"Burned it to the ground," I agree with a lethal softness. "Once I found out what Desmond had done to you all, I started gathering footage to take that fucker down. I went back and watched it all. I saw what you did for Silas. And after Sy told me what he planned to do instead of using my footage, I made sure he kept you as far away from Desmond's lair as possible. That's why he told you to get to Maria's café—not just to look after Jessica, but so we could look after you, too."

"We did go back to Desmond's lair, though," Bea recalls thoughtfully.

I smirk. "Yeah, well. Sy and I weren't accounting for how headstrong you women are. Just couldn't stay away from the excitement, could you?" I stroke a rogue tear from her cheek. "I watched you all—you, Jess, and Mar—bravely make your way through Desmond's lair to find Silas. I had emergency services on speed dial the entire time, ready to act should anyone get injured. I called them as soon as Silas went down, I promise."

"Why would you tell Silas to keep me away? We didn't even know each other."

I shrug. "I watched you save my best friend's life. And for that, I wanted to repay the favour, I guess. I saw you in the dungeons—you went in there without so much as a struggle to save your friend. I knew a person as special and selfless as you needed someone in their corner...I've been backing you ever since."

Bea finally looks into my eyes then, devastation and confusion pooling within her own. But then she leans up on her tiptoes to kiss me deeply, grounding me to this very spot. Her hands reach the back of my head and draw me into her desperately, like she's finally giving in and can't bear to be anything but as close as humanly possible.

I know the feeling well.

When she finally breaks us apart, I ask, "What was that for?", even though I don't really care and wish she'd do it forever.

"For protecting me and my friends," she whispers. "Even when we hated you."

I can't help but laugh at that. "I think it was only you who hated me, Honeybee."

She scrunches up her face for a second before saying, "I don't think Maria was too fond of you for a while...and I've definitely heard Silas use some colourful language when it comes to you."

I give her a knowing smirk. "Yeah, well. At least Jessica's always liked me," I say with a triumphant finger gesture.

"Jessica likes everyone," Bea goads gently, and then she's kissing me again. She tastes like ice cream sweetness and pink salt, and in this very moment, I finally feel like I'm home.

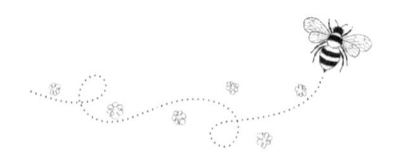

I park up outside Bea's house as the clock on my dashboard flicks to midnight. After the pretty heavy realisation we'd come to at the beach, we sat in silence on the damp sand for a long while, with her curled up into my side as the waves crashed and sang before us. It was freezing, and we'll definitely get a chill in a few days, but it was worth it.

Any time I get to spend with Bea is more than worth it.

"Do you want to come in?" Bea asks, staring out towards her front door. The words feel heavy.

"Yes," I chuckle quietly but turn in my seat to face her, taking her chin and guiding her eyes to mine. "But only if you forgive me. It doesn't have to be completely—not yet. But I need to know that you'll still be by my side in the morning, rather than trying to sneak out or running away from me as you secretly battle your true feelings. I can't take being blamed anymore, Bea."

She swallows before admitting, "I don't blame you, Artie. I couldn't, not after everything you told me. I'm sorry."

That's nothing short of blissful music to my ears. I slide out of the car and walk around to open her door. She takes my hand to jump down, and when she looks me in the eye, something in my chest hitches.

Our recent conversation has been far too heavy for my liking, so I lean down and brush a kiss along her bottom lip. "Race you," I whisper.

"What—" she starts, but I'm already gone, running up to her front door like an absolute child. I look back to see her rolling her eyes but grinning from ear to ear, and I can't believe how much I adore that smile.

I get to the door and lay my hand flat against the wood. "I win," I tease as she walks up behind me.

"Do you think you'll ever grow up?" she asks, unlocking the door.

"Not a chance," I boast as she follows me in, through the entranceway and into the kitchen. "Do I get to try another one of your special teas tonight?"

"Do you really want to hang out in the kitchen?" she hums, walking straight past me where I'm leaning against the kitchen island, and into her bedroom. But as she turns around to face me, it's not my Honeybee looking back. She's a siren, eyes all shadowed and enticing.

And I'm straightening off the counter, shaking my head without using words like a coherent human being, walking towards her and oh my god I've never wanted anything more than how I want her and she's beckoning me with the smallest of smiles like she knows just how much my mind is reeling—

"Are you okay?" she asks, voice full of smug power.

I nod, licking my lips. She smirks at me.

"I wish you'd look at me like that all day," I breathe.

But before she can ask what I mean, I take another step towards her and flick her chin up so her mouth meets mine.

There's nothing fast about our kiss. It's slow and deep and thorough, and probably the most sensual caress I've ever experienced. Bea's hands are at the base of my neck, keeping me where she wants me, as we walk deeper into the bedroom. A small thud breaks us apart for a moment, and I realise it's her legs against the base of her bed. She sits, looking up at me all doe-eyed and gorgeous, and my brain is screaming at me to tell her three stupid words that would change everything—but I don't want to change anything.

I want to stay here, like this, forever.

Instead, I whisper, "Are you sure?"

Now it's her turn to nod. Some of the tension I didn't know I'd been holding onto dissipates from my shoulders as I gently guide her backwards until we're lying together. I take a second to admire her, my eyes tracing invisible lines down her face. I don't want to miss anything; don't want to ever forget a second of this moment right here.

"How's your arm feeling?" she asks as my eyes catch on the freckle underneath her eye. I glide the pad of my thumb across it, down her cheek, and over her lips before cupping her chin. Her pulse thrums beneath my fingertips as I stroke the side of her neck.

"Perfect," I murmur, although I'm not talking about my aching arm. I lean down to press a tender kiss to the dark freckle that's had me captivated for weeks now. "You're perfect."

I think she starts to disagree with me, but I kiss the sentiment right from her mouth.

Her hands rake through my curls and mine do whatever they can to keep me grounded to this moment, attempting to remember every single insignificant detail.

Her scent: brown sugar and sea air.
Her skin: smooth and flushed.
Her kiss: gentle yet lingering; so intimate it takes my breath away.

But before I know it, Bea takes control and we're tangled together, and time is completely devoid of all meaning. Minuscule details pass me by, but one thing's for sure—I'll never forget how I feel in this very moment.

Just me, my Honeybee, and what I imagine dreams are probably made of.

Chapter Twenty-Four
Bea

I don't know what came over me when I asked Artie what I had on the beach. It hadn't been my plan to air everything out with him there and then—it just kind of...happened. We were at the end of the best date I've ever been on, and I was so sick of not knowing why I'd been hating this man for the past year. I needed to know before I got in too deep—if that was even possible.

But then he told me everything and I couldn't stop thinking about how I'd got it *so wrong*.

When he pulled up outside my house, I wanted to make up for all our lost time. Make it up to him for being such a bitch, probably. Make it up to myself for putting me through such pointless feelings of hatred, wasting the best part of two months ignoring what my heart had been begging my brain to give into.

So I invited him in, and I made up for it *plenty*.

By the time we're drifting off, it's almost 5 am. I'm lying in the crook of his arm, watching the dark sky outside my bedroom window as he talks me through the constellations he's mapping across my shoulder.

"I used to fear the night," I murmur absentmindedly. "When the panic would be at its highest. When everything was too quiet, too still."

Artie hums, still tracing little lines and circles along my flushed skin. "I used to think that too, actually. I'd call Silas whenever I couldn't sleep—which was almost every night, really. He's the one who taught me the stars' names. But if he didn't answer, I'd look up out of the window and remember something my mother used to tell me when I was scared of the dark. Here, look at the night sky." He shifts me slightly so he also has a good view of the window. "Most of us would call it black. A big dark pit of despair. But if you really look, it's blue. Midnight blue, and indigo, and azure, and even violet in some places. Then it's littered with burning stars to keep us company, brightening the coldest hours and offering a slither of solace that we might not be as alone as we once thought. What was originally bleak and lonely turns into something a little magic, as long as you can focus on the colours."

"That's beautiful," I whisper, like I'm worried too much noise will scare away my newfound magic. But then I realise he's just mentioned his mum, and I can't help but pry. "You hardly ever mention your parents."

"You're right," is all he says, and I understand to drop it. I don't like talking about family life either. *All in good time.*

I'm about to nestle down deeper into the duvet when Artie turns to me, his face shadowed by darkness but eyes glittering. He strokes his thumb over the darkest freckle beneath my eye and whispers, "You're mine."

I take his hand from my cheek and move it in front of my lips, kissing the palm, so he can feel me move my head up and down. I *am* his, completely. Utterly. Gone. Could never be anyone else's. Everything just kind of clicked at the beach, and my true feelings shone brightly against the horizon. But just for fun, I add, "Only the freckle, or do you want all of me?"

That makes him chuckle quietly, a lyrical rumble through his chest. "To be able to call every inch of you mine would be my greatest honour," he growls earnestly, and I nod again as if to say *You can take me for all I'm worth.*

"And I'm yours," he continues, and I hadn't even thought about it but him saying those words makes me feel giddy. I keep his hand steady and smile into it, his thumb stroking my cheek idly. "Goodnight, My Bea."

I beam so brightly that I feel the corners of my eyes crease. *That's my favourite nickname yet.*

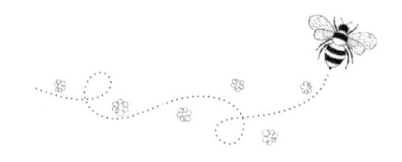

When I wake up at around 10 am, my eyelids are sandpaper. I groan and cover them with the crook of my arm. I turn over to the cooling space beside me, rubbing my palm over the empty mattress. No Artie.

I sit up begrudgingly, instantly irritated that he's making me get out of bed to see him. *Now who's sneaking out?*

"Morning, lover," Artie croons when I find him in the kitchen. I squint at him, and he laughs. "Too much?"

"Definitely," I groan as he comes around the island and plants a kiss on my temple, leading me to sit on one of my kitchen stools. "Why are you so excitable already? Don't tell me you're a morning person."

"Would you kick me out if I said yes?" he teases.

"I think I might." He slides a cup of tea in front of me, watching expectantly. I glance at the label—English rose.

I take a tentative sip. "Wow, how did you make it like that?" I ask because that's almost as good as I make it. And by that, I mean definitely better. "Tell me your secret right now."

Artie smirks, looking positively proud of himself. "No."

"No?" I affirm incredulously, only forcing his grin wider.

"No," he repeats. "If I tell you, you won't have a reason to keep me around. This way, you can't kick me out." His eyes flare as he whispers, "*Ever.*"

I throw him a levelling look over the lip of the cup. "You'd be happy being nothing but my tea brewer for the rest of your life?"

"It would be my honour." His voice is completely sincere, and it takes me back to the same sentiment he offered last night, which makes something in my chest sing.

"Well, I think I can find some other use for you," I say innocently, taking another sip.

He smirks knowingly but turns back to the stove.

"What are you making?" I ask to change the subject. *It's far too warm in here.*

"Something you can't," is all I get, and wow that's rude.

"I can make pancakes," I insist flatly, but as he passes me my plate, I can see the doubt in his eyes. "I can! It was the blender that was the problem."

It *was* the blender's fault. The only thing I can be blamed for is trusting him with a stupid story about how I tried to make pancakes one time and ended up with batter all over the ceiling. Who on earth doesn't keep that little plastic circle-thingy locked in the lid of their blender?!

Apparently, I don't. Because it was my blender.

Anyway, I *knew* he was waiting for the perfect time to bring that little anecdote back up and make fun of me. And here he is, taking full advantage with a sickly-sweet smile plastered on his face.

"Mhm," he exaggerates and I scoff.

"My pancakes would've rocked your world," I grumble, rolling my eyes as I take my first bite of chocolate chip pancake. Yes, they're *also* better than mine.

"Well, it's probably for the best I haven't tried them yet, then. I don't think I could take much more of your world rocking," he smiles cheekily, tucking a piece of hair behind my ear and stroking the pad of his thumb over my cheek. "Do you usually blush this much in the morning, or is that because of me?"

"I'm not blushing," I utter defiantly. But that smug, completely gorgeous half-grin he's giving me wants to make him blush right back. So I give him my most seductive look and propose, "How about you keep making me tea and pancakes each morning, and I'll keep rocking your world every *single* night."

His eyes blaze as his jaw almost hits the floor, and I chew my pancakes with my eyebrows raised, waiting for his snarky comment. But nothing comes, just a gentle palm on my thigh, his fingers squeezing deeply enough to leave little white marks.

"What, nothing to say back to that?" I challenge. "Have I left the king of jokes completely speechless?"

His gaze is heavy as he leans a fraction closer and says, "Not speechless—just nothing suitable for the breakfast table, Honeybee."

Yep, there go my cheeks again. And yep, he notices.

But he doesn't laugh. Instead, he leans over and kisses the fuchsia staining that I'm sure has made its way across my entire face, lingering for a second to breathe me in. He smells like pine and sweet batter.

"I wanted to ask you something," Artie sighs, taking a pancake off my plate, ripping a piece off and popping it in his mouth. "My sister invited me to Janie's first ballet class this afternoon. I know watching a load of kids jumping around in tutus probably isn't your idea of exciting Sunday plans, but I know it would mean the world to Janie—and to me—if you came."

I bite back a sympathetic grin, because that really *does* sound like the most boring Sunday plan, and I have absolutely nothing else on and only want to spend more time with him. "Of course, I'd love to."

"We'd only have to stay for a while, and they'll probably be going out for dinner to McDonald's or something but we can bail and go somewhere nicer. Or I could make you dinner, or we could order in and watch a movie—"

"Artie, I said I'd go," I interrupt, smiling at his weird spirally moment.

He visibly relaxes at that, then laughs. "Alright then, cool. Are you finished?" he asks as I put my knife and fork down on the empty plate. I nod, swallowing my final mouthful of deliciousness. "Good," is all he says before hoisting me up over his shoulder in a freaking fireman's carry and walking me back into my bedroom.

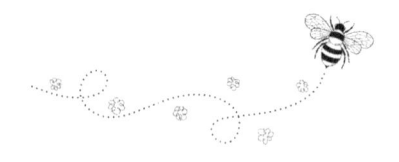

Eden, Jackson, and Hector are already sitting in the dance hall when we arrive at Janie's lesson. The teacher has put a handful of chairs around the room for parents to watch, but most of them are throwing us strange glances. Like maybe a five-year-old's dance lesson doesn't warrant the entire family coming to watch.

"Hey Bea, what a lovely surprise!" Eden coos as we join them. She stands and leans over her husband to kiss my cheek as I'm shucking off my coat and scarf, but I don't miss the raise of her eyebrows as she glares at her brother.

When I glance at him, his eyes are still locked in a returning stare. I look to Jackson for answers, but he just shrugs with a hopeless smile before gently guiding Eden back towards her seat. Begrudgingly, she breaks eye contact with Artie, and everything's back to normal.

I grin at Jackson, and he dips his head in acknowledgement. I'll have to get some tips from him about how to deal with the twin thing later.

Not that I think I'm like Jackson. *Not one bit.*

"Uncle Arth!" Janie calls over from the other side of the room, catching all our attention. "Bea, look!" She spins in a baby pink tutu to show it off and points to her hair, which is loosely fastened with the glittery clip I gave her.

"Oh, my goodness!" I gasp, feeling my heart triple in size.

"She hasn't stopped asking when she can see you again," Eden smiles at me. I give her a grateful grin back and Artie, who must sense how much this means to me, rests his chin lovingly on my shoulder as my eyes turn glassy.

The class is absolute chaos from start to finish, with children screeching and prancing around with very little ballet to be seen. But Janie looks like she's having a ball, and Artie never moves his claiming palm from my knee. I let my head rest against his shoulder as we laugh and joke with his family. It occurs to me that I've never experienced this kind of dynamic before, and I don't think I ever want to let it go.

As the class is wrapping up, Eden says she's popping to the bathroom before we leave and I join her. I lean against one of the small sinks as Eden washes her hands. "What?" I snip jokingly. She's been giving me a suspicious smirk since we arrived.

"Nothing…"

"Just say it," I laugh brightly.

"Oh, fine," she huffs like it took longer than a second for her to give in and share her thoughts, "I've just never seen Arthur as happy as he has been these past few weeks. It's lovely. You're good for him."

I move out of the way so she can dry her hands. "He's good for me," I return earnestly. There's something about Eden that makes me feel like I've known her my entire life, so I continue, "But don't you think—"

"Sorry, no time for your overthinking or dismissive thoughts. I'm starving." But as she ushers me out of the bathroom, she grabs my hand before we join the group and squeezes. "You're good for *each other*, Bea. Don't let your brain ruin a potentially wonderful thing."

We meet up with Jackson, Artie, and Hector just as Janie comes sprinting up to us, a large sparkly pink puffer jacket over her tutu. "Do you guys want to join us for dinner?" Eden asks me. "It'll be hectic, probably, but fun!"

"That sounds lovely," I start, but Artie slides a hand around my waist, bringing us closer together as he shakes his head.

"Honeybee and I have other plans," he says, giving me a secret smile as I hit him on the arm for using that stupid nickname in front of other people.

"Honeybee?" Eden asks, because *obviously*.

"That's her preferred name," Artie muses, still staring into my eyes as he talks to his sister. Those damned green pools are going to be the death of me. "She actually prefers when people call her that."

"Don't listen to him."

Eden snorts. "Oh, don't worry I won't. Why do you think he's the only person on earth who calls me *Edie*?"

"She likes that nickname; she's lying," he whispers to me.

"Shut it, *Artie*," Eden croons.

"Don't call me that."

"Why's Bea allowed to call you Artie, but no one else is?" Eden goads, and Artie finally stops looking at me to glare at her.

I decide I need to diffuse the tension, so I add, "It's actually Dream Boy now, anyway."

"DREAM BOY?" Eden shrieks, her cackle lighting up the sunset-painted sky.

Artie turns his attention to me, eyes wild with vengeance. He just shakes his head before turning back to his sister. "She's joking."

"Yeah, right. I'm having T-shirts made." I've never seen Eden look quite so giddy as she does right now, and it's infectious.

But Artie simply tightens his grip around my waist and guides me in the opposite direction, calling over his shoulder, "We have to go, bye!"

I rush to wave back at them all before I lose sight of the children. "Where are we going?" I ask, falling into step beside him.

"Mine," he shrugs simply. Indeed, we are walking in the direction of Bluetine Park.

"But you just told your sister we had plans."

"I have plenty of plans we can enjoy at mine," he smirks.

"Artie," I reprimand. "You yanked me away before I could even say goodbye properly. I bet your sister and Jackson think I'm so rude now."

"Eden won't think anything of it, Honeybee. She'll know it was all my idea."

I fold my arms defiantly. "Even so."

Artie dips his head slightly to catch my attention. Despite myself, I give in and slide my eyes to his. "You're so beautiful when you're mad at me," he hums, eyes gleaming in the last of the evening sun.

"So constantly, then?" I deadpan.

"Twenty-four, seven," he affirms with a definitive nod. "It's a wonder how anyone around you gets things done."

I snort derisively at the cliché, giving him a garish smile before asking, "How about now?"

"Still radiant," he sighs longingly, using his arm around my waist to draw me into him again, closing the gap I'd made just a second ago.

"You are so full of it, Artie Avila," I smile.

"Full of what? Adoration for you?" He throws me a cheeky look. "Why yes, I think I am."

I scoff, but I can't hide my joy. I feel somewhere close to cloud nine. "Your talent for getting yourself out of trouble is astounding, you know."

"I know," Artie boasts. "I think I might be the luckiest guy to walk the planet."

Chapter Twenty-Five
Bea

A week had passed since our conversation at the beach where I decided to let go of the blame I'd been unfairly holding against Artie. A week of...absolute bliss? A week of sleepovers, secret jokes, and the sweetest kisses.

We'd fallen into a routine of him driving me the quick route to work and picking me up again with my own car so I could drop him back home and head off to my house calls right away. I keep telling him it's absolutely ridiculous that he's taking time out of his day to meet me at the hospital every day, but he won't entertain the idea of leaving me to it. He says he misses me and he likes seeing me for our little drives.

I'll dismiss the sentiment every time, but I must admit, I like seeing him too. It breaks up my day, to see his silly grin waiting to open the car door for me after every shift. He also gives my mind something to hold onto when it all gets too much. Whenever I feel the rising panic start to creep over me, I find the nearest clock and count the hours until I get to see a friendly face.

Driving with him in the car makes me slightly braver too. I focus on him while passing through the toughest places, and he keeps his hand on my knee the entire time. That silly little touch has the power to make me feel invincible.

I've been home for one measly hour this week, only to pick up spare scrubs and an overnight bag with my skincare and toothbrush. My house feels so empty now, so boring.

It's fun and light and happy at Artie's, and I'm always laughing. Sometimes it feels almost too good to be true, but then Artie kisses me so thoroughly that it knocks any doubts right out of my head.

I think he can see them within me, those nagging feelings of anxiety. Whenever he spots them, he makes it his mission to ground me and help me through them. He'll dance me around the small living room and burst into laughter when I knock something over. He'll bring me a cup of tea and sit with me until everything feels lighter again. He'll talk me through everything but also respect my silence if I don't speak back.

Yeah, it's blissful here.

"Okay, do you need anything before I go?" I ask, wrapping my stripey scarf around my neck twice and tucking the edges into my coat.

"How long are you leaving me for again?" Artie asks, amusement dancing along his lips.

I put my hands on my hips before conceding, "Like...twelve hours."

"An entire night?" He strokes his chin as if in deep thought. "I *think* I can keep myself alive until sunrise. I'm feeling pretty confident."

"Good luck with that," I drone, turning on my heel towards the door. I don't get very far at all, though, because I'm being tugged back by the hem of my coat.

"Where do you think you're going?" he asks as he stands from his office chair to tower over me, cupping my jaw with his hand.

"To put your survival skills to the test," I murmur onto his lips between kisses. "I might not come back at all."

"I'd have to track you down," he admits onto mine.

"That's possessive..."

"I just don't think I'd ever be able to let you go if I knew you weren't coming back." He chuckles quietly as he draws himself away from me, scanning every inch of my face before landing back on my eyes.

"What's funny?" I ask.

A quick shake of his head has a loose curl falling in front of his glasses. "I have no idea what you're doing to me, Honeybee."

"I hope that's a good thing?"

"Oh, it's the best." Another peck. "I'll miss you."

"I know you will," I wink, although I don't want to go anywhere anymore. I want to stay and explore what exactly he means. Still, I reluctantly straighten my coat, head out into the dwindling sunset and jump into my waiting taxi.

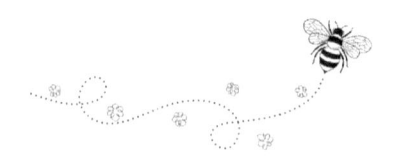

Artie and I made the decision that I'd stay at mine tonight as I need some more clothing and honestly, it was getting slightly ridiculous how much time we were spending together. But right now, as I'm lying on my sofa watching a rerun of some weird reality TV show I have no interest in, I'm wholly regretting the idea.

I will not call Artie. Absence makes the heart grow fonder, Bea. Stay strong.

I shake my head at my foolishness, tuck a blanket over my legs, and turn the volume up louder because I can't trust my brain not to overthink when it's quiet. I pick up my current crochet project so I don't grab my phone and start texting people asking them if they still like me. I'm making a sunflower potholder for Jessica's new house. Well, I'm trying, at least.

It's past 11 pm by the time I drag myself into the kitchen, bundled up and wearing my oversized blanket like a cape. My phone rings as I flick on the kettle.

"Hello?" I say to the screen because it's a video call, although the image is completely black.

"Hey," Artie replies, voice gruff with sleep. It's comforting, that low voice. Like a soothing melody suddenly encompassing me with its gentle rhythm. "What are you doing still awake?"

"It's only eleven, Grandpa." I laugh, ripping open a packet of sleepy-time tea.

"Uh oh, looks like you've been spending too much time with a night owl," he hums, and the phone light reflects off him just enough to show me the tiny curl of his lips. He's in bed, glasses off, eyes closed, grinning at me. The light hits his shoulder and I see that he's topless. *What I wouldn't give to be nestled into that bicep right about now.*

"The night owl who's in bed by eleven?" I ask, carrying my steeping tea and phone into my bedroom. "Maybe we've swapped bodies."

"What a treat for me," he purrs and I blush brightly. "Sorry, I don't want to keep you if you're on your way to bed."

"Wait," I rush out. "Why'd you call me?"

An exhale, somewhere between annoyed and pitiful, sighs through the phone. "Can't sleep," is all he says, but it's heavy with implication and my heart breaks for him. "Don't think I'll be able to sleep properly without you by my side ever again, Honeybee."

"Do you want me to come over?" I ask, already mentally making a list of all the things I'll need to take with me.

"No, I don't want to make you drive all the way back over here."

"It's not a big deal," I insist. "Or you could come over here if you want."

He shakes his head and his curls bounce in the darkness. "I'll only keep you up waiting for me. Can we just stay on the phone for a bit? Put your phone up against the pillow, I'll do the same—it'll be like we're together, but not." A brief pause before he smirks and adds, "That sounds weird. Have I completely creeped you out?"

I hide a smile behind my cup of tea and shake my head. "No, that sounds nice. I like you a little weird, anyway."

He chuckles, and I don't know if it's the half-asleep state he appears to be in or something else, but he says, "I *adore* you, full stop," and my entire world shifts on its axis.

I excuse myself to brush my teeth so I'm not tempted to ask him to clarify what *exactly* that means. When I get back from primping and a quick pep talk in the mirror, Artie already looks asleep through the screen. I slide into bed carefully so I don't disturb him, flick off the light, and turn towards my phone on the pillow next to mine.

"Goodnight," I whisper almost soundlessly, fighting the urge to stroke the screen like a true weirdo.

"Can we talk for a while?" Artie asks, his voice heavy.

"Of course! Sorry, I thought you were asleep already."

"Not without you next to me," he rasps and I bite my top lip. Suddenly the distance between us seems completely too far. "Tell me something I don't know about you."

I groan because it's too late to be conjuring up answers to team-building exercises. "I'm...Uh...Oh, I'm *extremely* competitive. No one ever wants to play games with me. As soon as you've tried playing Monopoly with me once, it's over for us."

A low hum sounds through the phone, and I wish I was with him to feel it against my cheek. "I'd wipe the floor with you at Monopoly, Buzzy."

"Yeah, right—wait. *Buzzy*?" I deadpan, ignoring his incorrect statement in lieu of the worst nickname I've ever heard.

He chuckles—a low, delicious rumble—and concedes, "Not my finest work, but I've been brainstorming new ideas. I thought you'd be pleased."

"Honeybee is better than Buzzy!"

"Really?" he asks as if that's not a given. "Okay...what about Buzzykins or Cuddlebee? Bumblepuff?"

"*Artie.*"

"What about something simpler, like Sunshine?" he continues. Then he drops his voice even lower and purrs, "Hello, Sunshine. Eh?"

Butterflies erupt in the pit of my stomach at that one, utterly betraying me. I ask flatly, "Do you ever turn off?"

"Not with you around," he muses and I laugh despite myself because that was smooth as heck.

"I thought you were tired," I chide. He nods. "Right then, no more talking. Goodnight, Mr Avila."

"Goodnight, Queen Bee of the Honeycomb."

"You're ridiculous."

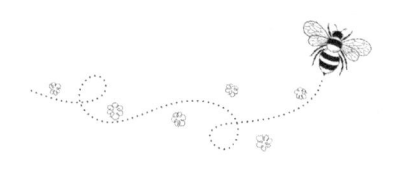

I wake up to Artie still sleeping within my phone screen, and I watch him for a second as my eyes readjust to the sunlight pouring in through my window. It seems in the haste of getting into bed last night, I forgot to draw my curtains. And now I'm awake on a Saturday at 6 am. Perfect.

"Hello, Sunshine," he purrs through the phone.

"Morning," I yawn. "How did you sleep?"

"Good enough. Your snoring is quieter on video."

I gasp, mouth making a perfect O. "I do not snore!"

He lets out a throaty chuckle. "Just teasing, Honeybee." He rubs some sleep from his eyes with the heel of his hands. "Thank you for last night, I don't know what I'd have done if you hadn't picked up."

"Fallen asleep on me later?" I smile, trying to lighten the mood and steer the topic away from his nightmares. But then I do my best to bite back my balk as I realise I've just assumed he'd even want me to come over later and oh my god he never even invited me and what if he thinks that I'm being presumptuous and—

"Indeed," he interrupts my thoughts with a quiet hum. "I'll let you go for now then, but I'll see you later. Shall I pick you up from the hospital?"

"Yeah, if you're not busy with something more important."

Backtrack, Bea. Backtrack!

"I cannot think of a single thing more *important* than you. Already looking forward to it," he admits before we say our goodbyes and hang up.

I place my phone on my nightstand and lay on my back, smiling like a goof up at the ceiling, doing a small happy dance. There's just *something* about Artie Avila that makes me feel on top of the world.

CHAPTER TWENTY-SIX

Artie

HAVE YOU EVER LOOKED at someone and thought 'Wow, I am *so* in awe of you'? Like completely, utterly, foolishly fascinated with everything about them. Don't want to ever look away in fear that you might miss the tiniest smile or quirk of the brow you enjoy so much?

That's how I feel when I look at Bea. I'm in awe of everything about her.

Like the little squeal she made when I carried her into her bedroom the other morning? Core memory. Burned into my brain forevermore, just how I want it.

And I can't stop thinking about her. Even when she's right next to me, like she has been for the past forty-eight hours, my mind is completely focused on her. Probably not the best idea when I'm supposed to be thinking about other, slightly worrying things—like how I haven't heard from Damian Wolfe since I told him I'd deleted my tip—but I'm powerless to stop it. My brain is no longer my own—it belongs to Beatrice Di Menna.

I think my heart might be following suit, too.

Looking at her now, sitting cross-legged on my sofa intently painting a canvas, I don't think anyone could blame me. She's divine. She's amazing. She's all mine.

Before I picked her up from work earlier, I took a quick trip to the craft store and bought half its stock as a surprise. "I've planned a craft night," I boasted proudly as I slid into the car next to her.

"A what?" she gasped happily. "Are you purposefully trying to embarrass me?"

"Yes. Will you make me something to display in my home forever, so whenever anyone comes over, I'll be able to tell them about the gorgeous artist behind it?"

"Are you going to make me something in return?" she challenged, lightly pinching me on the leg.

"Ow! Yes, *obviously*. I've been watching tutorials and everything." She scoffed, but it's true. I spent half my day looking for beginner-friendly homemade gift inspiration, then the rest of the day watching videos on techniques. Not to brag, but by the end of it, I was feeling pretty confident.

The rest of the drive to mine was full of her excuses, but once I got her home and she saw all the paints and yarns and fabrics laid out on my coffee table, her face lit up with excitement. She's been painting something on her canvas for hours now, but she won't show me what it is. I have to wait until it's finished, apparently.

The sun has long set by the time Bea puts down her paintbrush and cocks her head to examine her masterpiece.

"Finished?" I ask hopefully.

"Mhm," she murmurs, although her squinting eyes indicate she might take that back any second, so I jump up and move her paint palate away before she can be tempted.

"Can I see?" I ask and she rolls her eyes playfully.

"You're like a dog with a bone." She shifts in her seat and holds the canvas by the sides with her fingertips. "It's still wet, and I'm really not a very good painter. It's for fun, really—"

"Just show me, Honeybee," I urge, leaning over to sneak a peek. She tilts the canvas sharply and gasps as she hits it into her shoulder, smearing blue paint over my T-shirt she'd changed into earlier.

"Oh no! I have to fix it again now," she grumbles, but I grab her hand.

"It's fine, I'm sure it just adds character." I gently lower her wrist and guide the canvas towards me. "Show me."

She does, and I have to stop myself from melting on the very spot.

"It's the night's sky." Bea points at different colours smeared across the canvas behind the bright stars. "Midnight blue, indigo, azure, and violet." She looks up at me then, grinning from ear to ear.

"It's gorgeous," I coo, unable to stop myself. She's actually painted me the night sky, with the colours my mother used to describe it. *How'd she even remember me telling her that?*

"It's okay," she starts, but I cut her off.

"It's *perfect*, Bea. No one's ever given me something so special before."

Her eyes gleam. "No one's ever planned something so special for me before, either." Leaning over to kiss me, she whispers a quiet "Thank you," onto my lips.

When we finally break apart, I only say, "Well, my gift's going to look disappointing now," as I lift up my small bouquet of air-dry clay flowers. All different shades of yellow. "Careful, they're still drying."

"Oh, Artie—they're beautiful!"

"Not too bad for a beginner's attempt," I smirk humbly. "I made them because, well, this right here?" I gesture to indicate the entire room—her sitting cross-legged on my sofa, her belongings dotted around my apartment, her presence lighting up a previously desolate space, "I think this is my yellow."

Her eyes soften as she takes in my words, glistening tears threatening to spill over her lashes. "Your yellow?"

I nod as she gently places the flowers on the coffee table before sliding into my lap to pepper mini kisses all over my cheeks, forehead, neck. "You're my yellow, Honeybee."

They're not the three words I wanted to tell her, but judging by the look on her face, I don't need to elaborate. Her lips meet mine again, with the absolute urgency of two magnets destined to always find each other. She repositions herself atop me, but her foot catches on the coffee table and knocks one of her flowers onto the floor.

"Shit!" She scrambles off me to fetch it, smoothing out the petals one by one. "I think I saved it."

"Not destined for the craft morgue quite yet, then?" I tease, pushing the rest of the flowers to the far side of the table and guiding her back towards me. She yelps as she falls into me, but then she's giggling and I want to record it to use as my ringtone.

"No way. I'm going to keep them forever." Her hands find my curls as mine caress her thighs, grounding her to this very spot. I bite back a groan as the temperature in my apartment reaches astronomical heights.

"Can I keep *you* forever?"

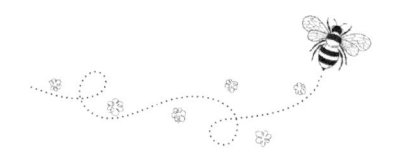

I drop Bea off at the hospital early this morning before coming straight home. She's getting so much more confident at passing through certain areas of town, it's only a matter of time before I'm no longer needed for moral support. I think my heart might just burst with pride when that happens...although I will be a tiny bit sad to say goodbye to our daily drives. It's become one of my favourite times of the day.

It's not until I'm alone in my apartment that I realise just how little I have to fill my time with these days. I fall back into my office chair, head lulling back as I look towards the ceiling. I suppose I could do what I've been putting off these past few days...

With a pained groan, I log onto my computer and open my damned email inbox. Ninety-seven unread messages. Yikes. But one sticks out like a sore thumb, and I open it regretfully.

Not good enough.
Not quick enough.
Not feeling generous enough.
We will be seeing you soon, Mr Avila.
- D.W.

Shit. There's only one person who might be able to help, so I find my phone and dial Silas's number.

"Hello?" he answers straight away, and I wince at the thought of involving him in something like this. But I'm desperate.

"Do you know someone by the name of Damian Wolfe?" I ask.

"Damian Wolfe?" Silas repeats, tone turning slightly more urgent. "*The* Damian Wolfe?"

"Is there more than one?"

"God, I hope not. Why are you asking—holy shit, Artie. Please tell me you're not being stalked by Damian fucking Wolfe?"

"I deleted everything surrounding my tip to the police, but he's emailed me saying it wasn't good or quick enough." I read the entire email out to him for good measure.

Silas makes an exaggerated noise. "Sounds like he's coming for blood. I'm sorry, Arth."

"What do I do now?" I ask hopelessly as I scrub my face so hard my glasses go flying towards the other side of the room. "You're the expert, right?"

A humourless chuckle. "In my experience, killing the bastard seems to be the only way to keep them down. But otherwise, keeping your loved ones close is vital."

I sigh in agreement, massaging my temples. How the fuck am I supposed to explain this to Eden?

"And Artie," Silas continues, interrupting my thoughts. "That includes Bea."

That stops me in my tracks. "I don't know what you are referring to," I say, completely unconvincing.

"Yeah, you do. Let me know if you need any backup, and call if you need advice. I'd come back and help, but with Jessica…I can't put her through something like that again."

"Of course, you two stay away." *The last thing I need is more people around me that Damian can hurt.*

"Tell Bea," Silas warns. "She won't take kindly to being kept in the dark."

"Will do," I affirm, even though that's the absolute last thing I want to do. "A pleasure, as always. Give my best to Jess!"

"Bye, Arthur."

And then he's gone, and I'm left alone to stare at my ceiling. I blow a deep sigh from my mouth, wondering what the absolute fuck I'm supposed to do now.

I stand, pace for a while, fill my empty apartment with colourful curses, before slapping on my bravest face and making a plan.

Eden, Jackson, and the kids are easy. It takes me thirty minutes to find and book them a holiday at their favourite family-friendly hotel in Spain. To be fair, it only took that long because I had to call Eden for their passport information, and she spent most of the time arguing my ear off.

"The kids have school!"

"It's term break next week, I checked."

"What about my business?"

"You can work from Spain—isn't that the whole point of being the boss?"

"Jackson would need to book annual leave!"

I sigh at that, tapping my keyboard a few times to access the private network his business uses for holiday entitlements. "I've taken care of it."

"How?"

"Don't worry about it."

"I hate when you say that," she sighs.

"Why, because you know I outsmart you in every way?" I add a smirk because I know she'll hear it and hopefully annoy her enough to stop wondering why I've just gifted her family a two-week, all-expenses-paid trip out of the country.

I guess it does, because she ends the call with a giddy little laugh and lots of thanks.

I lean back in my chair with a satisfied sigh. Good—four less loved ones to worry about.

Silas and Jessica are fine, far away from Fayette Bay. The inner circle is nowhere near here, either. Really, it's just Bea and Maria to think about.

I do some searching and book Maria and her new accountant on a business course out of town, emailing both of them a fake page that says they won it in a raffle. It lifts my mood the tiniest bit thinking of them arguing about who entered the café into the competition in the first place.

That just leaves Bea.

My Bea, who will probably never forgive me once I tell her I've got another crime lord chasing after us. I should probably start coming to terms with the fact she might not be mine for much longer...

Serves me right.

By the time she walks through my door, I'm back to pacing. She wasn't booked for any house calls today, so Maria met her at the hospital after her shift and they went for lunch. I thought not picking her up would've given me more time to think through a plan, but all it's done is made me more anxious.

"Hey," she sings as she locks the door behind her. "You'll never guess what Maria told me. She's only won a *raffle*—"

I've been waiting for Bea to come back all day, but as soon as I see her face, I lose it. I grab her by the waist and pull her close, burying my face deep into her hair. Because if I'm about to lose *her*, I need one last memory to hold onto.

It's honey and brown sugar scented, my memory. It's warming sunshine and beautiful melodies. It's the feeling of home and security and trust, all about to be wiped out within a second.

"Artie? What's wrong?" Bea asks, stroking a firm hand up and down my back. It's reassuring and heart-shattering all at once.

"Maybe we should sit down," I say, taking her hands in mine. I give them a squeeze and lead her to the sofa, guiding her down next to me as I sit. Another squeeze. Maybe, if I can squeeze her just tight enough to permanently join us, she won't walk right out of here in the next five minutes.

"You're scaring me," she admits with a nervous laugh.

A sigh. "I know, and I'm sorry, Bea. But there's something I need to tell you."

"Bea?" she repeats, hand to her chest and smiling. "No silly nickname? Who's died?" I don't smile back and her face falls. "Oh my god, someone really has died. And I've just made a joke about it. Who? Artie, who's died?"

"No one's died," I say with another squeeze, "but I've let you down, and I need to tell you about this so you can get away from me and keep yourself safe."

She looks as confused as ever, but she clasps my fingers back reassuringly. "Tell me."

Every instinct within me is screaming at me to *not* do that, but I have to.

If only my safety were on the line, I'd probably already be making some smart-ass remarks to Damian, practically goading him to come and get me. But with Bea to think of, I can't risk that.

So I tell her everything.

By the time I'm finished, her mouth is partially agape. "So, this Damian Wolfe guy is coming after you because you sent an incriminating tip about him to the police? And he's the man behind your attack." I nod and she hums. "What are you going to do about it?"

"Nothing? I've burned all my bridges with the police, and going to them about this would probably put me in more danger anyway. I'm pretty much powerless to do anything but sit here and wait for him to find me, and hope to high hell I can get away without any life-threatening injuries." I add a tiny smirk, but the joke doesn't land. Neither of us are laughing.

"Can you hire a bodyguard?" she suggests.

"Could do. But the most important thing for me right now is to get everyone close to me out of harm's way. I need you to go home, Bea."

"No," she says simply, stone-faced.

I'm physically taken aback at that. "No?"

"No," she repeats. "This Damian Wolfe didn't say anything about hurting me, did he?"

"Not in so many words, but—"

"Then I'm not going anywhere. It's better to stay together than be in two separate houses. What if he turns up on my doorstep while I'm all alone over there? I'd bet you'd feel pretty stupid then." She makes her tone lighter for the last line, but the mood still doesn't change.

"You need to go home," I push.

"Do you want me to go home?" she counters.

No, I do not. I want her to stay forever, never leaving me to deal with a bad night again. But if Damian came here...

But what if he *did* go to Bea's house? What if that's his plan...

"I don't want you to go," I say truthfully. My head hurts.

"Then I'm not. We'll face Damian together."

"I don't know, Bea..."

"Artie, you have helped me more these past weeks than I ever thought possible. It's thanks to you that I've had the courage to start working at the hospital again. You're the reason it doesn't take me three times as long to drive through town anymore. Let me help you this time." Her eyes are glassy and she's biting her lip as she smiles at me. Somehow, I feel lighter just by looking at her. But something's still eating away at me.

"I don't want to drag you down into another one of these messes," I whisper.

Bea strokes a light touch down the side of my face and neck, stopping her hand right over my thrumming heart. "You're not dragging me," she affirms. "I'm coming along for the ride."

CHAPTER TWENTY-SEVEN

Bea

I KNOW WHAT YOU'RE thinking, so you don't have to tell me.

I know I'm an absolute fool for staying here with Artie, and I know I promised myself I'd never get into another position like this again. The tiny voice in my head keeps telling me to get out as fast as I can, and maybe that is the smart decision...but I don't want to. I meant what I said last night—Artie *has* changed my life in just a few short weeks. I let fear control me for a full year and I'm just tentatively crawling out the other side because of him. I won't let that fear win again.

I push the thoughts of Damian Wolfe and crime lords to the back of my mind to focus on the task in front of me. I'm making us pancakes for breakfast—although I have *nothing* to prove—when Artie emerges from his bedroom, rubbing sleep from his eyes. He gives me a wry smile and I return it, stroking his curls as he leans down to give me a kiss on the cheek.

"Something smells nice." He sits at the breakfast bar and I place a cup of hot coffee in front of him. "Magical woman," he groans before taking a sip.

He didn't sleep well last night. I know because every time I'd been jostled from sleep by the faintest of noises outside, I'd look over to see him still wide-eyed and staring at the ceiling. I guess even me being here couldn't chase away the nightmares this time.

"What do you want to do today?" I ask, wiping the side clean of batter splatter. "I've taken some emergency time off work, so we can do something to take your mind off of everything if you want."

"You took time off work?" he asks over the lip of his cup. "They just let you do that?"

"Yeah," I shrug. "I was surprised too, but I think Helena wanted me off the phone. She told me she'd get cover for however long I need it."

Artie appears impressed, and the look only intensifies as I slide a neat little stack of pancakes over to him.

"I told you I could make them," I say with a resounding smugness.

"My Honeybee strikes again." His voice is a low, gravelly hum.

I grin at him over the rim of my own mug. "So, what do you want to do?"

"To be honest, I was just going to spend the day figuring out if there was any way to hack into Damian's systems."

"Oh, okay." I turn to pile the washing up in the sink so he doesn't notice the disappointment that I'm sure is shading my face. "I'll stick around though, if that's alright with you."

"I'll do that." I hear him come up behind me before wrapping his arms around my waist. He nuzzles my neck and I allow my eyes to roll closed, savouring the warmth of him pressed against me so casually. "And it would be my honour."

"You're happy for a man who's basically been handed a death sentence," I hum, breathing in his warm pine scent.

"Oh, that? Already forgotten about," Artie murmurs into the crook of my neck. "What's the worst that could happen?"

I have to laugh then, because it's such an Artie Avila answer. "To not care in the slightest that someone's coming after us is incredibly on brand for you."

"No," he corrects before spinning me around so I'm pressed against the sink, his arms braced on either side of me as he leans in close. "I don't care if Mr Wolfe comes after *me*. If anyone even thinks about getting too close to *you*...all bets are off." I watch as his pupils dilate to swallow the green usually residing there. "I care about you, and anyone coming after you is as good as dead already."

I'm still trying to calm my heartbeat, which I'm sure he can hear after that admission, and steady my breathing as he smirks secretly, pushes off the sink, and tugs me away so he can start washing up. I collapse clumsily into his office chair, watching his curls bounce along the nape of his neck.

"I care about you, too," I blurt out, for what reason, I'm not entirely sure. His shoulders flex slightly before he turns around, and I'm entirely certain he's going to say something completely sarcastic to make fun of me. But he's not smiling when his eyes meet mine.

"I care about you more than I've ever cared about anyone before," he confesses quietly.

"Me too," I say, and it's the truth.

Last night, when he told me about Damian's message, I think I felt my heart physically break. But not for me—for him. For Artie, who's been through enough. Who's been suffering in silence for so long, much like me.

Maybe that's why I chose to stay. My head was screaming at me to run, to walk out of the door right that second. But my heart told me to stay. I think I needed to stay so Artie didn't spiral back down into the place he'd been hiding in for so long, behind silly jokes and a goofy grin.

Eden's words ring back through my head: *You're good for each other.*

I think we might be perfect.

Once he's done with the washing up, Artie rounds the island and I stand, making room for him to get to work. He hooks my fingers with his before I can get too far, grinning at me. "Want to help?"

A few weeks ago, if you'd told me I'd be sitting next to Arthur Avila learning about code and various software programs hidden from usual internet searches, I'd have laughed. But that's exactly what I'm doing—controlling the mouse while he's in charge of the keyboard.

"Click that little box with the black square in it," he instructs, pointing. I feel rather important with such a high role. I do as he says and he types something instantly. His fingers move so quickly I'm almost surprised they're not smoking.

"What are we looking for, anyway?" I ask.

"Any crime lord worth anything will have their data encrypted, but that can only go so far in protecting their interfaces. Depending on how good Mr Wolfe's personal protection team is, we might be able to access his files by breaking through their firewalls." I nod along like I know what he's talking about. "If we can get in, there might be something concerning me in there. Emails to hitmen, instructions of how to dispose of my body—fun stuff like that."

He smiles innocently as I roll my eyes. "What if you can't break into Damian's accounts?"

"I have a very specific way of approaching everything in life," he explains with a wicked grin. "I just keep trying until the code eventually gets sick of me and lets me in."

I chuckle. "And that works?"

"It did with you."

"Oh please. You did not have to try that hard to wear me down," I pout dramatically.

"Honeybee, you convinced yourself you hated me for an entire year. I've never dealt with code as hard to crack as you."

"Not even my doorbell video camera?" I deadpan.

Artie lets out a snort. "That was the easiest. I probably cracked that in less than thirty seconds."

"No way!"

He looks at me, suddenly giddy, and takes the mouse off me. And yep, within thirty seconds, he's showing me the outside of my house through the traitorous doorbell stream.

"Well great, now I need a new doorbell!"

"I wouldn't bother, they're all the same. Easy to crack, even easier to manipulate." He shrugs as if this is common knowledge.

"What security system would you recommend then, Mr Know-it-all?"

"Me," he says simply.

"You."

A happy hum. "I'll keep you safe, Honeybee."

"And what about when you're busy?"

"I'm never too busy to look out for what's mine."

I beam as he squeezes my thigh and throws me a wink, the look in his eye telling me he's completely genuine. And that makes me smile even brighter.

But before I can challenge the possible logistics of him being my personal round-the-clock bodyguard, a message pings through on the middle screen. Artie's attention is torn from me, quickly reading it and typing something back.

Then three more messages appear, and the entire chat window scrolls too quickly for me to make sense of what's being said. Half of the messages are just numbers, letters and symbols jumbled together.

Artie must feel my confusion as he stops typing and points at the screen. "My inner circle," he clarifies. "We met on a hacker's forum years ago. We help each other out whenever one of us is on a heist. They're sending possible encryption keys for Damian's accounts. I'll copy and paste these into here," he points to a password box on the screen closest to him, "and keep my fingers crossed that one of them is a match."

"Ah." I still have no idea what he's talking about but it's definitely hot when he talks gibberish.

I watch him sidelong as he goes back to typing. I've never met someone so willing to talk everything through, even when he's under as much pressure as he is right now. It's like Artie's never too busy to put my mind at ease. His kindness warms something deep within me, and I have to stop myself from leaning across and holding him.

Back on the screen, every single password he tries causes the login box to wiggle back and forth like it's physically shaking its head.

Every. Single. Password.

All wrong.

By the time he finally leans back in his chair, rubbing his eyes beneath his glasses, he looks utterly defeated. And a little pissed off. We sit in silence for a few minutes before he runs a hand down his face and asks, "Want to grab something to eat?"

I look back and forth between him and the computer screens. "We're done? I thought you were working all day?"

He shrugs. "Bored; hungry," he groans with a charming grin. But my eyebrows are still pinched, so he continues, "Kyra is taking over for a while, see?" he points to the group chat, still reeling with messages. "Then Johnny will jump in, and if they're still struggling, we'll have to let Aaryan have a go."

I look at him quizzically as he laughs, a smile tugging at my own lips as I watch his delight. "Aaryan means well, but he's known for his mistakes. We like to joke about it whenever we can—he hates it. It's hilarious." His eyes darken a shade. "I'll introduce you properly, if—*once* we get out of this mess."

I tilt his chin up to look at me. "*Once* we get out of this mess, I'd love to meet them."

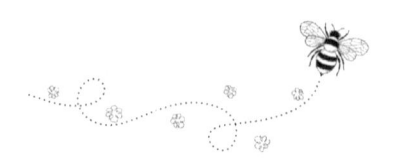

We settle on a small diner overlooking Temmistone Port for lunch. It's so peaceful here, with the gentle breeze knocking little sailboats together, groups of children sitting along the quay looking for crabs, the miles of deep blue water stretching out ahead of us. I wish I could come out here more often.

It's beginning to drizzle outside, so the diner is busier than usual with people trying to get away from the weather. Artie and I managed to snag a table near the window before the clouds darkened, so I'm trying to avoid the eyes of the dozen customers waiting for us to give up our seats.

"How are you feeling?" I ask Artie over our small table and sandwiches, because he's barely said two words since we left his apartment, and his eyes are more distant than I've ever seen them.

My voice snaps him out of whatever thought he's losing himself in, and he gives me half a smile—*half a fake smile.* "All good. You?"

"I'd be better if you were honest with me," I probe gently, nudging his leg underneath the table with mine. "What were you thinking about?"

A smirk. Again, it's not completely honest. "You don't want to know."

"Then why'd I ask?"

His eyes slide to mine, and heat pools in my chest. Okay, maybe I don't want to know. I'm pretty sure I'd prefer to know nothing about any of this. But, since time travel is impossible and there's no way in hell I'm leaving Artie to deal with any of it by himself, I steel my spine and hike my eyebrows up, waiting.

Artie bites the inside of his lip to stop from laughing. "I like you when you demand things of me." He picks my hand up from next to my plate and brushes a kiss across my knuckles.

I tug my hand away defiantly. "You like me all the time."

It's his turn to lift his eyebrows. "Is that right?" he drawls.

Taking another sip of my raspberry tea, I challenge, "Is it *not* right?"

"God, Honeybee. It's impossible not to."

He looks like he wants to clear the table and pull me towards him, so I avert my eyes and ask again. "So what were you thinking about?"

"I told you—" he starts, but I cut him off.

"I do want to know!"

But then he stares at me with a glint in his eye—a challenge. "You really want me to say it in front of all these people?"

All the blood rushes from my brain at that. "...What?"

"Very well," he croons, smirking like an evil villain. His voice is far too loud for diner conversation, and it's only then that I realise my mistake. I grab his hand in a bid to beg him to *not* do this, but it's too late. With his cheeky smirk still in full force, he announces, "I was just thinking about how unreal you'd look in my bed right now."

CHAPTER TWENTY-EIGHT

Artie

I shouldn't have lied. Well, *technically* it wasn't a lie. I have pretty much been thinking about Bea in my bed nonstop for the past few weeks, ever since the first night she slept next to me in my fuzzy pyjamas. And it was hilarious to see her cheeks turn the deepest shade of burgundy as she dragged me into the hailstorm because she couldn't bear to be in the diner a second longer with everyone staring at us.

If only she knew how often people stared at her anyway.

But regretfully, a naked Bea was not what I had been imagining when she asked me at the diner. My mind had been otherwise preoccupied with the message I'd received as we'd been waiting to be seated.

Unknown

> Really, Mr Avila? Trying to get into my system is an interesting move. A foolish one, but still. Tell me, what's it going to take for you to realise my threats are true? Perhaps Nurse Di Menna would enjoy a quick house call.

Artie
> Stay away from her.

Unknown
> I thought as much. You cannot change your fate, Arthur. But hers will depend on your actions in the meantime. Don't do anything you'll come to regret.

So yeah, I was in a bit of a bad mood. Feeling sorry for myself, too. I really wanted to get into Damian's files today. I *needed* that little win. I can't stand the waiting around, wondering if I'm going to meet another underling with brass knuckles every time I step outside, or if it'll be a takedown-from-afar this time.

I steal little glances at Bea as I drive us back to her house. She's looking straight out the window, cheeks still flushed crimson. I can't help but smile to myself, despite all the guilt currently clawing at me from within, because she's *so* mad at me.

And she's *so* cute when she's mad at me.

Does that make me the worst person in the world? Here I am, sitting next to a girl who has quite literally got my heart in a chokehold, putting her in this much danger. It's enough to make me feel sick.

Me? I've probably done enough in my lifetime to warrant an early grave from a disgruntled crime lord. Stupid games: I've played them all.

But Bea? Innocent, too-brave-for-her-own-good Beatrice Di Menna? I'd rip out the throats of anyone who dared come near her.

Well, I'd get Silas to do it. I'm more of a puppeteer than a fighter. A manager to the wrestler. I'll be in his corner, but he's more muscular than me. Silas is the brute strength, but the brain? That's all Arthur.

When we arrive back at Bea's house, she practically jumps out of the car while it's still moving. I chuckle as she slams the door, storming right into her house without a glance back. If it hadn't been her idea to stick together, I'd wonder if she'd even let me in.

But then it dawns on me—should I go home?

I probably should let her cool off and keep her away from Damian's prime target. I stare at the steering wheel, wondering how much more I'd piss her off if I left.

As if she reads my mind, a text chimes through the centre console of my car.

Bea

Don't you dare drive off.

Call me weak, because within a second I'm walking into her warm home, locking the door gently behind me before kicking off my shoes. The faint scent of cookie dough candle rolls over me invitingly, and I find Bea in the kitchen standing over two mugs of steeping tea. Her eyes flick up to me with such an icy glare I'm pretty sure my blood freezes, before looking down again.

"How long are you going to pretend like you're angry with me, Honeybee?" I drawl, hoping it'll drive her wild.

Her eyes lock on me before narrowing. "Oh, I'm *not* pretending."

"You're mad at me for a joke?"

"You told the entire diner that you were thinking of me..." she hisses the last words like she's afraid her neighbours will hear through the walls, "*in bed*."

I smirk. "I told you; you wouldn't want to know."

"That's not what you were thinking about, Arthur." Her tone is ice cold to match her stare now, and I take a step back to get away from the bitter words.

"Don't call me that, and what do you mean?"

Don't read too much into the fact that I just told her to stop calling me the name I've been begging everyone to use for my entire adult life. It's not important.

"Well, I'd hope you wouldn't look so *desolate* when really thinking about such things," she bites out, sliding my cup slightly towards me on the counter, but not enough that I don't have to lean over the entire island to get it. "So, you're either lying about what you were thinking about, or thinking of me in bed is the most horrifying image your brain has ever conjured up."

Ah. I see my mistake now.

"So, which is it?" she demands, her eyes still piercing into my very soul. She's tapping the side of her mug rhythmically, mimicking the sound of a ticking time bomb. "Which is the lie?"

I circle the island gently and put my cup down before placing hers next to mine. I take her reluctant hands and rest my forehead on hers. She looks up at me with big, unimpressed eyes.

My god, I'm a finished man.

"Okay. I didn't want to worry you, but Damian messaged me while we were at the diner and it put me in a bit of a funk," I confess. "Since that wasn't my idea of the best lunchtime conversation, I made up a small white lie about what I'm definitely usually thinking about."

"Artie," she scolds, her eyes full of pure grief. "Show me?"

I go to object, but she moves my hand towards where my phone is in my jeans pocket. I slide it out, unlock the screen, and hand it over willingly. Bea takes a second to read the short thread, a shallow crease forming in between her eyebrows.

Finally, she hands the phone back to me. "You should've told me straight away."

"I know."

She sighs. "This isn't going to work if you keep things from me, okay? We're a team in this. I don't want to be kept in the dark again." I nod wordlessly. "Can you promise me, Artie? Promise no more secrets between us."

"I promise," I whisper onto her skin as I pepper her hand and forearm with kisses. "I'm sorry, Bea. Truly. I'm going to get the inner circle to stop looking right away."

But she pulls away from me abruptly. "What? No way. You can't just give up. We need to know what Damian's plan is."

"Not at the expense of putting you in danger." I shake my head because antagonising Mr Wolfe is simply not an option anymore.

"He's coming for us anyway, right? If we can get a head-start—"

"It's not going to happen, Bea."

We engage in a tense staring contest for a long moment before she glances away. "Fine. But let's forget about it for now, okay?" She clears her throat lightly, running a hand through my rain-damp hair. She presses her lips to my forehead, and I want to cherish her for being so understanding. Worship her.

"I don't deserve you." *True.*

"No one does," she hums softly, and I chuckle. "Going back to earlier. Exactly *how* often are you thinking of me, again?"

I grin at her sultry expression, desperate to lighten the mood. "Like ninety-eight percent of the time." I edge closer to drag my fingers up her arms to her shoulders, then to her neck. "In all honesty, I can't stop thinking about you. Your image takes up my entire day. I think I might want to have you in my arms every single waking second."

She hums a pleasant response, closing the space between us. My hands tangle in her hair, pressing our lips together so tightly neither of us can come up for air. Our coats are abandoned somewhere on the kitchen floor, my blue jumper discarded on the way to her bedroom.

As our forgotten tea gets colder, we only flame brighter. The open curtains let the early spring sunset paint the entire bedroom in crimsons and roses and maroons, but I hardly notice because I'm so lost in the very essence of Bea. Once the sun's long set, we fall asleep in each other's arms, only to wake up a few hours later and ignite again.

Somewhere during the youngest hours, I realise I am completely powerless to this woman. She can take me for all I'm worth. I'd probably beg her to do it, too.

If I die soon, I'll be happy to have been able to call her mine for just a short while.

No, I'll be *ecstatic*.

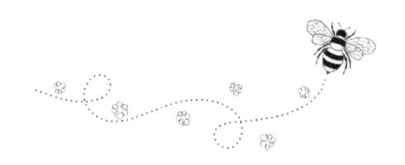

I wake up with Bea still in my arms, thick hair tickling my nose as she snores softly on my bare chest. My brain is mush from exhaustion, eyes burning. But I'm happy. *Definitely happy.*

I snuggle into Bea's warming scent of sugared strawberries and a hint of salt. God, I could get drunk on that smell alone. I trace a line with my fingertip up her arm and over her shoulder, the soft skin warm like a peach sitting out in the summer sunshine. I could bite it.

"Morning, you," she murmurs, diving deeper into the crook of my arm.

I smile at her, although she's not looking at me. "Hello, Honeybee."

"What time is it?" she asks, words muffled by my muscle.

"Like nine, I think? Misplaced my phone last night."

Bea lets out a long groan, and her breath is hot against my skin. "We have to start going to sleep earlier."

I smirk. "Absolutely. Shall we say, tucked up in bed by eight tonight?"

"I'm serious," she says, pinching me.

"Ow! Me too—the earlier the better, I say. What about seven-thirty?"

"I'm just saying that it's probably not healthy to stay up until five every morning." Another groan.

"But the hours between midnight and five are my favourite with you," I say truthfully. When the worst-case scenario daydreaming finally lets up and I can enjoy a slither of peace with my girl.

"Shall we compromise and move those hours earlier?"

"I hear five pm is the new midnight," I muse in agreement.

"Dinner at four," she agrees. Her grip on me tightens as she stretches the sleep from her entire body.

"Fuck dinner," I hum to make her laugh. It does.

"I like dinner."

"I like you."

She hums happily, snuggling into the duvet with her eyes closed again. "What's for breakfast?"

"I'll have a look at what I can whip up, shall I?" I tease.

She gives a *mhm* sound but doesn't bother looking at me, and I'm certain she's almost asleep again. I give her a peck and slip out of bed, grabbing the first thing I can find to wear before entering the living room. Which, it turns out, is a fluffy pink robe hanging on the back of Bea's door. It's short, but it covers everything important.

The living room is cool but bright, with most of the curtains still open. I start making eggs in one pan and bacon in the other, flicking the kettle on to boil water for Bea's morning tea. I hum a happy tune, not completely hating the freedom that this robe is offering me when the door knocks.

I look up towards the sound, then to the bedroom, then back to the front door. It knocks again.

There's no sign of Bea emerging to save me, so I pad as quietly as I can towards the entranceway and check the peephole. Instantly I'm smiling. Oh, this is going to be *so* good.

"Good morning, you son of a gun!" I holler as I swing the door open wide, arms outstretched. Silas looks me up and down before pinching the bridge of his nose. "What are you doing here?"

"Are you going to let me in and stop showing the entire street what an absolute idiot you are?" Silas asks, voice low. He's trying to hide his laugh; I know it.

"Where are my manners? Come in, come in."

I follow him into the kitchen, rushing to turn down the stove. He sits on one of the stools, staring at me through low eyebrows. I beam at him.

"So what are you doing back in the Bay?" I ask, plating up three portions.

"To offer moral support."

"You're very kind, but I don't need—"

"I know you don't need any," Silas interrupts me, pushing his sandy blonde hair away from his flustered face. "I came to see Bea. Which I thought might be a given since this is her house." He sniffs as casually as he can. "Jessica's busy with her art students, so I thought I'd come back for a few days to make sure everyone's...coping."

"That's very nice of you, but I have it covered."

"I know you do," Silas assures, hands up. "But you can never have too much muscle with these kinds of guys."

"So, you're my bitch?" I smirk, probably to counteract the heaviness of this conversation.

"I'm your backup," Silas growls.

"My bitch, gotcha." I round the island to knock on Bea's bedroom door, calling through that breakfast is ready. A groan is all I hear back.

"Are you going to change into some clothes?" Silas asks, dragging a plate towards him and tucking in.

"Why? Is pink not my colour?" I ask, spinning to give him a good look.

Silas closes his eyes and I swear I can almost see him vibrating. Before I can antagonise him anymore, Bea appears from behind her doorway wearing my T-shirt. It swallows her, making those legs look longer than I've ever seen them. I hide my grin behind a fist as her eyes bulge at Silas, then pinch as she takes me in, in all my pink marshmallow fluffy glory.

"Silas! What are you doing here?" she asks, bouncing over to hug him while looking at me with startled eyes.

"I came to check on you," he says with a slight edge to his voice.

"That's sweet of you," she replies, coming up behind me and taking her plate. She smiles at me with rosy cheeks, and I have to lean down to kiss her. It's like I have no other choice. My hands are tied.

"I'm not loving this arrangement," Silas cringes as we come back up for air, eyes firmly pointed down at his plate.

"Why not? Can't you be happy for us?" I goad. Bea elbows me in the ribs lightly.

"You're far too good for him, Bea."

"Ouch," I say with a hand over my chest.

"Why don't we all let Bea decide who's good for her?" Bea interjects, looking between the two of us. Silas and I only nod in agreement. "Good. Sy, are you staying here?"

Silas takes a long moment to think. "I was planning on it, but I don't want to impose if you're going to be here...together."

I almost do a spit-take. I can't take him seriously, all shy and uncomfortable. Bea shoots me a look that says *Don't, or you'll never see me in your T-shirt again.* I sigh because she really does look sublime. It might be my favourite look on her.

"You can stay here, Sy. Artie and I will stay at his," she decides with a satisfied smile.

Silas jerks his head up at that, though, a dangerous twinkle in his eye that has me rolling mine. I cringe as he chortles, "You and who?"

Bea looks from me to Silas before getting the joke. But then the traitor matches Silas's expression and repeats, "Artie..."

"Don't," I warn him.

"Why, *Artie*?"

"Don't call me that," I groan.

"You let Bea call you Artie, why can't I?" Silas hums, far too amused.

So I bite back. "Because I'm not in a relationship with you," I say. "And I'm certainly not sleeping with you."

Silas makes a disgusted noise and Bea paces back into the bedroom, muttering something about being surrounded by children.

"Artie, for fuck's sake—"

"Stop calling me Artie."

"Then stop telling me you're sleeping with my sister!" Silas shouts, exasperated.

"She's not your sister," I remind him helpfully.

A muscle ticks in his jaw. "You know she's as good as. I might not be able to keep her away from you, but I *really* don't need to be included in the details."

"You know, *technically* it was you who told me to look after her."

I think he might start steaming from the ears at any second. "I swear to god—"

"Alright, alright!" I concede. "I'll stop."

"Fine."

The tension between us as we finish our breakfasts is heavy. I'm biting the inside of my cheek to stop from laughing, because I think Silas might just be furious enough to knock me out if I even think of making a sound.

Thankfully, Bea returns only a few minutes later fully dressed in tight jeans and my blue crewneck from last night. She must feel the tension too as she looks at Silas and asks, "Why don't we go to the café for a catch-up? You'll never hear the end of it from Maria if you don't pop in."

He nods at her, jaw still hard-set.

"It's settled, then." She pokes out her tongue at me and I wink. Guess my invitation got lost in the mail.

CHAPTER TWENTY-NINE

Bea

"And then he says to Andrew, 'I'm not paying for a glass of water that came from the tap,' all grumpy and Silas-like!" I can barely get my words out; I'm laughing so much. Artie's smirking, too, watching me intently from his pillow. He's lying on his side, stroking a light finger up and down my bare stomach. "You should've seen Andrew's face—he was the colour of those squeezy ketchup bottles Mar puts on each table!"

Lunch with Silas and Maria had been just what the doctor ordered. It was so refreshing to get out and stop thinking about everything going on, although I did miss Artie a whole bunch. I wanted to invite him to come with us, but judging from the smoke pouring out of Silas's ears when I came back from getting dressed earlier, I thought it'd be best to separate them.

Silas means well, and I know he does. He'd do the exact same for Maria. I can't be mad at him, but I wish he'd stop looking like he's about to punch Artie. Those two have a weird dynamic none of us can ever figure out. Artie swears they're best friends, and I think Silas might even call them that too if we forced it out of him, but that doesn't stop Silas from constantly looking like he's ready to rip Artie's head off.

After I gave Silas a quick refresher of where everything was at mine, I grabbed an overnight bag and drove straight over to Bluetine Park. Yes, I drove myself—the short way, all alone—to Artie's. I passed Desmond's old office. A tear might've leapt free as I did, but even so. *I did it.*

I wish I could've had a camera ready when I told Artie. I rushed through the door, adrenaline sparking through every nerve within my body, as I told him how long it took me to drive here. His face was a perfect picture of surprise and wonderment and admiration. He picked me up and spun me around, over and over until we were both dizzy, peppering me with proud kisses and praise. Then he ordered us a celebratory pizza and let me pick what film I wanted to watch. I chose a slapstick comedy.

"Did you have fun?" Artie asks, watching me with loving eyes. The world outside his bedroom window had faded to dark navy, but I feel lighter than ever. *Happier* than I have in a long while.

Excited. I probably shouldn't, considering the situation we've found ourselves in, but I can't help it.

"Lots," I hum, rolling to face him. His fingers continue to paint charged lines over my skin as I readjust. "Can I ask you a question?"

"Always," he murmurs sleepily. It must be well past midnight by now.

"Why am I the only person allowed to call you Artie?" I nibble on my lower lip, suddenly worried he might brush me off or realise he actually doesn't like me calling him that and ask me to start calling him Arthur instead. I hate that name.

Artie's mine.

He takes a long second before answering, and it's enough for my brain to go into overthinking overdrive. But then he whispers, "When I was younger, my mum came up with the nickname. My dad hated it, but Mum and Eden would always call me Artie. We were *Edie and Artie*, and we loved having similar names." I can just make out his quarter smile in the dark. "So when she died, I couldn't...I couldn't bear anyone calling me Artie anymore. It felt like a betrayal, as if I was letting others use *her* name for me. My sister doesn't mind so much, so I still call her Edie when we're together. But I've been Arthur ever since I was seven." He blows a deep sigh from his lips that disturbs my hair resting on his chest. "Losing Mum crushed our father, too. He kind of just...took a step back from life. So for the longest time, that name reminded me of the two parents I lost so young."

"Oh, Artie..." I start, but kind of trail off in the middle because it feels completely insensitive to call him that now I know why he hates the name. "Why didn't you tell me? I would've never kept calling you that if I'd known. I'm so sorry."

But he's still smiling at me, now stroking a thumb across my cheek. "Don't be," he says quietly. "It didn't take me long to realise hearing that name from your lips is one of my favourite sounds in the world. I never want to hear you call me anything else."

I take a second to let those words settle around us. Those beautifully vulnerable words that will forever mean the world to me.

"Thank you so much for sharing that." It feels like I know a completely different side to him now; one secret only I'm privy to. Then I whisper, "I love you," so quietly I think he might not hear me at first because he's silent, but he leans in to kiss me and it's the sweetest kiss I've ever tasted.

"I love you too, Honeybee," he murmurs onto my lips, and those are the sweetest words I've ever tasted, too.

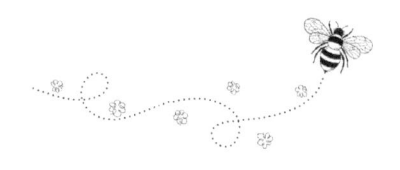

I walk out into Artie's living room, rubbing sleep from my eyes and yawning. The sky outside the large windows is powder blue mixed with a little lavender, and I protest quietly with a pout. Too early. *Damn my dry mouth.*

I fill up a glass of water and lean against the sink for a second while I down the entire thing. Artie and I must've only fallen asleep a few hours ago, and I've had nowhere near enough sleep to function properly. These late nights are really beginning to mess with my head.

As I walk past Artie's desk on my way back to the bedroom, I wiggle the mouse to check the time quickly. I left my phone...somewhere. The screen bursts into life, much too brightly for my delicate eyes, and I notice the account's unlocked. *Weird*.

The time is a few minutes after 4 am, and that makes me stifle another groan. But what catches my eye is the inner circle group chat reeling with new messages. They appear far too quickly, and I have to skim them to keep up.

Kyra
> Arthur, stop what you're doing and get online.

> I managed to get into Damian's account.

Aaryan
> Holy shit…

Johnny
> Calling Arthur now.

Aaryan
> Find anything useful, Ky?

Kyra
> I really need Arthur here to say this…

Right on cue, I hear Artie's phone buzzing on his nightstand. I step away from the desk tentatively, on my way to wake him up, but the next round of messages freezes me to the spot.

Johnny
> Tell us in case he's reading on his phone. He might be with Bea and unable to get to his computer.

Aaryan
> True!!!

> Wait, who's Bea?

Kyra
> Damian Wolfe isn't planning on attacking Arthur. He has an entire plan in place to target Bea instead.

Aaryan
> Who's Bea?!

Johnny
> Seriously, Aaryan?

I let out a small panicked squeak as I read Kyra's last message, covering my mouth in a bid to muffle it. Oh god...Artie.

I need to get Artie. He'll know what to do.

Silas. He should know, too.

Wait—I've left Silas at my house. What if Damian has gone there? To get *me*?

Damian only threatened *me* yesterday morning. How could he already have an entire plan mapped out?

Get Artie.

I only make it a few paces towards the bedroom before I hear them—the footsteps shuffling behind me. There's a split second before the bag lands over my head where I know what's about to happen, and I'm completely powerless to it. There's a sharp sting in my neck before my legs turn to jelly beneath me; my words fail me as I try to scream for help.

I'm drifting, drifting away into complete nothingness. Artie's vibrating phone is the last thing I hear before I completely float away.

Chapter Thirty
Artie

"What do you want?" I whisper-moan into the phone, head still half-concealed by my pillow from where I tried to block out the noise of relentless vibration earlier. I'm only giving in now to stop it from waking Bea up, who hasn't so much as stirred next to me thankfully. I haven't even checked the name of the caller, so it's a complete lucky dip as to who will speak next.

"Get the fuck up and log onto your computer right now."

I bolt up at the low, gruff voice almost shouting at me. "Johnny?"

"Get to your computer," is all he says before hanging up.

I throw the covers off my legs and almost run to the desk. *The inner circle doesn't call each other.* We've only spoken on the phone once, all of us, on a conference call to brainstorm a plan for one of Kyra's more difficult heists. Aaryan spent the entire time annoying everyone with knock-knock jokes, so we decided to cap it with group chat messages going forward.

So, Johnny calling me at 5 am is definitely worth jumping out of bed for.

I sit down at my desk, wiggle the mouse, and scrunch my eyebrows at the fact my computer is unlocked. *I never leave it unlocked.*

The group chat messages are empty, too. Completely gone.

Arthur
> Are you joking, Johnny? There are no messages here.

Johnny
> Don't be an idiot.

Kyra
> What do you mean there are no messages? We've been waiting for you for over an hour.

Arthur
> No messages that I can see…

Kyra
> Holy shit.

Johnny
> Fuck, Arth.

> Arthur
> ???

> Kyra
> Arthur...call Bea.

> Aaryan
> What's going on?

Within a second, my brain enters freak-out mode. My eyes dart around the apartment before reaching my bedroom doorway. No...

No, no, no.

Holy fuck, *no*.

She wasn't there. When I woke up; when Johnny called me and I sprung out of bed, her side of the bed was cold. The room didn't feel right, but my brain is only just catching up now to figure out why.

> Arthur
> Kyra, tell me everything.

A typing bubble pops up next to Kyra's name. Seconds feel more like hours, so I jump up and poke my head around the bedroom door. The bed's empty, duvet bunched at the bottom from where I discarded it a few minutes ago.

"Bea?" I call out to the numb apartment, just in case she's hiding somewhere. Thinking she's funny, about to jump out and throw a bucket of water over me.

What I wouldn't give for this to be a practical joke...

GEMMA NICHOLLS

No one answers my futile call, so I sit back down in my desk chair. Then I stand, because what am I thinking trying to sit at a time like this?

Kyra's still typing.

I grab my phone from the nightstand and call Bea. Her phone begins vibrating from within the bedroom.

Kyra

> I got into D.W.'s account last night. He has an entire folder saved onto his desktop with the initials AA-BDM. Clicked into it, and it's a planted decoy, obviously. But the plan is laid bare within it, how he's going to take Beatrice Di Menna and lure you into a specific location through her. No plans detailing what he wants to do with you once you get there, but I think we all have a pretty good idea?

Arthur

> I told you to stop looking.

Kyra

> Bea told us to disregard what you said and keep going.

Arthur

> Bea doesn't know what she's talking about!

YOU AND ME, HONEYBEE

Kyra

> She's right, though. We needed to get into the files so we had a better chance of beating Damian without you getting yourself killed.

> Johnny and I are working on cracking the rest of the files as we speak.

Johnny

> There might be something hidden in one of the encrypted files that we can use to get her back.

Arthur

> You had no right.

Kyra

> Bea wanted this.

Johnny

> Sorry Arth, but she's right.

Arthur

> She could be anywhere…

> They could be doing anything to her.

> I can't just sit here and wait??

Johnny

> Give us one hour. One hour to gather as much information on this fucker so you're not completely defenceless against him.

I'm pacing now. One hour. Can I really sacrifice sixty minutes before tearing the town apart to find her? *This is all my fault.* I should've known better; made her stay at her house with Silas to protect her. I should've known she'd find a way to tell the inner circle to keep going.

I should've done more to make sure they'd stopped looking. But those night-time hours...they were for us.

Not for Damian fucking Wolfe to steal the girl of my dreams right out of my bloody bed.

Frustrated tears spill over my lashes as I unlock my phone and call the one person I definitely don't want to admit this nightmare to. "Silas, get here. Now. He—he has Bea."

I hang up before he can begin the flurry of colourful insults he surely has saved for me. He'll be here within a matter of minutes, so he can berate me then.

He's going to be *furious* with me.

As expected, ten minutes later, Silas is barging through the door I'd propped open for his dramatic entrance. I'm still pacing, back and forth by the TV now, chewing the skin around my thumbnails until they're bloody.

I'm expecting him to punch me in the face, call me a *fucking idiot* or something. But he doesn't. He walks over to me, tense and rigid, and squeezes me into a tight embrace.

Oh. *Okay.*

I stand still, letting this six-foot-something man hug me so tightly I might burst, and I want to cry. I want to sob into his chest and tell him how much I screwed up bringing this danger into Bea's life. I want to blame him for ever introducing us.

"We'll get her back." Silas pushes off me, and I feel woozy for a second. I nod, wishing I had an ounce of his calming resolution right now. "Tell me what happened."

"We went to sleep around two in the morning, and by the time I woke up at five, she was gone and her side of the bed was cold." I shake my head. Three hours is a lot of time to have been in the dark. If only I'd answered Johnny's first call...

"Okay. Did they leave any clues?"

"Clues?" I ask helplessly.

Silas starts inspecting the apartment, searching high and low for god-knows-what. "You know, footprints, notes, anything to hint at where they might be taking her."

"I don't think so..." I start searching though, nonetheless. It's all I can do not to break down in a heap in the corner. I search underneath sofa cushions, around my desk, in all of the kitchen cupboards.

Silas and I must search for half an hour, with each passing minute only making me more unnerved. When he finally calls time on our mission, Silas grabs me by the shoulders and says, "It's okay. That was a longshot anyway when dealing with Damian Wolfe. But look," he angles me towards my desk, "we have the best hacking equipment in the country right here. We're going to find her, Artie." His voice is far too calm; it's making me even more on edge.

"Don't call me that," I say absentmindedly. Because Bea calls me Artie. That name is hers. Just like Honeybee is mine.

And now she's gone because of me.

In danger, probably. Scared, definitely.

I'm scared. I can't sleep without her. Hell, I can barely breathe without her.

"Right, Arthur. I know exactly what you're going through and how difficult this is going to be, but I need you to get it together. For me, for Bea, for all of us. I need you to be able to use this equipment like I know you can and come up with a plan, okay?" Silas asks, lightly slapping me across the cheek to wake me up from whatever self-deprecating trance I'm holding over myself.

It works, to an extent. "Okay."

He smiles tightly. "Thank you."

Silas disappears to make the coffee while I hover over my desk, convening with the inner circle. My fingers are raw around the nails from how much I've picked the skin, ending every tap of my keyboard with blistering pain. Thankfully, Kyra has most of the brainstorming covered and is more than happy to take the reins. Once we find Bea and I throw all this equipment in the harbour, I'll enlist her to take over the inner circle for good.

Kyra

> Okay. So we can rule police help out, correct?

Arthur

> Pretty sure Monty will have blackballed me on every single officer's email list by now.

Aaryan

> Even if we explain that it's a helpless victim who's never been near the hacker's game in her life?

Johnny

> Won't matter. I've heard Monty's one of the worst for holding a grudge.

Kyra

> And he double-crossed Arthur, anyway. We can't trust him.

Arthur

> Another plan that doesn't involve the force, then?

That sets off a slew of messages of new alternate plans. We spend hours conjuring up new ideas just for the others to shoot them down. Kyra thinks we should hack into every security system we can find within a ten-mile radius. It shouldn't be too difficult if we split up the area and each take a vicinity to search through, she says.

Johnny's convinced we'd better use our time by heading back into Damian's network, as there must be *something* in there we're missing. Silas, who hasn't stopped muttering to himself since he got here, reminds me that many of the biggest players in the business keep everything offline to stop the likes of us from finding anything out about them.

Aaryan—well, he's just being useless.

"I can't take this anymore," I say into my palms, covering my face to trick myself into believing this is all some weird nightmare I can wake up from.

"I know," Silas agrees before going back to arguing with himself. My fingers are too raw to mess with anymore, so I've resorted to chewing my upper lip. Drawn blood a few times, I think. I can barely taste it.

We all go back and forth on countless ideas for the entire day and well into the night, after the sun has set and the moonlight is casting a sombre glow across my living room. Across my sofa that holds so many new, fond memories. I hold my throbbing head in my hands.

Silas fans a gentle touch across my shoulder, trying to console me with rhythmic squeezes. It's not working.

"We'll find her," he says for the millionth time today and I've just about had it with those damned three words.

"When? Because I need her now. I need to have her sleeping in my bed while I'm sat in the corner of the room, never to sleep again to make sure no fucking crime lord comes back and steals her from me." I pause for a second before the next words come out, but they're so devastatingly true and I need the world to know otherwise they'll eat away at me forever. "I love her, Sy. She's my everything."

Silas doesn't reply, but simply claps a firm palm on my shoulder. I think that might be his way of giving me *some* kind of blessing—that I absolutely do not need—but I'm wrong. Because before I know it, I'm being thrust away from the desk by the back of my wheeled office chair, dragged into the empty space between the kitchen island and the sofa.

"What do you think you're doing?" I ask as Silas lets go and leaves me sitting in the no-mans-land of my apartment.

"Finding our fucking Honeybee," he growls.

Physically recoiling at that, I lock up the memory and make a note to tell Bea about it later. She'll be so mad that I have *Silas Knight* calling her such a ridiculous nickname.

Well—she thinks it's ridiculous. I think it's adorable, just like her.

"Don't you think I'd have a better shot at finding her, considering I'm the hacker out of the two of us?" I ask dryly.

"You haven't managed it all day," he replies in a matching tone.

I give him a quarter smile and he rolls his eyes. At least we haven't been completely devoid of humour through everything going on. Although it feels almost dirty to be smiling at a time like this, so I quickly let it fall from my face.

Silas opens the inner circle's chat and dives in.

Arthur

Right. Enough brainstorming, we need to get a plan in motion now.

> **Kyra**
> We've already done digital footprint analysis, so take Johnny's original idea off the table. There's nothing in Damian's files that points to where he's taken her.

> **Aaryan**
> Why don't you ask that conman friend of yours to see if he has any close contacts with D.W., Arth? Surely, they must've run in some of the same circles over the years.

"Hang on, that's not the worst idea." Silas pushes back from the desk, looking at me with contemplative eyes. "Desmond would definitely know of Damian…what if he still has information on him in his office somewhere?"

"Holy shit," is all I can manage.

But something in Silas's eyes tells me it's not quite the right time to celebrate yet. For the first time today, he looks panicked—a little clammy, maybe?

"Is everything okay?" I ask. "That was quite a range of emotions your brain just went through."

He lets out a deep breath. "You know how it is, going back to the scene of a crime. The scene of *your* crime."

Ah. Of course. It's entirely unfair to ask Silas to head back into Desmond's lair after everything he was put through. Bea could barely drive past the place for an entire year—a small bubble of pride flits through my chest at the memory of her elation just last night—so what am I thinking, assuming Silas will go back into the building willingly?

"Let's go." Silas breaks me out of my thoughts, already by the door.

Oh—never mind, then? I guess we're going.

I nod, quickly sending a message to the group to tell them the plan. I finish off with a quick instruction for everyone else, because four hackers are definitely better than one and we need all the help we can get.

Arthur
> For the first time in your life, Aaryan, you've been useful.

Aaryan
> See? You all underestimate me greatly.

Arthur
> We're off to Desmond's Deals to see if the conman had anything on Damian before he died. Kyra, check out the dark web and do some data mining. Johnny, keep looking through his network and see if you can't get a geolocation to track. Aaryan—keep an eye on the airlines.
>
> If all else fails, ransomware attack.

Silas drives us down to Desmond's Deals, the old storage container garage Desmond Rose used to operate his con game antics from. I've never been here physically, but I'm no stranger to the camera network.

I glance at Silas as he shoulders the door open. His face is grim with determination, and probably a little sorrow.

"We don't have to do this if you're not comfortable," I whisper in the darkness, jerking at his arm so he's facing me. "I can go by myself."

"No," he bites out, voice thick as fresh smoke. "Bea risked her life for me in here once. It's the least I can do to help find her now."

Silas leads us down to the office, flicking on lights as he enters the room as if he owns it. In the middle stands a metal desk, still with a full ashtray and an empty bottle of whiskey on it. The room smells of damp and rotting paper.

Silas smirks as he picks up the bottle, inspecting it. "Figures," he muses.

I head straight to the dark blue filing cabinets lining the walls behind the desk. They're dusty, covered in a thin layer of sticky tar, and so full that rogue papers are sticking out of the thin gaps. But when I try a door, it's locked.

"Damn it," I moan, but Silas is already rooting around in one of the desk drawers. He turns to me and spins a bunch of keys on his pointer finger smugly, eyebrows raised.

"Desmond Rose, that paranoid little prick," he murmurs, sniffing a laugh. "He taped his keys to the underside of his desk within the drawer. He told me he kept one hundred keys on this ring just in case anyone ever found it. All of these cabinets use the same key—we just have to find the right one."

"Are you joking?" I ask. "That's the most idiotic thing I've ever heard."

"Look who we're dealing with."

"If only he'd let me put all this stuff online," I grumble, taking the ring of keys from Silas and trying the first one. Nothing. "I practically begged him to let me back up all his files online. It would've been so much easier for me to keep track of everyone he held a grudge against. Do you know how many people he had me tailing?"

"I can give it a pretty good guess. Do you know how many people he had *me* conning?" Silas takes the ring from me and opens it to pour a handful of keys onto the concrete floor in front of him, closes it again, and hands it back to me.

"How'd you ever stand working so closely with that guy?" I ask, angrily thrusting wrong keys into the rusted locks over and over again.

"You worked for him longer than I did," Silas points out unhelpfully.

"I never met him, though."

"Do you want a gold star for keeping a safe distance?"

"I want my girlfriend back." I grind out. It occurs to me I've never called her that before, and I make a mental note to make a big deal out of it when I see her next. Because that's what she is—my girlfriend. Mine. Not some puppet for a loser crime lord to take and dangle as bait. I don't think I've ever felt this angry over something before, and I'm not loving the sour feeling it's leaving in the pit of my stomach.

Silas doesn't reply; he just tosses me an understanding smile to my silent apology for snapping at him. *Not your fault*, the curl of his lips says. *We all know I was the same with Jessica.*

He was worse actually. But now's not the time to bring that up.

Not when one of his keys finally makes a triumphant scraping sound within the lock, and the door to the furthest cabinet flings open.

"Yes!" he shouts, throwing me the winning key to unlock the rest. I do so quickly, each door pinging open one by one. Files burst out, flopping lazily onto the floor between us. Silas is already flicking through one as I tuck the key in my pocket for safekeeping.

We leaf through dozens of files before finding anything interesting.

"Hey, look at this." I tilt a file towards him so he can read his own name printed on its cover. "Care to take a look at the many, many ways you wronged Desmond Rose?"

Silas huffs a laugh. "No."

I point a finger gun at him to tell him I understand, but quickly put it away when I realise that it's probably in poor taste. Anyway—

"Bingo." Silas holds up a folder with big, red D.W. initials on the front.

I grab the file and Silas scoots closer to me across the cool floor. As soon as we look within the file, it's like we hit the motherlode. We catch each other's eyes, because to say Desmond had done his research on this one would be a colossal understatement. I'm holding a file containing the past five years of Damian Wolfe's criminal history.

"We need to get this back to yours so we can go through the entire thing." Silas flips it over so we can both see just how bulky the file is. It's thicker than many of the old books lining my old bookshelf at home. The one Bea made fun of.

Bea.

I push up off the dusty floor to stand. "Let's get out of here."

Silas nods and quickly follows my lead, sealing the door to Desmond's abandoned office firmly behind us.

CHAPTER THIRTY-ONE
Artie

We pick Maria up from the café on the way back to my apartment. Need all the help we can get, Silas reminds me, and Maria would be upset if we didn't tell her that her best friend is missing. He's texted Jessica, too, letting her know what's happening. Despite his best efforts to prevent her from getting anywhere near another crime lord, she's on her way.

She's braver than I am.

Silas sits in the armchair that Bea had all but claimed as her own, Maria on the sofa where Bea kissed me for the first time, and I'm pacing throughout the apartment filled with her happy memories and warm scent. Every second we waste in this cramped space is getting harder to manage. I feel like I'm drowning, painfully slowly, with no one to pull me up for air.

"This handwriting is atrocious," Maria muses as she flicks through her stack of paper. We've divided the contents of

Desmond's file into three to get through it quicker. Still, it's taking an age to understand the scrawled letters, numbers, and what we think might be symbols for a secret language.

"Here," Silas leans towards her, "swap with me. This is mostly print-outs, and I have a better track record with Desmond's writing."

They swap their stacks and we fall into deafening silence again.

My group of papers is all about Damian's sightings. It seems like he's been hiding in plain sight for quite some time now, but Desmond had someone tailing him whenever he was spotted around Fayette Bay. The printed pictures are all grainy, all blurry, and mostly useless.

A close-up of Damian's black, gelled hair. A blurry image of what I think might be a classic crime lord leather jacket. Nothing distinguishable or usable to tie him down to one particular spot.

That is until I flick to the last image. At first, it looks as futile as the rest of them. I can just make out Damian halfway through a door that's half covered by the pavement. The print-out is overexposed to high hell, zoomed in far too closely, but…the background. I recognise it.

"Hey, guys," I drawl, uncertain, turning the picture to show them. "Look at this."

Silas takes the paper and holds it closer so they can both inspect it. It takes them a second to see it, but then Silas's jaw goes slack and Maria's eyes widen.

"Holy shit, that's my café."

"You don't think—" Silas starts, but Maria cuts him off.

"I didn't even know there was a door leading to beneath my café." Her eyes dart left and right, like she's trying to figure out the hardest maths equation in the world.

"I mean, we should definitely check this out." I'm already pacing towards the door.

"Artie, it's three in the morning." Silas jumps up to grab my arm and hold me firmly in place. "I think we should get some sleep first."

"You two sleep. I'm going to find Bea," I throw back, zipping up my coat and shaking him off me. They both share a look I don't recognise, but that's fine because the door's halfway closed behind me already.

That is, until Silas's freakishly large hand lands on my shoulder, dragging me into my apartment. "Arthur, we might have just found Damian's lair," he urges with a level tone.

"Yes, *exactly*." His casual tone only highlights my manic one. "We need to go check it out—Bea might be there."

I look to Maria for help, but she glances away. *Traitor*.

"We've never been up against someone as big as Damian Wolfe before."

"What are you saying? You just want to leave her there—alone, scared, possibly hurt—until Damian's had his fun and is ready to tell us where they are?" My voice cracks, and the sane part of my brain knows there's rationality in their words, but my rising panic won't let me comprehend it. All I know is that Bea is being held captive and it's all my fault. "I thought you two were her friends. I thought you were *my* friends."

Tears spring free and race down my cheeks. The weight of everything—the guilt and the panic and the sleep exhaustion—has well and truly broken me down and battered me into the ground. If I didn't have the determination to find Bea safe and sound forcing me through it all, I don't know what'd be left of me by now. I stare at Silas through bleary, defeated eyes, half expecting a hardened face to greet me, but it doesn't. I'm met with pure sympathy.

"All I'm saying is we need a plan. Storming into a lair is not the way we want to go with this, trust me. It'll end with us probably dead, and Bea in even more danger. We need to be clever about this."

"Spoken like a true conman," I murmur, and he sniffs a laugh.

"Hey, I was once stupid enough to run after a girl right into the lair of a crime lord," Silas reminds me. "Who was there telling me it was a stupid idea, and that I was signing my own death sentence?"

I let out an annoyed grunt and fold my arms. "Me," I concede. "But you survived."

"Barely," he sighs. "Now, I have more experience with crime lords than any of us, okay? I think that gives me the right to appoint myself as the leader of this mission. And my first point of action is for us all to get some sleep." I try to cut him off, but he puts a hand up. "Ah-ah. No arguing. The lair is less likely to be armed in the daytime because they'll be expecting us to come at night."

"Makes sense," Maria mutters, dipping her head in approval. I look at her like she's gone a little mad.

"Thank you." Silas gestures towards her before looking back at me. "You and I will meet back here at 8 am before heading to the café, where we will check out this door as inconspicuously as we can. We will then plan how to get in once we have the layout down. Is there any way we can get into the cameras of the potential lair to make sure we're looking in the right place?"

"I can ask one of the inner circle," I yawn, scrubbing my face with my hands. All at once, the exhaustion has hit me. I feel like a gust of wind could knock me down for the count.

Silas nods. "Good. Mar, I'll walk you back to the café so you can get home before sunrise. Arth, I'll be coming straight back here afterwards and waiting up for Jess, so don't even think about doing anything stupid. I don't want to see you until the morning."

"Are you seriously ordering me to go to bed like a child? It's *my* apartment." I drawl and he shrugs.

"Yes, and I don't give a shit. Goodnight." He beckons Maria to follow him out the door, but she kisses my cheek on the way past.

"Goodnight, Artie. And good luck."

I bite back a wince at that name and give her a tight smile instead. They leave, and because I'm pathetic, useless, and powerless, I follow my orders.

Arthur

> Anything of note to tell me?

Kyra

YOU AND ME, HONEYBEE

> Nothing from data mining. The guy keeps himself squeaky clean.

Johnny

> Got a geo-location for somewhere near you actually, Arthur.

I almost laugh.

Arthur

> Let me guess, somewhere near the Twinkling Bliss café?

Johnny

> Oh great, you know of it. I love being the last one to know the updates. It really makes wasting my time worth it.

Arthur

> Just a hunch. Have you got the exact location and timestamps of the device?

Johnny

> Only since this evening. The device is still there, but unknown whether it's a phone or laptop.

Arthur

> Right. Any cameras?

> **Kyra**
> On it already.

> **Arthur**
> Excellent. We're headed there tomorrow to check it out. Need to sleep now, I'll definitely collapse if I don't. Call me if you find anything vital to the mission?

> **Johnny**
> Because that worked so well last time.

> **Kyra**
> We will. Take care of yourself, Arthur.

> **Arthur**
> Thanks.

I log off and drag myself into my room. But as soon as I see my bed, the duvet still balled up in a sad heap at the end of the mattress from this morning, I freeze.

Honestly, I don't know how I don't yell. I am so beyond my breaking point—I need sleep. But I *can't* sleep without Bea next to me on a good day, let alone when I know she's somewhere out there, in the hands of one of the most dangerous crime lords in the country.

In the hands of Damian Wolfe. The thought of it has me snarling at the empty room.

I scrub at my face again. My glasses are pissing me off.

I can't lie down. I can't even sit.

Fuck it.

I storm back out into the living room and grab my keys, leaving the door unlocked for Silas as I head into the stunted twilight.

Maybe it's the lack of sleep, or the utter terror racing around my mind that's making me completely irrational, but I'm almost jogging towards the Twinkling Bliss without a care in the world about the danger possibly awaiting me, or the fact that I have no weapons.

I don't even have my bodyguard.

But I still don't care when I reach that odd partially concealed door halfway beneath ground level. I shuffle closer to the steps leading down to the ominous door when something in the shadows next to me moves. A figure appears, and I have only half a second to freak out about imminent death before Silas steps into the light and I groan like a caught-out teenager.

"I knew I'd find you here," Silas whispers, his tone half smug, half grim. "You're a moron."

"Have you been waiting in the shadows just so you could pop out and scare me half to death?" I hiss, acutely aware that there are probably cameras around us.

"Yep."

"How'd you know I'd come?" I clock that he's not making an effort to turn me away, but I won't mention it. He's actually descending the concrete stairs with me.

A long moment passes before he admits, "It's exactly what I would have done."

We give each other a curt nod. *In this one together.*

"You're aware this is a trap, aren't you?"

"Yep." I blow a sharp exhale through tight lips. I'd figured that out on the short journey here. "This is my fight, not Bea's. Let him have me. I just need to get her to safety."

Silas agrees before bending down to pick the lock with a bobby pin he retrieves from his small bun. The metal door swings open with a low whine, and Silas claps me on the back. "You're a good guy, Arth."

I throw him an unconvincing look before stepping inside the pitch-black hallway. There's a distinct smell of damp hanging in the air, and every so often I hear an echoing drip, drip, drip. The floor is uneven underfoot, and we creep slowly to stop ourselves from being heard.

It doesn't take us long to find the first door. *Cool steel*, I determine as I run my fingers along its perimeter. Silas does his little bobby pin trick again to unlock it, but without any light to guide him, it takes us several frustrating minutes to get inside. I try not to focus on the tiny green light coming from the electronic keypad just above the lock, and how it'd take me half a second to disable it from behind my desk.

When the steel does eventually swing inward from Silas's manual magic, it takes everything within me to stop my knees buckling at the sight. Bea, lying unconscious on a small cot in the corner of the room, covered by a cheap grey blanket. My skin almost recoils at the look of the itchy wool.

Silas heads straight towards her as I hover in the doorway, too stunned to move. I watch him as he kneels next to her head, feels across her neck for a pulse, and dips his head in relief as he throws me a thumbs up.

She's breathing.

I cross the threshold tentatively, but I can't get much closer. Bea looks so peaceful, so *innocent*.

I forced this reality onto her. I'm the reason she's lying in this dark dungeon. How will I ever be worthy of sharing her space again?

"We need to get her out of here—" Silas starts, but a new noise hushes him.

Footsteps coming from the hallway. Walking slowly; dawdling. Not frantic and rushed but calculated and calm. *Cocky.*

The owner of the clipped footsteps chuckles quietly as he reaches the doorway, filling the frame with his sheer size and presence. "Gentlemen," he addresses us with a feline smile. "My men have a bet on to see whether you two would be stupid enough to fall for this," he muses. "You've just won me a *lot* of money."

"Happy to oblige," Silas pushes through gritted teeth. "How about letting us go for the trouble?"

"Silas Knight, are you bargaining with me?" Damian croons, looking him up and down. He hums for a second before continuing, "*Silas Knight*. I know who you used to work for."

"Then I'm sorry."

"Desmond Rose wanted me dead," Damian titters. "Always stalking me in one way or another. He used to send me threatening notes detailing how he was going to get his best worker—a

Mr *Knight*—to kill me if I didn't do what he wanted." He takes a step into the room. "Tell me, have you come to fulfil his wishes?"

"Desmond never so much as mentioned your name to me, Mr Wolfe," Silas declares casually as Damian begins moving in a semi-circle around us. A lion studying its prey before the lethal hunt.

"Leave Silas and Bea out of this," I interject, probably foolishly. Both their eyes fixate on me now, Silas shaking his head ever so slightly in silent warning, but it's too late. Damian's intense attention is already consuming me. "Your issue is with me, so let them go."

"Arthur Avila," Damian elongates my name like he's tasting each syllable. "I've been waiting to meet you."

"It's been a long time coming," I agree.

"Indeed, it has. I was quite surprised you decided to turn up in the middle of the night like this. I thought you might've been smart enough to wait for my signal. We've barely set things up for you." A smug chuckle. "Then again, you didn't listen to my countless warnings about your girlfriend, so why would you start using your head now?"

"Bea's innocent. She doesn't deserve to be here."

"And you thought the heroic thing to do would be to storm in here and whisk her away." *Not a question.*

"It's what's right."

Damian *hmphs*. "Silas Knight, you may go. Take Miss Di Menna and leave the way you came. As long as this little interaction remains between you and me, neither of you will ever hear from us again."

A sinister promise, laced with unwavering intent. I glance towards Silas, who's already staring back at me with regret in his eyes. I give him a look that I hope will tell him I understand and take a step back out of his way. Then I break into a grin, as wide as I can muster.

My girl and my best friend are about to be free, and that's something worth smiling about. They'll have Jessica and Maria to look after them, and they'll all be safe. I started all of this, and it'll end with me. Best case scenario if you think about it.

"How long before she wakes up?" Silas asks Damian, hoisting Bea into his arms. She's still wearing my T-shirt and fluffy joggers she wore to bed the night she was taken.

"No longer than a few hours," Damian drawls with a dismissive wave. His eyes are still fixated on me, probably to make sure I don't run. "Pleasure doing business with you, Mr Knight. Remember what I said about forgetting this interaction. There will be no second chances."

Silas ignores him, holding my eye for a long moment. I think he might be trying to tell me something, but my brain is so devoid of rest that I can't make it out. Before I can ask him to repeat the wordless commands, he's striding Bea quickly through the darkened doorway, sealing my fate that the crime lord in front of me has already mapped out.

Chapter Thirty-Two

Bea

It takes me a few long, groggy moments to truly wake up, blinking back a rough haze to make out where I am. My head's resting on a familiar pillow, and I'm encompassed by pine and vanilla; Artie's smell. I'm in Artie's bedroom.

There's a second or two where I believe it truly was all just a bad dream and that Artie's in the kitchen making pancakes and tea to surprise me with. But something heavy in my chest knows that's not the truth. That's not reality at all.

I kick the duvet away and stand up, shaky on my feet as I stumble towards the bedroom door. My eyes meet Silas first, standing behind the kitchen island, coffee pot in hand, a grave look on his face. Maria and Jessica are sitting on the sofa, but they both jump up as soon as they hear my footsteps.

"Bea, oh my god—are you alright?" Maria asks, running both hands up and down my arms. But I'm not looking at her. I can't tear my eyes away from Silas, who won't back down from my glare.

"What happened?" I ask him, voice barely a whisper.

"Why don't you sit down?" he suggests, and I can make out the faintest feeling of Maria guiding me gently to the sofa. But I can't move. Not without knowing.

"Where's Artie?"

A deep sigh. "He's with Damian. We found you in the lair and Artie gave himself up so I could get you out of there."

My vision tunnels before expanding to the size of a thousand suns, brighter than a burning galaxy. The atmosphere around me turns leaden, and it's nearly impossible to fill my lungs with air. I try anyway, desperately gulping as my world turns black around its edges.

Time warps between us, and I wonder how long it will last this time. My ribs feel like they might crack.

Artie.

Artie.

Artie.

"Bea. Breathe." Silas is in my face now, cupping my face with his hands as Maria waves a glass of water in front of my eyes. I think I can feel Jessica rubbing my back. I try to focus on all of them, but it's no use.

Artie.

My eyes flicker past their panicked expressions to the far wall of the apartment. I don't see it at first, but when my eyes finally manage to focus on it—

Midnight blue. Indigo. Azure. Violet.

My soul comes careening back into my body, knocking whatever's left in my lungs out in one fell swoop. My chest allows itself to expand again, just a fraction, filling the empty space with fresh air. I exhale heavily, grateful that my heartbeat ringing in my ears appears to be slowing down.

I won't take my eyes off that painting, though. The colours of the night sky I'd painted for Artie a few days ago. I hadn't even noticed he'd hung it up.

"Bea? Are you okay?" Maria's voice still seems distant, but I acknowledge the question with a flutter of fast-paced blinks.

I hadn't noticed until now, but my painting looks exactly like the sky had when Artie had taken me for a walk by the river, all those weeks ago when I came storming around to ask why he'd been spying on me through my doorbell.

When he calmed me down by asking me to watch the water while he monitored my pulse with his caressing thumb.

I'd hated him, but he still made sure I was okay.

I want to choke out the painful sobs slowly building in my chest. A dull ache roars beneath my skin as I turn towards Silas. "How could you let him do that?"

"He knew the risks," is all I get. But then Silas sighs, perhaps because he can see the panic turning to anger behind my eyes. "He knew it was a trap and he went anyway, because he wanted to save you from Damian."

Maria interjects then. "Silas told him to stay at home and we'd all come up with a plan in the morning, but Artie—"

"Arthur."

A bloated pause. "Pardon?"

"You call him Arthur." I fold my arms as an indication that I will not be expanding on my stance any further.

Silas clears his throat, ready to take the floor. "As Mar said, I told Arthur to get some sleep before breaking into the lair. I walked Maria to the café and waited to see if he'd try and sneak in without us knowing. He did, and that's why we both found you in the dungeon last night instead of following the original plan. I made sure he knew it was a trap before we entered, Bea. You meant more to him than his own freedom."

"Still not understanding why you just gave up as soon as Damian found you," I prompt coolly. I can't bring myself to look at any of them, so I stare at the wood grain patterns on the coffee table. "If what you're saying is true, you left Artie alone with Damian and walked away. He'd never give up like that on you..."

Silas takes a sip of his coffee before asking bluntly, "Would you have preferred I stayed so we all could be captured by Damian Wolfe?"

I comb my hair with my fingers helplessly, tempted to grab and pull. "I would've preferred someone to be with him, yes. This isn't fair on him."

"But you being held there wasn't fair on you, either." Jessica reaches for my hands and clasps them gently within hers, as if sensing my thoughts.

"I don't care about me!" I think I must be crying now, although I can't feel any wetness on my cheeks. They feel...fuzzy. Not quite attached to my face.

"Well, we care about you," Silas barks, although his tone is gentler than usual. "And so does Arthur. He knew if he didn't go with Damian, then we'd all be in danger. Arthur went into that dungeon to get you out—no matter what it took. He was fully willing to pay the price, and that's what he did."

"Are you serious?" I start, voice rising.

"Bea," he cuts me off. "We could go back and forth on this all day. What's done is done, and I have a plan. Are you going to listen to me, or waste time arguing?"

I suck my teeth for a second as I bite back my furious words still fighting to spill out. "Fine," is all I let get past my lips.

"Fine."

Silas sits in the office chair and wiggles the mouse to ignite the screens. We watch as he opens the inner circle chat and sends a message. I read a few lines higher—messages from last night, I guess—while he's still typing.

Kyra

> Arth—they have a camera system. Tricky to get into, but I'm working on it.

Johnny

> Nice one, Ky.

Aaryan

> How are you so good at everything?

Kyra

> :)

> Johnny
> Oh my god.
>
> Absolute IDIOTS!
>
> ...They're there already, aren't they.

I shake my head as I read. They *were* idiots. But then I take a breath and make an effort to still it. They were trying to save me, after all. I should maybe be slightly more grateful about that.

I'll consider it again when I'm not feeling so pissed off and shaky.

> Arthur
> Hi everyone, Silas here. I assume you saw most of what happened if you're in the cameras. Arthur's with Damian, I have Bea here with me. Open to any ideas on how to get Arthur back as soon as possible. Kyra, do you know how I could access the camera footage as well?

> Kyra
> Utter fools. How's Bea?

> Arthur
> She's fine.

> Once we have a plan to get Arthur back, then we can all discuss how much of an idiot he is.

Johnny

It doesn't look like there's anything fancy for us to do here, Silas. I think you'd probably have better luck getting him out than any of us.

Glad to hear you're safe, Bea.

Kyra

Me too. And Silas, Johnny's right. You've got more experience with this than anyone. The only one of us who's dealt with a real-life infiltration mission before is Arthur.

Aaryan

One of us, one of us...

Johnny

Shut up, man.

Aaryan

Rest easy, Bea.

"Are they right?" I ask Silas because he's far too quiet. He's clicking open every single link Kyra is sending through the group chat, but nothing's working. I sit next to him, take the mouse gently from underneath his palm, and work my magic.

A camera feed of an unfamiliar dungeon expands across the entire screen, transporting us back through the small, grainy moving images. *This must've been where I was kept.*

"How did you do that?" I swear he almost sounds impressed.

"Spent enough time watching Artie, I guess."

"Stupid hackers."

"Are Kyra and Johnny right?" I probe again, waving towards the screen. "About you being the best person to get him back?"

Silas sighs. "Yeah, probably."

"And you don't want to." It's a statement more than a question. I can see it clear as day, from his tight lips to how he's desperately trying to pinch tension from the nape of his neck.

"It's not that I don't want to get Arthur back, Bea. Of course I do. And I will—believe me, I'll do anything to get him back. But," he takes a deep breath before hanging his head and continuing, "I swore I would never get back in this game. I told Jessica I was done, and I meant it. I don't want to go back to how I was before." Jessica comes up behind him to run her hands through his hair soothingly.

"It won't be like last time, honey," she whispers to him.

I take a deep breath, resting my head on his shoulder. "I'm sorry I haven't been more understanding, Sy. I can't imagine how difficult this must be for you."

He lifts his hand to his face, and I think it might be to wipe a tear. I keep my head firmly down to give him a moment of privacy.

"I will bring him back to us, Bea."

I clasp his free hand with mine, looking up at my painting so proudly displayed on Artie's wall. "I know you will."

There's no other alternative.

Chapter Thirty-Three
Artie

"So, do you have a plan of what to do with me, or are you just keeping me here until something sparks an ingenious idea?" I ask, grinning as genuinely as I can at my captor.

Damian Wolfe glares at me from the other side of the dingy room, his minion between us whirling around to do the same. They led me into this large dugout space with unfinished walls and concrete flooring, littered with a few foldaway chairs and one very ominous-looking table in the corner, covered in a dark blue sheet.

We've been stuck in this stalemate—me sitting on my metal chair in the corner of the room, Damian sitting nearest the door, and this underling patrolling between us—for hours. Well, it certainly feels like hours.

"I'd be very careful with your words, Mr Avila." Damian stands, walking ever so slowly towards me. "You wouldn't want to force my hand now, would you?"

"You mean to tell me it's *not* a sure thing you're going to kill me? Score."

"Your mouth will get you in plenty of trouble," Damian muses, turning and nodding towards me as he gestures some secret code to his worker.

I tip my chin up to him as he comes storming towards me, bringing a thundering fist down against the bridge of my nose. My glasses clatter to the floor as the world turns black for a second, returning to colour just in time to see another fist swinging towards me.

And another.

Something like five impacts later, the dog's called off. He retreats, almost regretfully, making way for Damian's cocky expression to fill my throbbing vision.

"Any other smart remarks you'd like to make, Mr Avila?" he goads, and I wish so badly that I could bring myself to say something stupid.

Just for fun.

But it occurs to me that I don't want to die here, and if I'm right in thinking Kyra should've managed to get into the camera system by now, I'd never hear the end of it if I risked my life just for some stupid quip. So I suck both lips between my teeth, signalling my wilful silence.

Damian smirks grimly, turning on his heel to return to his chair. I throw a wink to the camera in the corner of the room just in case anyone's watching.

"*Is* there a plan, though?" I ask once he's situated back in his side of the room, half because I want to help my friends any way I can and half to distract me from the horribly itchy feeling of drying blood crusting my face.

"There is always a plan. *You* are not to know of it quite yet."

"Can I get an ETA? I hate surprises."

He sighs harshly. "Once my associate has arrived, we shall fill you in on the details. Now stop talking."

And that I do.

Associate...*associate*...ass-oh-cee-ate.

The question of who this mystery guest might be swirls throughout my head as we sit in the numbing silence. Almost falling asleep by the time the door opens again, I'm too exhausted to perk up at the new visitor. I watch the door idly through a sleep-deprived haze as the *associate* we've been waiting for steps from behind it. They walk straight up to me, picking my discarded glasses from the floor and balancing them back on my throbbing nose before giving me a grim look, eyes twinkling with something like satisfaction and greed.

"Arthur Avila," he barks, voice as rough as ever. His thinning hair is slicked back and he still has his work slacks on, but his badge is noticeably absent.

I can't help but laugh, bright and hysterical, as I take him in in all his stupid glory. "Monty Robinson. What the fuck are you doing here?"

He looks me up and down, then turns to Damian to shake his hand. They give each other a terse nod, obviously still working on their friendship. They whisper a few quick words, ignoring my chaotic glee. I notice the bodyguard looks just as confused as I feel, so at least I'm not the only one.

I take the opportunity to glance toward the camera again. I hope whoever's watching heard me say his full name. *If anyone's watching at all.*

"Arthur," Damian announces, finally turning back to me. "I believe you know my associate, Officer Robinson?"

"I knew you were crooked, Monts. Not this much, though. I'd give you a round of applause if my hands weren't tied. Don't suppose you fancy helping me with that?"

"I see you've been pissing people off down here already," he snarls at my smarting face.

I sigh longingly. "You know me—I can never seem to keep quiet, even when it's for my own good." I lift a shoulder as much as I can in a shrug. "But enough about me. Enlighten me, boss—why'd you tell me you didn't know who D.W. was when that was so clearly a lie?"

"I couldn't lose the one piece of evidence we had leading back to him," Monty spits, as if that's the most obvious answer in the world.

"They've been trying to catch me for years," Damian whispers with a wink. "We struck a deal once you went behind his back and deleted all the information he had on me. Thanks for that, by the way. Very convenient."

I look a little sheepishly at Monty, who's staring at me like he's thinking of one hundred ways to murder me.

"It was between him killing me and my friends or deleting the files, Monts. I did what I had to do. Surely you can understand that?" Although truthfully, he looks like he doesn't give a single care in the world.

A gruff *hmph* is the only reply I get, watching me like I'm nothing more than street vermin.

"Okay," I drawl. "So, what's the dream team got in store for me now? I mean, I did delete those files for you Damian—what more was I supposed to do?"

"Unfortunately, it's not enough that you deleted them, Mr Avila. The fact remains you fed them to the police in the first place. If I don't teach you a lesson, what's stopping others from doing the exact same thing? It's very possible that an officer smarter than our friend Monty here would've created copies once you mentioned them the first time, so deleting the files at such a late date would've been no use to me." Damian begins mapping out circles around me as he continues, "I'd say it's pretty lucky, actually, that Monty and I conjured up an unlikely friendship. Lucky for you, that is. Because if that information had been kept somewhere at the station in hard copies," he stops in front of me, leaning down so we are nose to nose, his dark eyes flashing, "You'd already be dead."

"I'm shaking in my boots," I trill, but no one seems to be in the laughing mood so I clear my throat, train my face into the straightest tedium and try again. "So, I'm lucky to still be alive. Thank you, Monty, for not thinking to make copies of the intel

I gave you—you're a real friend." I throw him a wink, and his murderous stare intensifies. "Am I free to go now?"

Damian and Monty share a look before bursting out in grim laughter.

"Sadly not, Arthur. You see, you really did get Officer Robinson into quite a sticky situation with the station, and they're thinking of rescinding his badge for forgetting to back up the intel on the county's biggest crime lord. You didn't think he'd just let that go, did you?"

"What's done is done," I say with a shrug. "Can't we let bygones be bygones?"

"I have a family to think about, dick." I can hear Monty's teeth grinding from the other side of the room.

I throw him another shrug. "I did warn you about this, Monts. I told you I needed that information back to save my friend—it doesn't take a rocket scientist to figure out that the hacker *might just* break in and steal it back from you." I raise my eyebrows at him with an exacerbated smile. "I don't know how much clearer I could've made it."

"Indeed, Officer Robinson should've made the copies and then my displeasure would be with him instead of you," Damian agrees. "But alas, he didn't. And I gave you ample warnings, Arthur, that I needed those files gone. You repeatedly ignored me and waited around until the last possible moment to delete them, which by that point they could've been copied and ready to use in my downfall. Then you chose to be even more of a fool by breaking into my system."

I roll my eyes dramatically. "So many theatrics, Damian. I mean, really! All this because I took too long? Last I checked, you didn't give me a definitive timeline. The files are gone. You're free. Monty's angry, but that's not our fault. I see no reason for me to be here, for us to still be in each other's lives at all. In fact, this all seems like quite a large overreaction to me. Why don't we all just walk out of this room together, shake hands like adults, and get on with our separate lives, eh?"

Wow, I even impressed myself with that sprinkle of maturity there. I think that's a solid argument for my case. Perhaps I could go into law once all this is over and done with. I give Damian a winning smile for good measure.

But he's shaking his head as he guides Monty out of the room. "I don't think so, Mr Avila. You were thinking of yourself when you deleted those files, and now I have to think of myself. Monty won't let my business fly under the radar without something in return, and you *royally* pissed him off. Now you will have to face the consequences. Sleep tight if you can. We'll see you in the morning."

And with that, they're gone.

I look to the corner of the room where the camera's red light is still flashing slowly, indicating the feed is live and being uploaded to its server. I stare down the lens for a moment before sticking my tongue out at it, silently begging for one of my friends to be behind their screen watching me. Not necessarily making a plan to save me or get me out of this mess, but to keep me company.

Hell knows I need it. Considering this might be my last night on earth, I'm feeling pretty alone in the world right now.

Chapter Thirty-Four

Bea

The plan is in place and everyone's ready to go. Silas is busy strapping a bulletproof vest to himself with the help of Jessica, who brought his emergency stash of protection with her. Once the vest is on, she rests her forehead between his shoulder blades with a devastating gentleness. I avert my gaze to give them some privacy, looking back towards the three monitors I'd been watching all night. They're still open on Artie's camera feed, maintaining the flickering image of him sitting in the middle of a derelict room.

Silas offered to take over multiple times through the night, but I didn't want to step away in case I missed Artie sending an important signal. So far, all I've caught is him sticking his tongue out at me. Yes, I did laugh a little—and yes, it quickly turned into me sobbing.

I watched Monty and Damian interrogating him; I heard their reasoning, if you could even call it that. When I told Silas why they were doing this, he hadn't been at all surprised. *That's what these crooks do, Bea. They're all unhinged and hungry for power. Nine times out of ten, they'll never have a true reason for hurting people.*

And that one line snubbed out any remaining hope I had of Damian having a change of heart and letting Artie go.

So now here we are: Silas getting ready to head back into the lair, and me sitting at the desk ready to feign the role of *Hacker*.

"Ready to do this?" Kyra asks through the left screen. We're video-calling so she can see my screens in real time and help me get through today without messing everything up. The only reason she's not taking charge of this whole operation is because Artie has the superior setup and software installed that we'll need. I asked Kyra to come over to run the mission, but it turns out she lives in South Africa.

Johnny and Aaryan didn't know that, either.

"As ready as I'll ever be," I press my lips together in a pathetic attempt at a smile. Kyra gives me a genuine one back, all toothy and wide.

She's gorgeous, by the way. She has bright blonde hair and round hazel eyes, with tanned skin that brings out the freckles on her nose. I'm slightly self-conscious just looking at her. The pang of jealousy radiating through my chest is quite inconvenient, to be honest.

"You'll be fine," she assures me, and Silas comes up behind the office chair and squeezes my shoulders.

"She's right—we'll *all* be fine." He kisses the top of my head. "Kyra is here to help you with the coding nonsense, and Johnny and Aaryan are on call for backup."

"And I'm here for moral support," Jessica cuts in, face grave.

"All you need to do is make sure I'm able to get into the dungeon, then out with Arth." *Simple as that.*

I agree absentmindedly.

"I'd better be off then," Silas announces, checking the time on the monitor over my shoulder—5 am. "Final test?" He clicks a button on the tiny earpiece in his ear. "One-two, one-two."

"Yep, all clear." I repeat the test to make sure he can hear me through my own earpiece. Silas gives me a definitive grunt to confirm our communication channel is open.

He relaxes his shoulders and lets out a sharp breath. "Right—showtime."

"Good luck." I squeeze his hand before he takes it off my shoulder.

"Good luck, Silas," Kyra's tinny voice rings through the speakers.

"Thanks, ladies. Good luck to you both."

"I'll walk you out," Jessica murmurs quietly as Silas picks up his weapons from the counter and shoves them deep into his coat pockets.

It's only when they're gone that I let my own shoulders fall, scrubbing my face. I am so far out of my depth here. One single failure on my part could cost Silas and Artie their lives...

"Stop worrying," Kyra says gently.

"I'm not."

She gives me a look as if to say *Yeah, okay*.

"I just...this is all in my hands," I mutter quietly, picking at my nailbeds. "What if I press the wrong thing and somehow doom two of the most important people in my life to a world of hurt? I'm not a hacker—I barely know how to set up a social media account."

To her credit, Kyra doesn't laugh at me. Her large eyes are full of genuine sorrow, and I feel somewhat validated. "Bea, none of us know if we're going to be able to help anyone. We all use humour as a coping mechanism, but it's only ever to hide the fact we're often petrified of messing up."

"So you all just hope for the best?" I laugh quietly despite myself.

"Yep. Johnny's the worst for it, too. He might seem tough, but he's a softie at heart. Absolutely cannot bear failing. He often asks me to jump on a call with him as a backup for his own heists." Kyra gives a shrug like it's no big deal. "I guess what I'm saying is that there's no shame in asking for help or needing some guidance. The inner circle is a team, and by proxy, that makes you one of us—although never tell Aaryan that I used his words to make a point."

"I promise." I sniff harshly because, at some point, I've begun crying.

Jessica walks back through the door then, alone. She's hugging her elbows, her face completely drained of colour.

I stand to draw her into a tight hug, and she breaks down in my arms. It takes a few long moments before we're able to let go of each other. Kyra interrupts our embrace with a small fake cough.

"Sorry guys, but I have eyes on Silas. He's approaching the main door now."

"Shit," I breathe, pointing the door out on the camera feed to Jessica, who's even more of a novice at this computer stuff than I am. "Here we go."

"Let's go, girls," Kyra smiles so casually, like we're not about to try and pull off an utter fool's mission. "Remember to breathe, follow my lead, and don't panic. Fake it 'til you make it, darlings. We've got this."

Jessica and I share a quick look before laughing along with Kyra, albeit more nervously.

No going back now. *Let's do this.*

I hold the button on my earpiece down. "We're ready. Good luck, Silas."

We watch Silas register my words, take a deep breath, and walk down the steps to the dungeon's door.

We have access to ten cameras situated along the feed: one pointed towards the outside of the door, four through various hallways, one in the room I was apparently kept in, one in what we assume is a crime lord's break room, two more in random empty cells, and one in the space Artie is currently sitting in. The only thing we can't find on the cameras is Damian's office, if he even has one.

He's still alone, staring aimlessly at the camera. He looks utterly defeated. I wish there was some way I could show him how desperately we're trying to get him back. To give him that reassurance that we're coming.

Hold on for just a little while longer, Artie.

Silas gets to the front door and reaches for his hair before appearing to curse himself out.

"*I don't have any pins to unlock the door with,*" Silas's voice hisses through my ear.

"He can't pick the lock," I relay. Jessica's wringing her hands together so tightly her knuckles have turned bone white.

"I think that's an electronic keypad next to the door. Do you know how to unlock those through Artie's software?" Kyra urges.

I rack my brain. *Yes.* Yes! Artie taught me how to do that.

"Give me a second, Sy."

I look down at the keys in front of me, begging my brain to focus. *I can do this.* It takes a few long seconds before my fingers begin moving on their own. I use tabs I don't remember ever seeing before, the weird switchboard thing Artie showed me once, and several keyboard shortcuts I have no business knowing.

But somehow, I *do* know them. It's like muscle memory, even though I've only done it once. Maybe it's some sort of fight or flight response, as an emergency brain backup feature to save my friends.

I see Silas try the door again and slip through as soon as it opens. *Thank you, subconscious memory.*

"Nice!" Kyra whoops through the screen, far too excited compared to the palpable tension felt in Artie's living room. "Bea, that was awesome! I didn't even need to tell you how to do that. Looks like you don't need me after all—shall I leave you ladies to it?"

"No!" Jessica and I both shout at the same time, forcing Kyra to burst out in a fit of giggles. I choke out a small exasperated noise, looking at Jessica's terrified eyes and shocked expression. Her flushed cheeks quirk at me before she goes back to tracking Silas through the tunnels.

"Is it strange that the lair appears to be empty apart from Artie and Sy?" Jessica asks.

Kyra leans forward, squinting for a closer look. "Hm, maybe. They could all be out, I guess. Or they could be hiding, waiting to jump out at the most opportune time."

It's my turn to lean towards the screen now. "What should we do if that happens?"

A simple shrug. "Nothing. We're supposed to look out for the boys, but we can't exactly shoot the baddies through our screens. Our role here is to watch and wait, and to help in any way we can."

"How are we helping if we can't protect my fiancée from being killed?" Jessica asks, voice strained.

"It won't come to that," I say, trying to diffuse the situation. "Silas is a master at this, he knows what he's doing."

"Yeah, it's Arthur I'm worried about," Kyra drawls, checking her fingernails.

"Okay, not loving this game," I reprimand flatly.

Kyra snorts but relents. "Fine. Jessica, if we see any bad guys hiding in the shadows, Bea will tell Silas to give him as much time as possible to react. Bea, Arthur is smart enough to get himself out of literally anything. They're both going to be okay—trust me."

"Need directions, Bea."

I shoot straight up in my chair and squint at the screen, suddenly regretting offering to be the one wearing the earpiece. "Take a left, straight ahead, and keep going until you see two doors on the right. He's through the second."

"Thank you."

We watch in silence as Silas follows my directions and nears the final door. My breath is caught in my throat, and I'm pretty sure Jessica's bitten her nails down to the quick. Kyra's leaning back in her chair and spinning in half circles, back and forth.

Silas reaches for the door handle. He twists it, rattles it, then takes a step back.

I use my super-strength muscle memory to unlock it for him, and he walks right on through.

This is too easy, the voice at the back of my head taunts. I push it away; maybe that's just how it is. Damian Wolfe is actually a terrible crime lord, only gaining in popularity through sheer good luck and happy accidents.

I dare a glance at Kyra, who's already looking at me like she's thinking the exact same thing. Only she doesn't believe it for a second.

There's no time to discuss, though, as Silas appears on the same video stream as Artie, smirking as he locks eyes with his friend. Artie bursts out laughing as Silas ducks behind him to untie his wrists. They share a quick hug and some quiet words we can't hear through the feed. Then they both look towards the camera.

In a completely uncharacteristic moment for Silas, he points dramatically at Artie, his mouth in the shape of a perfect O.

And in a completely characteristic moment for Artie, he waves at the camera and does a twirl. His face is caked with dried blood, and I have to admire him for a second. Someone with such sheer positivity like that should be cherished. I make a vow to do just that as soon as I can, for as long as I can.

Kyra snorts. "Stupid boys," she chides.

Despite the choking tension freezing the air around us, I let out a gasping laugh. Even Jessica manages a tiny smile.

"*Told you I'd bring him back,*" rings smugly in my ear. "*We're out of here.*"

"They're coming out," I tell Jessica and Kyra.

"Better hurry," Kyra warns, sitting up straighter in her chair. She sees them a fraction of a second before we do—the group of men hurrying down the tunnel, the exact same way Silas walked just a few minutes ago.

A panicked squeak escapes me. "Silas, four men are on their way towards you."

Silas hardly has time to react as the first underling bursts through the metal door, lunging at him with a glinting weapon in his fist. He ducks, pushing Artie behind him as he grabs for something in his pocket.

Gunshots.

The men fall to the floor like flies, Silas standing tall in the middle of them. But when he turns to look for Artie, who's backed himself into the corner, his face looks anything but victorious. Jessica's got her hand clamped over her mouth and tears threatening to spill over her lashes. I clasp her shivering knee.

"It's over," I whisper.

"He shouldn't have had to do that," she whimpers, shaking her head violently.

"I know."

"Ladies," Kyra warns. I wince but force myself to look back at the camera feed. *Click.* "More."

"*How many more?*" Silas asks.

Click. "Half a dozen. At least."

Jessica's up from her seat as soon as the next group enters the room, almost tripping over the four men that came before them. I see Silas hand Artie a gun behind his back before he begins shooting again. Artie takes it, examines it. Doesn't use it.

I'm not sure when I took my last breath.

"We need to get them out of there," Kyra muses, almost to herself. "Tell Silas to run. As soon as these guys are dealt with, they *need* to run."

"I think he's a bit preoccupied," I snap. Each gunshot rings through the cold apartment like a death march. And all we can do is watch powerlessly.

"Just do it." Her voice is devoid of all humour now and it almost makes me wince, so I follow her instruction.

Click. "Silas, you need to run. As soon as you can, just run."

I don't get a reply.

Back on the screen, Silas takes care of the six men on his own like some sort of superhero. The underlings barely have time to get past the threshold before they're sprawled on the floor, piling up on top of one another. It's...impressive, maybe? Unsettling, absolutely.

"Guess being a conman is like riding a bike," Kyra admires grimly.

She's braver than me to say something like that with Jessica in earshot, but I'm not one hundred percent sure my best friend's still in the room with us right now. She's tiptoeing back and forth between the sofa and coffee table, grasping her forearms tightly enough to leave fingernail marks.

"Bea, get the code ready to unlock the door in case Damian has locked them in again."

There's no point, though, as when I glance back at the footage I'm met by Silas and Artie being pushed back into the desolate space by Damian and Monty themselves. Monty grabs Silas and thrusts him to the floor, sending his gun skittering away across the concrete. Damian lunges at Artie, who ducks but not quickly enough and ends up on the receiving end of a cracking fist.

I wince and Kyra makes an *oof* sound.

"What's happening?" Jessica asks from the other side of the screen. Neither of us reply, entirely focused on the two evils picking our men up off the floor and slumping them into two metal chairs beside each other.

Jessica hurries around the desk to watch over my shoulder, bursting into angry tears at the sight. I grab for her but she slips away, digging the heels of her hands into her eyes.

Kyra's the first to break the silence. "Right then. How are we going to get them out of this one, ladies?"

CHAPTER THIRTY-FIVE

Artie

IF YOU'D HAVE TOLD me, even two hours ago, that I'd watch my best friend shoot ten people singlehandedly to save my ass, I'd have called you stupid. Because Silas Knight *hates* guns. Even the mention of a weapon disgusts him nowadays.

So what he just did—I know all too well just how painful that had to be for him, and the wave of grief smothering me is almost excruciating. I can see the aching in his eyes already, and I know I'll see it in Jessica's too.

If we ever get out of here alive.

And I...I did nothing. I saw the gun in my hands and froze, letting Silas shoulder the guilt of killing all those men for me without doing a single thing to repay the favour. I just stood back and watched. *Coward.*

"Gentlemen," Damian drawls as Monty binds Silas's hands behind his chair before moving onto my ankles. His hands are slick with blood from dragging the lackeys' bodies out of this room, making securing the ties trickier than usual. "How did you ever think *this* plan was going to work?"

"Sheer luck?" I croon half-heartedly.

That earns me a daggering stare and I smile sweetly back. Damian's eyes glower before turning his attention to Silas. "Honestly Mr Knight, your reputation had me expecting more."

"He's rusty. Taken the year off to focus on the family. I told him he should still be training—little heists here and there, you know the sort—but I guess he's been slacking." I tut. "Good to see he's been putting time in at the shooting range, though."

"Arthur," Silas growls quietly. "Stop talking."

"You should listen to your friend," Damian warns as Monty straightens and stands next to him. "What are you doing?" he asks the officer.

"What?" Monty's eyebrows pinch underneath the thin sheen of sweat coating his skin.

Damian stares at him for a long moment before gesturing towards us. "You haven't tied up his legs," pointing at Silas, "or *his* hands," which is directed at me.

I stretch my hands out in front of me to demonstrate his point. Silas gives me the foulest glare I've ever seen.

"I didn't have enough ties," Monty shrugs.

Damian looks completely taken aback by that. "Well, go and get some more?"

Monty huffs a curse under his breath before stalking out of the room.

There are a few seconds of silence as Damian takes a long, steadying breath before turning back to us. "He is the worst officer I've ever worked with."

"Why'd you think I let him go?" I ask as if we're nothing more than two old friends catching up.

"Shut up, Mr Avila." Damian pinches the bridge of his nose, and I get a quick kick out of causing the reaction I want. Anything to keep his anger on me rather than Silas. "As I was saying, *Mr Knight*. What made you come up with such a hasty plan of action? Did your time working under Desmond Rose teach you nothing?"

"Desmond Rose is dead because of me," Silas snarls.

"And yet, here you are. Failing so miserably at helping one of your friends." Damian makes a small, smug sound. "I warned you there'd be no second chances. If I were you, I'd have a long think about the company you keep. Your *friend* here is the reason why you'll soon be dead."

That makes me feel just wonderful.

"Arthur isn't the bad guy you think he is, Mr Wolfe. Did you hear what happened to me and my fiancée last year?" Damian grunts in confirmation. *Everyone in Fayette Bay had heard of that.* "Right. Arthur is the reason why most of my friends and I are still breathing today, but he's been putting a lot of the blame for the situation on himself. He gave Officer Robinson information on you to repent for sins he never even committed—it's all a massive misunderstanding. So, to answer your question, we wanted to get Arthur away from all this as quickly as possible.

He's not a villain; he doesn't belong here. Truly, if you want to punish someone, choose me."

Well, that was an unexpected turn.

"How very noble of you," Damian drawls, picking up the gun Silas dropped earlier. "But you're not the person who sold me out to the police, are you? Arthur Avila is of sound mind and body. I checked all of this out beforehand, and I understand he made his decision to turn in that evidence while knowing the risks. Besides, Monty wants him dead and I have to follow through to keep him sweet. So, while your speech was *just darling*, it does nothing to help his case." Damian sighs. "And quite frankly, it's just pissed me off."

Before I know what's going on, Damian raises the gun directly in front of him, clicks the safety off, and points the barrel between the two of us. "So, which of you two should I kill first? Who wants to be the honourable one and volunteer themselves?"

"I do," I announce before Silas can jump in and act the hero, and a vicious grin sweeps over Damian's face as the gun lands on me.

"Very well, then."

I will my eyes to close, to think of my Honeybee one last time before the chance is gone forever, but they won't. I'm literally staring down the barrel of a gun pointed right at me—

I'm plunged into complete darkness.

But there's no pain. I can still feel my body—my hands clammy, my lungs frozen in fear.

"What the fuck?" Damian growls.

The lights...the lights are off. I'm not dead. Not yet anyway.

Holy shit.

The lights are off and I'm not dead and there's a very uncomfortable piece of cool metal in my pocket, sandwiched between me and my foldaway chair.

I will not freeze up again.

Chapter Thirty-Six

Bea

"What just happened? Did we lose the feed?" Kyra asks urgently, straightening in her chair.

I barely hear her; my ears have been ringing and my vision spinning since Damian lifted his gun and pointed it directly at Artie's chest.

I'm mildly aware I'm hyperventilating, but I won't let the unwavering dread take me. I can't allow it to consume me—not this time. Not when two of my best friends are staring death right in the face...

"We have to do something," Jessica squeals quietly, the way she does when she's panicking.

"It's not like we can disable guns from our desks," Kyra adds unhelpfully, eyes flitting from side to side as she racks her brain. "Where did the light go?"

"I cut the power," I murmur, clicking off the program Artie taught me how to use when we played that practical joke on Monty a few weeks ago.

"Nice one," Kyra says with an approving nod.

"Is it?" Jessica asks, looking between us. "Now we won't know what's happening, or if anyone gets hurt—"

A ringing explosion crackling through the monitor forces me out of my seat. A flashing light flares across the blackened screen, and then there's a thudding that sounds like bones cracking and slumping onto the unforgiving floor.

"Holy shit..." Kyra breathes.

"Bea," Jessica whispers, tears streaming down her cheeks, "what have you done?"

"I—I," is all I manage, because what *have* I done?

I thought turning the lights off would stop Damian from being able to land the killing shot on Artie, but now we can't even see who's been hit.

Click. "Silas...Silas, are you alright?" I ask into my earpiece.

Nothing but static answers my plea.

I shake my head gently to Jessica. "Turn the lights back on, Bea." Her voice has dropped to a devastatingly quiet.

"I'm trying, but it's not—it's not working." Whatever part of my brain remembered how to turn them off has since frozen with fear and I'm blanking hard. Now I'm just pressing buttons, frantically hitting the keys like I have a personal vendetta against them.

We hear shuffling through the cameras, still without an idea of who's moving.

"I can't remember how to do it." Panic turns to anger as it bubbles through my clouded chest and up my throat.

A message pops up on the screen then:

LOCKED OUT. ENTER PASSWORD.

"Shit!" I'm suddenly overcome with the urge to empty the contents of my stomach onto the floor. All the tabs and software we had open are now hidden behind a lock screen. I take a steadying breath and will my mind to not panic—which is much easier said than done when I've potentially just killed Silas and Artie.

Oh my god.

"Do you know Arthur's passwords?" Kyra demands calmly. I can't see her, but her voice is still ringing through the speakers.

"No!"

"Then shit," she agrees.

"Try something he likes," Jessica chimes in. "Coding? Coffee? What are the names of his sisters' kids?"

But I'm shaking my head. "He's a hacker—surely, he'll have a password full of weird numbers and symbols. Right, Kyra? That's what all you guys use for your passwords?"

The apartment fills with the echoing sound of Kyra's relentless typing on her own computer. "You'd think, but it *is* Arthur. He's only a step up from Aaryan when it comes to his safety."

"Try Bea one-two-three," Jessica urges.

Kyra snorts, but I just scoff. "I'm not trying that."

"I'm using my software to crack the password, but it might take a while. If Arthur's smart, he'll have encrypted the password so this *can't* work—but again, it's Arthur we're talking about. It can't hurt to keep brainstorming while we're waiting," Kyra suggests, still typing.

"Silas managed to guess it correctly," I remember. *Last night, he logged in like it was his own damned computer.*

"There you go, then! Not impossible, so keep trying."

"*Please,*" Jessica whimpers, "try it, Bea."

I do, regretfully. It feels stupid and embarrassing to assume I'm important enough for Artie to use my name as his password, but I push my ego to the side and try it anyway.

Maybe it's another girl's name...

Or a pet. Let's go with an old pet's name.

Unsurprisingly, *Bea123* doesn't work. The command box shakes its head at me mockingly.

"Any luck, Kyra?" I almost beg, itching my brow.

"Starts with a capital H," she mutters.

"That narrows it down," Jessica grumbles. "Come on guys, *think.*"

"I'm telling you, it's one of those stupidly long passwords that look like someone's just bashed the keyboard five times and pressed save."

"H-o," Kyra announces.

"Home—homestead? Homer Simpson? Honey, I shrunk the kids?" Jessica rattles off a few more suggestions, but I've stopped listening.

I'm typing eight letters.

Hitting enter.

"I'm in," I breathe, and Kyra whoops.

The footage stream reappears, looking just as dark and frightening as we left it. Kyra's face pops back up, along with the rest of the software programs we'd been working with. I've never been happier to see a hacker's toolkit in my life.

"What was the password?" Jessica asks, clutching her chest.

"Honeybee." I want to laugh and cry and scream at the absurdity.

"Honeybee? What a stupid password." Kyra tsks, but Jessica nudges me with her shoulder knowingly. I don't acknowledge her, though, because I can't quite believe it either.

"You can ask Arthur about it later," Jessica tells Kyra, who's still muttering to herself about the stupidity of wildlife-themed passwords. "The lights?"

Right, the lights.

I follow Kyra's vague instructions on how she would control the power during her heists. Thankfully, something she says sparks my memory and I'm able to figure out the rest. Through the screen, the lights flicker back on—to display a completely empty room. No chairs, no Silas or Artie, no Damian.

The only indication it's even the same room as the one we'd been monitoring all these hours is the new crimson pool of blood glaring up at us from the floor.

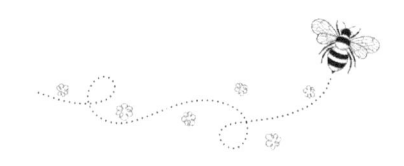

It might've been minutes since the lights came back on, although it feels more like hours.

Jessica's back to pacing, Kyra's typing frantically to update the other half of the inner circle, and I'm staring blankly at the screen, begging for an answer to jump out at me. Still nothing through my earpiece.

"Where could they have possibly gone without us seeing them?" I ask, glancing between every other camera feed on Damian's network. They're all still working. "If they'd have left the room, we'd surely have seen them on the hallway footage."

"Not if there's a blind spot in the system. Anything could've happened while we were locked out of the stream." The clacking of Kyra's keyboard is driving me insane, but I daren't say anything.

"They've killed them both and moved the bodies out of the frame so we can't see them," Jessica says through her silent sobs. She's gone straight to assuming the worst.

"If Damian had killed Arthur and Silas, he'd have no reason to move the bodies," Kyra says matter-of-factly. "Even if he didn't know we were watching—which he probably does—there's no need to move the bodies when you're a crime lord in your own lair."

"You think they're still alive?" I ask quietly, slightly afraid of the answer.

Kyra sighs. "Arthur's clever. I've never seen someone get out of as much shit as him. From what I've heard, Silas is basically indestructible—" I steal a glance at Jessica, who's not finding the funny side of that quip, "—so if any of us could get out of that situation, I think they're the ones to do it."

It's not a yes, but it's a little reassuring, nonetheless.

"So, what do we do now?" I ask.

"I want to go down there," Jessica announces, voice strong. When I meet her glare, her eyes are determined. "We might be able to help. Kyra can stay here and monitor the cameras; you and I will go find them."

"Woah, woah, woah. Let's not rush into any silly decisions here," Kyra warns through the screen, but my eyes are locked on Jessica. "This is exactly how Arthur got into this mess in the first place."

"She's right, though. Maybe we could help them," I hear myself saying.

Kyra blows a deep breath through her nose. "Why is it so difficult for you people to understand that heading straight into the heart of a crime lord's lair is *not* a smart idea?"

"They're in danger, Bea." Jessica already has her leather jacket on, flicking her dark curls out from the neckline.

"Bea, listen to me. Arthur would not want you to do this," Kyra urges.

She's right, of course. I know she is—Artie would rather die than see me put myself in danger. But how could I live with myself if something happened when I did nothing to stop it?

"Kyra, you have my number from the other day, right? Text me updates." I stand, grabbing my own coat from the counter.

"You two need to listen to me!" Kyra shouts, her voice filling the entire room. "You don't even have any weapons! Walking into that dungeon is as good as signing your own death certificates."

Defiantly, Jessica presses a small gun into my palm. It's freezing cold, like it's covered in the implication of death already, and I have an overwhelming urge to get as far away from it as possible. "Left over from Silas's stash," she says shakily. "Let's do this, Bea—for our boys."

Instead, I pocket the small gun and squeeze her hand. "Our boys."

"For the love of all things *sane*!" is the last thing we hear from Kyra before we're out the door and walking towards the café.

Jessica gives me a quick lesson on how to use a gun on the brisk walk. I'm hating every second of it, but I don't allow my clouded thoughts to get in the way of retaining as much information as I can. My chest feels like it's swallowing itself whole, but I can freak out after we have Silas and Artie back.

And there will be an after.

"Shit," Jessica mutters under her breath as we round the corner towards the dark door. "I knew he'd do this."

"Do what?" But then I see her.

Maria, hurrying out the café door waving her arms towards us. "Don't you dare!" she hisses.

Jessica smirks slightly. "She's making a big deal so the cameras will see her and be alerted if we try to get into the lair. Follow her lead; we don't need to draw attention to ourselves."

So we allow Maria to usher us into the empty café before closing and locking the door firmly behind us.

"You two are imbeciles," she snaps in greeting. "Silas told me you two would do this, and I was to stop you from putting yourselves in harm's way."

"How long have you been standing at that window?" I ask, a tiny smile tugging at my lips.

"Since he texted me this morning!"

"I can confirm that she hasn't left that window," Andrew calls from his usual spot at the counter. "I've been serving customers all day."

Maria just rolls her eyes.

"Oh, hi Andrew. I didn't see you there," I say awkwardly as Jessica's eyes go wide and she mouths *Andrew!* at me. I nod with equally expressive eyes.

"It's fine. For the record, I think you're all idiotic for even entertaining the idea of heading into that pit."

"Thank you for your input, Andrew." Maria throws over her shoulder in an overly sweet tone.

"You can join us if you want," Jessica says quietly to Maria. "I have a spare gun; we could always do with more backup."

Maria looks like she might be considering it, but Andrew is off his chair and by her side within a second. "Absolutely not."

Jessica and I look between Maria and Andrew, both equally confused. "Excuse me?" Maria asks him incredulously.

"You're not going into a crime lord's lair, Maria."

"You don't get to tell me what to do."

"I do when it involves you putting yourself in immediate danger."

"Why?" Maria asks, and it sounds like a challenge.

Before they can go at it again, Jessica cuts in. "Sorry guys, I didn't mean to stir up...whatever this is. But we have to go, and you can't stop us Mar. So, are you in or out?"

Maria takes a second to think, but Andrew steps between us, partially shielding her. "She's out."

Jessica looks at Maria for confirmation, who lowers her head a fraction. Then she steps around the tall, bossy accountant to give us both a tight hug.

"Look after yourselves, okay?" she mumbles into our hair.

"We will, Mar."

"I'll be waiting for you by the window."

"We'll come straight back," I promise, voice muffled by her shoulder.

Maria kisses both of us on the cheek before letting go, eyes glassy. Before I can change my mind and stay in the comfy confines of the warm café, Jessica grabs my hand and guides me back onto the street.

"Okay, ready for this?" she asks.

"No?"

She huffs a laugh. "Me, neither."

I match her tense smile. "Then let's do it."

Chapter Thirty-Seven

Artie

As soon as the room blackened, I knew who'd turned out the lights.

My brilliant, brave Honeybee.

Bea's face shining through my mind was all I needed to muster enough strength to reach underneath me, grab the gun Silas had handed me earlier, and shoot blindly in front of me.

The thud of Damian's body and the deafening silence that came afterwards were enough to let me know my bullet had landed where I'd intended it to.

"Holy shit," I gasp into complete nothingness. My eyes hadn't yet adjusted, and this was perhaps the darkest room I'd ever experienced.

"Took you long enough," Silas grunts next to me.

I ignore him. "We need to get these ties off." I hear a *ping*, followed by plastic bouncing across the floor. "Oh, as *if*."

"Not my first rodeo," Silas sighs, his voice much closer to me now. He's kneeling before me, fiddling with the tie around my ankles.

"How?"

"Just an old trick someone taught me back in the day." A knife appears from somewhere and he slices through the tie like it's made of butter. "Let's go."

"Could you be *any* cooler?" I ask in mock wonderment.

"Shut up," he drawls.

And because I don't want to test my luck too much, I zip my lip. God, to get out of here. To see Bea again, to hold her. To put this nightmare behind us once and for all. But then something dawns on me.

"Sy, what about Monty?" I ask, grabbing his arm.

"What about him?"

"Once he realises we're gone—that we killed Damian—don't you think he'll come for us?"

Silas appears to ponder this for a moment before growling under his breath and turning on his heel.

"Where are we going?" Heading back further into the stony pit was *not* how I wanted the plan to change.

"To move the body."

"Right you are," I agree, because he's the ex-conman and I don't know what I'm doing. "Move it where?"

Silas pushes me forward, and I almost trip over the body right at my feet. The ground is sticky, presumably with blood, and it's enough to make me want to retch. *Like I've never needed to do anything more, ever.*

"Do *not* throw up," Silas warns, walking around me to the other end. "Grab him and let's go."

"Go where?" I hiss, scooping the heavy legs up and backing towards the door. Blood squelches between my knuckles and I force a shaky breath.

"His office."

Thankfully, we find the office within a few minutes, and the lights are still working so we can see the damage my bullet caused in all its glory.

A single hole, right between Damian's eyes, crusted with drying crimson blood.

"Not a bad shot," Silas murmurs as we slump the body onto the rug. He squeezes my shoulder as I stare at the dead man in front of me uselessly. His eyes are still open, but they're fogged. "Let's go, Arth."

I try, but I can't move. It's like my feet are cemented to the floor, like the blood I stepped in a moment ago has fused with the fibres of the rug beneath my shoes, keeping me here forever. The price I have to pay for my actions, finally catching up to me.

"Arthur," Silas warns, his voice gentler than I've ever heard it. "We need to go now."

I make no effort to move—still can't—until I feel his hand on my flushed neck and his words close to my ear: "Let's go find Bea."

Bea.

My Honeybee.

I feel myself nodding. *Yes, let's go find Bea.*

"Oh, if only it were that easy," a low voice drawls from the open doorway behind us.

I feel Silas tense next to me as he hangs his head. "So close," he cringes before we turn to face Monty.

"Look, Monts—it's over." I gesture to the body on the ground. "Damian's dead. You've caught the guy you've been after for so long; you even know where his lair is to catch the rest of his team. Tell everyone at the station that you were the one to shoot him in self-defence and get your badge back. Let us go and reap the rewards for yourself."

"Let you walk out of here without consequences?" He laughs grimly, and it's the least humorous thing I've ever heard. "For you to run off and tell everyone you know about my involvement with Damian Wolfe? You must think I was born yesterday."

"You have our word that we won't tell a soul." Silas puts a hand on his chest to drive the point home.

"It's not you I'm worried about," Monty snarls, encroaching further into the room. "It's *him* that's the problem."

I look behind me to see who he's pointing at, giving him the biggest grin I can muster on the return. He doesn't look amused in the slightest, and Silas whacks me in the chest.

"Ow!" I grimace. "Monty, do you really think I'm that much of an idiot to double-cross you like that? I have no interest in this stupid game anymore. I just want to get out of here, get on with my life, and forget any of this ever happened. As soon as I walk out of that godforsaken door, I'll have forgotten all about you. I give you my word."

Monty seems to mull this over for a second, looking between me, Damian, and his shoes. *Come on*, I urge silently, *let us go.*

"No," is all he says before pulling a gun on me.

The next sequence of events happens in the blink of an eye; too quickly to even try and comprehend what's playing out before us.

One second, Monty has his gun pointed at my chest with his finger curled around the trigger.

The next, he's on the floor, coughing and spluttering against the blood quickly rising up his throat and pooling behind his teeth.

Monty dropped his gun as he fell, so Silas kicks it to the other side of the room before kneeling beside him, grasping his hand silently as the fire behind his eyes snuffs out.

I should probably have done the same, but my eyes are locked on the hallway just outside the door. There, both clutching the tiniest guns anyone's ever seen, stand Jessica and Bea.

Their faces, the picture of abject horror, are all white eyes and mouths in the shape of bullet wounds. Like they're trying to comprehend what's just happened, too. I look down at Monty, whose eyelids are being lowered by Silas, and find two shots to the chest.

They'd taken him down together.

Tentatively stepping over the body, I stagger my way towards them and scoop them both up in a tight embrace. "Thank you," I whisper, burying my face as far as I can into their comforting warmth.

"He was—he was going to kill you," Jessica stammers. Bea grips me even tighter.

"I know. You saved our lives." I kiss them both on the cheek, but as I do, I physically feel my heart shattering into a million tiny pieces.

They did this for me.

Two more innocent people I've dragged into my helpless mess.

Silas comes up behind me and gently draws Jessica out of my grip, enveloping her with his arms and resting his chin on top of her curls.

I turn my attention to Bea, giving my friends the privacy they deserve, to see her looking up at me with tears streaming down her face. I take my thumb and wipe one away. "Stop that," I murmur as I cup her face with shaking hands. "It's all over now."

"I need you to promise me you're never going to do something that senseless ever again," she gasps through jutting sobs.

"Not for as long as I live."

She nods. "Good, because I need you alive. I need you alive and breathing and telling me stupid jokes every single day. Okay?"

"I don't know why you're calling my jokes *stupid*," I start, but her tears are still falling thick and fast and I realise she needs my sincerest form of loving right now rather than my silly quips. So I wipe at the tearstains again and vow, "I promise you, Honeybee. I'm not going anywhere."

"Nowhere," she agrees, crushing her face into my chest as I hold onto her for dear life.

Chapter Thirty-Eight

Bea

We're sitting in the booth furthest away from the door at the Twinkling Bliss café—me and Artie on one side, Jessica and Silas opposite, and Maria at the head of the table. As soon as she saw us coming, she swept us into the empty café and locked the door.

Andrew brought us all a mug of steaming sweet tea before returning to his usual spot at the counter with a frown.

"You shouldn't have come in after us," Silas reprimands over the rim of his mug. It's the first any of us have really spoken to each other since the reunion, and I just roll my eyes at him.

"I told them not to," Maria mutters in a sing-song kind of voice.

"We saved your lives," Jessica reminds them helpfully and I point at her, agreeing with that very valid notion.

"We could've taken him," Silas drawls. "Right, Arth?"

"Hm?" Artie looks up from his still-full cup, eyes weary.

"I was telling the girls that they didn't need to save us; we could've taken Monty ourselves."

Artie agrees with the smallest smile I've ever seen on him. He looks up at me, then at Jessica. "You really shouldn't have come for me," he says, voice thick and painfully heavy. His eyes then land on Silas. "None of you."

"Don't be silly." Jessica sniffs a laugh.

"We weren't just going to leave you to rot in that dungeon," Silas sighs, looking around the table at each of us. "We help each other out, don't we? We're a team. The main thing is we're all safe and we can put this shit behind us."

I squeeze Artie's knee beneath the table. "We were always going to come for you. Just like you did for me." Tears prick my eyes as I watch him because I *need* him to understand what I'm about to say as the absolute truth. "It wasn't your fault, Artie."

"Absolutely not," Jessica agrees.

"Never," Silas chimes in, and Maria nods eagerly.

He presses his lips together in a tight smile before going back to playing with the handle of his mug.

"So what's going to happen now—with the bodies?" Maria asks Silas, our resident expert in this field.

His face turns grave at the thought of it, eyes shadowing as he clears his throat. He drags his phone from his pocket and begins skimming the screen. "Kyra's still in the security system and the bodies have already been discovered by Damian's second-in-command, Justin Seethly." I notice the colour drain from Artie's face as he grips his mug tighter. I stroke my palm up and down his filthy jeans. "Naturally, that *should* be a real shit-show for us. However, Kyra's done some digging and it turns out Damian wasn't best liked within his own organisation. She's skipped over the details, but it looks like his deputy has been trying to get rid of him for a while."

"What does that mean for Artie?" I ask, suddenly worried this might not be as over as I assumed it was.

"Kyra has wiped the camera feed and Damian's server of any trace of us. It's likely that Seethly will have already figured out it was us, so only time will tell whether he wants to act on that or not. It's no secret Monty and Damian weren't each other's biggest fans, so they might even put it down to a mutual homicide and leave us out of it."

A humourless laugh escapes me. "So what? We simply have to sit and hope that we don't get killed in our sleep by the new ringleader?"

Silas seems to contemplate something for a second before confessing, "I know Justin. We go way back, actually. We were paired up on some cases together when he was working under Desmond Rose."

Artie's eyes flick up at that. "I thought the name sounded familiar."

"Yep, so leave Justin to me. He's always been gunning for a ringleader position, and I bet I can keep him quiet by reminding him of his impending promotion."

I shake my head, not quite believing it. "We can just...get on with life, then? Pretend like none of this ever happened?"

Silas nods, but Artie shakes his head. "I don't think I'll ever be able to pretend like you all didn't risk your lives to save me today." He glances between the rest of our friends, lingering on their faces for a second before moving on to the next. "I am irreparably grateful for all of you—I have no idea how I'll ever repay this honour. I'm sorry for putting this on all of you."

"Just don't do it again," Silas warns with a wry smile.

"Yeah, it's a long drive from our new home!" Jessica agrees, laughing.

"And Maria lost an entire day's worth of business," I chime in.

"Oh, don't worry about that!" Maria starts, but Andrew swivels around on his stool behind her.

"My point exactly!" he calls over disapprovingly.

None of us can help it then—we all burst into laughter. Andrew *hmphs* and turns back around in a huff, which only spurs us on more.

"Okay, we shouldn't let you waste any more of your opening hours on us," Artie murmurs, wiping a rouge tear. "I'm exhausted anyway. Shall we go?" he asks me, and I follow him out of the booth—completely relieved he still wants me to come home with him.

"Text me later," Maria tells me, eyebrows raised.

"Me too!" Jessica leans over to kiss me on the cheek.

"Don't bother texting me," Silas adds flatly. "I don't want to hear *anything* from you two for at least a week."

"I'll fill him in," Jessica teases.

"I'm definitely texting you later." Artie throws him a wink, clapping Silas on the back as we walk past. Before we get too far, though, I toss my keys towards Silas, who catches them just millimetres away from his face.

"You guys can stay at mine tonight if you want. I don't think I'll get that far." I stick my tongue out at Jessica and Artie chuckles, pressing a kiss to my temple. Silas groans and scrubs his face, looking physically pained. Maria's still whooping as Artie and I walk out into the warming afternoon air, gripping onto one another tightly.

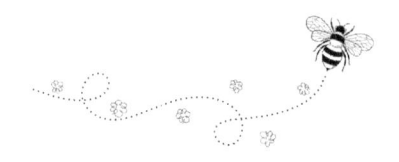

I collapse onto the sofa beside Artie, leaning my head on his shoulder. I went for a shower while he checked in with the inner circle and closed all the programs we'd been using. I told him he didn't need to bother with that right away—that he could join me instead—but he was adamant he wanted to get it over and done with.

"Feeling better?" he asks, taking my hand in his and rubbing the pad of his thumb back and forth over my knuckles.

"Getting there." I snuggle deeper into his shoulder, savouring the scent I'd been missing: vanilla and tree wood. "How are you doing?"

He takes a second before answering, and it's long enough for me to start freaking out. I want nothing more than for him to be okay. I *need* him to be okay.

"I'm getting there," he repeats my sentiment back to me, and it seems like that might be the best I'm going to get for now.

After everything, it feels like enough.

"Any word from Silas?" I dip a clean cloth into a bowl of warm water I'd made and begin dabbing the dried blood crusting Artie's beautiful face. He winces but doesn't move away from me.

"Yeah, he says it's all been taken care of. We have Justin's word that none of this will get back to us, and the organisation will deal with the aftermath. All we have to do is never speak of it again to anyone outside of our little group."

I chuckle despite myself. *Despite the fact I'm currently cleaning dried blood off my boyfriend's face.* "It almost seems too easy."

"I think we deserve a little easy, don't you?" Artie sighs, resting his head against the backrest and closing his eyes. He looks exhausted, *broken*.

"Definitely," I hum, leaning in to press the lightest of kisses to his lips.

Then I remember something and hit his arm lightly. "Honeybee?! Your password is seriously *Honeybee*?"

"No," he exclaims loudly, glancing over his shoulders to make sure no one's around to overhear. In his empty apartment. "My highly secure password is definitely not *Honeybee*."

He looks at me like I'm the irrational one and I scoff. "You need to change that."

"I have."

"Good." Although I kind of liked the fact I was important enough to be used as his password.

"Yep. It's now dream-boy-hunk."

I burst out laughing because *of course it is.* "That's still not secure enough!"

"What do you think I'm hiding on my computer that requires such high levels of security?" he teases. "Get your mind out of the gutter, Honeybee. There are no dirty pictures on there."

I roll my eyes. "Your software program thingies! What if someone breaks into your computer and gets you into this kind of trouble again?"

"I deleted them." He shrugs.

That throws me for a loop. "What do you mean?"

"I deleted all my software *thingies*—they're all gone. Factory reset my computer, changed my password, and said goodbye to all that shit."

"You deleted your entire career?" I ask, completely dumbfounded.

He nods so casually that I feel like I need to freak out enough for the both of us.

"I told you I wanted nothing more to do with it."

"I know..."

"That's it, Bea. I don't want any reminders of how I almost got the most important people in the world killed through my stupidity. I deleted everything but the inner circle group chat."

"But you're the best," I muse thoughtfully.

He smirks at me. "I'm the best at a lot of things," he agrees, drawing patterns along the back of my hand. "I'll find something else to excel at. It's no big deal."

"If you're sure..."

"I am. All I want to do is put this behind us." He stifles a groan as I go back to cleaning his clotted wounds. "Will you tell me something—I don't know, light?"

"Light?" I ask uncertainly. After everything that's happened, light-hearted topics are the last thing flooding my mind. But when he cracks an eye to look at me with a silent plea, I glance around for something to spark inspiration. My gaze scans the bleak bookshelf, Silas's now-empty weapons box, the light grey walls—*my painting*. "I actually never got the chance to tell you something..."

"Oh yeah?" Artie asks, expression turning hopeful.

"Do you remember our first call when I was showing you my craft morgue and you asked why I had so many failed attempts, and I said I was looking for my yellow?"

"How could I ever forget?" The smile that comes with those words is bright enough to light up a star-less space.

"When you told me I was your yellow, I don't think I truly believed you. To me, yellow had always been something like a hobby—a perfect book I hadn't read yet, a craft that required so much of my focus I couldn't think of anything else." I have to clasp my hands together to stop them from physically shaking. "But I get it now. Artie Avila—you are my yellow, too. My calming, beautiful, hopeful light after a year of the darkest dusk.

You've helped me in more ways than I even thought possible—to be honest, I was beginning to lose hope before you came along."

Artie tips my chin up to face him, and it's only then that I notice the glistening tears streaming down his cheeks. "I don't know where I'd be without you," he whispers lovingly.

"I didn't do anything," I say, shaking my head. "Not without the help of Kyra, Silas, Jess and Maria. I think I was probably just in the right place at the right time."

"Will you stop putting yourself down so much, Bea? You saved me—in so many more ways than just today. And I know you'll probably never truly understand why, but please believe me when I say you're my yellow, my midnight blue, my indigo, azure, violet, and everything in between. To have you by my side eternally would truly make me the luckiest man alive."

I grin at him adoringly, not knowing what to say because my head wants to tell him he's mistaken but my heart wants to sing with him forever. I feel tears prick in my eyes then, and I realise that if I don't lighten the mood, I'm surely going to start sobbing. Once that door opens, I'm not sure how long it'll take to close. So I ask, "Am I about to get lucky, too, Dream Boy?"

The corners of Artie's damp eyes crinkle as he laughs, dimple shining like the sun at daybreak. "We have the rest of our lives to be lucky together. Can we have a nap first?"

"Yes, *please*. I feel like I could sleep for a thousand years."

He stands first, gently pulling me with him and guiding me towards his bedroom. But as I help Artie peel off his filthy clothes and slip underneath the covers, one of his words is still playing in my mind—*eternal*.

It sounds silly, but I've never had anything that permanent before. No parents, no siblings, no pets. Nothing to call mine for longer than a short while.

But he said it...

"Artie," I whisper as we hold each other underneath the sheets. The lowering sun paints the room with streaks of amber, gold and saffron. "Do you really think we're *eternal*?"

"Yes," he whispers back quickly, as if it's the easiest question he's ever had to answer. "You and me, Honeybee—forevermore."

And when he seals that declaration with a kiss to last just as long, I believe him.

Epilogue

Six months later

"What about him—he's cute!" Artie coos, pointing to a ginger kitten darting around his cage at our local animal rescue centre. "He looks like the perfect Duck."

I splutter a loud laugh at the seriousness in his voice. "That's a terrible name for a cat."

"What's wrong with Duck the cat?"

"How many cats have you ever met called Duck?" I deadpan, folding my arms across my chest.

"Exactly!" Artie exclaims before turning around to the mewing cat and calling, "Duck, Duckie!" in a high-pitched tone.

Obviously, the cat comes running to nuzzle against his finger through the bars.

Artie gives me a *told you so* look that has me rolling my eyes. "He *is* cute," I relent, extending my hand out for the cat to sniff.

He licks the pad of my finger before returning to Artie. "I guess you're his favourite."

"I'm everyone's favourite."

"Probably because you're so humble," I chide, which earns me a cheeky wink.

We get Duck home within the hour, and he's off exploring his new space before I can remind myself of what he looks like. I can't blame him—our new home is massive.

I have a room specifically for my crafts, and Artie has his own office where he can teach his computer software training courses in peace. He's often in there all day, even when I pop back in between shifts at the hospital.

Still, he's never too busy to drive me to work, even though I don't have trouble driving through town anymore and actually look forward to my hospital shifts. He says it's his favourite time of the day and he won't give it up for anything. The mornings and evenings are for us only.

"What time is everyone arriving later?" Artie asks as we walk into our kitchen. He flicks the kettle on and throws two teabags into our designated mugs—vanilla chai for him, sweet ginger for me.

"Around six. That'll give us enough time to get ready and for me to start preparing everything." I'm hosting my first dinner party at the new house tonight. Artie's in charge of catering, like he promised all those months ago, but I've got hostess responsibilities covered.

"What exactly are you preparing, again?" Artie asks, his words sickly sweet with amusement.

I glare at him flatly. "I have to lay the table, pick out the wine, create the perfect ambience...there's *lots* to do." I make a hand gesture as if I'm reading a never-ending list.

"Right," he says, straightening from where he was leaning on the kitchen island to pass me my tea. "I don't have to start cooking for a few hours; anything I can do in the meantime?"

"Would you be able to make the bed in the spare room ready for Silas and Jessica while I set up the kids' table for Janie and Hector?"

He salutes me in answer, pressing a kiss against my temple as he walks past. "I love seeing you so passionate," he murmurs against my skin.

I take a slow sip of tea, grinning a little behind my mug. I just love doing nice things for my friends, and without so much worry plaguing my every thought nowadays, I have plenty of time on my hands to organise these things.

Duck decides to make his reappearance then, gleefully trotting into the kitchen with a wad of white felt between his teeth.

"Look at that, he's making friends already," Artie croons, bending down to pluck the wool from the kitten's mouth. He holds it up for me to see, and I groan as he cackles. It's a half-finished felted animal carcass—because yes, the craft morgue did survive the move. Artie said he couldn't live without it. He's even managed to sneak some of the half-finished knick-knacks around the house as decor. "Oh gosh, he's found another duck to play with."

"That's a cow," I remind him flatly.

"A cow that I named Duck." His voice is dripping with glee; his smug smile showing just how proud of himself he is.

"Don't tell me you named our kitten after one of my failed crafts," I grimace.

"Why? That's exactly what I did."

I shake my head, taking the felted cow from him and straightening a few wispy fibres Duck—the *kitten*—had managed to pull out from its body. "How am I still surprised at your incapability to act seriously for even a second?"

"Hey, I can be serious when I need to be."

I scoff and roll my eyes for good measure, because no, he can't. *And it's one of his qualities I admire the most.*

But then he hooks my chin with his finger and drags my eyes up to meet his, whispering onto my lips, "I could show you the most serious side to me if I wanted to."

He nuzzles my neck, and I carefully crane it to give him better access. He nips at my exposed skin lightly, and all coherent thoughts leave my brain. "I dare you," I breathe.

Leaning back from me ever so slightly, I catch his crystalline eyes darkening. He pulls his phone from his pocket and plays a gentle ballad through its speakers, leading me into a loving slow dance around our homey kitchen.

"Honeybee, I am so *seriously* in love with you," he announces softly, his words sparkling in the small space between us. "If someone were to ask me what my favourite thing about you is, my *serious* answer would be this:

"There's not one single thing I can pinpoint as my favourite. Sometimes, it's laughing with you. Other times, it's little touches with you. It's looking around the room for you, filling up my phone with notes of all the silly things I want to tell you when you're not with me. It's experiencing the smallest moments of life with you, and not wanting to share them with anyone else. It's adopting a Duck with you. It's about being there for you in your hardest moments and celebrating every one of your wins. I'm *serious* about you, and us. That'll never be a joke to me."

Then he kisses me because I'm quite obviously speechless, and it's deep enough to suck any and all air from my lungs; sweet enough to have me thinking of honey and sugar and the purest of wishes coming true.

THE END

Acknowledgements

And just like that, I'm writing the acknowledgements for my second book. I truly cannot believe we've reached the end of You and Me, Honeybee. I feel like I might need to cry or do a little happy dance. But first, I have some special people to thank!

Firstly, the biggest thank you to everyone who read and loved my first book, The Long Con, giving me the courage to continue with my author journey. Every single review and message is so special to me, and they really are the cherry on the cake that is being a writer.

To my real-life Artie, Brandon. Thank you for your undeniable support and constant belief in my dreams. Even when I'm doubting myself, you're my biggest fan cheering me on from the sidelines. Without you, absolutely none of this would be possible.

To Albie, my own personal *yellow*. Thank you for making life that much brighter with your infectious smile and sweet personality.

Thank you to my mum, for your constant unwavering support and love.

The biggest thank yous to my early readers, Eleanor, Kacey, Nicki, and Holly. You all accepted this book in its roughest form and helped me turn it into something magical, and for that, I'm eternally grateful.

To my proofreader Sophie, for not laughing at some *questionable* spelling and grammar mistakes I'd missed despite countless readthroughs. Thank you for not laughing and for the sweetest comments.

Thank you to Bia Shuja for another killer cover.

I can't *not* acknowledge Bea and Artie here, for being the easiest characters to create and fall in love with. I'm truly going to miss working with them every day.

And finally, thank you to any reader who chose to pick up my second book and give it a go. The fact that you're here right now means everything to me; you're making my dream come true.

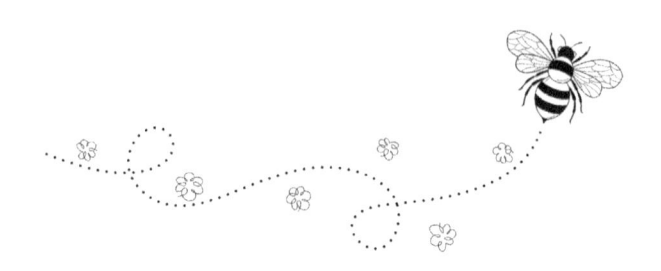

About the Author

GEMMA NICHOLLS is a professional writer from sunny South England, now residing in rainy South Wales. She's always been passionate about writing, creating stories, and finding new worlds to take her away from reality for an hour or two. She loves romcoms, fantasy, and any book where the love interest leans against the doorframe in *that* way.

Gemma lives with her wonderful boyfriend, their son, and their two wild tuxedo cats. She drinks far too much coffee for her own good and hopes that her books will put a smile on people's faces, giving them a safe space to escape reality for a little while when they need it most.

For the latest information on new releases and other fun stuff, come say hi on Instagram:

@gemmanichollswrites

Printed in Great Britain
by Amazon